THE ATTACK

A Novel of Terrorism

In America

THE ATTACK

By

Kurt Schlichter

Paperback Edition ISBN: 979-8-9892066-2-9
The Attack - Kurt Schlichter - Paperback - 010124 – v60

For Irina

ACKNOWLEDGEMENTS

I want to thank various people for their help and guidance on this project. Of course, we start with Irina Moises, who worked as my editor throughout. It was Regnery editor Harry Crocker III's offhand idea that I do a book on terrorism in America post-10/7 as a novel and not as nonfiction that got me thinking about this project.

I got input from many other people, like veterans Matthew Betley, Jim Hanson, Russ Smith, Seth Goldberg, Patrick "Kit" Bobko, Josh Steinman, and Tom Sauer. My former battalion commander, Colonel (R) Bill Wenger, and Dr. Seb Gorka both took the time to provide their thoughts on the manuscript. Much of the White House background stuff came from Dan Bongino's recent memoir. Hugh Hewitt's consistent coverage of the Gaza War, made possible by ace producer Duane Patterson, introduced me to many guests who helped provide me with some perspective on the enemy. Larry O'Connor and Glenn Reynolds have been big supporters. Drew Matich and @GMFWashington, pros in the entertainment field, provided a bunch of story notes that I incorporated into this final version.

There is another guy who you know and who I will not name who read it over and provided important thoughts – thanks!

Thanks for the guidance from my agent, Keith Urbahn, as well as my regular cover artist, Sean Salter, *aka* Salty Hollywood. He's done another incredible job.

Thanks to everyone who has followed me on Twitter/X, and all the Gladiators at *The Schlichter Arena* on Locals.com, as well as everyone who reads my columns at Townhall.com!

Finally, I always thank Andrew Breitbart because he is the guy who pushed us to create conservative cultural content. Thanks, Andrew.

PREFACE

This is a change of pace for readers of my eight (so far) Kelly Turnbull *People's Republic* novels. It was the result of an off-the-cuff book idea I passed on to my agent, Keith Urbahn, in the wake of the October 7, 2023, Hamas terrorist attack. The idea was simple – what about a nonfiction book about how that could happen here?

Because it could.

Harry Crocker III at Regnery suggested that it might be interesting as a novel, and I started thinking about the best way to do it. My mind went back to my first book, *Conservative Insurgency*, which I had done as a faux oral history. Harry was right about doing it as nonfiction – too dry and too distant. I wanted the reader to *feel* it. But a straight-up novel would be too sprawling – you would have to force a protagonist to Forrest Gump it way too hard to cover all the different facets of a massive terrorist strike that I wanted to address.

But an oral history-style novel, with short stories as told by the participants, could let me talk about every aspect of a terrible attack here at home. Think of it as *World War Z* – one of my favorite books – with terrorists instead of zombies. But Max Brooks was not the inventor of that particular format, just a skilled practitioner. You need to go further back, at least to the (real) oral histories of Studs Terkel and to General Sir John Hackett's remarkable and influential *The Third World War* from

1978. To the extent that this book bears similarities to these forbearers, it is intended as a tribute.

The Attack is the result. I wrote it quickly, lest it be overcome by events. Regnery was unable to publish it because it was pausing fiction, so here it is via Amazon like the Kelly Turnbull novels. It was three months from idea to published book.

Understand that everything here is all plausible – I spoke to people in the know. I was also concerned that I not give out information helpful to the savages. I obscured some things and excluded others because I do not want to assist anyone who would do us harm. However, do not imagine that they could not think up everything I discuss here and worse. And believe me, there is worse.

I hope *The Attack* helps make people think and inspires them to act before this nightmare becomes real, at least on the individual level, because there are bad people out there who want us dead. While this story is fiction, that part is not.

KAS, January 2024

THE ATTACK

INTRODUCTION

In the five years since the events of August 27-29, those three horrible days (and those that came after as the country tried to pick up the shattered pieces of normal life) have been referred to in many ways. Some people reference the dates – you occasionally see "A27/29" or such. Referring to it by the dates is simple because everyone in America who was alive and aware during that time remembers them. Everyone understands 9/11, and that feels like the right thing to call what happened that morning in 2001.

But limiting it to the initial three days fails to recognize that the nightmare actually began long before then, and the killing itself continued on afterward, albeit at a much lower level at home and much more far away. In the end, reciting the dates is unsatisfactory to express what it means. The effect of what happened to this country – and to us personally – was simply too great to be encompassed by dates.

Similarly, the event cannot properly be identified by a place name like "Pearl Harbor." Americans were murdered in 49 of 50 states, tens of thousands of them. Many more were wounded. It was not one discrete event but thousands of smaller events happening all at once, and collectively those events have changed the United States and every citizen in profound ways.

We needed another way to refer to it, yet what word or phrase can do it justice? Even English – perhaps the most flexible and expressive language in the world because of its greedy devouring of foreign vocabulary – comes up short of expressing the horror of it and its impact. It calls for something more, but what word or combination of words can do it?

Most of us refer to it simply as "the Attack."

There have been many books about the Attack, mostly scholarly works or after-action reviews directed at security professionals. There has been little straight history and almost no pop culture references. There has been no major movie about it, no Netflix series. The stories of the people who lived it have never fully been told.

Perhaps living through it was enough, for the Attack touched more Americans directly than any historical event since World War II. Almost none of us does not have a personal connection to someone who was killed or maimed. We all know the names of the famous stars, athletes, and politicians who were murdered. That was, of course, part of the enemy's intent. They wanted to shake us to the core of our souls, and they succeeded in that. Of course, it is impossible to know if they felt that the wrath they drew down upon themselves was worth it.

The story of how the Attack came to happen, of the three days of major bloodshed and what happened after, is so massive that it could encompass many volumes, but here I am limited to just one. I decided that the best way to tell the story of the Attack was to let individual people tell theirs. For every interview you read, I conducted maybe a dozen more. After all, millions saw the violence happen before their eyes, and everyone else watched it unfold on television or the internet. I attempted to select the small stories that, put together, would tell the big story – or at least begin to.

We all have our stories. You have yours, and I certainly have mine. And through it, perhaps, some of my own story will be told. Like so many others, I lost people.

I have tried to let these individuals tell the story of the Attack and thereby help us to understand what happened five years ago. To the extent I have succeeded, the credit is theirs. To the extent I have failed, the blame is mine.

The Author

BEFORE

1.

Eagle Pass, Texas

Master Sergeant Arturo "Artie" Jimenez of the United States Border Force stands looking at the infamous border wall. We have parked on the shoulder of the main security road that runs parallel to the barrier from the Gulf of Mexico about 1,954 miles west to the Pacific, ending 200 meters into the Pacific at San Diego. It went up in a year, and Mexico did not pay for it – at least not directly.

"The Wall" is really two walls. The barrier facing Mexico is solid reinforced concrete 22 feet high and topped with razor wire. Then there is the interior dead zone of 100 feet back to the second barrier, a cyclone fence 12' high with a concertina crown. In some places, like Eagle Pass, it is electrified.

Signs face the Wall from outside near where we stand in both English and Spanish:

> *"STOP!*
> *YOU ARE ILLEGALLY ENTERING THE UNITED STATES OF AMERICA.*
> *DEADLY FORCE IS AUTHORIZED."*

It is hot, over 100 degrees. Msgt. Jimenez leans against his USBF armored SUV, a loaded M4 carbine hanging from a sling around his neck, looking less like a policeman than a soldier.

That is intentional. He takes a swig of Desani water, wipes his forehead with his sleeve, and begins to speak.

If you had come here five years ago, a month before August 27th happened, none of this would be here. You would see lines of illegals crossing the Rio Grande. But you can't even see the river now in most places. It's all walled off.

We were processing thousands of illegals a day. When I say processing, it was just that – not deporting, not taking into custody, but processing. It was the process of checking them into the United States and then letting them go.

They were not just Mexicans. In fact, we used to shout when we actually got a *Mexicano* – "Hey everybody, this one's from Oaxaca!" It was people from everywhere. I mean everywhere, countries no one ever heard of. What the hell is Tajikistan anyway?

It was a business. The cartels found something almost as lucrative as fentanyl and coke. *Pollos* – the chickens. They would take thousands north a day, move them up to the line and bring them across then hand them straight over to us. The coyotes would teach them what to say, the magic words to claim asylum: "I'm afraid of persecution." Bingo, say the magic words and you're inside the US of A on parole. We were just checking them in, then handing them off with a piece of paper with a hearing date five years in the future. The parking lot was littered with those papers.

They would get picked up by the NGOs, the non-governmental organizations spending government grants. Here's a cell phone, here's some cash, here's a free flight somewhere. Some would lay up in town – the town was totally overrun, but the Vice President, who was supposed to be the border czar, never showed up. We knew why. It was no secret. They wanted the border open. We could have stopped it. Hell, when Trump was president, we *did* stop it. But the brass understood what their bosses wanted, so they made us understand what *our* bosses wanted. And they wanted those bodies to keep flowing.

It was a hard job. Little kids without families. The girls who were raped – there was a lot of that. But the thing we noticed was that more and more of them were really sketchy, from sketchy places. Afghanistan, Syria, Iran. They just kept coming and once in a while we would get pings on our watch list, but most flowed right through.

We knew there was something up. We knew it and reported it. The other ones – Venezuelans, Nigerians, Chinese – they were nervous when we processed them. They were told we would be harmless, that we would let them go, but they were normal people – well, not all the Chinese, but that's another story. They were nervous, and they were deferential. But these Muslim guys, all of them males in their twenties or thirties, were cold. They said what they had to say, but they hated us. You could tell. They scared the other *pollos*. The rest of the detainees stayed away from them, and the Arabs kept to themselves. And after they got their phones and cash and swag bags from the do-gooders from the NGOs, a lot of them just disappeared. Some took our free flights into the interior, but a lot of them just vanished. Now we know what happened, but we were so busy processing the new ones that we did not pay attention to what happened to the others after we let them go.

Still, we guys on the line reported that something was going on. We were supposed to send up intel notes when we heard or saw something unusual, and the intel ops guys were supposed to collect these spot reports for analysis. Then they would write their own formal intelligence reports. The investigation after the Attack showed that these reports went up the chain and they mentioned the Arabs, but no one in DC cared.

I remember making a spot report about a talk I had with a coyote we nabbed. He was Mexican and he knew he would get charged then bail out and disappear south – the *federales* did not patrol their border! Anyway, he was in a good mood because in

24 hours, he would be back home having a *cerveza* and laughing at us gringos.

I was killing time between busloads, and he was cuffed to a bench, so I asked him in Spanish how business was going. He told me it was great. He thanked the USA for making him rich – he was going to cash out soon and buy a nightclub in Michoacán. Then he said that human trafficking would be the perfect job except for the damn Arabs.

I asked him what was up with them, what was the problem? And he got this look. Now, he worked with the cartels, and we all know what they did before they got waxed afterward, so he did not scare easily. But he looked scared.

He said, "*Amigo*, just stay clear of them."

I asked him why, but he clammed up. I wrote it up and sent it up the chain, but no one listened to me or anyone else.

On August 27th, I was visiting my wife's family outside St. Louis. It was Central Time, so everything started there at 11:00 a.m. I was actually at a Target walking to my car when I heard a burst of what I knew was rifle fire way off in the distance. But that was it, and I thought all these gun-loving Missourians were just going off. I got into my car and drove back to the in-laws' place, about 15 minutes, radio off. I go inside and everyone is gathered around the TV. All hell is breaking loose. I remember the same feeling when 9/11 happened, except I was a young Marine at Pendleton and we were watching it happen on the TV in the barracks dayroom. I knew in 2001 that I was about to go to war, and I felt the same way watching the ABC special report, "America Under Attack."

It was not long until what I expected to happen happened – the news anchor announced that all active and reserve military and federal law enforcement were to report to their units. I was packed by then with a couple days' stuff – I carry a go-bag with a uniform and a Kevlar vest in my trunk – and, of course, I had my duty Glock 19 and five mags. I told my wife I would see her soon, and I could tell she was scared. But her dad had his Palmetto Arms AR-15 out and I knew he knew how to use it. He had been a paratrooper.

I went to the federal building to join up with the rest of us federal LEOs. It had not been attacked, but there were a lot of guys on the perimeter waiting for our turn to get hit. You could hear shooting in the distance.

There was no Border Patrol unit in St. Louis, so I found the U.S. Marshals and when they found out I was a Marine NCO back in the day they had me build a platoon of orphan feds, Postal Inspectors, IRS agents and the like – any rando who carried a badge and a gun. We drew AR-15s and shotguns – it was pretty clear that this was not going to be law enforcement but urban combat. I knew what that meant. I was in Fallujah.

We went out in support of local police. We came under fire near the Arch, where the terrorists had hit the park. Bodies were everywhere. We helped the cops dig the cell out of an apartment building where they holed up. Five or six cops got whacked. Those SLPD boys did not take anyone alive. I saw one of the dead tangos dragged out – not gently – by his feet. Apparently, instead of being taken alive, he had shot himself in the back of the head twice. I looked at what was left of his face and he damn well could have been one of the assholes I processed and let go.

Then we got sent to George Washington High School. You heard of that? Over 300 kids. They hit it at lunch when the kids were in the cafeteria.

Well, I saw it all firsthand. They took their time with those kids. They had plenty of it – 911 went down and no one knew that the terrorist cell had a whole high school for three hours. The terrorists were gone when we got there – it was a recovery op. I don't want to talk about it more than that. I still have nightmares.

I fought for three more days all around St. Louis, mopping up, then finally left and went down to Eagle Pass to rejoin my people and help with Operation Shut Down. We went from thousands of illegals crossing the border to nobody crossing in just a few days. We were not gentle. Not after what happened.

Later, I went along with the Army as a liaison during one of the incursions into Mexico to take down the cartels that had brought so many of the bastards in. I don't want to talk about that either. I'll just say payback is a bitch. Damnedest thing – one of the prisoners – one of the very few prisoners – was that same coyote. He asked me to put in a good word for him because he had warned me about the Arabs. And I did, but I don't know if it helped. Maybe he is running his club in Michoacán. Or maybe he's in a pit with his buddies.

You know the rest. The Wall went up almost overnight and the United States Border Patrol became the United States Border Force. We went from law enforcement to paramilitary, and we stopped playing.

You know the three warnings? If they are regular illegals and they get past the Wall, they get three warnings – we yell "¡*Pare o disparo*!" three times, then bang. If we suspect they are cartel, they don't get any warning. They get lead. Word has gotten out. We do not see many crossers – my last arrest was a couple guys trying to get through and, thankfully, they stopped and gave up on warning number two.

You know, some people ask me how I feel about that. Shooting first, asking questions later and all. I just tell them that I saw what happened at George Washington High School.

2.

Dubai, United Arab Emirates

Charlie is waiting in a beautiful bar overlooking the Persian Gulf high inside the Burj Al Arab Hotel, a sail-shaped structure on an island at the end of a fifth of a mile-long causeway extending out from the city. It is shaped like a gigantic yacht mainsail, and the inn attempts to live up to the Burj Al Arab's unofficial designation as "The world's only 7-star hotel."

Charlie – not his real name, of course, and he requested that his nationality not be mentioned – selected the location for our meeting precisely because it was a high-visibility venue. It was unlikely that one of the remaining active American Reaper Teams might choose such a public place to kill him, as they had done to so many others.

But also protecting him was his cooperation following the Attack. Charlie has survived in his business of moving money for questionable people with questionable purposes because he understands the necessity of flexibility when it comes to loyalty. One of the agents he assisted following the Attack arranged our meeting.

His English is slightly accented – it is the language of business, though he speaks Arabic, Farsi, and others as well. As he talks, Charlie sips an orange juice – it is unclear if it is spiked – and his eyes ignore the view, preferring to scan the other patrons and anyone entering the bar.

You know about *hawala*? The word means something like "trust" in English. It's a system to transfer money without actually transferring money. It's hundreds of years old. Basically, you have two *hawaladars* – money brokers – in different places, sometimes on different continents. If you want to transfer money to another person, you go to a nearby *hawaladar*, who contacts a *hawaladar* nearby the recipient. You pay the principal to your broker, and then the other broker pays the person you are sending money to out of his pocket. The brokers take a small commission and settle up between themselves later. There's no actual money moving, and no paper either. It is on the honor system. Billions move like this every year.

You see the advantages? It's fast and the commissions are less than banks charge. But the appeal to some people is that it is invisible. Money transfers among banks are all watched, and closely. Your NSA uses artificial intelligence to look for suspicious transfers, or so it is said. But with *hawala*, there is no transaction to look at, no money moving at all.

I used it. I was a wizard of *hawala*. I had contacts almost everywhere. I even acted as a *hawaladar* on occasion. It was one of my many skills. My work was always on the edge of the law, but nothing could get done without people like me. I think the best word in English for what I did was "facilitator." I facilitated transactions that might otherwise not take place.

You see, even before the Attack, the Middle East and the Third World in particular were not a free market. Not at all. The West likes to talk about free enterprise, but between sanctions and end-user regulations and so forth, not to mention the graft in these countries, nothing is easy. Certainly nothing is free. Everything is, what is that word? Sketchy.

At the time, I was working on obtaining oil and drilling products for Iran. There were sanctions by the U.S. and others in effect, but sometimes they were enforced and sometimes not. After the Hamas War, enforcement tightened again, and that was good for business. I would locate buyers for sanctioned oil, and sellers of sanctioned drilling equipment, then arrange the money flow.

Sometimes we would launder the money through one of my companies – I often used construction companies because they typically worked with large amounts and you could establish credibility by announcing in the press that you had big projects so no one would be suspicious, even though the big projects never happened. A five-million-dollar apartment complex in Tehran? It got announced, it got paid for, but it is still a vacant lot.

Other times, I would use high-end *hawaladars* – I am talking millions of dollars. Many were right here in Dubai. My connections were good, my reputation impeccable. They might need sanctioned drilling control mechanisms, so I would create a drilling company in Oman to buy it from a Western manufacturer and would provide an end-user certificate. I would transfer the money from Iran via *hawala*, pay it through the company, get the goods, and abandon the company once the equipment was shipped out. If anyone cared to look, and they never did, it was just another bankrupt drilling enterprise.

It was good business, and I was pleased with it. But so were the Iranians. Too pleased.

I had a contact I called Afshar – not his real name, but I never asked. I also never asked exactly who he worked for, though his cover was some company with a forgettable name. I believe he was actually with the Army of Guardians of the Islamic Revolution, what you Americans called the IRGC, the Islamic Revolutionary Guard Corps.

We would meet here in Dubai over tea – never alcohol – and talk for a while about our families. That is how business is done here, slowly. You build relationships. But this day he seemed eager to get to our business, barely going through the normal pleasantries.

Was I able to do work in Libya and Sudan? I was surprised, but this was a surprising business. In fact, I had done small deals in both countries, to the extent either failed state could actually be called a country. Afshar had products that he needed to move to Sudan for what he called "processing." There was a factory being set up there where the work would be done. Could I facilitate the money transfers?

I asked him about the amounts, and he took out a piece of paper. There were 12,000 units at $450 for each one "processed," or $5,400,000. This was a substantial number, not my biggest deal but still large. My end would be in the area of $250,000, a respectable amount. I said I could help.

Now, *hawala* is based on honor, but I was not about to rely on the honor of Libyans and Sudanese I did not know. I arranged to fly out to meet the prospective *hawaladars.* Libya was still chaos, with armed militias on the streets. I hired a platoon of guards. It never occurred to me to wonder what 12,000 things someone might want from Libya.

I flew to Khartoum and satisfied myself that the local *hawaladar* had the capacity and – I hoped – the integrity to do what I needed done. I was in my hotel room when Afshar called. He was in Khartoum as well, and he told me to be ready as he was picking me up. He wanted to show me the factory.

We drove out to an industrial part of town where there were many non-descript buildings and warehouses. The factory was unmarked but surrounded by a fence and guarded by armed men, serious ones and not local. Inside, there were dozens of workstations and many tools, but no one was working because the product had not yet arrived.

I complimented him on his factory – which was owned by a front company – but confessed that I did not know what I was looking at. He told me that the 12,000 items were 12,000 folding-stock AK-47s from the Libyan war that needed to be refurbished. I guess the businessman in me took over my common sense – the wise move would have been to nod, go home, and withdraw from the deal. Instead, I asked why not make a deal with the Taliban for 12,000 of the brand-new M4s the Americans left behind when they fled. No need to refurbish them, and they would probably be more profitable. But then Afshar said something strange that I should have paid more attention to at the time. He said, "No, then the Americans will be able to trace them."

I facilitated the payments, and took my share. Then they asked me to help move the guns to Venezuela. I assumed the weapons were for the Venezuelan Army, or maybe local guerillas.

I was paid handsomely for this, and I was proud of my scheme. I decided to use Nigeria as the waystation. First, I arranged for a weekly flight into Lagos by the Venezuelan national oil company, Petróleos de Venezuela, S.A., supposedly to transport oil drilling gear. That went on for a few weeks, every Wednesday, establishing a routine.

Next, I went to Lagos myself to vet my *hawaladar* and grease the right palms at the airport. For four successive Mondays, a Sudanese transport with a manifest of oil drilling gear – it was my go-to cargo – took off for Lagos, and the cargo was off-loaded into a warehouse. Some labels and paperwork changed, and on Wednesday it was loaded on the Venezuelan plane and flown out to South America.

Each shipment was 3,000 refurbished rifles, plus ammunition. I would later help arrange some other flights of various equipment that I suspected, correctly, were munitions of various types. I made a great deal of money. Afshar was greatly pleased with me.

Arms were not my usual stock-in-trade, but I told myself that this was a one-time deal. I truly had no idea what they were intended for. Had I, I would have pulled out of it. I swear on my children.

Then Afshar called to meet again and I agreed, but I told myself no more arms trafficking. Even before the Hamas War, the Israelis were coming after the people who armed the Palestinians and I did not want to turn over the engine of my Mercedes and find myself a martyr, though 72 virgins could be interesting.

But he had a completely different question for me, one I never expected. He wanted to know if I had many *hawala* contacts in the United States. I did not – I stayed away from the Americans. Afshar was looking for one or more in a number of large U.S. cities. He assured me the amounts were not large, but there would be many transfers, and that it was very important "for the faith."

That scared the hell out of me. I wanted nothing to do with it. He pressed, and I gave him names who might help him. One of them was my friend Omar, who was more adventurous than I. Afshar still wanted me, but I pleaded that I had no such contacts myself, and he finally relented.

This was all well over a year before the Attack. Afshar called once or twice after that occasion to ask to meet, but I either gave an excuse or let the call go to a voicemail that I immediately deleted. I saw Omar once after recommending him, and he thanked me profusely for the referral to "our friend," but neither he nor I said any more about that.

On August 27th, I was in Egypt on normal business. It was about half past 7:00 pm local time and I was in a tea shop talking with my customers, when someone shouted, "Allahu Akbar!"

I nearly dove under the table, expecting that some fanatic was about to blow himself and us up, but then other patrons began shouting. The television was on and it was reporting that the United States was under attack. Shootings, bombings, planes crashing. The whole tea shop erupted in cheers, but I felt sick. I instantly thought of Afshar, and I hoped with all my heart that the guns I helped ship played no part.

I excused myself to go to my hotel, nauseous. Outside, people were beginning to gather in the streets, cheering and hooting as the news grew more and more terrible. Everyone knew the Americans gave Egypt billions of dollars in aid every year, yet this was their gratitude. The TV pictures of the revelry were directly responsible for the aid cut-off, and the subsequent famine and riots.

But it was less a riot than a party that evening. Luckily, my hotel was close enough to walk to, since a taxi would be useless with the throng gathering to celebrate. The Arab street, not just in Egypt, was ecstatic. I remember smiling old women offering sweets from a tray as I passed through the Orman Gardens on my way to the Nile Ritz-Carlton.

I sat in my room and watched the horror on American CNN for two days until I could get a flight home. Outside, Cairo was delirious with joy. I remember going downstairs to the restaurant and one man at the next table was excitedly telling his comrades that this was certainly the deathblow for the Americans and their Zionist puppets as well.

I disagreed, but kept silent. I knew a bit about Americans, and I was afraid, especially after their new president was sworn in.

For a month I lay low at home, watching events unfold. I assume that Afshar was in the IRGC command bunker in the mountains when the Americans struck because I never heard from him again.

I watched as the Americans took vengeance on the drug cartels that smuggled in the men and weapons. And I was afraid.

Then, one day, I was talking to another friend about how everyone was too frightened to do any business for fear of drawing America's wrath when he asked me if I had heard what happened to Omar. I had not.

Omar was shot twice in the chest and once in the forehead with a .45-caliber pistol outside the Dubai Mall in front of his wife. Only Americans used .45. Omar was the first of several people I was acquainted with killed by US Reaper Teams.

There was clearly a .45 bullet or three out there with my name on it. I had a choice to make.

Loyalty is important, but loyalty to family comes first. I was not about to leave my wife a widow, my children fatherless, for the sake of a man incinerated in an airstrike on an underground bunker.

I knew who to talk to if I needed to talk to Mossad. Everyone did – they made sure you knew how to reach them when, as I was, you were desperate and they were your only way out.

I met Avi, an Israeli Arab I believe, and told him I had important information for the Americans, but I wanted a guarantee of my safety in return. The Americans were, as Michael Corleone did at the end of *The Godfather*, settling all family business. Bodies were piling up in every Arab and European capital, and at least in the Emirates, the police were either unable or unwilling – most likely both – to arrest any suspects.

Avi told me he would pass on my information to the Americans, but he could make no promises. And he told me that we were now "friends," and that in the future he would expect "help." I understood and agreed. I was debriefed in a CIA safehouse here in Dubai for three days. I told them everything. I held nothing back. When I finished, I waited for the bullet, but they were good to their word – at least that day – and let me go.

I just worry that one day, someone in America will decide that the man responsible for moving the weapons to Venezuela needs to die too.

3.

Masada, Israel

We meet on the high, parched mesa overlooking the Judean desert and the Dead Sea. The ramp the Roman X Legion built to reach the fortress is still there against the west face of the cliffs. When the Romans finally broke through the walls in about 75 A.D., they found nearly a thousand Jewish defenders had committed suicide rather than be taken alive. This place teaches the critical lesson that Israelis must remember – victory or death.

America has learned that lesson, though whether it retains that wisdom is uncertain.

The late fall weather is warm but not unbearable, about 80 degrees Fahrenheit, and there are throngs of tourists. The crowds are likely one additional reason why David, who will not give his last name, selected this location to meet. Where he sits, he can watch the entrance as he talks, ensuring he is not being followed. Old habits die hard.

David, still lean and fit and probably around sixty, spent decades in Israel's intelligence community. He refuses to identify his precise organization, but the individual who arranged the meeting suggested that it was some black branch of Mossad. His job, he says, was simple: find Israel's terrorist enemies and stop them by any means necessary.

After the Attack, he found the Americans who sought his and Israel's assistance in eliminating their own terrorist threat took "by any means necessary" to a whole new level.

America inspires fear when it is struck and lashes out. But that fear fades and Americans then fall back into their old ways. It's a cycle. In 1981, the mullahs released the U.S. embassy hostages the day Jimmy Carter left office because they feared Reagan. But it soon became clear to them that Reagan was a paper tiger. Their catspaws blew up the Beirut embassy, then the Marine Barracks, killing hundreds. Reagan did nothing other than have an aging battleship lob 16-inch shells into the Shouf Mountains. Eventually, the mullahs attacked U.S.-flagged ships in the Persian Gulf in 1988, and the threat to America's oil supply was too much to bear. Reagan sank their Navy in an afternoon. The mullahs behaved for a while, sort of.

Clinton tolerated Bin Laden's attacks in Africa and elsewhere. He did nearly nothing about them. He could have killed bin Laden. He didn't. They grew bolder. They executed 9/11, and America conquered Afghanistan and then Iraq. For a while, the forces of jihad were frightened and on the run. Then the Iranians helped their Iraqi puppets murder hundreds of U.S. soldiers with IEDs. America did nothing. In fact, Obama sought to cater to them. Then they pushed America too far and Trump killed Soleimani. They behaved briefly, then once again got bolder. There was no pushback from the next administration.

You must understand your enemy and mine. I fought them all my life. They are serious about their beliefs. You cannot reason with people who think it is justified to rape and mutilate and murder and broadcast it on the internet. But you must respect them enough to believe what they say – at least to each other. To the infidels they may offer *tawriya*, or deceit. But sometimes they are honest, like when they talk about cleansing Israel from the river to the sea. And also when they talk about killing Americans.

We did not believe them, and October 7th happened. The savagery we experienced that day reminded us that our enemy was cunning and dedicated. It was *serious*. But America took no lesson from it, to its great grief. Some truths are difficult to face.

America has always been blessed with two oceans that kept the savagery of the world at bay. This allowed it, and Europe too, to indulge in fantasies about those people from outside. Blame the noble savage fixation of the West – oh, the damage that Rosseau inflicted on our civilization! The power and prosperity of the West not only kept its people safe but created space to indulge the sophomoric notion that all people thought like, and aspired to be like, the West. But that is not true. It never was. That's why you have a peace rave where those young people all probably thought that our country was too hard on the Palestinians, that we Zionists created their anger and fury, and it could be obliterated in an orgy of rape and slaughter by the very people for whom they were dancing for peace.

But, as with the Holocaust, there was denial by those people who embrace the savage outsiders over their civilized neighbors. I was there and saw what Hamas did. I never had any illusions to shatter in the first place, so none of it surprised me. But hope for peace meant that many Israelis were shocked. Afterward, they rallied to do what had to be done.

I am convinced that it was not Israel's response but America's that brought about the Attack. Predictably, the American elite initially stood with Israel, but it quickly grew disenchanted as Israel did what it had to do. Rubble and dead children in Gaza are aesthetically displeasing, but they are consequences of war. The problem stopped being that Hamas had murdered 1400 Jews. The problem became that too many in power in the West were too soft to continue to make the case for victory to the Hamas caucus in their countries. This was especially true in America, where Hamas supporters were prominent members of Congress and embedded deep in the bureaucracy. Our enemies saw weakness.

Of course, we here were focused on Gaza and Judea and Samaria, and on Hezbollah to the north in Lebanon. I wish I had spent some time specifically considering the threat to America, but there were American agencies – many of them – who were supposed to be doing that. The most glaring issue was obviously the southern border. For political reasons, the border was left essentially open. People coming over would claim asylum and be allowed in with a court date some years away. They would be given food and shelter and transportation, even cell phones. Do you imagine your enemies would have not taken advantage of it? There were warnings, but the administration took the risk. Maybe those in power did not even see the risk – again, no one is more blind than the man who will not see.

Our enemies saw. How could they not? And the weakness America showed around the globe inspired them. You Americans have no idea about what a terrible blow to your reputation you suffered retreating from Afghanistan in disgrace as you did. The jihadi enemy looked at that and they believed that if they could inflict one great blow, America would retract and retreat. Then they would erase Israel – as I said, "from the river to the sea, Palestine would be free" was always about the extermination of the Jews – and, next, they would finish their work in Europe. In the final battle, they would sweep across the Americas. Whether it was messianic Shias in Iran, or the Sunnis most everywhere else, they believed it.

This sounds fanciful to Western ears, but what matters is that *they* believed it. The 72 virgins for the martyrs? Again, it sounds like idiocy, but they believe it. That they may rape and torture and murder infidels? They believe it. Our weakness is that we find it nearly impossible to imagine people who believe all this, until it is too late and we are surrounded by mutilated corpses.

We saw indicators. We did not put them together in a comprehensive picture. We just got glimpses. Much of it we passed on to the Americans. Some of you got it. Robert O'Brien, the prior National Security Advisor, went on your Fox News as early as the prior December warning that, "What they did to Israel on October 7th, they would do to us if they could." But the administration in power did not put it together either. I think that it did not want to.

All the evidence was there. For instance, we knew of training bases in Syria, Iran, and Libya. That was nothing new. It was not clear that they were connected – some were Shia, some were Sunni. But these were churning out significant numbers of fighters. Young men were rotating in for short periods, a few weeks or so, and then they disappeared. Normally, the trainees would go to a militia somewhere, Hezbollah or what have you. Not these. They were phantoms. They came in without names and then vanished. Thousands of them. We were baffled. What were they doing?

We managed to capture one of the trainees. He was an educated Palestinian living in the West Bank and had supposedly left for schooling as a civil engineer. He came home, got on the phone and told a friend he was at a camp somewhere in Libya. So foolish a trained operative would assume we were listening because we always were. But that was the point. He was not a trained operative. He was a drone, a worker bee, with one simple task to perform.

We had one of the units of Mista'arvim – Israeli military who look and act like Arabs to infiltrate and operate in Arab areas – take him off the street. Under interrogation, he turned out to be a near amateur. He had a little military training in terms of infantry combat, and some tradecraft for urban operations. He was just taught the basics of the AK-47 as well as hand and rocket-propelled grenades. What was also striking was that he was taught how to operate a body camera and to upload the footage to social media.

Otherwise, the young man knew nothing. He was told he would be paid to train at the camp for an important mission. Of course, he was already indoctrinated into the martyrdom cult from his schooling and Palestinian TV, so that was reinforced. But he had no specific mission. He was told to wait at home and he would be contacted and given instruction. He chose a false name at the camp and was told not to talk about himself to the others. There were thirty in his class, Sunnis, but he could tell from their accents that they were from all over the Arab world and beyond. He thought some were from Nigeria. And there were ten classes underway while he was there.

He was to await a call from someone who would give him a codeword, then he was to do whatever he was told. We turned him, and set him up as an informant. When he got the call, he was to talk to us. We let him loose a couple days later. Apparently, they knew we had taken him because he was found carved up in Jenin two nights later.

We had nothing. We had other matters to investigate and let it go. That is, until May, three months before the Attack. Our AI monitors many things. Without giving away too much detail, we are able to see trends using artificial intelligence. We started to get info that a significant number of families throughout the Arab world were reporting their sons as missing. That was odd. And we also noted that a lot of military-age Arab men were flying into the socialist nations of Venezuela and Nicaragua. But then, people from around the world were coming to Central America to start their trips north to the United States. They were all using their own passports – why bother with the expense and risk of flying on fake documents if you are planning on dumping your documents before the cartels help you cross the border? – so we thought little of it.

In retrospect, clearly they were being prepared for a mission not too dissimilar to the Al-Aqsa Flood operation. The principle of these attacks was demonstrated in Mumbai in 2008, when ten terrorists from Lashkar-e-Taiba murdered 166 people and wounded hundreds more, in the Pulse nightclub murders by an ISIS supporter, and in the Las Vegas shootings that your FBI failed to ever explain – and I cannot speak to what I know of it.

It is simple but brutally effective. Arm young men who would generally be willing to fight to the death with automatic weapons and unleash them on civilians. The killers will kill until they themselves were killed, and if there are many such events, the authorities will be stretched to the breaking point.

The majority of the fighters did not need to be particularly well-trained because their targets were civilians and their main threat would be civilian law enforcement usually armed with pistols. Of course, we saw that in reality they often came up against trained American civilians armed with AR-15s and other rifles thanks to your Second Amendment. Your Founders were wise – I wish more of our people had firearms on October 7th.

Some of the terrorists needed more training. The special units that attacked fortified locations, like the White House, or whose primary mission was to take hostages, actually trained as a unit then shipped out immediately to lessen the risk of disclosures while waiting at home. After all, they actually knew something about the mission. Others were trained on anti-aircraft missiles, or on constructing IEDs. It was mostly Iranian sleepers who had been in-country for years and who had established relationships that worked with the radical students and groups, like Antifa.

And then there was the leadership cadre. They got enhanced training. The terrorists had a classic cell structure, with a very flat hierarchy. Each group of about five had a cell leader. He was the point of contact for those men once in America. He bought a vehicle with cash, made sure everyone had mobile phones for communications, and he led them during the Attack. He also picked up and distributed the weapons and ammunition. But the only other person he knew outside his cell was his contact, who was in charge of 20 or so groups and usually only communicated with them by phone. That leader would give the cell leader his assignment and weapons. There were a couple levels higher above that, but not much. This was not an operation that required continuous coordination. It was designed to fire and forget, like a bullet.

The regular fighters knew nothing, not even that they were part of a larger attack. They got to America, lived in a motel together, and waited. One day, their cell leader got a call and went out, then came back with AK-47s, some grenades, body armor, and their GoPros.

He would also have the mission – attack this school, or that mall. Much of it was patterned after the Mumbai Massacre, from the multiple attacks to the torture of captives. While some cells were assigned to take hostages, most were told only to do so if surrounded. Otherwise, they were told, "Kill every infidel you see."

The targets were selected by Iranian sleepers over the years, and set out in target packets to be handed to the cell leader right before the strike. The emphasis was on the lack of security, the potential for mass casualties, and the psychological impact on the American public. At the cell level, the fighters had no idea they were part of something bigger. It was a surprise – most thought they were the only cell instead of one of thousands.

There was a beauty to their plan because it required no command or control. They would simply need to be let loose to rape and kill, and broadcast their crimes until they were themselves killed.

The challenge for some of the cell leaders was holding back their cells. On the first day, only some of the cells activated. The others wanted to get in on the action. But it was important to attack for three days in a row. It demonstrated the American government's impotence. Day One, attacks in public spaces. Day Two, when Americans were ordered to stay home, attacks on residential areas. Day Three, attacks on infrastructure.

The U.S. government would promise each day that it was over and each morning it would begin again, but somewhere new. The government was protecting public spaces on the second day when the terrorists began attacking people in their homes. Then the third day, the government was protecting homes as the terrorists attacked infrastructure.

It was asymmetrical warfare, like on October 7th. They put their strengths to your weaknesses. They leveraged your government's dysfunction while preparing the Attack and then while executing it. I know they were stunned by the success of it. They expected thousands of casualties. They did not expect how many they actually killed, or the reaction to the videos that were supposed to break America's spirit.

They believed their own false narrative about their enemies, just like America and Israel believed theirs. They expected weakness and capitulation. What they got was ruthless retribution. You Americans are a dangerous people when attacked, even an academic man like yourself. And we in Israel, including myself personally, understand what you went through as a country and personally.

I know what the terrorists thought because we grabbed several of the planners and operators involved in the Attack. In Israel, we do not execute our terrorists, so we got a chance to talk to these guys in depth. They were shocked at how the United States responded. And I expect that after we gave them to the United States – America was polite enough to phrase the extradition demand as a request – they were shocked when America wrung whatever information they had left in them out of them and then shot them in the back of the head.

4.

State of Oaxaca, Mexico

The man they once called "El Cochino" – the Pig – has re-invented himself as a gentleman farmer, the patrón *of a small village far south of the United States border and of Mexico City itself, where the nation twists east into the Gulf. He is not thin, but he is no longer the 400-pound behemoth he was when he was the leader of* Los Chicos Malos, *an infamous organization affiliated with the once-feared Juárez Cartel.*

He is still accompanied by lean, watchful men with weapons. It is understood that the author will not identify his current location with any greater specificity.

"I have," he laughs mirthlessly, "unpaid debts others may wish to collect." He pours himself a shot of Tres Tribus mezcal, an Oaxacan agave liquor similar to the better-known tequila of Jalisco, and knocks it back before he speaks.

You know, they wrote *corridos* about me. Really! Songs! I was very well-known as someone who never gave in, who fought when pushed. But I was generous too. No one who ever worked for me and gave me loyalty wanted for anything. And the regular people, *campesinos* and the like, never had anything to fear from me. I would help them. So, they repaid me with songs.

Much about what was said about us was unfair and wrong – lies to cover up their own corruption and complicity. I do not deny that I ignored the law, but what is the law but a tool to make the lawmakers rich and everyone else poor? They say I was a bad man, but I deny it. I was simply a man living on the terms other men set, and when I angered them it was because I played their game better than they did.

They talk about the cartels as if they were one giant group, but there was no such thing. Mexicans are too independent, too stubborn to all work together in one giant organization. A cartel was really an organization of organizations, many smaller groups. *Los Chicos Malos* was just one of many such groups that made up the Juárez Cartel.

The cartel was centered in Ciudad Juárez, on the border south of El Paso. I was within the leadership circle, I admit. I was respected as a man who could make things happen, who took care of business, and who could be relied upon for sensitive tasks. I was respected by my peers, and my voice carried weight. We were strong when we were forced to be because it was a serious business and it demanded discipline. We were blamed for many horrible acts, but we did not do violence lightly like some other organizations.

The border was our business, as it had been for hundreds of years. A border is there to prevent people on one side from getting what they desire, and to prevent people on the other from giving it to them. We never forced a pill or a powder down anyone's throat or up his nose. We simply responded to the demand of the *gringos*. If not us, someone else would have become rich giving them what they wanted, so why not?

As for people, the *gringos* wanted them too. I had been to the United States when I was younger, before the Drug Enforcement Administration (DEA) decided to persecute me. I saw what the migrants did, slaving away for pennies in rich Americans' fields and factories. Yes, the *pollos* wanted to go north, but the Americans – despite what they said out loud – wanted them to come.

If they did not truly want what we provided, they could have shut down the border with a snap of their fingers. And they did, after the Attack, so you can see the hypocrisy. I do not claim we were innocent. I just reject the easy lie that we acted alone and forced our drugs and migrants on the United States against its will.

Our relationship with the United States itself was delicate because it was a giant that we dared not anger, for it could squash us in a moment. Perhaps during decades of experiencing only its patience, we forgot that as had others in the past. Centuries ago, America invaded our country and stole most of the southwest United States. A bit more than a century ago, Pancho Villa pushed too far and killed some Yankees and the American Army under Black Jack Pershing invaded and hunted him throughout the north. He could not catch the wily Villa, but the humiliation of foreigners tramping across our soil while we were powerless to eject them never left us.

We, in our business, had clear lines that we would not cross. Mexican officials, most of them corrupt themselves, were fair game. But not Americans. The DEA wanted to put us in American prisons, from which there was no escape, but still they were off limits.

In the 1980s, one cartel broke that rule. It kidnapped and tortured and killed Enrique Camarena, an American DEA agent. They were fools. The Americans struck back. They kidnapped Mexicans for trial in America. They did not admit it, but they killed some of those they thought involved. Worse, they shut down the border traffic. Their hand was always on the spigot, and when someone crossed the line they turned it off. That could not be tolerated. We, the cartels, acted to placate the angry giant. Soon the wrongdoers were punished, some by us, and not gently. Like an angry Aztec god, America required a blood sacrifice and we saw that she received it. When the Americans' thirst for vengeance was satisfied, things returned to business as usual.

Decades passed, and the new generation forgot that lesson, much to its regret.

I must be clear with you. It is a lie to say we helped the terrorists. That is, we did not know what they had in mind. We had no inkling. If we had, we never would have worked with them. And I know you have suffered. On my children, we did not intend that.

It was just business as usual. These were not huge deals in the scheme of things. A few thousand men from the Middle East? Why, we were passing tens of thousands of them north already, among the millions of migrants who crossed over the border. It was the best business one could imagine. With drugs, you had to find mules who were willing to, or could be convinced to, risk twenty years in a federal penitentiary to carry over a backpack of fentanyl. But the *coyotes* for the *pollos* need not even cross the border themselves! You bring them to the border, point out where they walk to, then have them give up to the Border Patrol and say their magic words to claim asylum and you have earned five to ten thousand dollars a head.

We knew the Arabs – I know they are different and have different names, but we called them all "*árabes*" – from their trade in heroin and other drugs. They did us favors, we did them favors. When they asked to move bodies north, we thought little of it. After all, we are not political. We believed they were doing what we were doing, getting paid as transporters of migrants. We had no idea that these were *sicarios*. If we had, we never would have allowed it.

I was asked to help with certain shipments of items to the north, sealed in trucks. I believed they were precursor chemicals for meth labs out in the American countryside, though I thought them foolish for taking the risk of brewing the drugs in the United States when we could do it cheaper and without the risk of the police in Mexico. We got such chemicals from China, though with fentanyl they actually made it there and shipped it to us already processed.

I saw the sealed shipping containers and the Chinese bills of lading. They were listed as containing routine items, like bicycle parts or toasters. The *árabes* insisted we not look inside, and assured us the chemicals were specially packaged in a new way so that the drug dogs would not detect them. I did not like it, and I demanded they accept the risk if the items were detected, and they agreed. It seemed to me they had a lot of faith in their new packaging, but in reality the dogs would not detect gun oil or ammunition or missile fuel.

We had friends among the Americans. In Mexico, we offered silver or lead. We can buy you or kill you. For Americans, as I mentioned, we were limited to buying them. And they were expensive. But the *árabes* were paying the costs, so I spent what I needed with my friends at Customs. I would tell them the time and the truck number and I told them to walk their dog around the trucks. I half-expected the dogs would alert, but they never did. My American friends waved the trucks through, free of suspicion because the dogs had cleared the cargo, and off the vehicles went into the interior to be turned over at prescribed meeting points. I must have sent two dozen through without a hitch on our end, though I understand the American authorities did discover some of the weapons later and did nothing.

After my group completed the shipments, I thought nothing more of them. Why would I? I had other things to do, other business to attend to. In August, the hot season was winding down and the next few months would be very busy, so I set about organizing for the next flood of migrants coming up north. I knew when to expect them because other elements of our cartel guided them up from the Guatemala border.

It was a good time for us, for we were making so much money. And it was clean, or at least cleaner. Drugs had a dirty reputation, but helping hungry peasants get to the promised land? That was something to be admired. I would go to a club in Ciudad Juárez and they would cheer for me when I walked in. I would buy drinks for everyone. And, of course, the women overlooked my weight – I was never lonely.

I did not hear about the Attack on the television or radio, but in a phone call from one of my men in the United States on a smuggling run – I think menthol cigarettes, which America banned even as it was legalizing weed. He sounded panicked, and I told him to calm down and tell me what was wrong. Maybe he was in an accident or was being arrested.

No, he told me. He was caught in a gun battle in Oklahoma City. I heard shots in the background and the line went dead.

Was it a rival cartel ripping us off? We all tried not to do wet work in the United States, and while cigarettes were profitable, they were hardly worth killing over.

I found out later that my man had been unlucky, trapped on a freeway by terrorists who blocked the road and walked down the lanes killing everyone in their cars. I wonder if we were the cartel that helped them cross over.

It soon became clear that something big was going on in America, something like 9/11 but worse. One immediate effect on us was the closure of American airspace, followed by the closing of the border – at least the official border crossings. It was not for a few days that the Americans became serious about illegal entry, after they found that many of the killers had been detained by the Border Patrol and released after claiming asylum.

The big men in the cartel met with our chief the next night as the bloodshed to the north switched to the murders of families in their homes. We were no saints, and I will not pretend that families were never targeted, and this disgusted even us. But we did not understand that we were connected to it.

We did not appreciate the effect this had on the Yankees. We told ourselves that this would mean business would slow for a time, and that we should lie low and wait it out. On the third day, when they attacked infrastructure and transportation, we worried that the lull might last longer than we originally thought, but we still assumed it would pass. But it did not.

It was serious enough that the heads of the cartels met under a flag of truce, something that rarely happened. By then, we were getting an inkling of what was coming. There were news reports that the *sicarios* had come over the border, as had their weapons. But we knew nothing of that, until someone remembered the favors we had done for our Arab friends. Could it be true?

Our contacts among the Arabs would not answer our calls. They had gone underground. I began to think they might have the right idea. My contacts among the Americans were scared, but not of us. And they were angry. They were angry at us – when you know how feared we were and you had contacts tell you to go to hell, you knew things had changed. We had no idea yet how much.

The new American president came on the television. We had loved *El Viejo*, the man he replaced. This new *presidente* was something else. He closed the border. He rejected all pending asylum applications, ended any new ones, and ordered all illegals out of the country. Then he explained that the evidence showed that the cartels were behind the smuggling of terrorists and weapons into America. He told the government of Mexico to dismantle the cartels and deliver their leaders for justice, or America would do it itself.

By then, America was under martial law and they were shooting terrorists.

Of course, the government could not take us on. We *were* the government – it functioned only to the extent we allowed it to. Plus, Mexicans are poor but proud, and they would not submit to the demands of the Yankees regardless of what we had done to it by facilitating the Attack.

The cartels came together to provide a united front and sent word that any retaliation would result in America paying a heavy price. I argued against that, loudly, because I knew Americans and I could see what was happening. The bombing of Iran was a warning. But the leaders of the cartels had so much to lose, and many of the members had nothing else but their cartel jobs. I at least had my village and my villa because I had always intended to retire there before I caught a bullet.

When another group captured those frogmen and tortured them and put it up on video to scare the Americans, that was the moment I started driving south. It showed desperation, and I knew it would backfire. The idiots! They thought the Americans were just *gringo federales*.

I was on the road south when Operation Border Justice began. The Americans had their information gathered over decades and they used it. Airstrikes annihilated much of the leadership. The special forces teams hunted others, and the American Army and Marines poured into the country.

The Mexican military disintegrated. Our *sicarios* tried to fight, as they had fought the Mexican forces, but these were not policemen. These were soldiers with tanks and artillery and drones. Our fighters were swept away, though the insurgency continued for a long time.

The Americans were brutal, more brutal than we ever were. We made examples out of people, true, but you kill one man in a horrible way and you save a hundred who learn not to fight back. But the Americans killed anyone who resisted indiscriminately with their planes and shells, including women and children who were nearby. And they shot prisoners after a show trial.

I know America suffered, but its overreaction was an even greater crime, in my opinion. Yes, the three days of the Attack were bloody, but if you count annual deaths from fentanyl, the same number was attained every three years. If the Attack merited war, why not fentanyl? But America, I think, felt guilty about the drugs because it was complicit. In this, America felt it was innocent, though the Arabs have their own grievances, so America felt justified in unleashing all its power against innocent Mexicans.

For my part, I knew I was hunted. The DEA had a thick file on me. I got my lap-band surgery and changed my face. I hid deep in Mexico. I was not the only one who saw what was coming and got out, but during the first years after the Attack, the Americans found most of them. It has been quiet for the last couple years, and I now live a quiet life. I believe the Yankees have forgotten about me. Or so I hope.

One month before this book went to print, the Toyota SUV that El Cochino was riding in on a country road outside of the village of Güila was struck by what news reports say was an American R9X Hellfire missile. The R9X is designed to minimize collateral damage and does not contain an explosive warhead. Instead, on terminal approach to the target, the missile deploys six large, razor-sharp fins, which has led to the weapon's nickname – the "flying Ginsu." Footage uploaded to the internet shows the mangled remains of a man who appears to be El Cochino, albeit much thinner than he appeared in his photos from the time of the Attack.

As is typical when asked by the press, the Pentagon spokesman stated, "We do not confirm or deny our participation in particular strikes, but we reiterate that it is United States policy to hunt down and kill anyone who participated in the Attack in any substantial manner."

5.

Kansas City, Missouri

Richard "Richie" Cunningham went from being walked out of the offices of the Department of Homeland Security to being a deputy director of its successor, the Department of American Security, with personal responsibility for the agency's operations in the Midwest. His firing by the agency after he provided information to the Attack Commission on the failure of the federal government to prepare was reversed by the new president, who renamed, and began the process of reforming, the agency.

Cunningham, who looks nothing like Ron Howard, has a nice office in the new headquarters building – it was moved from D.C. to Missouri as part of the effort to get the bureaucracy closer to the people it serves. But the office barely looks lived-in. Cunningham believes a leader leads by going where his people are instead of summoning them to appear before him. His desk is clear except for his tactical vest, which he carries with him in whatever vehicle he is riding in. "I will not get caught short again. Because something will happen again. There's no doubt."

One big question we had right after it happened was how all these various guys came to be working together. You look at the terrorists and they were not all the same. Sunni, Shia, all sorts of countries and non-countries – there were Palestinians, too. Most of them would have killed each other given the chance, but they all worked together to execute the Attack. That was the main thing I was trying to understand by talking to them.

I switched modes from trying to predict what would happen to figuring out what had happened once the Attack took place. I had been predicting it for years, and that pissed off my bosses. But it was so obvious. We were on the ground in the Middle East and we were infidels. The bad guys were mad. And we left the back door open for them. Was it crazy to think they might walk in? But the brass did not want to hear it. My famous memos – the ones I gave the Attack Commission? I wrote one or two a week for a year documenting the fact that we were going to get hit. They saved my ass when the old Department fired me. I was suddenly this heroic whistleblower. No, I was doing my job! But I knew enough about bureaucracy to cover my ass with paper.

I was a HUMINT guy in the Army – human intelligence – back when I was younger, and I talked to a lot of detainees in Kabul and Baghdad. I got it in ways a lot of other folks at DHS didn't. See, I understood that the enemy was *serious*. This jihad martyr virgins crap – they *believed* it, enough to die for it. Not all of them, of course. Did you know only 94% of the killer teams actually went out and killed people? Some just said, "The hell with this!" and took off and disappeared.

Others enjoyed the Great Satan's delights a little too much. Miami was a bloodbath, but one of the kill teams went out the night before to The Cinnamon Panther gentleman's club, got wasted, and got locked up after a brawl when one of them tried to launch a jihad to conquer the G-string of a dancer named Lady Blue. Four idiots not being able to hold their Bud Lights probably saved 200 lives.

The point is that most of them were really dedicated to their cause, and most Americans could not really accept that. It was so alien to us. It was crazy, so most of us treated it like it was an act, like these guys were just playing an angle. We could buy them off with words or cash or something. Nope. Not happening.

Because we were unwilling or unable to take them seriously, most people in the government thought that they would not really do something massive. Now, this is only a couple decades after 9/11, and a year after October 7th. I think they treated the warnings that I and some others gave as evidence of paranoia not just because they did not understand but because they did not *want* to. And there was the political impact – if you took the threat seriously, you would have to address the open border and Iran, and the administration was not going to do that.

They chose to take the risk. They chose poorly.

I wish I could say I saw the precise outline of their plan. The pieces were out there, but at the time we had no effective synthesis cell to look at them. I knew the numbers coming across the border. I knew there were occasional weapons arrests. And I knew about the two walk-ins, one on each coast, who wanted asylum and residency and talked about how they were trained and sent here.

But they were low-level guys. They did not know anything except they were trundled across the border and told to wait. Look, we have always had sleeper cells. The Russians in the Cold War? You would be surprised. That *The Americans* TV show was onto something. The Chinese. Oh, they had plenty of boots on our ground. Still do. And the Iranians? We not only had sleepers but hit teams. They were planning to kill the Trump administration guys who waxed Soleimani even before the Attack. Of course, they tried it during the Attack and they got smoked because we had security on our officials.

And then there were the radicals and the college kids who got indoctrinated. That was no secret. They were loud and proud about wanting the downfall of America, But again, if you take them seriously, then you have to react. Could you see those administration hacks coming down on leftist activists? Hell, many of them were leftist activists!

The point is there was always an excuse to ignore the evidence. And they ignored it.

When the Attack happened, I got called out like everyone else. I did not have my gear in the truck and I went out on ops with street clothes and a pistol on the first day. That's why I carry all this gear with me everywhere.

On day three, I got called off the running and gunning and back to operations and intel. We needed to figure out what happened, and the best way to do that was to talk to the prisoners. I was a natural for the interrogations, having dealt with the same kind of guys overseas. I knew a little Arabic too. We had to hop on it because the military commissions were running fast, and you had to get them before they got gone, if you know what I mean.

There's been some criticism that we did not keep them around longer and squeeze them for more intel. I don't know about that. I probably interrogated a hundred of them, and maybe five had something interesting to say. Those guys got a temporary reprieve and a more focused debrief, so to speak. The other 95% did not know much of anything. That was intentional. They were like ants, following basic instructions until they dropped dead. And the queen was not taking the drones into her confidence.

The thing that got me about the worker bees was that they were all different but the same. They hated the Little Satan, Israel, and they really hated the Great Satan, us. They might cut each other's throats in a heartbeat, but the thing that unified them was the desire to murder us. The organizers were smart. They tried to put, say, Yemeni guys together on a kill team, or Palestinians, or Somalians. But regardless of their brand of Islam or their hometown, these guys were all on the same team when it came to the big picture. And since we looked at those divisions as indicators, that they worked together was part of their deception plan.

What I never got over is how, in personal interactions, there are really no people more hospitable than Muslims. That's a cultural thing. You treat guests well. They are very pleasant and friendly. But man, you cross the jihad line and these guys are savages. They would sit and brag about raping women or chopping up little kids as if it was the greatest moment of their lives, and you had to hold it together. I had some experience with it, but sometimes I lost it. Once I asked this guy talking about what he did to the teenage girls at that school in St. Louis what the hell his mother would think. He looks at me like I'm the idiot, and tells me that he called his mother *during* it and that she told him she was proud of him. I didn't drop any tears when the MPs dragged that piece of shit outside for his nine-millimeter comeuppance.

It was the higher-up guys who were interesting. They had a very flat hierarchy – one guy would oversee dozens of these little kill cells. He would set them up in some apartment or motel and have them wait. Just before D-Day, he would arrange the delivery of weapons and gear and then hand over a target packet. That was their command and control. He would report up to a superior, and that guy was directed from the outside.

The specialty teams had more interaction. Some were set up to shoot down aircraft and they needed to get their missiles. Some were assassination teams with a death list – several politicians or officials or celebrities. For example, the assassins in Washington would have ten targets on it and they would just go all the way down the list and then go on a shooting spree against regular civilians after they finished.

The bombers took a lot of support because you needed the explosives, and the vehicles, and places to assemble them. So there were some sleepers who spent months setting that up. They rented empty garages and then trucks and cars – they never stole them. That meant money. They needed fake documents, like driver's licenses and credit cards, so that was sophisticated. I expect the cartels helped with that.

The explosives were tricky for them because we watched those materials pretty closely. If you took a little, it was a bigger deal than a large theft because you have some Emulex go missing from a mine explosives locker it's a red alert since the mine owners know they can go to jail. But if a whole train car of ammonium nitrate goes missing, everyone assumes it's a screw-up and the car is sitting lost in some railyard because who would steal an entire train car? Well, we found out. The key train cars are all GPS-tracked, so the trackers being disabled was kind of a red flag. But again, if you admit there's a problem, people look at you for a solution. So you deny there is a problem. Bureaucracy is a beautiful thing!

We really should have seen the infrastructure attacks coming. The Day One attacks on public locations were basically the same mass shooter scenarios we had seen dozens of times, except times a thousand. The home attacks on the second day were pretty much a repeat of the Gaza attack on Israel. And the third day, when they went after infrastructure, that was really the part of the operation that was supposed to cripple the country, which it nearly did.

You can lose tens of thousands of people, and that's bad, but the country goes on. But screwing up the power supply? That's existential, and we knew, we damn well knew, that bad guys were looking at the power grid. There were over 160 attacks on the grid, physical attacks, in 2022 alone. You know those transformers you see? You don't just go down to the local giant power transformer store and pick up a replacement. China builds them, and they take months to build assuming the Chi-Coms will even sell us a replacement. And you can put one down with a rifle.

They did, too. When the Attack hit, after the public venue attacks the next day the cops and soldiers guarded public venues. The terrorists hit private homes on the second day, right where our forces weren't. So, on the third day we focused on residential areas and that day the terrorists hit infrastructure. They always hit where we weren't – asymmetric warfare. The power companies hired private security and would put an unarmed minimum wage guard sitting in his 2009 Toyota Corolla in the driveway of a substation with a cell phone and tell him to call 911 if something went down. There were a lot of dead security guards, and a lot of dead transformers. So we had power outages, and that ramped up the chaos.

And the food supply – what a disaster. In most big cities there is a zone where they have all the giant reefer warehouses where they keep the food before distributing it to the supermarkets. In Los Angeles, there's a tiny city called Bell which holds most of them. The warehouses are massive. You hit the power substations supporting those reefer buildings and suddenly the meat and veggies start spoiling. Add the cyber screwing up the logistics and there's no resupply. You got millions of people with nothing to eat.

An American city at the best of times has about three days of food on hand for its population. Do you know what you have when you have an American city that has not gotten food delivered for three days?

Mogadishu.

It was a miracle it was not worse. The good thing about Americans is that people act on their own and we improvise. That's what saved us. That and martial law.

Of course, all hell broke loose after, with bureaucrats pointing fingers. I got fired, then rehired and promoted. Here I am, doing the same job as before with at least some support from up high. But I worry. It's hard to be on your toes forever. I see people relaxing, thinking maybe we are overacting, that it can't happen again. Well, those bad guys over there across the ocean, they may be quieter now, but they still want to kill us all.

6.

Cambridge, Massachusetts

Robinson Hall is a squat, two-story building from the year 1900 that holds the Harvard History Department. Most of the faculty is new, having joined over the last five years. The arrests and the purges, both voluntary by the school and forced by the federal government, have dramatically changed the focus of the Department. Today, it is again about education – "To study the past to understand our present and future." But five years ago, the History Department's mission statement was very different: "To leverage visions and interpretations of the past to uproot systemic racism, sexism, and transphobia in the present and to train leaders in the struggle to decolonialize the future."

Professor Donald Hersh, who holds the Andrew Breitbart Chair in American History, was a graduate history student at Harvard and one of the few current faculty members present at Harvard before the Attack. He has made the study of the events surrounding it his focus.

It is somewhat unusual for a historian to study events that he lived through himself. Historians typically look at times and places far removed from their own personal experiences. But I was a percipient witness to the events that I now teach to my students about. I understand that this may mean my findings are biased by that personal experience, but as a percipient witness to the events I can testify based on what I saw and heard myself. It is just like you have your own story among the ones you are gathering for this book.

I was warned not to go into the Harvard Ph.D. history program for two very practical reasons. The first was that there were very few jobs for historians. You could teach, but a tenure track position at a fine college was quite rare – a handful a year among the most prestigious schools. I figured the Harvard credential would solve that problem. The name itself was something special, so special that there was even a name for the moment when an alum lets it be known that he or she is a graduate – "Dropping the H-bomb." Of course, most alumni enjoyed that moment immensely. I figured with a doctorate from Harvard, I would instantly be a competitor for any faculty position anywhere.

But there was another practical reason to avoid Harvard. The politics of the faculty and the student body. It was not merely liberal. It was radical. Once Harvard had at least allowed in token conservatives, like Ben Shapiro, but no more. The admissions office at Harvard and the other Ivies curated the student body to, in effect, curate the future ruling class. I did not understand that. I thought that if I simply focused on my work and research, I would not be affected by the zeal and excesses of the radicals. The administration would keep them in check. I did not realize that the radicals were, in fact, in charge. Just look at Harvard's former president, a woke activist and plagiarist with a wafer-thin curriculum vitae. I was somehow accepted into the program, and I ignored my misgivings and matriculated.

I originally wanted to study the Israeli-Palestinian issue. That was interesting to me – I had family in Israel – and it seemed less esoteric than devoting myself to the twelfth century or the like. Perhaps I could even help contribute to a solution to the problem of peace.

I proposed this as my focus to a faculty advisor team and there was an awkward silence. I was not sure what the issue was. One of the professors told me that I might not be the right person to focus on this topic. I "did not have the indigenous perspective," and my work "could be interpreted as giving voice to settler narratives." For good measure, another professor, a man dressed as a woman who I was expected to pretend was a woman, added that they – everyone always made introductions with their preferred pronouns – was concerned that my topic "ignored and therefore devalued trans and gender non-conforming voices."

The advisors were gentle but insistent. Several students of Arab or other descent were allowed to take on the topic as their focus, but for me it was the twelfth century. I agreed to reorient my work and told myself that once I had tenure I would be free to pursue my actual interests. This really was a paper chase – a race to get that diploma and use it to find a position somewhere else because it was clear I would not fit in on the faculty here.

But it was also clear that I would not fit in among the student body. Students are naturally activists, but they are also scholars and young people enjoying life. Studying and fun are both important too. But in the Harvard hothouse, the activism took on more and more focus.

I expected to find brilliant minds among the undergraduates that I taught as an assistant, but they were closed-minded, emotional, and resistant to any ideas outside the dominant narrative. I received complaints because I offered balancing perspectives – some I did not even agree with – to the prevailing set of ideas. In most cases, they were shocked to find that anyone could articulate a position that was different than what they believed, and they were outraged by it.

The indoctrination was endless. Putting aside the uniform progressive perspective of the classes, there were endless teach-ins and rallies. It seemed like every day I was invited to add my signature to whatever letter of concern was being circulated. Obviously, the United States was a primary target – it was a capitalist dictatorship built on indigenous genocide, slave labor, and systemic racism, and it was a stain on human history. But while they hated America, they also hated Israel. When October 7th happened, I was shocked and horrified to see my students celebrating, chanting "From the river to the sea," denying the Hamas atrocities, and cheekily waving placards with paraglider silhouettes. This was a reference to what some terrorists used to fly into Israel to rape and slaughter rave attendees who were about the same age as my students.

And I came in for special suspicion because I was Jewish. Many friends at many other schools, prestigious schools, told me that they were experiencing the same thing. Now, there was some pushback. Some rich donors cut off the school, though with a multi-billion-dollar endowment that meant nothing. More effective was several corporations and big law firms announcing that people associated with anti-Semitic protests were unwelcome. Interfering with students' futures in America's elite organizations got their attention, but they simply took their radicalism underground. And when it was hidden, it turned even more pathological.

I found it frightening but fascinating. I wanted to see what was really happening. I was not observant then, and I stayed out of politics, so I could pass as an ally – I just could not be a leader, because my voice was supposed to be subordinate to other voices of those higher on the intersectional hierarchy of oppression. I began attending the meetings, which were not quite secret but not quite public. The speakers and their agenda were much more radical than I imagined.

I remember one woman – the women were always the most strident and vicious – haranguing the students.

"Do not believe that decolonialization is a metaphor or a symbol!" she said. "It is not. It is action, concrete action, where blood tomorrow will be shed in an act of accountability for the blood shed by settlers and their stooges yesterday!"

I watched some kids, perhaps realizing that they were not prepared to buy into this, ask what should happen to the Jews in Israel. They were attacked and belittled for failing to focus on the pain of the Palestinians. But occasionally the instructors were honest. "They will suffer justice, and it will be beautiful, and we must not allow the oppressors to set the terms of resistance." Everyone understood what that meant. It meant that rape and torture and murder were allowed if the right oppressed people did it to the right oppressors.

And they made it clear that this moral construct applied to America as well. America too must be cleansed. Every meeting or event began with a land acknowledgement reciting how the ground Harvard was built upon was stolen, and how it would be taken back. They often referred to America as "Turtle Island," because, they claimed, some tribes thought North America was created on the back of a giant turtle. And, ominously, they began to refer to Americans – normal Americans – as "settlers."

This went on for months and got worse over time, with the rhetoric ticking up in its bloodthirstiness. I observed it and then went home and documented it. I am not sure what I intended to do with my research, but I felt I had to bear witness. These were supposed to be the best and brightest of America's youth, and they nodded along with this moral madness. Not all of them seemed to accept it. There was some subtle eye-rolling and most of them probably forgot it as soon as they went back to the dorm and cracked a brew. But there was a sub-set, about a tenth maybe, that seemed to fully embrace it.

I began sharing my *sub rosa* observations with others at various different schools. My experience was their experience. There had to be some level of coordination among the organizers since their narratives were nearly identical. Obviously, there was money funding it. And there were the outside organizers. They were shadowy, not part of the faculty. They would often observe the proceedings, but never speak to the groups directly. Like a cult, they would help select the students most susceptible to the message and bring them inside the clique. They would use social pressure and love bombing, feigning the acceptance of people who were broken or hurting, and turn them into monsters.

I was never able to get so far as to be invited into the inner circle. Being Jewish and male made me suspect, so I started claiming to be a genderqueer two-spirit and using xe and xir as pronouns, but it did not help. I did get a lot of disturbing direct messages on Twitter though.

In retrospect, we know what this was. They groomed a hardcore of supporters at America's most respected universities. At Harvard, there were maybe a hundred in the hardcore with another thousand allies willing to do supporting tasks and minor vandalism. It was the hardcore who would commit violence. The faculty members and grad students doing the organizing were interacting with Iranian sleepers, many of whom passed as Americans.

They trained for direct action too, with the hardcore taken out into the country to learn to shoot, make firebombs, and how to use knives. It was exciting for them. Most of them were affluent kids who came from prosperity, lived through their screens, and had never been in a fight. This was *real*. It was also quasi-spiritual. None had any religious grounding – they had a void and the enemy understood how to fill it with their Frankfurt School dogma. The worst of the hardcore were as fanatical as the most dedicated jihadi.

And this was all indirectly subsidized by the United States government in the form of loans and grants. It happened at a hundred universities across the country, though with varying levels of success.

Was there any warning about what was coming? We heard cryptic rumors about the training for the select few, talk about "direct action," and the like. But there is no evidence that anyone, even the faculty organizers, knew that on August 27th there would be a massive terrorist attack. What they knew was that at some point in the future, the oppressed would rise, that the oppressors would be eliminated in a just rebuke by those they held under their boots.

The first day of the Attack, Boston was struck hard in many places but Harvard was not touched. We know now that the terrorists avoided striking the colleges where they built an infrastructure – though they went on murder sprees through dorms at schools that were not organized. Obviously, they wanted to avoid killing their own minions, but there was another reason. The violence people saw on their iPhones or televisions – though most of the young people did not even have a television – was purely abstract, like a video game. If they had to contend with dead bodies in front of them the first day, many more might have run away from their cult.

But that first day, the organizers knew what to do without even being told – they sought to "contextualize" the violence and to "explain" how this was the cry of long-oppressed peoples. They began their pro-terror rallies and gatherings within hours of the first killings. What we understand today is that the sleeper agents then reached out and told the local organizers that this was the revolution. This was the time to strike. The sleeper agents helpfully provided targets and instructions for their university warriors. Sometimes, they provided weapons too. They also did this with the Antifa chapters and other radical organizations that they were cultivating.

Why did so many young college students, from good families and with bright futures, join an orgy of blood and violence? Programing, but also the excitement of being part of a great, violent change. Do you remember the chaos of the first day? It really seemed like everything was collapsing. The President was missing. Planes were falling from the sky and bombs were exploding. The police could not regain control. Everything seemed to be falling apart, and for those awaiting the collapse of the United States, it seemed that the time had come.

That was how, on the second and third days, so many of our young people joined in.

7.

Los Angeles, California

Joshua Levy stands outside the rebuilt Holocaust Museum near Pan Pacific Park on the west side of LA. He helped raise the millions of dollars it took to repair the damage to the building. He is armed, carrying a Beretta PX4 Storm pistol on a custom leather holster hanging off his designer belt.

He seems to know everyone, shaking hands, suggesting their people and his people arrange lunch. The only time he is not talking to the author or an acquaintance is when he stands silently for a moment contemplating the Wall of Remembrance memorializing the tens of thousands murdered in the Attack.

"Never again" means never again. That's my motto.

Look, I was a liberal guy. My family was in the entertainment industry and everyone I knew was left of center, even progressive. Oh, we hated Trump. Hated him! He was closer to Israel than any other president ever, but that did not matter. He was a Republican, so he was an anti-Semite. We knew because of course he was.

You have to understand that many of us in the U.S. really did not see ourselves in terms of religion. Many of us did not practice, except to show up at the synagogue on the holidays. The Orthodox were as alien to us as any other religion was. A lot of us really found our faith in politics.

So, our faith was shattered when October 7th happened and we turned to our allies on the left and expected – though, in retrospect, why would we? – them to stand with us. More Jews were murdered in one day than at any time since the Holocaust. There was no question about it – Hamas bragged about it, filmed it. They uploaded videos! They were proud of it! Who could deny it was an atrocity?

But, at best, our allies shrugged. Others celebrated. They cheered! They told us – sometimes in so many words but sometimes to our faces – that the Zionists, the settlers, had it coming. And it began to dawn on us that *we* were the Zionists and the settlers they were talking about.

It turned out that in the hierarchy of oppression, Jews were at the bottom. The same people standing by us as we called out anti-Semites on the right were now chanting, "From the river to the sea." It was like they turned on a dime. Anti-Semitism was bad one day, but the next day it was mandatory. Our heads spun.

We were told that as good allies we should support the Palestinian resistance. Some of us did! They were so deeply inside their own ideology of oppression that they nodded and went along. It cost some of them dearly.

I was never a go-along guy. I thought it was an outrage. I was on the left myself, but I was also in Hollywood, so I could smell bullshit. And I did. It was all bullshit.

Some of us fought back. We had a woman in our company who got on Instagram and called us "Jewish cockroaches." She got canned. But a bunch of big stars and directors on the left signed an open letter slandering "the Zionists" knowing that there would be no repercussions. It had lots of talk about Palestinian children, but none about dead or kidnapped Israeli ones.

I was often on the host committees for the President and for some of the progressive senators, and I raised a lot of money for them. The President was fine on the Gaza War at first, backing up Israel, calling terrorists "terrorists" – though he would not name

Iran – but as the war went on, he started backtracking. He started calling for a ceasefire when that would only give them time to rearm and regroup. He said nothing about the hostages. I texted his campaign people and asked, "What the hell?" except I did not say "hell." No response. I called up some of the senators I had helped raise big bucks for. Only a few took my calls, and they started telling me that it was a complex issue, that there were nuances.

Nuances? The bastards wanted to wipe Jews off the face of the Earth!

That is when I saw that there were cracks in the Democratic Party. All of us were Democrats, and our families had been for generations. But now we needed the party and the party was worried that the progressives might not be happy if the party was seen as too protective of the Jews. It was clear. We were not part of the new coalition.

I was angry, of course. I was especially angry at the denial. The leftists would ignore the atrocities when they could, then excuse or even condone them if pressed. We put up posters of the hostages, including little babies, so that people could see what the media and our administration were ignoring. The progressives would tear them down and laugh while they did it.

A big star did a showing at the Holocaust Museum – the old one they blew up – of a video collection of the terrorist uploads and camera footage. Horrible, but it had to be seen. Like when Eisenhower made his camera crews record the camps specifically so no one could come back later and deny it. So, we showed it.

And outside the Palestinian sympathizers were waiting, and they attacked us. There was a fight. The cops barely intervened. We were lucky no one was hurt. But the hate they had for us was incredible. I had never felt it before. I never imagined it was possible in America. But I started to realize that if they could get away with it, they would pull an October 7th here. They hated us that much.

There were more outrageous actions, like when a mob trapped Jewish students in a library at a New York college and the authorities told the students they could go hide in the attic. That really happened! If someone pitched me that in a script, I would have called it too on the nose.

Where was the FBI, the Department of Justice? They should have been rounding these punks up. But no. The administration's answer was a task force to fight Islamophobia! It was not Muslims being threatened in the streets!

This anti-Semitism was tolerated, and the radicals got the message. It got uglier. A Jewish man was killed at a demonstration here in Los Angeles. A rabbi was stabbed in Detroit. If it was anyone else being targeted, the authorities would have called these "hate crimes." But they did everything possible not to do that when the victims were Jews.

Synagogues were damaged. Kosher restaurants were trashed. The Palestinians' supporters marched on the campuses, chanting, "Gas the Jews." The college administrators did nothing. Maybe they were afraid. Maybe they agreed. Jewish students were attacked, while Jewish fraternity houses and clubs were vandalized and even burned. Families pulled their kids out of college.

Many of my friends hoped it was just temporary. America will come to its senses, they said. They thought it would blow over. It was a cope.

But for me, "Never again" meant something. I learned from history. No one was going to protect me but me. I was one of the ones who went out and bought a gun. Me and a gun – I had never shot one before and I gave a lot of money to gun control groups. I thought guns were for right-wing knuckle-draggers, and I thought it was a lie when they said they just wanted to protect their families. Well, here I was, with a gun, ready to protect my family.

Luckily, I had some connections. I got the weapons trainer for *The Destructonator* movies to train me just like he trained the stars. I got my gun permit thanks to a Supreme Court that I had been outraged at just about a few months before. And I was going to Oak Tree Gun Club every week to train because I knew, I just knew, this was going to get bad.

It got worse, here and elsewhere. There were beatings, there were murders. The Orthodox community could barely go outside. The authorities shrugged. The communist district attorney refused to charge the thugs they caught, though in fairness he never charged anyone. Some of my friends were too scared to say anything, while others told the loudmouths like me that I was helping the Republicans by talking about the situation. As if that, and not the pogrom against us, was the issue.

I was at work the first day of the Attack, getting ready to go to a breakfast meet with a producer who allegedly had a star attached – she was a "tentative maybe" – for a feminist reboot of *Dirty Harry*. That was a nonstarter – audience appeal aside, I just did not feel Emma Stone for the lead. But I was going to hear him out – well, them, since they insisted they was a nonbinary two-spirit. It was one of those meets you need to do, in this case because to have turned it down would get me painted as transphobic or whatever. I was already making enemies. Some big names would not work with me because I insisted on calling out the anti-Semites.

We were at a trendy coffee place on North Bedford in Beverly Hills, and my companion was nibbling their elderberry and lemon scone, and I hear gunfire. By then, I knew what real guns sounded like. People started running down the street and screaming – some were bloody – and it was a zoo. My companion ducked under a table, but I had my piece and I went to the door and looked outside. I saw one – black shirt, green headband, AK-47 running across the street at the next intersection, pursuing people, shooting. He disappeared around the buildings and I could hear gunfire. If I had had a shot, I would have taken it.

I somehow got home and the family and I settled in. My gun was on the kitchen table. We lived up in the Hollywood Hills then. We could not stop watching the news. They reported that a car bomb had destroyed the front of the old Holocaust Museum, and then the killers had gone after the schoolkids and patrons who were inside. I felt sick.

I was home from work for two weeks. Of course, with the cyber-attacks and power issues, nothing much happened. We were down to some old cans of Campbell's Chicken Soup before our Whole Foods got resupplied. I stood in line for six hours to get my ration – one shopping bag full. The next day I sat in line all day for gasoline and never got to the pump. You know I had my gun in my belt the whole time.

The terrorists did not come into our neighborhood, but the radicals drove through screaming and yelling, smashing car windows, telling us the revolution was here and that we settler pigs would pay. I busted off a cap over the heads of what had to be a bunch of college kids with Palestinian flags and kitchen knives. They drove away, but I can't forget their faces. Remember the Manson girls in those old photos? They were *happy*. It was insane. I think if they had known about the Manson family they might have carved swastikas in their foreheads too. It would have been on brand.

Other people I knew were not so lucky. I lost several friends. One was a sit-com actor you know, shot down in Beverly Hills not far from where I was. It could have been me. Another was a movie composer. They came to his house and butchered his family and then him. I knew some acquaintances who were killed, one shot down in a 787 while taking off from JFK and another who had called me a "racist" for not supporting the Palestinian cause. She was raped and murdered in New York. I sometimes wonder if she tried to explain that she was on their side while they butchered her.

I got why they attacked Jewish sites, like the Museum and the Jewish community around Fairfax. But at first, I did not get why they attacked the most liberal part of one of America's most liberal cities. And then I realized that their hate trumped their politics. Liberal, conservative, Jewish or Christian, they hated us all. And they literally wanted to wipe us all off the face of the Earth. Being a good Democrat was not going to save you.

I'm not any kind of Democrat anymore. Neither are my parents. I can't forgive the party. I understand the party's predicament, but right is right and choosing wrong set the conditions for what we went through. Now, I'm one of those gun-carrying, right-wing knuckle-draggers, and I raise money for the politician who takes the hardest possible line against the terrorists. Liberalism is a luxury when someone is targeting you for genocide.

When I say "Never again," I mean never again.

8.

Peterson Space Force Base, Colorado Springs, Colorado

General Leon Dugan looks more like a shopkeeper than what he is, the Army four-star in command of the U.S. Northern Command (NORTHCOM). NORTHCOM's mission is the protection of the continental United States. Dugan was a military intelligence officer – in the past, the NORTHCOM commander would have come from the combat arms community, like the infantry or aviation. But not now. Now, America's first line of defense is its spooks.

General Dugan's job is much more than just overseeing military forces. His primary mission involves "integrating intelligence community, law enforcement, and other civilian assets into a unified and proactive defense posture." His command identifies threats before they can mature. The task fell to NORTHCOM during the post-Attack reforms after it became clear that no one else had been performing it. The price for that failure had been unbearably high.

All the pieces were there, every single one of them. We had all the pieces, or at least inklings of all the pieces. But no one put them together. There was no one entity looking at the big picture, just many entities looking down inside their own silos. America missed what was happening.

Remember, the terrorists understood us. We had hunted them for decades after 9/11. They knew what we were looking for, and they let us see what they wanted us to see.

They understood the Israelis too. The October 7th massacre should have been a warning. It was a masterstroke of asymmetrical warfare. Asymmetricity is how a nominally weaker force defeats a nominally stronger one by carefully applying each of its limited strengths against the limited weaknesses it identifies in the stronger. Look what Hamas did. First, it did its intelligence preparation of the battlefield, what we call IPB. It did careful reconnaissance of Israeli Defense Force (IDF) fortifications and dispositions. It observed the IDF routines, as well as those of the police agencies. It sought out weaknesses in the barrier systems that kept out the terrorists, including electric fences and remotely targeted guns. And it analyzed the layouts and defensive capabilities of the local communities and kibbutzes.

What did it find? First, it found – and this was over an extended period – that the Israeli defenses were designed against small, discrete groups of terrorist infiltrators, maybe five to ten individuals. The physical barriers and remote weapons were designed to deter them or delay them long enough for the IDF to dispatch ground forces to eliminate the intruders. The failure of imagination on the part of Israel was regarding the number of attackers and, importantly, the number of attacking groups. The defenses fell because they were designed for one or maybe two groups at a time, not fifty or a hundred at dozens of points across the length of the border. Hamas surged its limited forces all at once and overwhelmed the IDF's defense for several hours, which was all it needed to conduct its massacre.

The second thing Hamas did was train its forces at a cell level for their specific task, but it kept them totally in the dark as to anything else. Each cell knew it was being trained for *something*, but it did not know what. The members of each cell certainly did not know, until just before the Attack started or maybe even after the assault was underway, that it was only one cell of dozens. And, of course, the senior leaders in Hamas knew the Israelis were listening to their mobile calls, so everything they said on their phones were things they wanted the Israelis to hear. They presented as shooting some rockets, but nothing more. Their actual substantive communications were conducted face-to-face.

The third thing Hamas did was utilize what it had on hand as far as equipment for maximum impact. It made a virtue of necessity. Old-school AK-47s were perfect for this kind of attack – light, simple to use, and deadly against unarmed or lightly armed targets. They used the folding stock model because those guns were easier to conceal and to use in close quarters. Civilian trucks, cars, and even motorbikes were perfectly adequate to transport them to their targets once they breached the walls. They cleverly used drones to drop bombs and take out the remote guns.

Fourth was their use of deception and timing. Like with the cell phones, they used their rocket launches to draw Israeli attention away from the real operation. And they knew that IDF protocol, and civilian protocol, was to take cover in shelters when the rockets flew. They fired off rockets overhead and the real targets, instead of being on alert, took shelter. They were not out and ready to respond to a ground attack. That the Attack was executed on a holiday ensured there was reduced manning.

Finally, they selected an asymmetrical objective in that they sought to electrify their supporters and terrify the Israelis. They would put what strength they had against primarily civilians and some outgunned IDF forces to run up the casualty count. They also fed their fighters Captagon, a kind of amphetamine popular among Syrian fighters, that made them more aggressive and lowered inhibitions against atrocities, although their indoctrination from childhood did that too.

The brutality of it, and the way they ensured that the scenes of the carnage were uploaded to the web, were deliberate choices. They demonstrated to both their side and to the Israelis that they were not powerless. They also knew the horror of the initial assault would fade and that the focus of the world would become the Israeli response, which it did. They likely expected the world to restrain the Israelis more forcefully than actually happened, much as Bin Laden did not expect the American response to 9/11 and the attackers of August 27th did not expect our response to that atrocity. At the end, while we did not truly understand our enemy because of its alien mindset, our enemy did not fully understand us.

But it understood enough to pull off the most massive terrorist attack in history.

What did they see when they looked at America? What did their IPB entail? First, they had been looking at us for decades, particularly the Iranians, who have had a presence here in the form of sleepers since the Shah fell. They examined our defenses. On the borders, the defenses went from limited in scope under Donald Trump to effectively none under his successor. The border was not merely open, but the United States government was effectively assisting the people breaching it. Our enemy probably could not believe its luck.

Through connections formed within the drug trade – much of the world's heroin flows through the Middle East – they came to an arrangement with the Mexican cartels to move men and equipment into the United States. That solved enormous logistical problems.

Inside the United States, they found a country utterly unprepared for a mass assault. All of America was a soft target, although the fact that Americans could be, and sometimes were, armed did disrupt a number of their attacks. The long-term sleepers did the reconnaissance. They carefully scouted targets and the Iranian Revolutionary Guard Corps (IRGC) planners in Iran created hundreds and hundreds of target packages. Each one had information and maps that could be given to a cell and allow the cell to execute its mission. The Israelis found these same kind of target packages on dead Hamas terrorists. American law enforcement actually had several of these packages in hand before the Attack, but they were in the hands of different agencies and made no reference to other simultaneous attacks, so no one understood their significance. Some were not even translated until after the Attack.

Like Hamas, the terrorists trained to the cell level, so an informer could only implicate a few members. And the cell members knew nothing until the Attack was about to begin. We had members of various cells in custody before the Attack, but none that had received their mission yet. All we knew was they had undergone training and come to America.

The specialists were different, but the training most of them received was limited because for the vast majority of the terrorists, they just had to know how to take an automatic rifle and kill everyone they saw. Again, they selected the AK-47 because it was cheap and simple to use. We know they considered using the M4s left in Afghanistan, but understood that they would be too easy to trace, though afterward Iran was not shy about hinting that it was behind the Attack. They did consider buying weapons here, but buying guns is not as simple as the media claims and besides, civilian "assault rifles" are not actually assault rifles in that they are not automatic weapons.

The key was mass. America's anti-terrorist efforts were targeted at small groups acting alone. The enemy saw we were vulnerable to mass in terms of attackers and discrete attacks. What was unimaginable, and was not imagined, was the sheer audacity of the numbers – ten thousand killers? That was an Army division. Nearly two thousand separate attacks over three days? Unprecedented. But it could be done because there was no border and because the nature of the attacks required no coordination after the initial orders.

As in Israel, the beauty of the plan was that it eliminated the need for command and control. The targets for each of the three days – the three phases – were identified long in advance and documented in targeting plans that gave the cells everything they needed to conduct their strikes. Day One, public places. Day Two, Americans in their homes, Day Three, infrastructure. The successive waves of attacks struck at new targets just as Americans struggled to secure the targets attacked the previous day.

The killers were fire and forget assets – that was the advantage of martyrdom. They *expected* to die. There was no need for an exit strategy, resupply, medical evacuation, or anything else needed to support an army. They would kill until killed. The ringleaders – it was a very flat cell hierarchy that had minimal contact with individual cells even as the cells awaited activation – did not have to provide leadership once they handed over the target packets and weapons. Each cell simply executed its mission and shot or otherwise slaughtered civilians and first responders until it was shot down itself.

And, as in Israel, reveling in the atrocities was part of the plan. They believed the effect would be to cause America to withdraw from the world, and that there would be internal support by the American left. They were partially right on that last count. Their Antifa and college student allies were a supporting effort, but it was important because the message was that "American elite, your sons and daughters and others are with us."

And then there was the cyber component the third day – they wanted our internet up the first two days to spread images of the carnage. Our cyber defenses are shockingly weak and they had probed us for years. We do believe North Korea, Russia, and perhaps China – though the CCP categorically denies it – assisted with improving the Iranians' cyber skills and targeting. In any case, we were prepared for internet vandals and ransomware thieves fairly well – not very well prepared, but somewhat prepared. We were not prepared for the kind of massive, targeted cyber-attack we suffered. Again, asymmetricity.

What did we know about the Attack before it happened? A lot, in retrospect. But we did not know it as a coherent whole. Everyone had pieces of the puzzle, like the blind men in a cave feeling an elephant. Except in this case, the blind men refused to even talk to each other.

For example, the old Central Intelligence Agency had significant information, but the CIA did not share it. It attempted to analyze the raw data in the context of its own sources, and that let the enemy's deception plan work. The CIA knew that there were training camps, but it assessed them as unrelated because some were Sunni groups and some were Shia groups. The idea that they might combine under Iranian leadership was never really considered, though Hamas was Sunni and the Shia Iranians were Hamas's patrons. And the CIA did not even consider the information showing that some of these guys might be here already, waiting for D-Day, since the Agency was not supposed to be doing domestic work – though it never had a problem doing so when the Agency felt it was politically useful to do so in other contexts.

The FBI knew that there were Iranian sleeper cells in America. There had been threats to former Trump officials here in America to avenge the killing of Qasem Soleimani, the head of Iran's IRGC, back in 2020. Plus, there were other jihadi sympathizers around. Yet the FBI was oriented away from these threats and onto "white supremacists" and "domestic extremists" who did things like attend school board meetings. The FBI's focus was on "insurrectionists" and traditional Catholics. The Islamic radical threat, which had actually killed thousands of Americans, was made secondary as a political choice by a series of administrations.

Shockingly, there was almost no federal attention paid to Antifa and other leftist direct action groups, Palestinian sympathizers, or the college-based radicals. Antifa had shown its capacity for organizing and violence, but the administration, for purely political reasons, refused to recognize it as a threat. It did not help that the children of prominent Democrats were involved in these organizations. The stepdaughter of the former Vice President actually raised money for a pro-Hamas group; her stepmother famously tweeted about raising bail money for rioters in 2020.

The Border Patrol was seeing Arab, Afghan, and other Muslim military-age males coming across in shocking numbers. In fact, the ten thousand terrorists were only a fraction of the number of such people coming, so they blended in. A very few popped on watch lists – their biometric data came from Israel or from our Iraq and Afghanistan databases of enemy combatants. The ones who came up hot got sent back to Mexico and then just snuck over and avoided detention the next time. A number of them were among the dead after the Attack.

We had local police coming across cells, raising the alarm, and being ignored. For example, the Chicago Police Department reported to Homeland Security that five guys were living in a hotel room and one stabbed a woman for not covering herself and then started shouting about how the infidels would pay. The leftist DA let him out without bail and he disappeared. The next time they saw him was when he was shot dead during the Evanston massacre.

Agencies got approached by several cell members who wanted permanent asylum in exchange for telling what they knew, but it was always nothing. They had gone to train in Syria or Libya or wherever and then got helped to get here. Okay, that's not good, but what was your target? I dunno. Who is the next higher leader over your cell? I dunno? Do you have guns? No. Not a lot to work with.

The guns illustrate another problem – corruption. The cartels knew the Customs agents who were dirty. They waved the trucks through, even walked the drug dogs past and got a clean bill of health. The corrupt agents never knew what they were letting into the country. A thousand rifles. Hundreds of thousands of bullets. Hundreds of crates of grenades. Dozens of shoulder-launched missiles. They waved them through and earned their ten thousand dollars for their vacation house fund. Once again, the drug trade corrupts everything around it.

We had so many pieces of the puzzle. Everyone knows about the stolen train cars and truckloads of explosive precursors they used to make the truck bombs. There were other indicators. We had a California Highway Patrolman pull over a van near Kettleman City with a Jordanian and fifty AK-47s plus ammo the week before the Attack. He refused to say anything, and no federal agents talked to him until after the Attack. Atlanta cops recovered a couple ground-to-air missiles that we think were supposed to have been used at Hartsfield International three days later. The two Syrians would not say a thing.

And there were more esoteric indicators. There were several reports from local cops of interacting with Middle Eastern individuals lurking around public venues and infrastructure sites that were later targeted. And there were the four Arabs in Alaska who were driving to Anchorage the day before the Attack. They slid off the road and got attacked by a grizzly who shrugged off their AK rounds and mauled them into chunks. That bear was why Alaska was the only state with no casualties during the Attack. If I could, I would hang a Silver Star around its neck.

The terrorists were able to evade the kinds of surveillance we mostly relied upon. We had signal intercepts that indicated something was up. In the 48 hours before the Attack, there were a bunch of calls back to the Middle East with young men saying goodbye to their families. They were flunkies, so there were no tactical details. The cadre did not use phones for any kind of substantial communications, only to set face-to-face meetings and even those they kept to a minimum. They also avoided the mosques, so what informants we still had were out of the loop.

We could not pin down the money. We are very good at identifying and tracking unusual bank system transfers, but they relied on the *hawala* system to move the majority of the money.

Sadly, the dollars to fund this – and it took a lot – was not an issue because the former administration paid the Iranians billions for a few hostages.

But our best intelligence source is not signal or cyber. It was human, HUMINT we call it. A human in the enemy camp can not only tell you facts but can shed light on what the facts mean. I cannot tell you what HUMINT assets we or our allies had before because it is still classified, but they did not help. The cell structure negated their effectiveness. Even the Israelis, who are very good at it, were caught unaware on October 7th, and on August 27th as well, because almost no one asset knew enough to illuminate a significantly bigger picture.

The Intelligence Synthesis Cell here at NORTHCOM is designed to remedy that shortcoming going forward. Because of the scope of the disaster, the whole law enforcement and intelligence community got revamped after the Attack. They gave the military the intel synthesis mission because the civilians dropped the ball, though it makes them mad when you say that. Our skill is military intelligence, and we look at this as a war, not a law enforcement operation. We bring reps of dozens of organizations here and force them to interact and share information and analyses.

We try to think big picture. In fact, many of our people are not military. They are civilians who could not get into the military. Some are actually on the spectrum, but they see patterns others cannot. We use AI too, and we use red cells. The red cells sit around all day and think of how they would launch terror attacks on the U.S. A lot of them are brainiacs and nerds, to be honest. Their job is to come up with their own plans and plots, to think asymmetrically. Then we look to see if our data shows indicators that someone is executing those plans. It's like *Three Days of the Condor*, but none of them looks like Robert Redford or Faye Dunaway.

I cannot tell you if we have found and stopped any new attacks. That's classified. I can only say that, five years later, every single day we are here watching, determined never to get caught short again because we failed to put the pieces of the puzzle together in time. Of course, we said that after 9/11, too.

THE FIRST DAY

AUGUST 27TH

9.

Austin, Texas

Inside his sleek, modern office at Excalibur Industries, company co-founder David Keener walks unsteadily to the art deco coffee cart by the window, surveys the options, and offers his visitor tea. "It's not cruelty-free," he explains, smiling grimly. On the wall is an old picture of him and several other Silicon Valley entrepreneurs with Barack Obama, and next to it, a recent photo of him with the current president – a man who is the antithesis of Obama's cosmopolitan leftism. "That's my journey," he says when he notices his guest staring.

Keener will not describe what he and his four-year-old company do in detail, but open sources disclose that Excalibur oversees classified military and intelligence systems that leverage AI to identify, target, and help neutralize terrorists and their networks.

I was a Silicon Valley demigod. Not a god, like a Zuckerberg or an Ellison, but a tier or two down in the tech pantheon. I got write-ups on *The Information* and the *SiliconValley.com* sites as one of the guys to watch. VCs – the venture capitalists – took my calls because I had a track record of success. I was rich by most any standard in human history, but not yet rich enough to buy a serious house in Atherton. That would come. I thought I was the king of the world, and beyond the reach of the world.

August 27th was the second day of Techfest in the Moscone Center. It was one of the last technology conventions to stay in San Francisco after the city had started going to hell. But what did I care about that? I did not walk the streets. I either drove my Fisker up to the valet or, like that day, got dropped off out front in a Chevy Suburban by a limo company that surcharged me for the carbon credits it supposedly bought to offset the climate impact of my ride. That was the kind of thing that I used to justify lifestyle.

The world was going to hell around me, and I never had to notice, so I didn't. My little world was fine. I was too busy enjoying myself with girls, the occasional microdose, and with my political posturing. I just sort of adopted the same casual leftism that my social set embraced. None of us saw politics as being particularly important except as a social signal, and certainly none of us ever let our Chablis socialism moderate the vicious capitalism we practiced.

I was speaking in front of about 5,000 of the biggest names in tech at 10:30 a.m. that morning. A few of the industry gods were there, and most of us demigods – it was a regular technology Olympus. But I was not worried. It was no big deal. I had this. I was dressed casually, of course. Lawyers wore suits. I had Paul Kruize jeans, a custom shirt that cost more than my dad made in a month when I was a kid, and – thankfully – I was wearing very expensive sneakers. My fashion sense probably saved my life.

My current start-up was Leftoverture. It was an app that used proprietary AI to match people with leftovers and facilitate some guy using his car to make the exchange. Say you cooked lasagna and had half a pan left but wanted something else for dinner the next night. Leftoverture solved that problem. It identified other leftover holders, let you choose what you wanted, and facilitated the trade. Our slogan was "Second day is not second best." Leftoverture was my contribution to mankind.

I remember being driven into San Francisco and getting off 280 and looking up from my phone for the first time in an hour and realizing that we were in the city. There were street people everywhere, but there was nothing unusual about it except that it was already sunny. That was pretty unusual. Yet, I felt somehow unsettled. Were the homeless looking harder at me than they normally did? Tech bros were both loved and hated in San Francisco. I could not put my finger on it, but there was a feeling of unease lurking in the background of my mind.

I ignored it, and we got to the Center. It is right in the middle of downtown, and there was a lot of security – most unarmed – whose job it was to turn around the junkies and hustlers who might wander too near the important people and their gathering. I got out of the SUV and walked up the front walk to the entrance. I did not have to line up for my credentials like a schmuck. There was a long line of people queued up to get theirs. Instead, some D-girl using facial rec software scanned me as I came up the entryway and was waiting to hand me my badge, which I looped around my neck. It was golden – "SPEAKER" – and as I walked inside people whispered and pointed.

It was 8:43. I remember glancing at the Norqain Independence Skeleton watch I wore on my left wrist.

I headed toward the back of the center, to the VIP area, passing the vendor hall and the ballroom where I would stand up in just under two hours and extol the virtues of casserole swapping. Every few seconds was another "Hi" or a handshake and a quick agreement that we needed to set up a meet. I knew about a third of the people who knew me.

I remember the normality of it all, normal for me at least. Techfest was thousands of people talking and dealmaking about technology. It was an insular universe, and I was one of its minor deities. It never occurred to me that what happened next could ever happen. My imagination, which had made me rich, failed me. Of course, our collective lack of imagination failed us all.

I got into the vast green room and suddenly felt a bit diminished. It was the who's who of tech. Not just the guys you read about but the guys you don't know about unless you are in that world, the wizards who made Silicon Valley work. There must have been 300 doctorates just in that one large room. Remember the Manhattan Project to build the atomic bomb? How they got all the best physicists and other scientists together in one place, Los Alamos? It was that kind of concentration of pure talent, along with the hangers-on and hustlers. But it was also a deeply frivolous gathering in some ways, oblivious to the real world.

I took a bran muffin – it was bespoke, but it was still just a bran muffin – and a cup of some barely drinkable Nicaraguan enviro-conscious tea, and began making my rounds just as the clock hit 9:00 a.m. Pacific Time.

"Leftoverture sounds like another winner," Raffi Awad told me and a couple other folks who were standing with us. He had a slight accent. I knew him from around town as a guy always on the make, successful but a couple tiers below me. At that time, he was at Premiericon as its "Chief Impact and Synergy Officer and Vice President for Human Outreach." Premiericon was some kind of video delivery system that promised every kid with an iPhone camera and a dream the chance to be an influencer.

"We think Leftoverture is a game changer in the delivered meal space," I replied, trying to be subtle about how I was scanning the room for someone more interesting to talk to. That's when we heard it. The pop-pop-pop. Then more and more pops.

Raffi froze and went pale, even as I laughed and made some joke about how the PA system better be fixed before it was my turn to go onstage. There was more popping.

"What is that?" somebody asked.

"Kalashnikovs," Raffi sputtered.

"What?" I asked. I didn't know.

"AK-47s," he said. "I grew up in Lebanon."

More popping.

"I don't understand," I said. I had never shot a gun, but I played *Call of Duty* and knew what an AK-47 was, and what Raffi was saying made no sense to me at all.

"There is someone shooting," Raffi said, voice quivering. "More than one."

That got my attention, as did the sudden increase in the number of pops. If that really was shooting, there was a lot of it.

I froze and listened, and now the rest of the room was doing the same. There were a few individual pops that sounded different – probably guards trying to fight off the attackers with their handguns. Those pops stopped pretty quickly.

Everyone just stood there, unsure of how to react, as the popping got more intense and louder.

The main door flew open, and someone shouted, "Mass shooter!" That broke the logjam. People screamed and yelled and went for the exit doors. But there were only a few exit doors.

"We have to go!" said Raffi, grabbing me for some reason and pulling me toward the rear doors that presumably led out to the backstage area. The escapees had pushed the exit doors open and were flowing out when the popping became blasting.

I looked back at the front doors and people were dropping. First, one man in black gear, then another and another, each with a gun, pushed their way inside and began firing into the crowd.

Bullets were flying, and a woman in front of me got hit in the stomach and fell down screaming. I pushed past her – what could I do?

Raffi was behind me and suddenly he stumbled and fell. I glanced back long enough to see a bloody splotch over his kidney. It was madness as people ran and clawed to get to the back doors. But the gunmen must have seen it and the bullets came at us. I was hit in the side, near the hip. I fell and three or four people fell dead on top of me. The men in black approached – I could now see their green headbands clearly. They seemed to be outfitted like SWAT guys with gear and body armor.

They were shouting in accented English at the people in the room to be still, and most were. There were only three of them in the VIP room, but I could hear a lot of shooting outside. They seemed to be gathering the survivors up and taking them toward the far corner of the room. Some of the wounded were not as lucky. They were shooting them.

One of them walked over to Raffi and I heard Raffi screaming, "I am Lebanese, I am an Arab!" and then something in another language. The shooter screamed something back in the same language – he was furious. And he shot Raffi in the face. Not once, but many times.

I lay still under the dead people who fell on me. One twitched, and the gunman shot her. Her brains sprayed across my cheek but I was paralyzed with fear and that saved me because I did not move.

Satisfied that everyone on the floor in front of the rear door was dead, the gunman joined his comrades in gathering up the dozens of survivors. They were shouting and screaming orders, and the unwounded survivors were crying and begging but complying.

With their eyes on their prizes, I had an opportunity. Maybe it was the risk-taking entrepreneur in me, but I took the chance. I pushed myself up and slid out from under the bodies and I ran to the doors. Thank goodness for those sneakers. I heard a shout and heard the shots, but I dodged the bodies and went straight through those doors and into the backstage area.

It was wide and brightly lit, full of storage shelves and carts and the moving parts of a convention center. But there were no people. The staff had fled, as had those lucky enough to escape earlier.

Now, I was alone and fleeing down the hall while behind me the massacre was continuing. It was only after a minute or two that I realized that my hip wound was serious. I guess it was the adrenaline, because there should have been no way that I could have run as far or as fast on it as I did, wounded like I was.

I finally came to a real exit, one to the outside world. I laughed at myself for pausing because there was a sign that said, "EMERGENCEY EXIT ONLY – ALARM WILL SOUND."

I pushed through into the sunlight and into chaos. There was a burning San Francisco Police Department cruiser smashed up against a bent lamp post, smoking. The windshield was riddled with bullets and the two cops, a woman and a man dressed like a woman, were in the front seat, both very, very dead.

People were running and screaming, and I could hear Kalashnikovs shooting. Now I was an expert just like Raffi was.

I ran away west, and did not stop until I reached the Tenderloin. I passed a lot of bodies but never encountered another killing squad. Near a flophouse hotel, The Excalibur, I finally collapsed. A pair of guys who were clearly junkies came outside, dragged me in, and bound up my wounds. I declined their kind offer of painkillers and sat out the next 48 hours with them. I only came out after I saw the soldiers on the streets and flagged down an ambulance. I left my hosts my expensive watch. I ended up at a crowded Army combat support hospital set up at Oracle Park.

My hip still needs another operation. Every time I take a step, I think of the bastards who did this to me, and to my whole community. We all know what happened in the Moscone Center. They murdered all those hostages, horribly. They essentially wiped out an entire generation of Silicon Valley. Of course, that was the plan. They considered it a two-fer – you get to kill the colonizers and you also gut-punch America's tech capacity.

After that, you can probably understand why projects like Leftoverture stopped appealing to me. Let's just say my politics did a 180-degree turn. I took the same AI tech that I used to exchange half a tuna sandwich with some day-old chow mein and applied it to figure out terrorist networks and logistics. I still have not shot a gun, but Excalibur tech has helped kill thousands of those sons of bitches. And we keep improving it so it can help kill thousands more.

10.

Washington, D.C.

The Library of Congress Special Collections for Attack Research limits access to some of its videotapes to academics and scholars. There is a small niche market on the internet for Attack materials, the more explicit the better. Much of the material uploaded during the Attack was cached and can be found if one digs deeply enough into the dark web. What is not available are the relatively few confessions of captured terrorists.

The librarian inserts the disc into the air-gapped computer, which is hooked to a monitor. It is not available online and has not been uploaded to ensure it never gets out. Besides the desire to avoid delighting leering weirdos, such a tape would have endless propaganda value to the remaining jihadis still loose in the world.

The author may not record it, but he is allowed to use his speech-to-text program to transcribe it. Under the agreement with the Library certain portions that might identify specific victims have been redacted.

The video begins. "Statement of Hashir Al-Husayn – September 8." Al-Husayn sits, apparently alone, in a windowless room at an institutional metal table, his hands cuffed. He is smirking. He also looks as though he was dragged behind a truck for several miles. His English is lightly accented.

The librarian walks to the door. Is he leaving?
"I have no desire to ever listen to that piece of shit talk again,"
the librarian says before he steps out the door.

By Allah, the just and the merciful, I wish to make this statement. Perhaps my son will see it someday and know that his father was a warrior and a martyr. I know I am destined for paradise. And you are destined for hell.

You think I am afraid? I do not fear you or death. But you fear me and death. We have shown this to be true. We have shown the world that we can strike you in your cities and your homes. You tremble at our power.

I will tell you everything to show that we do not fear you. I will tell you everything but you are still powerless in the face of our holy warriors.

I first came to your degenerate country a decade ago. I went to school here, at your Florida International University in Miami and went home to Jordan an engineer and hating you even more than I did before. Your dogs, your pork, your whore women. The Jews parading around, and the homosexuals. You are disgusting. And I saw how you looked at me, the Arab, the one who was lucky to be allowed to come here. I took back my dignity, didn't I?

In Jordan, I married, had a son, but what was my life? Frivolous. Meaningless. I was working below my station, not using my engineering skills, but across the Jordan River in Israel, they lived fat off of what they stole from us. And you Americans supported it. You gave them their money. You gave them the bombs that murdered our children.

When the resistance struck, I would cheer and have my wife hand out sweets. Every shooting, every stabbing, every bombing brought us that much closer to the day our holy land is purified of the filth of the infidel.

When the brothers in Hamas struck in Operation al-Aqsa Flood, I was in ecstasy. The audacity, the cunning! We Arabs had struck back, not through our weak and traitorous leaders who are in league with the *yahud*, may Allah curse them, but through Hamas. I watched the videos and celebrated.

Then the evil Zionists, with the help of you Americans, began their butchery of the children of Gaza. The merciless bombing, the poison gas, the bombing of hospitals and schools – may they be cursed. And I was ashamed, for I was doing nothing.

Then a man at my mosque, a very respected man, took me aside and asked if I was truly committed to my faith. I said I was. He said my knowledge of English and my stay in America were a help, and that my time as a conscript in the Jordanian Army was useful too. He asked if I was ready to wage jihad. I said I was. He told me not to answer so lightly. The way of jihad leads to martyrdom. He instructed me to think on it for a week, and if I was ready to find him.

I thought on it and at the end of the week I was ready to take the path of jihad even if it led to martyrdom. I was proud to be asked. He told me to wait. I did not wait long.

One day a man came and dropped off an airline ticket to Libya via Sudan. I was to use my own passport and my story was that I was interviewing for an engineering job. I told my wife that I was leaving, and had to slap her to make her stop asking me where I was going and when I would return. I instructed her to take my son and go live with her family until I came back.

In Libya, I underwent training. Everyone trained on weapons and knives and other skills. I had been a sergeant, so I knew the AK-47 and I actually helped train some of the others. These were brothers from around the world. We did not speak of our real names or homes, but we shared our desire for jihad and trained, though we were not told for what.

I was told that my skills and intelligence meant I would be a leader of five men. I was proud. I stayed for more training as the regular fighters went home to await the call. Other men stayed for the advanced training as well. But we did not receive a specific mission.

Much of the advanced training had to do with America, how to rent a room, get a car, obtain phones. I was also trained how to conduct reconnaissance, and to choose targets and how to evade capture. There was much emphasis on discipline. We would be given a mission and it must be accomplished exactly as planned. One or two of the students did not show the commitment, and did not follow instructions. One stood up in class after being corrected during lessons on border crossing and began shouting. One of the cadre drew a pistol and shot him dead.

I was an excellent student – all of them said so. And I would not return to Jordan. Instead, I would fly, via Sudan and Turkey, to Nicaragua. I used my own passport, which I would dispose of before we got to the American border. In a house in Nicaragua, I was introduced to the four men I would be leading. Amir, Hasan, Abdul and Arif – I am not sure if those were their real names, nor where they were from, but they were all dedicated to jihad. I told them that this was a matter of life and death, and I expected them to obey my commands.

We went north by train and bus and met our guides. These were criminals, drug smugglers, but they had an arrangement with us and they were paid to take us over. We were surrounded by peasants from other countries, even some Russians and Chinese. We kept apart, praying and talking only to ourselves.

The guides ensured we destroyed our papers and then took us across the river. We were taught exactly what we needed to say to the American border police. We said we are political refugees from our home nations seeking asylum. That was all we said. We were each given a paper with a date for an asylum hearing on it years in the future. Then we were released to a charity group. They gave us money and phones, which I collected from my men, and asked where we wished to fly to. We chose Miami.

Florida was different from other states because the governor did not tolerate asylum seekers gathering together in a single area. I knew this and there was a plan. I texted a number when we arrived and shortly after I was delivered $5,000. We were to find a place to live and wait until called.

We lived in a one-bedroom apartment, eating, sleeping, and praying, for a month waiting for the call. I had to slap Arif for pestering me to allow him to go out. We could not take the chance. And then the phone rang.

I met with my contact, who had a car. We drove around Miami and he showed me our targets. He also gave me our weapons, ammunition, vests, and cameras. He handed me a paper with Facebook, Instagram, and other accounts and passwords that we could use. He also gave me a bag of pills. Finally, he gave me another $5,000 to buy a vehicle. That afternoon, I bought an old Chevrolet Blazer.

It was two days until we would strike. We were joyous as we cleaned our weapons and prepared our gear. I took them all, unarmed, past our targets the morning before and gave them instructions. We prayed and purified ourselves.

But I had to slap Arif again. He said we should go out and debauch ourselves since we would be martyrs soon. But we had been trained against that. Others had done that in the past and drawn attention. We would not need whores when we would be with our virgins soon enough.

I denied the men phone calls home, telling them our families would hear of our glorious mission soon enough. At the time, I had no idea that we were just one small part of something great and beautiful. It was right not to tell us the plan, to keep the mission secure, and this allowed us our great victory.

It was vital that we strike at the time directed, 12:00 p.m. on the 27th of August. That had been drilled into us in our training. And, Allah be thanked, we did.

That morning, we took the pills, the amphetamines, and left our apartment ready for martyrdom.

There is an island called Dodge Island in Miami Harbor. You reach it by bridges off the road called A1A, which goes to South Beach. This is where the cruise ships dock. There were two ships loading up that day, with thousands of passengers on the dock waiting to go aboard.

Arif drove and I was in the front seat. All of us carried ten magazines of bullets, including the one in our AK-47s. I told them to turn on their cameras and ensure they were feeding to the internet.

We drove toward the crowd and drove through some orange traffic cones. I remember a woman security guard blowing a whistle at us to stop. And at exactly noon, we stopped and got out of the Blazer. The Americans just looked at us, confused.

I yelled, "Allahu Akbar!" and I shot into a family in their matching Hawaiian shirts that was nearby with their luggage. They all fell, the man, the woman, their brats.

The others were firing into the crowd on automatic. It was impossible to miss. Of course, none of the infidels had a gun to shoot back with because they were getting on a ship. Then we tossed grenades.

We must have shot and thrown grenades at them for two minutes before a police car came. I shot at it and it crashed into a palm tree. By then, everyone was running in all directions, including into the ship. It was harder to hit them running, and another police car was coming.

I shot at it too, and it stopped and the policemen got out and shot at us with pistols. We had to shoot back and many people escaped us because of those policemen. We finally killed them both and I shouted to get back in the Blazer. I looked and Hasan was running up the gangway into the ship. I blessed him, and hoped he had good hunting inside.

As we left I passed wounded infidels crying in the street. I shot only the ones I felt might live, because I did not want to waste ammunition. I had shot six or seven magazines, and there were what looked like hundreds of bodies on the ground.

Arif got in the Blazer and I turned to Abdul to tell him to stop wasting ammunition on the wounded when a bullet struck him in the side of the head. It martyred him instantly. Oh, happy he now is in Paradise!

There was an American in shorts and a t-shirt firing on us with a pistol from behind a car. I shot back and he took cover. I grabbed Abdul's remaining ammunition and rifle and threw it in the Blazer, then the three of us drove off. The man fired at us as we left and shot out the rear window.

There were many police cars coming in, but we were among many cars leaving Dodge Island. Arif turned toward South Beach. All of us were excited and proud. We killed many of the infidels, and the internet connections had uploaded perfectly. We looked at Hasan's video feed, and he was still slaughtering infidels in the halls of the ship. We laughed as he paused to rape some whore after he shot her husband and children.

There were many police and other vehicles headed to Dodge Island now. We continued toward South Beach. It was the home of whores and homosexuals. I turned on the radio to see if there was news of our glorious mission yet, but the news gave us an even greater gift. It told us that we were just one of hundreds, perhaps thousands, of attacks across the Great Satan.

We began to drive up the main street, where there are many restaurants that are open to the streets. People were gathering in them, watching the television. We would open fire as we drove. We shot anyone we saw.

A police car followed us. We shot it up, but more were coming. They fired at us and the front tire blew out. The Blazer was useless, so we got out. Arif was martyred by police on the sidewalk. Amir ran into a hotel and I heard shooting.

I continued down the street on foot and I stopped to throw a grenade into a bar where there was a crowd when I saw that several of them were pointing guns at me. I went to take cover behind a palm tree but fell and struck my head. As I got up, a tremendous man – a weightlifter – punched me in the face. Then the whole crowd was upon me.

I prayed that Allah, praises be upon him, would allow me to be martyred, but who can know his plan?

The police came and took me. I was overjoyed that the Attack had been more successful than I ever imagined, but my joy was doubled to hear of the second day, and then doubled again on the third day.

I was smiling even as your military commission sentenced me to death. They said we killed over 265 infidels. When I heard that I smiled.

I am done. Will you at least let me pray before I am martyred?

The video ends as two military policemen enter the frame and lift him out of his chair as an unseen voice says, "No."

Hashir Al-Husayn was convicted by a military commission of murder, attacking civilians, conspiracy, and several other crimes. He was executed by shooting on September 8th.

11.

Stanford University, California

Dr. Simon Weary is a psychiatrist at the Hoover Institution at Stanford University. The Hoover Institute is not a medical school but a conservative think tank on the Bay Area campus. Since the Attack, Dr. Weary has made that event his research focus and provided his expertise to anti-terrorist officials, politicians, and for the first time here, to the general public.

Fear is not just psychological. It is also a physiological phenomenon. When you are afraid, your body releases hormones like cortisol and adrenaline while your blood pressure and heart rate increase. You breathe faster and blood flows to your extremities so you can fight or flee. It is unpleasant, and people seek to avoid the feeling of true fear. Artificial fear, like seeing a horror movie or riding a roller coaster, is fun in small doses. But real fear – terror – is something humans seek to avoid at all costs.

It is what our enemy counted on.

You must understand the Attack as primarily a psychological event. I know that seems strange to say, with so many thousands dead and injured in the physical world, but that damage was a consequence of achieving the true objective. You can achieve an objective using various kinds of power. Military force is one way. You can also use diplomatic and economic power to achieve an objective. Certainly there was some attempt by the terrorists to cause actual damage to American infrastructure. After all, the third day was focused on infrastructure attacks. But even those were a supporting effort, not the main one.

At heart, the Attack was what military people call an "information operation." It used the power of information – of the targets' emotions, to be more specific.

The Attack was designed to shape their enemy's perceptions and emotions to achieve a particular goal. That goal was to break America's spirit. The goal was to so terrify America that America would respond by allowing the terrorists to win.

If you look at the correlation of forces regarding the other elements of power – diplomatic, military and economic – there really is no comparison between us and them. They had no diplomatic power to speak of, and no economic power. They had no significant military might in purely terms of destructive power. American military might, from individual soldiers to atomic weapons, was much greater than what the terrorists had access to.

Their only real power was information power, if they set the conditions to use it. They assessed us as mentally weak and attempted to use terror as a weapon against us. What the terrorists sought to do was convince America, by creating collective fear, that resistance was futile, that we could never match them for ruthlessness, and that we must not try lest we provoke them further. They wanted to create such terror that we would allow that terror to dictate the terms of our surrender to them.

The key part of the word "terrorist" is "terror." Using terror as a weapon is as old as mankind. You find an enemy and you sow fear through acts of unrelenting brutality. What else explains the terrorists' notorious baby and blowtorch video? But understand that was the normal state of man for most of human history. Romans were masters of terror. In the ancient world, people dreaded the sack of their village or town. They knew what that meant to the losers, and they understood that they were at the mercy, such as it was, of the victors. It was accepted and understood as man's fate.

But over recent centuries, that collective memory has faded in the West as we became ever more civilized. In some ways, we became weaker because we stopped expecting these kinds of horrors to be visited upon us.

Now, there were modern exceptions. Nanking, Dresden, Hiroshima are examples. These were all horrors, but they are well-known because they are anomalous.

It is especially true for Americans. Such atrocities didn't happen in America, at least not recently and not between the settlers. Even in our own civil war, Sherman's actions in burning through Georgia on his March to the Sea were relatively tame in the grand scheme of atrocities. He torched plantations, destroyed farms, ruined crops, and made tens of thousands homeless. It is still remembered today, but it was nothing like what the ancients faced.

What happened between August 27 and August 29 was something out of man's past, an ecstatic, violent, and primitive orgy of hatred visited upon parties that felt themselves innocent. And, in the great scheme of things, we were innocent. In the Attack, the enemy was psychologically inoculated against anything like what we call "humanity." When you were raised in a cauldron of hatred, when hatred is seared into you from your earliest days, when that hatred is unleashed and multiplied by the humiliation your people have faced over decades, you are going to get something like we got during the Attack.

Let's take the Palestinians, since their cause was at least a significant, if superficial, motivation behind the Attack. In 1948, Israel declared itself a nation. Jews had lived there for thousands of years. The Arabs, now Muslim, had lived there, too. The Arabs found this development utterly intolerable, particularly because one of their three holy cities, Jerusalem, was threatened. Six Arab armies declared war on Israel and invaded. The Jews, a people who had been scattered across the globe, and who had just escaped extermination a few years before in the death camps of Europe, fought back and defeated them. This defeat broke the Arabs. It was an honor society and it was beaten.

Think about their humiliation for a moment. Against all odds, this pariah people had broken the strength of the Arab world, shaming them before their own people and the people of the world. Remember that the Palestinians were the artists and the engineers, the lawyers, and the teachers, of the Arab world. Not all of them, but many of them, and many had to find work in those fields in other Arab countries. It was shameful. Not only religious pride but ethnic pride was implicated, a powerful and toxic mixture. The humiliation of it, a proud people forced away from their lands in defeat to a tiny, hated minority, grew and grew.

And there were more wars. In 1956, the Israelis humiliated the Arab armies, and then in 1967, it captured all of Jerusalem, a holy city of Islam. It also took the Golan Heights as well as the Sinai. In 1973, the Arabs attempted to fight back. They came close to overrunning the Israelis, but they were again totally defeated. There were more wars in Lebanon, where the Israelis did what the Israelis wished to do and the Arabs could not drive them out until they decided to leave. There were *intifadas* and terrorism, and a compounding hatred among the Arab Street, fueled by the Iranians and their bizarre Shia millennialism. All of it built and built and built. They hated Israel with an unquenchable fury, and they hated America just as much for supporting it.

In Iran, *faux* Palestine, and elsewhere, the training of hatred, because it was trained, in the population began even as children. Whether in schools, in their mosques, on children's shows, or at their parents' table, the message never changed. The Jews must be killed, the more brutally the better, and Palestine reconquered. From the river to the sea! The Americans were likewise the enemy, and they must be murdered wherever they are found. The media rarely reported the true depravity of the terrorist war waged on Israelis even before October 7th. The terrorists were cheered by their people, and their mothers beamed with pride that their sons had been martyrs by blowing themselves up inside pizza parlors packed with Israeli teenagers. Those who fell into their clutches were tortured, raped, and mutilated. The Palestinians passed out sweets to celebrate the barbarism.

Think of the psychological twisting that makes a hero out of someone who invades a house and butchers a family. You add religious fervor to ethnic humiliation and sexual repression – rape is a component of this – and then create a moral framework that not merely allows but encourages these acts, and you will get these acts. If you define everyone as a settler, everyone becomes a target. This frees you from the constraints of morality and allows you to indulge your hatred. The acts of evil allow you to expiate your own personal sense of humiliation.

Americans are used to walking the streets, working, living their lives in relative peace. The terrorists attempted to shatter that peace, to unbalance our sense that we are secure. They hit people on streets, in restaurants, in airplanes. They attacked skyscrapers. They invaded our children's schools. They selected targets for the sheer number of defenseless people they could kill, but also for the information element – the message was that you are not safe, that you live at our discretion, that everywhere you go in your country you should be afraid. They tried to strike in all fifty states for a reason!

Some people try to call it madness. It is not. Do not think of them as insane. That gives them a moral pass for choosing a barbaric moral framework. They are not mad. They are evil. And they are usually fully prepared to die in perpetuating their evil, either from pride or what we see as ridiculous promises of paradise with their virgins and so forth.

Of course, this makes them the perfect candidates to carry out an assault like the Attack. These are people who can be aimed at a target with the assurance that over 90% of them will murder and rape everyone they see until they are killed.

Americans were not always unfamiliar with battling the wrath of displaced, conquered people. Look at the Indian wars. The idea of noble and peaceful savages living in harmony with nature and others is ludicrous. The atrocities the Indians inflicted on those colonists they encountered as they were pushed back and overrun were unspeakable. Whole families of settlers were butchered, and the butchers' own families celebrated it. They reveled in the murder, cheered on the torture. The settlers fought back brutally. America had forgotten that. It was certainly not taught in schools because it ruined the preferred narrative.

Israel relearned this lesson on October 7. It and the rest of the civilized world were stunned not only at the level of what civilized minds saw as senseless savagery – as we have seen, the savagery made sense to the savages – but also at the pride behind it. Look how it was broadcast to the world through the Internet. The West's own communications channel was turned against it and used to amplify the terror.

So, it was not that hard for the enemy to create an army of young men willing to carry out the Attack. They wanted to do it. For many, it was the culmination of their short lives. Look at the footage of the mothers of the killers in the Attack celebrating their son's martyrdom. Keep in mind that this indoctrination worked especially well on the far left of the Bell Curve. Most of the killers – as distinct from the leaders – were low-IQ individuals. Sadly, for my research at least, I had only the shortest of opportunities to talk to the captured ones before their date with the pistol. I could not give them formal intelligence tests, but in just talking to them it was clear most were below average in terms of intelligence. And those who planned it were above average.

There is the sexual aspect. The rapes of women and men, and of male and female children, during both the October 7 assault and during the Attack are notorious and distinctive in their savagery. The settler dynamic allowed them to dehumanize their victims, and their religious teachers taught them that the infidels were their sexual property by right. And there are stories of them continuing their rapes even up to the moment the authorities closed in and killed them still in the act.

Another factor was the sexual repression of their culture. I would expect that a staggering percentage – staggering for us at any rate – of the killers were virgins, at least in terms of male-female intercourse. Many were probably sexually abused or may have abused animals. The "goat screwer" epithet was not entirely invented – they had no normal sexual outlets until marriage, and many (but not all) were poor and not very bright, and therefore had few such prospects. Those who were homosexual by definition hid it – those that did not would be murdered. And, again, note the virgins reward. Hatred and sexual aggression plus the chance to inflict the greatest possible humiliation upon the settler enemy was too much to pass up.

In some ways, the participation of American college students and American radicals was even more frightening. The actions of the Middle Easterners were understandable, if repellant, but having so many college students and other radicals accepting the savagery as necessary and good, and to some extent participating in it, was horrific to our minds.

We had seen behavior like it with Charles Manson and his followers, but not on this scale. The demonstrations and anti-Semitism campaigns following the Gaza War became more extreme over time and even saw murders, but few people were expecting the level of violence that would manifest during the Attack.

Why did they do it? It filled a psychological need to belong, partly. How can you better show you belong than joining a murder spree? It also filled the need to distinguish themselves by transgressing societal norms, and what is more transgressive than a rape and murder spree? Some joked, before such jokes stopped being funny, that these young people were living out their daddy issues. That assessment was not wrong.

But did it break us? We clearly did not fully understand our enemy, perhaps because it was too great a leap to accept what is so manifestly unacceptable as true. We did not want to believe our enemies were capable of the crimes they had shown us many times, to the grief of the Israelis, they were not merely capable of but enthusiastic to commit against us. And they saw this, and our unwillingness to respond to it. What we thought was civilized behavior – not going into their lands and exterminating the barbarians in detail as a Roman consul and his legions would have done – they interpreted as weakness and cowardice.

They did not understand us either. They thought that exponentially increased terror would lead to exponentially increased submission and withdrawal. But that is not how the West works, even the modern West. Hitler thought the Blitz would break the spirit of the British as he sent the Luftwaffe over London. It solidified their determination. And 9/11 did not make America withdraw from the Middle East. Instead, America went into the Middle East even harder, occupying Afghanistan, annihilating his organization, and eventually putting several bullets in bin Laden's face.

In the end, terror did not lead to America being terrorized, but rather, energized and ready to inflict terror of its own. And, as the few remaining ringleaders hide, they are the ones feeling fear.

12.

Cincinnati, Ohio

Pete Warren is a multi-generational Ohioan and a multi-generational police officer in the city of Cincinnati. His grandfather and father were cops, and neither ever went into command – something they were proud of. They walked – or drove – a beat. That is what Pete Warren was doing on August 27th.

It was a normal day, with a little rain in the morning, but it was clearing up. Just an average Tuesday morning. I had been on the job ten years and had the seniority not to work nights. I liked Tuesday mornings. Nothing happens on Tuesday mornings. The crooks are still in bed. Even the junkies in the bad areas are still in their rooms. Nobody says, "Hey, Monday night! Let's go nuts!"

Some cops like trouble. I did when I started. Getting aggressive, charging and barging. I did my share of super cop stuff. But I was a little older, with a family. I had nothing to prove. I was Fred Warren's kid for the first few years, but now I was Pete Warren with my own reputation. I was a training officer, which is the closest to command I ever wanted to get. I liked to teach the new guys and gals how to do the job. There are two ways to learn, through your mistakes or someone else's. The smart guys learn from someone else's.

I was in the car with Kalya Jordan, who is finishing up her rookie year. She's driving. We're in the south part of the city. Nothing is happening. We started at six, got coffee and a maple bar – we never eat doughnuts on the job! – and then we answered a few calls. We ran off a bum, refereed a traffic dispute between two lawyers who got in a fender-bender, and took a theft report about a shoplifter. It was one of the illegal aliens being housed downtown, which meant we could not touch him. They were effectively exempt from the law. Why arrest them and spend four hours doing paperwork when nothing was going to happen? That border nonsense really bit us in the end.

So, it was dead, just the way I like it. We are starting to think about lunch. It was one of those days. Until it wasn't.

We get an all-cars call, shots fired, Christ Hospital. It's this big old red brick building up on a hill overlooking the city, less than a mile from the Ohio River and the Kentucky border.

It happens occasionally. A lot of times it's some dummy whose gun goes off, or someone offing his cheating wife. We are lights and sirens when the next call comes in, an update – mass shooter.

Okay, that changed everything. The rule on mass shooters is this – you put bullets into them. That's the one inviolable rule. You find the mass shooter and you put him down. I'm no hero, but that's the time you earn all those "Thank you, officers" from little kids and handshakes from their parents. I raised my paw and took the oath and now the bill was coming due. Like I said, I'm not a hero, but if I was one of those pieces of shit like that cop in Florida or those Uvalde guys who would not go in, then I would eat my own gun. I just couldn't face anyone, or myself, if I didn't do what I had to do.

I took the Remington pump off the rack and put a handful of double-aught shells in my pocket. I would have preferred a rifle, but you go to war with the army you have.

I told Kayla that we were going in hard, that she had the pistol so she would suppress the guy and I would try to put him down with the buckshot. We would not be waiting for backup.

Now, this was kind of counter to normal law enforcement. It was more like what soldiers do. My old partner Jimmy was in the Army Guard and he explained it this way. Cops try to use force to *de-escalate* the situation. We don't really have military weapons. You just get a bunch of cops there and the guy gives up because there are so many and more are coming. Soldiers try to *escalate* the situation with firepower and win that way. Now, the problem is when you are cops and you meet guys armed like soldiers who don't give a damn. Remember the North Hollywood shootout? Two bums with machine guns came out of a bank and lit up the Los Angeles Police Department? The normal model works 99.999% of the time. This was the .001%, but we did not know that yet.

We were first on the scene and we pulled up, got out and ran inside, guns up. We did not carry tactical vests then, just our regular ones, so that was a problem. But it was our problem.

The front windows were shot out, and I just knew it was going to be bad inside.

It was. It was a bloodbath. There were a lot of dead and a few wounded lying all over the floor. I heard shooting back in the building. A lot of shooting. Not just one gun, which is weird because we were first on the scene. A nurse ran up to us, hysterical.

"There are three of them!" she screams. She's covered with blood, hers or someone else's I don't know.

I ask her where the shooter is – the number did not really process – and she points down the hall. More bodies.

"Oh, damn," Kalya says, looking at the carnage. I've seen plenty of murder scenes, accidents and such, but this was something way past all of them. Still, we can't stand there and feel our feels. The job is to find the shooter and stop him.

I mean "shooters."

"Come on!" I yell and we move down the hall.

I'm using my radio to update dispatch as I go. I report mass casualties and I report three gunmen. Then it occurs to me – we're two of us going toward three gunmen. Of course, I did not know it was actually four.

We get to a T-intersection. Kayla goes right and I go left and there he is, among all these bloody doctors and patients on the floor. Some asswipe in a black shirt with a tactical vest full of mags, a green headband, and an AK-47. Thankfully, it's not yet pointed my way.

Sometimes your training kicks in and I yell, "Drop it!" like this is a regular arrest.

He doesn't flinch. He brings that weapon around and I pull the trigger.

The buckshot knocks him back and I rack again – fast – and by the time I let him have it again Kayla is dumping a mag into him. It seems like forever but he finally goes down.

I rack as I move forward and Kayla drops her mag and reloads as we come up on the body. He's spitting blood out of his mouth but there's a 9mm hole in his forehead. The guy is done, but standard operating procedure – SOP – kicks in and Kayla cuffs him. We try not to touch anything because the shooting team needs the scene pristine. Like they were going to investigate any shootings that day or the next.

The asswipe gasps and finishes bleeding out. I call in that the shooter is down, then hear more shots. I correct myself – *one* shooter is down. I ask dispatch where backup is and that's when I find out there are attacks all over the city. We might get some backup, but don't count on it.

I tell Kayla we need to move even as I'm stuffing shells into the tube of the 12-guage. We're still in the old world – what I should have done is take the asswipe's AK with me, but you don't touch a perp's gun at a shooting scene.

People are running past us as we go, screaming. There's a ton of shooting and a lot of dead people. I have a weird thought – lucky we are in a hospital.

We come around another corner and there's another one. We start exchanging fire. He's spraying at us and I'm blowing off shells. He goes down, and Kalya yells – there's another one behind us coming up the hallway. We shoot it out with him and he ducks around a corridor.

I look over and Kayla is sitting on the floor against the wall, shot in the side. That girl had heart. She's reloading a mag as she's sitting there bleeding. There's shooting from the direction of the terrorist that is on the run.

"Go get them," she says. The guy we just shot moans and starts moving. Kayla unloads on him. No command to surrender. She just wastes him. She realized what's up before I did. This was not police work. It was war.

I run down the hall and hear over the air that there are units on scene clearing the hospital from the other direction. The terrorist who ran from us exchanged fire with the guys coming in from the rear entrance and then comes running back toward me. He sees me just as I shoot. I aim at his face because I'm not sure if those vests have Kevlar – they at least have mags that might stop my buckshot.

The guy staggers and I put another into him and his head is looking like a dropped watermelon. He's face-down – to the extent he still had a face – on the floor and I put another in the back of his head.

The fourth one got killed by the other units. I informed dispatch and they told me to get in my vehicle and prepare for redeployment to another active scene. I took another guy and we ran through the bloody halls out front to my car. Luckily, Kayla left the keys in it and the motor running.

We were Code Three toward downtown when it occurred to me that I was in three officer-involved shootings and I had left the scene. But there were about a dozen shootouts going on around town, and dispatch told us all that this was happening across the country. These were terrorists, and in Cincinnati? How the hell did the politicians let that happen?

We got downtown and joined up with the guys on the ground looking for a cell that was running through the streets killing businesspeople and shoppers. I traded in the shotgun for an AR-15 and put on a vest with a Kevlar plate. Good thing, too.

One of them had crossed I-71 and was running through Smale Riverfront Park near Paycor Stadium, shooting everyone he saw. He met up with a squad and shot it out then ran back the other way. We were chasing him so he ran into us coming back. I caught a round right in the plate – 7.62x39mm. Luckily it was at a distance. Knocked me on my ass. I got back up and joined back in the shooting. I guess it was adrenaline because it only started hurting later.

I don't know if I hit him, but that piece of trash went down with a couple dozen bullet holes in him.

Later, I went in after the SWAT team breached at a high school where they grabbed some kids. It was bad, but we went in earlier than in some other towns and they did not have the chance to hurt all the kids, but they hurt enough. The guys who did it? They all died in the shootout or shot themselves rather than be taken alive. That's my story and I am sticking to it.

We did not go off-shift for probably a week. We grabbed sleep for an hour wherever and whenever we could. I did not see any action the second day when they hit the suburbs. The third day I was out patrolling the suburbs with the Army Guard guys when they hit the power grid and the rest of the infrastructure. They always hit us where we weren't. The first day we did not expect anything. The next day, when we protected public places, they hit homes. The third day, when we protected homes, they hit infrastructure. I was dreading the fourth day. Thank the Lord they were spent after that.

Sometimes I think about how it was just a normal Tuesday. We were living our normal lives. Then this happened. Where the hell were the people in Washington who were supposed to be doing their jobs?

I'm still doing mine. They wanted me to sit for the sergeant's exam afterwards. Hell no. I wouldn't take a medal either – I just did my job. I told Kayla to take her medal and to take the sergeant's exam. Me? I'm just going to keep being a regular cop driving around in a patrol car doing cop stuff. But now I have an AR-15 and a tactical vest in case this ever happens again.

13.

Seattle, Washington

Diedre Jimenez-Coleman completes the Channel 8 nightly news broadcast and takes a seat just off the set, opening a can of Fresca. There are rumors that she is in talks with Fox about a national gig, but she will not comment on them. "I am focusing on my job delivering the news to the people of the Northwest," she says, delivering the statement with well-practiced confidence.

The anchor has been in the television news business in the Seattle and surrounding regional markets for fifteen years, with her first twelve as a reporter covering everything from sea otter birthday parties at the aquarium to political scandals and street crime. But she never covered anything like the Attack, before or since.

It was a regular weekday. I was getting ready to go to a Seattle City Council meeting with my crew and cover a vote on a proposal to remove the words "men" and "women" from all city statutes because not doing so was trans genocide. This was taken very seriously at the time, and they tossed around words like that without thinking about it because they did not have any idea what genocide really meant.

The hearing started at ten and we figured we would roll out in the van at about quarter past nine and get set up. It was no big deal and very routine. I had on a red dress but running shoes, because you can't see those on the air and I was going to be on my feet a lot. Thank goodness, as it turned out.

Jeff was my cameraman and Frank was my tech, two very solid guys who had been in the business forever and had seen it all – well, almost all because no one had ever seen anything like what was coming before. I got a Fresca from the fridge in the break room and I was walking downstairs when my editor runs up to me.

"Mass shooter at Pike Place Market," he says.

"Great," I said, and that sounds insensitive but what I meant was this was a real story, not just a bunch of politicians fighting over nonsense. Of course I was not happy about a mass shooter. But I was excited that I was going to get to do my job.

It's about ten minutes from the station to Pike Place Market. This is a giant outdoor kind of fish market, farmer's market sort of place, with a big neon "Public Market" sign up overhead. There are lots of stalls and storefronts. You can do your marketing there, but also get coffee or breakfast or whatever. It was going to be packed on a rare sunny Tuesday.

We're getting close and listening to the scanner. It's chaos. The cops are very confused, asking questions, trying to pass information. There are a lot of casualties – they alerted the hospitals that this is a mass casualty situation. Apparently the shooter is not in custody. Worse, there's more than one shooter. Now, in these things you often get a report that there is more than one shooter because different people call 911 and report different things from different perspectives, like that *Rashomon* movie. Two shooters happens, but it is unusual. Even more unusual is that there may be more than two shooters.

We get close and there are a lot of ambulances and emergency vehicles, and there are people running past us. That's not good. Where is the perimeter? The cops usually surround the scene so no one gets in or out, but where are the cops?

I'm yelling at Jeff to find a place to park. Frank, who was monitoring the scanner while Jeff drove, yells, "Shut up!"

I was stunned – that was not like him. "Listen," he says.

The scanner is reporting shooters – plural – at the police headquarters. I don't understand – that is nowhere near Pike Place Market. How did the shooters get there? It did not occur to me for a moment that there were two attacks.

What I did not know was that at nine a.m. they launched twelve attacks in the Seattle area. I was still thinking this was going to be the usual mass shooting. Nut kills a bunch of people, then himself, then I spend a week listening to politicians spew into my microphone about how we have to ban guns.

We get so that we simply cannot drive further and Jeff and I jump out. Frank's job was to stay behind with the van to produce and transmit the video signal to the satellite.

We get out and there are people running past us, panicking. Usually people will look you over – hey, a news crew! – but not that day. They were scared and we were just in the way. We start going upstream, like salmon, and I hear it.

BANG BANG BANG BANG BANG!

I have never been a war correspondent, but that sounded like a war to me. The shooting up ahead just went on and on.

I could see the "Public Market" sign and went toward it with Jeff carrying the camera behind me. We pushed forward, through the escaping people, never thinking that we might find ourselves inside the story.

We got close. There was no perimeter of cops, but there were empty cop cars, doors open, lights flashing. Behind us, some ambulances were inching forward – it was faster to go on foot – but there was no one in front of us. There should have been an army of cops. Inside the market there's shooting.

I look at Jeff and he shrugs. We go forward.

We found a pile of bodies at the entrance, just normal people shot down. It must have been a dozen. I had never seen anything like it. Jeff was getting it all, but I knew that it would never get broadcast. Too graphic. I have an earpiece where I can hear Frank. I tell him what we see. He says back, "Diedre, this is going on everywhere."

At that point, I am still thinking that he means that these shooters are running around the city – though there is still shooting here at the Market – and I tell him that this scene is still active. He tells me it's happening all over the city and the country.

That's when I figured out it was terrorism.

The ambulances are pulling in behind us, but no more cops. The medics start checking the bodies. I see two cops coming out of the market, pale and scared. One is shot in the leg and the other is helping him with his arm around the wounded one's shoulder.

The one that is okay hands off the wounded officer to the medics and reloads his pistol. I do my job and stick a mic in his face while Jeff films it.

"Officer, can you give us an update on the situation?" I asked.

"Get the hell out of here! We got multiple shooters with automatic weapons. We need backup. We have officers down inside!"

There is a burst of gunfire from the market, just a whole flurry of shots from different guns. A paramedic comes up to the cop as we are taping.

"Are there wounded inside?" he asks.

The cop nods.

"How many?" the paramedic asks.

"A couple hundred."

The paramedic just blinks.

"Wait, what?"

"There are at least a couple hundred casualties," the cop says. There is another flurry of shots.

"Keep out, it's not secure." He turned and ran back inside with his pistol in his hand.

The paramedics looked at each other and it's clear they had never been in a situation like this. But who had?

"These people are all dead," another one says, looking at the bodies around the door. "Headshots."

They look at each other and grab up their bags and they follow the cop. Jeff and I follow them.

We took a lot of footage inside, most of which no one outside the station or law enforcement has seen. Horrible scenes. The killers came in multiple entrances at once and trapped a lot of people. They just went through and shot everyone. When they could, they shot them in the head to make sure. There were bodies everywhere, and a few wounded who lived by hiding behind something or under bodies.

We came across the corpse of a dead terrorist within a couple minutes. He had a bullet wound in his head and that was from a citizen who was concealed carrying. He was in the black shirt and green headband uniform, and Jeff filmed him on the ground while I reported. That was the first image nationally of one of the killers, about forty minutes into the Attack. My big scoop.

There is still shooting going on and we are pressing forward. We are trying to get to where the shooting is. There are bodies everywhere. I had seen bodies before because I had been at countless crime scenes. This was different. At mass shootings, you cannot get inside among the bodies because of the perimeter. But there were no cops on the perimeter. There were no more cops to spare because they were trying to respond to all the other attacks too, including the one on the police station. The terrorists did that in a lot of cities apparently.

We were in the middle of it, walking through the carnage. Dead men, women, children, and cops too. There was blood all over the ground.

We finally found ourselves close to the shooting, but it was hard to figure out who was where. That's when it hit me for the first time – maybe we were in danger ourselves. We were standing by a fishmonger's stall and there's gunfire nearby and

Jeff is just filming, because he was a pro, and suddenly I see a terrorist down the aisle of stalls. He just runs out in the middle and starts shooting the other way, I guess at cops, but he's backing up toward us.

I pull Jeff, who is still filming, into the stall and we take cover behind the rack of salmon and crabs. We get down low. The floor is rough cement, and there are streaks of blood on it. There are a couple dead fish sellers lying there.

We are hiding and I am whispering into the mic narrating it while Jeff is filming and the terrorist comes up running, stops, turns, and fires his machine gun back at the cops. Then he runs away as the cops fire back at him.

I know it sounds cold, but you need to understand that I have a job to do as a reporter. I turned to Jeff and said, "Please tell me you got that."

He did. It went to the van where Frank sent it off on the uplink and that was the famous clip you have probably seen a million times. It probably got me my current anchor job.

We stayed low until the cops came by, and we were probably lucky they did not shoot us when we stood up. They told us to get the hell out, that the terrorists were still around. We ran – thank goodness I had sneakers!

We stayed at the scene until it was secured a couple hours later. They finally killed all four of the Pike Place Market gunmen, but there were other incidents all over the city. We did not have enough crews to cover them all, so we drove from one to another. We were there at the Angela Davis Elementary School when the SWAT team went inside late that evening. They had been held back because the terrorists had said they wanted to negotiate and used the time to kill those kids with knives. We got the footage of the cops coming out crying and some throwing up.

The only time I told Jeff to turn the camera away was when the cops dragged out one of the terrorists alive, at least for the moment. I did not want any of the cops to get in trouble.

We thought it was over by midnight. I grabbed an hour of sleep in the van and started up at the Emergency Operations Center (EOC) at the King County Sheriff's Department. It looked like an Army base because all the police and sheriffs had their rifles and tactical gear. I covered the press conferences they gave every few hours. I just could not believe the number of dead, including the kids at the school. I was numb. I am supposed to be objective, but I was really just emotionally drained. I had not processed what I had seen.

Jeff and I were there at the EOC when the Vice President spoke. The whole place was basically stunned that she was so disconnected from reality. The whole place was just silent as she finished, and then everybody just went back to work, but you could tell they did not think they were getting any help from Washington, D.C.

And then the second day started. They hit a variety of Seattle suburbs. I went out again. I had not even been home to change, but I had an extra pair of jeans and a shirt at the station. I went to three or four attack scenes. The Army was on the street later that day, and they put up perimeters, but we still got to some early enough that we saw and filmed pretty awful things. It seems horrible, but I had seen so many dead people that what really struck me was the dead doggies. I saw one family dog just cut up and I started crying. It was the first time I had cried.

As media, we were exempt from the stay-home order and we covered the third day too. The power was off for a while, but we operated on batteries so we could still do our reporting. When the internet went down, that knocked us offline for a while. I took that opportunity to go home.

I got stopped at Army roadblocks because of martial law, but these were troops from Joint Base Lewis-McChord a half-hour south and they recognized me. "You're that reporter who almost got waxed!" one said. He was pretty impressed.

I got home and took a long shower and then slept for twelve hours. I threw away my sneakers. They were soaked with blood.

14.

Detroit, Michigan

There is a cliché in Hollywood action flicks that the bad guys pick on the wrong guy and come to regret it. Dale Axely is the quintessential wrong guy. He spent six years as a member of the United States Air Force Pararescue (PJ) force. These Special Warfare airmen have a primary mission of rescuing and medically treating American forces shot down or otherwise trapped behind enemy lines. Their two-year selection and training program – of which one candidate in five completes even after the rigorous assessment to be allowed to try – graduates them as not just certified EMTs but as skilled parachutists, scuba divers, and professional-level climbers. PJs do not just treat their charges – they protect them. They are trained on every individual American and common foreign weapon system, and they train and operate with Delta Force and the SEALs, who respect them as peers.

I had been out about three years and finished my degree and I was looking for work. I was a business major and wanted to get into a tech company and start working my way up. Being Michigan, there were not a lot of those, and I thought I was going to have to move to California. But Quizzle – it does multi-media optimization products and platforms – got a bunch of tax and regulatory concessions from the state and they decided to come to Detroit. They seemed like a good fit and I aced the campus interview at the university so they asked me to come in to their new headquarters. It was huge, a skyscraper that had been a General Motors or Chrysler building back before Detroit went south a few decades ago. The first ten floors were done, but the last twenty were still being renovated. I figured there was going to be a place for me so I put on my suit and went.

I got there and went up to the tenth floor. My appointment was at ten a.m. I was there early, because in the military if you are not there fifteen minutes early you are late. I was proud of my time in the service, and I got to do a lot of cool things, and some scary things too, everything from helping a Panamanian farmer's wife give birth to shooting it out with ISIS holdouts in Syria and some other stuff I still can't talk about. But I was not Mr. Military Guy. I don't look like one, and I don't talk about it unless someone brings it up.

Still, it's on my resume, and that always got brought up in interviews. I had passed the on-campus one, but now I was set to talk to the next level of management, which was guys about three or four years younger than me who had basically graduated college and gone to work at Quizzle. They did not understand what a PJ does and I gave them the short version, which was basically Air Force SEALs, and then I tried to move on to my actual qualifications for the job.

After the first round, I got asked to wait and they sent in a couple more senior people. They told me they liked my skills but they worried that I might not fit in the culture, being military and all. I knew that discrimination on account of military status was a No-Go, but I didn't want to drop that. I explained how I worked with a diverse group of professionals to make impactful contributions for our shared mission. That seemed to impress them. They told me to wait in the interview office while they talked. It was eleven o'clock.

I was sitting there checking my email, because I hate wasting time, when I heard it. Kalashnikov shots. I know what an AK rifle sounds like. What the hell was one doing in the Quizzle offices?

I figured mass shooter, but I heard two sets of shots overlapping. That meant at least two shooters. Then the shooting stopped.

I open the door and people are in the hallway, confused. I take it upon myself to call the police and hope I was just overreacting to someone playing a video game really loud. That could happen – people were using Razr scooters to go down the hallways and I had passed a "Recharge/Refresh Space" with a juice press.

I told the 911 dispatcher that shots were fired at this office and the dispatcher seemed baffled. She gave another address and asked if that was nearby. It wasn't. That was my first inkling that this was not a unique occurrence.

I walked down the hall to where a crowd of confused and worried people were pushing the elevator button. Nothing. Now I was sure this was no false alarm.

"There are people here with guns," I told them, including the people interviewing me. "You need to find a place to hide."

I knew they had no weapons. I did. I had my concealed carry permit and I had a SIG Sauer P229 Centurion in my bag. Of course, by then it was in the pocket of my suit with three extra mags of Speer 9mm hollow points and my Leatherman tool.

A voice came over a loudspeaker. It was a woman, and she was barely holding it together. She told everyone that some men had taken over the building and that no one was going to be hurt but we all needed to come down to the fifth floor immediately and do as we were told. Use the stairs.

Fifth floor, not the first. They were smart – make it hard on the SWAT team.

To my amazement, most of the people started heading toward the stairwell door. I guess I should not have been surprised. At the university, everyone conformed to authority. I got into the stairwell and listened. There was shouting – I heard Arabic. I knew what that language sounded like. There were a lot of Arab immigrants in Michigan for some reason, and I thought it might be some of them.

I started heading upward. The lady who was interviewing me told me to wait because I was going the wrong way.

I mentally wrote off the job and ignored her.

I went up and up, figuring I would get to the top and wait for the cavalry. The doors were unlocked because there was work going on, though I did not see any workmen. I went to the top floor and went around a corner from the door. I got out my phone and decided to take a chance. I called a buddy in the intel community and hoped he was somewhere he could pick up. He did on one ring.

No formalities. I gave him the situation. He told me that fit the pattern. There were several kinds of attacks going on. Mass casualty attacks with gunmen, attacks on airliners, and hostage situations. They were grabbing schools and workplaces.

"The hostage situations – how are they going?" I asked.

He paused. "Look, none are resolved. Everything is total chaos. But the other attacks are designed for mass casualties immediately. They are broadcasting it on the internet. The terrorists seem bent on getting killed. They might be interested in an actual hostage situation where they get away, but that would be a break from their pattern. They might want to just spread out the killing over time, emphasize our powerlessness, maybe take their time with the hostages and broadcast that."

I told him thanks and he asked me what I was going to do.

"I think my options are pretty limited."

"Most of the teams are four-man, but not all. You armed yet?"

"Yeah."

"Good luck."

I checked the P229's chamber to ensure a round was seated, and opened the stairwell door. I heard footsteps coming up.

I looked around. There was nothing really on the floor, just some tarps, paint cans, and piles of drywall. The footsteps were coming closer and I heard some Arabic words. The accent was familiar.

I slowly let the door close and continued to look for options. I saw one.

I used a fire extinguisher cabinet on the wall as a step to climb up and push an acoustical tile on the false ceiling up. We do a lot of rock climbing in the PJs. I knew the false ceiling could not support my weight but the HVAC duct might be able to. I jumped, got a hold of it, and pulled myself up, then used my foot to kick the tile back into place. Then I heard them step onto the twentieth floor.

They were laughing and joking in Arabic. I did not know enough of it to translate, but I knew whatever they were saying was not good.

They were doing something on the floor beyond searching it for stragglers, and I was not sure what. I thought about what I would do if I were them. What I would do is secure my defensive position, but with four guys they probably could not spare one or two to guard this top floor. I would use Claymore mines or something like that. My guess was they were planting some kind of explosives to take out a SWAT team trying to come in from the roof.

That would be suboptimal.

And so was my current position. The HVAC duct was not meant to hold a 200-pound PJ for an extended period. It groaned, and they heard it, made some comment about it, and went back to work. But it was clear that the sands in the hourglass of that thing holding me were running out. I figured I was coming down one way or the other. It might as well be on my terms and timetable.

I got out my weapon and I visualized what I planned to do. We're trained to visualize actions if we have no time to actually rehearse them. I ran it a couple times through my head, including one time where the false ceiling did not break cleanly through.

I was ready.

I dropped off the HVAC duct legs first and went straight through the acoustical tiles of the false ceiling to the floor. Their AKs were leaning against the wall and they were messing with a couple backpacks with cans and colored wires inside. It took me about a second to get my bearings. It took them three or four, which was plenty of time for me.

They looked over and went for their weapons. I drew a bead on the first one and shot him twice in the forehead. The other got his hand on the folding stock of his AK-47 before I shot him twice. They twitched for a moment before I shot them each in the temple, then exchanged the depleted mag for a fresh one.

The bags did have explosives. They were not hooked up, but it looked like there was some sort of field expedient cell phone command detonation system. I separated the explosives from the electronics just to be sure.

Then I picked up the better-looking of the two old Kalashnikovs and checked the chamber. Next, I took one of their vests with a basic load of mags and slipped it on.

Now I had a machine gun. Ho ho ho.

I moved down the stairwell as silently as I could in my business shoes. I had the Kalashnikov up and in front of me, with the stock unfolded for stability. There was no optic, which was not optimal, but at these ranges iron sights would do. Down I went, floor by floor. I was at the tenth floor when I heard some shots. Not enough to be the massacre I feared, but enough to hurt some folks.

I got to the door at the fifth floor, covering it. I figured the floor was probably laid out like the tenth, with a long hall and offices branching off. I figured there was likely a guard at or near the door. There would be at least one other somewhere near the door. They had numbers, I had surprise.

I visualized my moves over and over, maybe five times, but that muzzle never left the door. There was shouting, and another burst from far off followed by screaming, crying, and more harsh Arabic commands.

No more time to wait.

I had the rifle up with my right hand and I used my left to open the door.

There was one about five meters away. He turned, smiling to greet his friends. His smile vanished as I shot him three times then put a fourth in his head as he wriggled on the floor.

Then I saw that I had been wrong about the floor. It was not a tight, constricted hallway with offices but one of those open-plan collaborative environments. And at least two hundred people were huddled on the floor.

"Where is he?" I yelled. One woman pointed across the floor. I saw a black-shirted guy moving and I ducked behind the foosball table before he fired at me. I raised my rifle and acquired him.

Boom. I hit him once and he staggered and I followed up with three more. He fell back against the Keurig table.

The whole place is screaming now as I get up and look for other targets. I see a couple bodies on the floor. I see some women they had assaulted crying.

"Are there more?" I shout. Somebody yells, "One!"

I move across the floor, sweeping for a target. Then I see the last one, and he has a woman he's holding with the rifle barrel against her. He pulls back behind a cubicle wall.

This is not time for the rifle, so I lose it and draw the SIG in a two-hand grip. I move past the Keurig and pivot to put a cap in the head of the guy I just shot. I'm not having a live enemy to my rear.

The last guy is shouting in English about how he will kill the whore if I don't give him my gun. I come around and try to get a bead on him. He's hiding behind her and I can't shoot him in the face without him pulling the trigger and taking her along for the ride.

I had dealt with guys like this before. He would kill her in a heartbeat, and hope I would kill him.

I decided to use that.

"You speak English?" I asked. I had the weapon up, waiting for a shot.

He told me to go to hell.

"I'll make you a deal," I said. "If you let her go, I'll kill you."

He seemed confused. I went on.

"You want to be a martyr, just like your friends? Or do you want me to shoot you in the spine and you get to live in a wheelchair being the bitch for all the boys on the cellblock?"

"Shut up!"

"You shoot her, and I'm just wounding you. But if you try to shoot me, I'll kill you! I promise!"

"I'll kill her!"

"Then you won't be a martyr!"

"Shut up!" He started raising the weapon at me. The instant the barrel came away from the woman I fired.

The round hit his shoulder and pushed him back. The woman screamed and bolted as his grip loosened. True to my word, I put two in his chest and one through the bridge of his nose.

I took a minute to ensure the floor was clear, then organized the people to gather the injured. I spent the next few hours helping the wounded, since no ambulances were available. No one alive when I got to the floor died in that building.

Oh, Quizzle offered me the job. I declined. I re-upped and I've been back in the PJs ever since. The civilian world is just too dangerous.

15.

Carbon County, Montana

"Storm's coming," Robert "Rob" Cleaves said, looking toward the angry clouds approaching the Hellroaring Plateau from the west. He has his fishing gear and a Glock 47 9mm pistol on his hip, which he was allowed to keep when he retired from the United States Secret Service several years before.

Most agents refuse to speak about their protectees even after they leave the job, but Cleaves does not subscribe to that norm. He feels he was wronged. His book, A Family of Lowlifes, *about his years protecting the First Family, was a minor bestseller. However, this is the first time he has spoken publicly about the events of the Attack, as the Secret Service refused to clear that chapter of his book for publication. At his request, certain details that might disclose secret tactics, techniques, and procedures have been omitted here.*

Working on the Presidential Detail is the highlight of an agent's career. The assignment is intensely competitive, and so is staying on it. One little screw-up and – whoosh! – you're in Detroit chasing junkies running off Xerox copies of twenties at the local Kinko's.

I liked the job, but not the principal. You know, POTUS. Look, everyone on the job hated the whole family. The President, the doctor – we had to call her "Doctor" – and especially his scumbag son. Maybe "hated" is too strong a word, or maybe not. He treated us like hired help. Snapped at us. Never bothered learning our names. Not being a woman, I never had the experience, but there were rumors that when he was the Vice President he used to swim nude in front of the female agents. Trump got a bad rap in the media, but everyone on the detail loved him. This guy, though...what a jerk.

But I was not paid to like the principal. I was paid to protect him, and I would take a bullet for him in a heartbeat. We all would. That was the job, and we were the best in the world at it. And we sucked up a lot of abuse and cleaned up a lot of messes for the protectees. Remember the coke they found in the West Wing? Come on. You didn't need to be Sherlock Holmes to figure out that mystery. You could be Mr. Magoo.

Tuesday, August 27th, was a regular day. Hot and muggy, but clear. We got an intel brief every shift change. Nothing unusual. There was supposed to be some small demonstration about climate change or some such nonsense outside the gate, maybe fifty people for a couple hours, but we would not even see them from the White House.

Tammy Hernandez was our newest addition to the squad, just a couple days on. She was with me when the President came downstairs into the West Wing to head for the Oval Office. He liked to sit there and look out the window. He talked to the squirrels. The guy was old, ancient. He could barely walk some days. I think when he did a speech or an interview, one of his private doctors juiced him with something. But he was never a nice old man. He was always mean, and we agents were definitely there to take crap. Sometimes literally.

He had that damn dog with him. It was huge, like a German Shepherd or something. It bit people left and right. There was bad publicity so they announced he was leaving the mutt back at the beach house, but he would sneak it back to D.C. because he loved having it around. I think it was mostly because everyone was scared of it. I was. I still have a scar where that son of a bitch bit me on the hand when I tried to pet him.

Anyway, the dog, of course, wanders off into the Cabinet Room and takes this enormous crap on the rug. It's like the size of a small dog itself. And Tammy is just staring at it like, "What the hell?" And I say, "Well, new girl, enjoy!" She sighs and goes off to find something to clean it up with.

Our job was to hang close, but not too close. The West Wing is not the big, expansive place like you see on TV shows or movies. It's cramped and small, and everyone guards his turf. Woe unto you if you somehow think that merely because you are protecting the life of the President that you have any authority whatsoever in the anteroom where the secretary sits outside the Oval Office.

Now, to say the President was not very busy was an understatement. I accomplish more in a morning of retirement than he did on the average day as leader of the free world, and most of what I do is sit and fish. He would roll in at nine and they would often call a lid – that means announce that there were no more events so the media folks could relax – before noon. In the afternoon, he was napping or watching *Matlock*. Every day at three, one of the serving staff would take a vanilla ice cream cone upstairs to him.

Mind you, he's in the middle of an election campaign, but he's not even running a Rose Garden campaign. He's running a Lincoln Bedroom campaign. It sure makes life easier when your own Justice Department is trying to lock up your opponent.

That morning, he got his security briefing. I was not inside, but everyone came out laughing and smiling. We had had some bad days – Afghanistan, Ukraine, the Gaza War – so I knew the difference. No one saw what was coming that day.

Then the campaign types came in and what a shifty bunch of weasels they were. I tried to ignore them and they ignored me.

At about 11:00, his secretary tells me, "He's meeting FLOTUS in the dining room at 12:30 p.m." That was later than usual.

Turns out there are a bunch of Wisconsin cheese tycoons coming through just before noon and, well, Wisconsin is a swing state so he was going to meet with them for five minutes of face time.

Of course, the curd wranglers were all cleared in advance and basically given a colonoscopy before coming into the Oval Office. The door was open for this meeting, and I was outside just observing. It was always possible one of these dairymen was going to have a schizo break and lunge for the principal's throat. That would be a bad idea. I had my Glock, and there's a discrete closet nearby with some heavier stuff.

Everyone else is flapping their gums about cheddar, and the President is asking if they make Velveeta and it's getting awkward.

Anyway, that damn dog is lying on the carpet – he never crapped in the Oval Office – and suddenly he alerts, right at noon. I see it, but no one else notices. Then I hear the noise.

It's gunfire.

Look, most personal security details are concerned with one or two assholes trying to cap the principal. We're a little different because we plan for a lot of assholes coming to cap the principal. This is open source, so I can tell you that we have a CAT – our counter-assault team – and it is designed to take on a multi-asshole attack. It's the Secret Service's Delta Force. You have to try out, and most people don't get on. If you get it, that's your thing. You do not get a chance at the protection team, and I wanted to do protection so I did not try out. But they are badasses. Most are vets, with some special ops types. They are trained and equipped to stand and fight it out while the guys in suits like me spirit away the principal to safety.

Well, that day there were a whole lot of assholes. Forty-nine, to be exact, all with AK-47 automatic rifles, plus rocket-propelled grenades.

It was the Secret Service's finest hour. They hit us at several locations at once, trying to overwhelm the uniformed Secret Service on the perimeter. They needed to move fast to get into the White House before we could do what we needed to do and secure the President and a couple other key folks – everyone else was on their own.

Those uniforms fought hard – most could not get to long guns, but they never retreated. They fought it out, Glocks against multiple attackers with superior weapons. They died where they stood, no retreat, all heroes. And they took some of the bastards with them.

I'm going for the President before he and the Gouda magnates even realized that they are in a combat zone. I'm pushing these guys out of the way and the President is looking at me like I am nuts.

All of a sudden, this burst of fire hits the windows. They're bulletproof, of course, but now there is line of impact holes across it. Everyone drops except the President and me. I grab him and start pulling him out of the room.

Hernandez is at the door, her Glock out, telling everyone to stay down. One of the cheese guys gets spooked and tries to run out the door where I'm heading with POTUS, and Hernadez clocks him in the head with the butt of her automatic. Lights out, Windows reboot.

There is only one person who matters, our principal. If you get in our way and only get hit upside your head, count yourself lucky.

People are running back and forth in the halls, staff and guests. We don't care. They are not my principal. FLOTUS and the Veep are someone else's problem. I have to get the President secured. Nothing else matters, including my ass.

We were taking him to a semi-secret stairwell. I don't want to be too specific, but I never liked the route because we had to pass a door to the Rose Garden. Hernandez is first and she turns and engages out the door with her Glock – some of them had fought their way that close already.

She blows off half a mag and I yell, "Take him!" I have a full mag. I push the President ahead to her and she pulls him out of the doorway just as bullets spray inside from outside. She hauls him away and it's just me at the damn open door. I gotta hold that door, no matter what, even if it means getting smoked. I'm Hodor and the monsters are coming.

I step out with my Glock 47. It's a modified Glock 17 originally made for government agencies. I'm running Secret Service-issued 9mm hollow points and hoping they do the job. I pivot out and there are three of them plus one on his back that Hernandez capped.

I start blazing away. One goes down, then another. It takes all 17 rounds in the mag plus one in the pipe to do both because they are in armor. The third dives behind a rose bush about ten feet away just as I go dry. I still squeeze the trigger a couple times before I realize the slide is locked back. Then I figure out I'm dry and drop my mag. That's when the third guy figures that he's got me and starts standing up. There's no way I'm going to reload, flip the slide, acquire, and shoot the guy before he ventilates me with 7.62mm x 39mm.

I'm dead. But I keep going through the motions.

Then something pushes past me, fast, a black blur. It leaps on this terrorist schmuck, all fur and teeth. It's that damn dog, and he is messing that boy up. I read they hate dogs, so maybe it screwed up his chances to get his virgins. Anyway, I send the slide forward, take aim, and did him with one in the brain pan. He drops and I swear that dog looked at me like he was bummed out to lose his chew toy.

The CAT guys from the Hawkeye presidential team were there and they did not bother with "Excuse me" as they pushed past me into the Rose Garden, all geared up and packing their Knight Armament Company SR-16 Mod 3 rifles. All four terrorists on the ground got a safety tap in their heads – this was no game. The CAT boys are hard. Those boys held the White House, outnumbered and outgunned, and they ran up the score of dead tangos.

Now it was my job to get back to the principal. I run through the corridors, basically bulldozing the straphangers out of my way, until I see Hernandez trying to get the President to go down the stairwell to the emergency shelter. He won't go. He's yelling that "It's dark!"

He may be in charge of our country but when the shit hits the fan, I am in charge of him. I push him ahead down the stairs, but I am holding him by his upper right arm. He's shouting and screaming and fighting me, so finally I let him go so he can walk by himself. He takes two steps and promptly tumbles like he's on the Air Force One stairway.

He's in a heap at the bottom and he's screaming in pain. I've been around old people and I'm thinking, "Don't have broken your hip, don't have broken your hip."

Well, he broke his hip. Not my fault, but somebody had to get the blame. Hence my early retirement.

Anyway, there's an emergency level three clinic down there that can do anything. That's where they did the surgery, but he was out of it. Just totally non-functional.

And so was the Veep. I mean, we all knew she was a mess, but we had no idea. They brought her downstairs and she's in tears, babbling. The chief of staff grabs her and says, "Madame Vice President, the President is incapacitated," and looks at her expectantly.

I swear, I saw it myself. She looks at the chief of staff and says, No." And then she and her minions run into her emergency office and shut the door. They will not come out.

I just look at all this and think, wow, our country is screwed.

16.

Washington, D.C.

A plump rat interrupts our interview, scurrying out of a hole in the plaster next to an ancient, government-issue file cabinet and pauses to watch us for a moment, unafraid. Federal Bureau of Investigations Special Assistant Deputy Director for Operations and Interagency Synergy Peter Kilpatrick picks a red Swingline stapler up off his desk and throws it at the insouciant rodent. He misses, but knocks a hole in the plaster.

Kilpatrick shakes his head. "Kind of sums it up, huh?" he tells his visitor.

The 25-year FBI agent does not worry about the damage to the wall because the J. Edgar Hoover Building is being abandoned. He is one of the last personnel to remain, and in a few weeks he will shut the lights off for the last time in the once-storied law enforcement agency.

I was one of the old breed. I did a hitch in the Marines, and saw some action in Afghanistan, then got out and the Bureau hired me right up. I wanted to bust down doors and arrest bank robbers and terrorists, all that kind of stuff. And I did, for a while, until the end of the Bush administration. I guess I can talk about it now because, well, what are they going to do to me, right?

Then, under Obama, the Bureau changed. We stopped hiring military and law enforcement and started hiring people off the street to "change the culture." And did they ever. They hired these woke kids right out of college, gave them badges and guns, and what do you think they would do? By the 2010s, we were focusing on the new threat, which was basically any Americans who the Democrats didn't like.

The whole Trump-Russia thing was a huge embarrassment to those of us who wanted to be law enforcement officers, but you have to understand that most of the leadership was *proud* of it. Then the BLM and Antifa riots started and FBI special agents were out there kneeling. And if you've seen the pictures, a lot of them were fat. Of course, then January 6 became the big focus and we were out chasing grandmas for taking selfies in the rotunda.

But some of us knew that our real enemies were still out there, waiting, inside the U.S. We told the chain of command this was going to bite us, just like all those mass shooters who were on our radar did. But the seventh floor didn't care. They had their orders, and they were happy to carry them out. All the while, the reputation the Bureau built up over decades was getting flushed down the toilet with normal people. You know how much it hurt to go up to regular, hardworking Americans, show your creds, and have them flat-out tell you, "I won't talk to the FBI?"

Some of us hid, hoping to ride it out somewhere where people were still doing the job. I joined HRT – the hostage rescue team. Selection was a major bitch. The HRT used pretty much the same selection process as Delta Force. Ruck runs cross-country for miles, no sleep, total stress to see how you reacted. I don't know how I made it, but I did. The training was amazing. Shooting with Delta, fast-roping from choppers – we had our own – and diving with the SEALs. We trained with Tier 1 special ops from around the world. We did missions in Afghanistan and Iraq too.

But the woke crap even seeped into HRT. We were spending too much valuable training time on DEI classes. I remember the seventh floor sending a memo asking why we did not have more "differently-abled" operators. Standards dropped so we could meet quotas. We ended up letting sub-par agents join just to check boxes, and they made sub-par operators.

I tried to keep away from the flagpole as much as possible, but whenever I would come here to HQ from Quantico there would be something that made me want to punch a wall. I remember walking in here one time and there was this huge display downstairs about J. Edgar and the focus was on how he was a trans pioneer.

On August 27th, I was in command. We were deployed to a small town outside Nashville, Tennessee, to take down a preacher and father of eight who had been illegally praying outside an abortion clinic. We figured he probably had some guns because he was a normal American guy, but did we really need to send in the Team? We told higher that the local office should just call him up, ask him to surrender, and he probably would – the guy did not have as much as a jaywalking ticket in his jacket. You might think we would learn from Waco, but no.

Nope, they told us, you gotta go in and go heavy. We were sending a message for the administration, and the message was that the FBI was coming if you stepped out of line. No wonder the good guys were retiring in droves. I thought about it since I was nearing my twenty.

So, we bust down the doors of the guy's house at about 10:50 a.m. when most of his kids were at school – and it was a fight with the brass to wait that long. Some of the new guys were excited to do it, too excited. I had to directly order that no one shoot the family dogs. A couple of the new guys loved doing that on political raids to show the dissidents who was boss.

Anyway, the wife is crying, the kids too young to go to school are crying, and this guy is hooked up and as I read him his rights, he says, "I forgive you." That gutted me. I spent my whole life defending the Constitution and now I'm busting people for illegal praying. I wanted to puke.

The local office starts investigating the scene, executing the search warrant, and we're hanging around doing security. We have a plane set to take us back to Virginia in like four hours, so we're in no rush. About 11:15 a.m., my executive officer, my second-in-command, comes up to me all agitated and says, "I just got a call from HQ. We're alerted. Some kind of terrorist thing."

"Nothing more?" I ask. My XO shrugs and tells me that's all they said. I spot a TV in the living room, turn it on, start flipping channels away from the Sunday School Network to Fox or CNN or whatever I hit first. It was CNN, and the girl looked stricken, pale as a ghost.

"We are getting reports of multiple mass shootings from across the country," she says. "And at least two airliner crashes."

"Holy shit," I say. "Mount up," I yell to my guys.

We load up and start tearing off to the airport. I get through to FBI ops and they tell me to just get the team back to Quantico because all hell is breaking loose. I'm pissed. It's the Super Bowl and we're Tom Brady and we're sidelined.

We head straight to the general aviation area at Nashville International. It takes us an hour to get there, and the whole time we're listening to the radio. You remember. It was chaos. It turns out there are shooters in Nashville and we thought about helping, but the local yokels had it covered. We see cops with lights and sirens going every which way. Guys are calling their families, worried. It's a shit show.

Coming to the airport, there's something wrong that I can't put my finger on. We pull into the general aviation area past a scared gate guard who now has a shotgun and roll up to the plane. We roll out to load up and our pilot walks up to us.

"Don't bother," he says.

Then I figure it out. Nothing is taking off or landing. The national airspace closure order was in effect.

We try to get special permission to fly, but it's chaos at the FAA. Who the hell do we call anyway to get an exception? We're not going to just take off – the only planes I saw were F-16s patrolling and they seemed to have missiles on their wings. I made the command decision – we drive.

It's 625 miles and ten hours, my executive office says. I tell him that we better start now. We are in five black SUVs and I tell everyone to haul ass on their own and to rally at the compound at Quantico ASAP. Everyone heads out east.

Four of the SUVs got there. One got off the highway in Cumberland Country outside of Knoxville, ran into a roadblock of locals looking to make sure no terrorists hit their burg. Now, you see a bunch of good old boys with rifles who outnumber you ten to one, and that's your cue to deescalate. But the senior guy was one of those guys who liked killing dogs to show he was boss, and he thought flashing his tricked-out M4 would cow the country boys. It didn't. They shot that SUV 200 times, killed four of our operators. That was one of the few events that actually got a full investigation afterwards, or would have, if every single inhabitant of the county had not denied seeing anything.

There was no time to mourn. We got back to Quantico and started deploying in squads. Three of my squads, top operators, got taken to provide personal protection for seventh-floor brass. Of course, none of the FBI brass was targeted. In fact, the rumors are true – later, the investigation found that the terrorists had considered hitting the J. Edgar Building with an AMFO truck bomb day one, like they did in Vegas and elsewhere, but they made a conscious decision not to because they thought the FBI would do more damage to the American response if it was fully operational.

I was assigned to New York City and helped breach the Empire State Building hostage stand-off. There were eleven terrorists in there, with automatic weapons and rocket-propelled grenades. They dug in and then uploaded what they were doing to the hostages. That was bad, but seeing it in person was worse. We lost several NYPD guys and one of ours in the fight. In law enforcement, the criminal usually wants to live or will off himself, but it's very rare that he really wants to take as many of you with him as he can. They did, and they were on meth as well so that made it worse. It took us eight hours to dig them all out. We were less a hostage rescue team than exterminators. But we did exterminate them. We killed all of them. And we carried almost 400 bodies out of there.

I did two more hostage situations, a bowling alley in Long Island and that school in Newark. They always has the same playbook. One terrorist who spoke English would pretend to negotiate for a while, while the others were using their knives and such on the hostages. Usually, in a hostage situation, we have all the resources we need – negotiators, drones, surveillance equipment, and all the warm bodies you want. But when there are fifty hostage situations? No, you only have yourself. And that gets people dead.

The second day we thought it was over, but they started hitting homes. We went in and hunted the terrorists with local cops and citizen militia. Day three, when they hit infrastructure, what was there for us to target? We stood guard.

Afterwards, we did a lot of raids and arrests, particularly on Antifa types and BLM and college radicals. I'm proud of our work during and after. But we hardly covered ourselves in glory before the Attack. The hearings at Congress were brutal, but you know, they were right to ask us how the hell we missed ten thousand killers waiting for a "Go" signal inside our country. Just like all those mass shooters we missed – we had the pieces, but we failed to put them together. Of course, we were told not to look too closely – didn't want to oppress anyone, did we?

Before the Attack, the Congress was going to appropriate about a billion bucks to move us out of this old rat trap building into a swank new FBI complex. Afterwards, fat chance. We're lucky they gave us as long as they have to shut the doors and parcel out all the various FBI missions to other agencies. The new Federal Counterintelligence Agency will do the spy versus spy stuff. The Federal Criminal Investigations Service will chase the bank robbers and video pirates. FCIS – hardly rolls off the tongue. Can you see Efrem Zimbalist, Jr., saying, "I'm inspector Erskine of the FCIS?" Or Clarice Starling? Now the psycho killers all come under the National Profiling Agency, which isn't even technically a law enforcement agency at all and has no badge-and-gun agents, just shrinks and profilers.

Well, we have about thirty days until the official shutdown of the FBI. I'm sad, not about closing out what it is but about losing what it was. It kills me to say it, but for the last thirty years, going back to missing the 9/11 terrorists, we have let America down. And there are consequences for failure. I guess we in the Bureau are lucky that the consequence for most of us was just losing our jobs.

As Kilpatrick finishes the interview, the rat comes back, looks up, then casually slips back into his hole.

THE SECOND DAY

AUGUST 28TH

17.

Denver, Colorado

Major General Trisha Starr is the adjutant general of the Colorado National Guard, heading a nearly division-sized collection of different Army and Air Force units.

She sits inside her office at the Guard's headquarters underneath a framed flag – the "colors" of the 193rd Military Police Battalion. It has several battle streamers, including Afghanistan and "Attack Response 27-29 August."

She points up at it, clearly proud of it.

My unit gave me that when I rotated out of command a year after the Attack. Best job I ever had in the Army. If you would give me back my battalion, I would take these stars off in a second and go back and do it all over again. See, when you are a light colonel, you wear a silver oak leaf. You're a big deal, but you're approachable. Troops will talk to you, and you can get out of headquarters, dodge meetings, and go lead soldiers. Not like I'm stuck doing now. Once you make O-6 – full bird colonel – and you have that eagle, everyone looks at you differently and troops stop talking to you. A general? Forget it.

I was an Army National Guard "M-Day" soldier as the commander of the 193rd. That means I was a part-timer, you know, one weekend a month, two days a year. Ha! I had a full-time cadre of troops on active duty running the unit between our monthly drills. I was on the phone with them for two hours a day every day working for free even while I was a bank vice president. But that's what commanders do. Luckily, my bank supported me. Not everyone's employer did, or does even today.

In Denver, the Attack started at about 10:00 a.m. I was in a meeting, and near half past I see people outside in the offices start running around. That does not look good. It goes on for a minute and I finally call time out and open the door to ask what's up.

Terrorists, someone says.

I was a new second lieutenant military police platoon leader when 9/11 went down, and I ended up doing a tour in Guantanamo and a tour in Afghanistan. I just knew this was bad.

I did not know the half of it. There were attacks going on all over the country. Shootings, bombings, planes being shot down – all of those here in Colorado too, including a jumbo jet shot down at Denver International.

I canceled the meeting and got on the phone to state HQ.

"This is Colonel Starr. You want me to mobilize?"

They told me no, but I knew how things worked. I called my senior full-timer, a major, and told him to initiate the recall roster. The 193rd was mobilizing. If it was a false alarm and no order came down, I would just pay the troops by making the 27th and 28th their drill days. Two hours later, I got a call ordering me to mobilize my battalion. I reported mobilization complete one hour and three minutes later. HQ had no idea how I brought up 500 troops in sixty-three minutes.

The first few hours was a lot of waiting, though we were busy issuing equipment, including M4s and M240 machine guns. Military Police units are very heavily armed. I saw that the cops were fighting it out with terrorists with automatic weapons and the hell if I was going to not have fire superiority. You are not supposed to issue crew-served machine guns in a civil support operation. Well, this looked like a war to me. I issued the machine guns.

We got our mission in the late afternoon – point security throughout the city. Now, the civilians were issuing the assignments and we had some issues because they would tell us that we need a squad at such-and-such and I'd have a couple vehicles show up. That was a squad. They meant one guy to stand there with his gun. Nope, not how we worked.

But we got through it. I wanted to do patrols, but the cops were doing that. We freed them up for that by securing fixed locations. That night, while there were still some terrorists loose and the stay-at-home order was in effect, none of us saw any action.

That would change.

The next morning I am making the rounds of my various security positions, just dropping in and making sure the company commander is taking care of them, and my command sergeant major, who went everywhere with me and was on the web looking for intel, says, "Hey, the Vice President is speaking." He plays it on speaker.

The following is the verbatim transcript of the Vice President's speech at 10:00 a.m. Eastern Time on August 28th.

My fellow Americans,

I speak to you this morning from the White House on behalf of our President, who is recovering well from his minor injuries. He will be back at work soon after leading the response to yesterday's tragedy that occurred.

I want to confirm to you that the situation yesterday, where many people were tragically hurt or killed, is fully resolved. The danger has passed but now begins the process of processing our shared grief in order to allow the light that is in us all to shine again once more undimmed.

There are many rumors and much misinformation about yesterday's events, and we should look only to the trustworthy and approved information sources of our recognized and official free press for information, and avoid sources of misinformation that spread misinformation and hate. I urge you to embrace the love within us, not the anger, to seize the opportunity to become our best selves in the wake of this terrible tragedy, and to search within ourselves for solutions.

I know that many Americans are feeling many feelings today – sadness, hope, even joy in our shared experience as Americans experiencing a situation.

To those of you who have lost loved ones, we are sorry for your losses and we grieve with you. But what is lost can be found again in the kingdom of our hearts. We must embrace, laugh, smile, and dance. This will show the people who caused us such grief that our unbroken spirit remains unbroken and that they cannot break it.

It is important to not forget that those who have suffered so much include indigenous peoples, black and brown Americans, those who reject the gender binary and those who embrace the beautiful rainbow of identities that arches above our country.

This is not a time for hate, but for love, as we begin this journey for justice together. I wish to especially shout out loudly and clearly to our Muslim citizens and others, including undocumented migrants, and to assure them that the number one priority of my administration...of this administration, shall be to fight the scourge of anti-Muslim hate. Nothing could be worse than compounding this tragedy with that tragic kind of tragedy.

Understand that there will be accountability for these events, and that the people responsible will be held to their responsibility for the crimes they are responsible for. But we must not seek mindless vengeance or lash out in anger. As I once watched the Reverand Martin Luther King, Jr., tell a crowd, "Justice is not just for us."

We must redouble our efforts for justice of all kinds – racial, environmental, nutritional – and today I want to redouble our efforts to ban the kind of weapons of war that have caused so much tragic tragedy to our children and to the men, women, and gender nonconforming individuals of our country.

Thanks to the efforts of the federal government under our President and myself, we have ended the situation. The temporary national stay at home order means just fifteen days to stop the spread of this situation. We can soon return to our lives and living them loudly and unashamedly.

As Americans we share so much in common, such as America itself, which helps define and expand what it means to be American. And that experience of being American, which is something we all share, is the essence of America.

We're kind of stunned, and then Sergent Major, who was as NCO as an NCO can be, busts out, "What the unholy hell was that bullshit?"

Pretty much summed up how I felt. She was the top of the chain of command? Not good.

Things were calm until just after eleven. No one expected the terrorists to switch focus, but it made sense. They hit public places on Tuesday, so the government ordered everyone to go home, so they hit people at home.

The 911 call center crashed as people in the suburbs called for help, and those college bastards helped jam the 911 lines with fake calls before they joined in the killing themselves.

After an hour, the cops were totally overwhelmed and I said, "Screw it." I stripped down the point security teams and assembled two-vehicle mobile squads and vectored them into the suburbs where the violence was worst. And I drew an M4 and went myself.

We were in Highlands Park in the south part of the city and the houses are very close together. That meant they could go from house to house quickly, just killing everyone. We had no idea where they were. Sergeant Major gets on X, Twitter, whatever it is, and finds a terrorist feed – they put them up faster than Twitter could take them down – and he sees a street sign in the background of one. A whole team was just shooting everyone.

We put it in the nav and it's a minute away.

Charge!

We roar in, my Humvee and Humvee gun truck and the first thing we see is a tango – you could tell the terrorists because they wore body armor, black shirts, and a green headband – and he's trying to drive off in a Kia Sorrento just as we are driving in.

Advantage, Hummer.

My driver, a kid from Mexico who I swore in as a citizen, just plowed into the front of the Kia. I guess the tango didn't wear his seatbelt because he flies through the windshield onto the hood and is there moaning.

I roll out with my rifle and Sergeant Major gets out, walks up with his SIG and blows a hole in the terrorist's head. Seemed harsh at the time, but remember that the CSM had been watching their videos to get a clue about where they were and saw what they were doing. He was just ahead of the power curve when it came to taking prisoners.

We move down the street. There are bodies everywhere, adults, kids, dogs. People are screaming in this black house. My driver and I move through the kicked-in front door. There's a bloody little girl in the hall, clothes ripped off, and this tango is trying to pull up his pants. He looked at us like, "What?"

He's not going to be much use to his virgins where I shot him.

They would not go down easy. They would fight, just spraying and praying, so we would have to pin them down with fire, maneuver on them and take them out. The gunner on the gun truck was useful because he could suppress the hell out of them. One of them ran into a house and took a hostage. We were not going to wait and rushed in. He shot the old lady and we shot him.

There were dozens just in that neighborhood. We fought all day, securing one area, moving to another. My driver got shot in the gut, and Sergent Major in the left arm, which did not stop him since he was carrying his pistol.

I formed up my own ad hoc force with Army, cops, and civilians with weapons. We swept through. It was hard, a real fight. They were in platoon strength. I maybe had a company-sized element, pretty much the minimum to take on a defending enemy force of that size.

These guys fought right up until we killed them. The two we took alive were wounded bad. But even then they were not running away. They were trying to find more people to shoot or blow up with a grenade. People would hide in their cellars and they would drop in grenades. They would use propane tanks from the BBQs or would try to cut the gas lines and try to blow the houses up, or just burn them. Lucky it's so hard to burn a modern suburban house.

It was not like fighting soldiers. Soldiers fight – I don't want to say fair, but they fight other soldiers. These bastards fought everyone, including the unarmed. They just wanted to pump up the body count and they did. All those poor people, trapped in their homes.

Now, a good many of the tangos knocked on the wrong door and got shot at for their trouble. If they took fire, that screwed things up. They had to react to the shooter and that took them off their primary objective of killing innocent people. So they just bypassed anyone able to resist if they could. But this was not out in the country. This was a lot of affluent, usually liberal, people who mostly did not believe in guns. Well, they believe now.

18.

She works in an office now, at an urgent care location as a physician's assistant. Today, Cheri Williams dispenses pills and diagnoses colds for mostly routine maladies, but five years ago, she was a veteran paramedic with the Kansas City Fire Department (KCFD), and she was on duty on August 27th.

I was on the job about six years. We had our own vehicle, me and Mac. All shiny and red. I wanted to be in one since I was a kid. I guess I was a tomboy. I liked action and adventure. I got it.

Our job was to get to the scene, stabilize the patient, and get them ready for transport. Sometimes we would ride along to the ER, but most of the time we would turn over the patient to the ambulance crew. Other times, we worked with fire crews and police.

We responded to everything. Car wrecks, shootings, falls, fires, heart attacks. Everything. You could not believe some of the trouble people can get themselves into. Sometimes Mac and I would get into the truck after a call and just look at each other and say, "What the hell was that?" and start laughing. Horrible stuff. Arms off, legs off, eyes out. Impalements, decapitations. Some were straight-up accidents. Some you are wondering how the guy got this far in life without getting himself offed. I remember one guy who tried to pull a baseball glove out of a woodchipper – man, stay the hell away from woodchippers! You had to laugh or you might cry.

We got jaded. We saw ugly stuff, but we also helped people. That was important to us. We were first responders. People thanked us for our service, like we were soldiers. They would bring little kids up to shake our hands. They bought us coffee. They appreciated us.

And we were good at it. We were proud of the team. We knew how to work under pressure. If we got to you and you had a pulse, damnit, you were getting into the meat wagon alive no matter what. You might buy the farm in the hospital, but when you left us you were going to be breathing if we had anything to do with it.

If we did not have that attitude going into the Attack, I don't know what would have happened.

We were working northwest KC the first morning. Routine day. Sunny, hot. We did some runs. One older lady had to go to the hospital and the family could not move her. Not unusual. A guy broke his femur falling into a ditch jogging. Normal stuff.

It kicked off at 11:00 a.m. Central Time. Our call was to the airport, which is up there in the north. A shooting. We have zero idea what's happening but we hit lights and sirens and we're going up I-29. Then we hear another call. Mass shooting, downtown. Well, we're committed so we keep going and the airport call gets upgraded. Mass casualty, shooting. Two mass shootings?

Then the call goes out. Plane crash. A freaking airliner. And then more shootings. What the hell is happening?

That's how it started and it did not end for 96 hours.

Airport Fire was responding to the plane crash. We saw it there, a mile from the runway, burning like hell because it was full of fuel. Someone shot it with a missile on take-off.

We get to the terminal and push through the people and cars and then through the line of cops – very hyped-up cops – and the whole area inside is full of dead and wounded. The terminal was a bloodbath. The terrorists walked in and started shooting at the people lined up at the ticket counters and security. They kept shooting until they ran out of bullets. Then the airport police gunned them down. It was that moment that I put it together – terrorists. This was all part of a plan. But I had no idea it was happening across the entire country.

I had never seen anything like it. I mean, when you have hundreds of people dead and wounded, where do you start? We began triage. We would look at a patient and evaluate – can he or she live? Headshot? Nope, move on. Gut? Chest? Maybe. And family members are screaming at us to help and their kid has brain matter dripping out of his skull and I have to get to the woman with the arterial bleeding and maybe save her life with a tourniquet. Why her and not my kid? Because your kid is gone, let me do my job.

We were out of QuikClot in about a minute. We enlisted anyone who was unhurt, and a few who were hurt, to put pressure on wounds, to make field expedient tourniquets out of their belts, anything. We are basically trying to stop the bleeding. Just stop the bleeding. That's all. Don't die here. Stay alive until we can put you in the ambulance.

Of course, what ambulances? Every ambulance was out on a call. I grabbed the driver of some Hertz rental shuttle and told him he's an ambulance and we sent him off with two dozen wounded folks and some civilians with some medical experience. There are a half-dozen hospitals in northern Kansas City, some without emergency rooms. Well, they all got patients that day. Of course, the blood banks ran dry and how do you refill them when everyone has a stay-home order? Actually, I thought of the solution. I had dated an Army sergeant from Fort Leavenworth for a while and I knew it was mostly Army schools, so the soldiers were not getting put on the streets. I told the fire chief to go tell their general to line up his troops and stick 'em. He called the general, the general ordered his guys to line up, and they gave blood. I'm pretty proud of that.

The last of the wounded was medevac'd six hours after we got there. There were still active shooters in the city and at least one hostage situation. We drove down, stopping for coffee at a Waffle House. Waffle House refused to close. Just refused. They were feeding the first responders. We got food and coffee and rolled. We treated some patients, including cops, but while it was pretty bad compared to before, it was nothing compared to the terminal.

It was only then that we realized this was happening everywhere as part of a coordinated nationwide terrorist attack. But we did not have time to think about that. We went to the station to re-up medical supplies but most of it was gone. We literally went into a CVS that was somehow open – though I'd have broken down the door – and filled a cart with stuff. We left a written IOU from the KCFD, and they were fine with it. People were really coming together.

We thought it was over. About 24 hours in, Mac and I were talking about how we were supposed to go off-shift at noon when we get this call. Shootings at such and such. I check the map app. It's a neighborhood – regular houses and stuff.

The second day was worse. They went after people in their homes. And they took their time when they could.

We had to sit outside the subdivisions, waiting for them to be cleared. The cops would go in and get in these massive gunbattles and it would take hours. We were supposed to just sit there. Screw that. We went as far as we could inside without getting shot. Remember, these were active crime scenes. The cops would roar in and the terrorists would be hiding and let them pass then hit the firefighters or paramedics, or just start killing regular people again.

The first house we got to was a McMansion. Very nice, well-decorated, and the dad is lying in the hallway shot up. The mom is holding the kids, or her body is. Of their kids, only one has a pulse and his right arm is pretty much missing.

Another time, we walk into a house and the mom is on the carpet screaming, gut shot. We think it's just that, you know, getting shot hurts. But we could see that they sawed her three kids' heads off in front of her, then wounded her so she suffered more. You don't even want to know what they did to dad, but you can find it on the dark web. They filmed and uploaded everything.

There were a lot fewer wounded than we hoped. Every house we hoped there would be someone alive, and often when they were, they were mutilated. We had an old lady with her eyes gouged out – they did a lot of that – just sitting in her TV chair. They left her alive to suffer.

The rapes were terrible. Inhuman. Girls as young as six, torn and bloody. Old women, teens, moms. They would make the men watch if they could. Most of the women they murdered after, but we had to treat some survivors. What do you say to them? And they raped men and boys too.

It never ended. There were always more the next block over. The wait for an ambulance for the wounded was endless. There were not enough for what was happening.

We treated so many gunshot wounds, hundreds of them. People would get shot running, or escape after being wounded. A lot of cops got shot, and a lot died. The cops were incredible. They hunted these bastards down and just took it to them. By then, most had drawn long guns so you had these extended firefights. Mac and I got trapped in a house for an hour, flat on the floor, while a squad of police fought it out with one guy in a house across the street. They shot the guy in the liver, and he was alive. We get called over to treat him.

Mac is like, "I can't, I'll kill him." Mac was a big guy, tough but sensitive too, more than me. I never saw him mad like that before. There were other wounded to treat, so I went over to the terrorist. He was cuffed and it looked like the cops beat the living snot out of him. Oh well.

I'm trying to be professional and I'm trying to stop the bleeding. Liver hits are pretty painful. He should have been screaming in pain, but he's screaming at me. I'm an infidel whore, he's going to kill me, he's going to kill all of us. I don't get it.

One of the cops sees I'm confused and tells me they are on meth. They're drugged up. If he feels it, he doesn't care. I patch him and give him to the cops. I hope his drugs wore off and he suffered for a while before the Army blew his brains out.

Mac and I went on all afternoon and all night as they hunted down the second-day killers. We were on coffee and adrenaline. It was real meatball medicine. Stabilize and evacuate, like a war zone – which is what it was.

We didn't talk. Mac and I just worked. We grew more and more numb. Raped thirteen-year-old girl. Man with his hands chopped off. Woman scalped. Gunshot wound to the back. Raped thirteen-year-old boy.

Triage. Treat. Stabilize. Hand off for evacuation. Go on to the next.

We stayed on the next day, each of us covering the other to let the other have an hour of sleep in the cab of the truck. I woke up Mac after an hour, then I remember shutting the door and going out and then someone pounding on the door. Mac had let me have two hours. That was who he was.

Who he was changed after that. The same with me. We both changed. I think it made me stronger. But I think it broke Mac. He was such a gentle man who maybe felt he could not live in a world like this. One day, a year after, he wrote out a long note with some instructions, unlocked his front door, sat down in the chair where he loved to watch the Chiefs games and dialed 911. He politely told the dispatcher that there was a single-shot gunshot wound, victim deceased, and gave his address. He hung up and shot himself in the head with a hollow point so it would not go through and make a mess someone else had to clean up.

I made sure that Mac's death was recorded as being due to the Attack. His name will go on the Memorial when it gets finished along with all the others.

I guess I count as one of the wounded. I stopped being a paramedic and got qualified as a PA. I did not think I had anything more that I needed to prove as far as being a paramedic. I think I was tested and I passed. This new gig is good – I'm still helping people. But in my trunk, I carry a full trauma bag just in case it happens again.

19.

Bucks County, Pennsylvania

Thomas "Tommy" Ferguson sometimes does his own commercials for his air conditioning company on Chris Stigall's morning radio show as "The HVAC King of Philly." He still lives in a large house in the Crowne Pointe Estates subdivision, a gated community where most folks grew up with money and commute into the city to law firms or finance companies.

Tommy does not have a college degree – he says he has "a masters in freon." But he built his company from the ground up, employing nearly 500 people.

I started my own company because I wanted to hunt deer. Deer hunting is a religion in Pennsylvania – a lot of schools out in the country just make opening day a holiday because none of the kids are showing up anyway. That was me. I grew up near Chambersburg, which got burned down twice by the Confederates in the Civil War. And I lived to hunt deer.

I was not going to college, no way, and the military was out because I am half-deaf in my left ear, so after high school I got taken on at a heating, ventilation and air conditioning company and started learning the trade. The great thing about HVAC is everyone needs air. Good times, bad times, people need to be warm and they need to breathe. I got pretty good at it too, including the people part. If you're nice to folks, it's easier for everyone. It got so people would call in and ask for me by name, which I think rubbed my boss the wrong way.

I would do whatever needed to be done. That was just the way I was raised. Late-night calls, holidays, you name it. Tommy was there with his toolbox. But the one little thing I wanted, the one tiny favor I asked, was to let me have opening day off. Let me get my buck, and then I'm good to go. I don't think it was much to ask, and for a few years my boss always made sure I was covered for opening day.

I guess he thought I was getting too big for my britches or whatever, but one year I casually mentioned where I'm going to go hunting on opening day and he tells me no, I'm working and that's that. I thought he misunderstood, but he didn't. I was working, or I was finding another job.

Look, I'm a nice guy but if you push me there's going to be a problem. I quit right then, but I didn't go get another job even though everyone in town wanted to hire me. I started up my own company because I was never going to ask anyone for a day off again.

Gail was not happy, especially with a kid on the way, but I got a truck and put out a shingle and pretty soon I had more work than I could do. I hired on more guys and some gals, and we kept growing. I never missed opening day.

Billy and Wendy come along and our little house was, well, little, so we decide to move into this new subdivision, Crowne Pointe Estates. It's a gated community, so none of the crime from the city is going to come out here. It's pretty and safe. Nice houses, well-kept lawns. But some of the neighbors were a bit, well, snobby. I did not have a degree. I did not drive a BMW. I parked a work truck in my driveway and I know people talked.

Everyone was polite to our faces, but my real friends were my hunting buddies back home. No one else hunted in Crowne Pointe Estates. When I went to a Fourth of July picnic or a Christmas party, I would start talking about deer hunting and I might as well have been speaking Swahili. Of course, they lined up when I had extra venison – I always made sure that someone ate what I shot.

The day of the Attack, the first day, was like any other. It was sunny, and being August it was all AC calls. I was at the office doing paperwork – I sometimes took a service call myself just to keep in the game, but not that day. Just before noon, Brenda – my secretary since we started – comes in with a cheesesteak sandwich. That and my Pepsi were lunch. I remember looking at the calendar and thinking, "Just two months" – deer season is in late November to early December.

Sometime after noon I'm finishing up my lunch and I hear a bunch of sirens and think there must be a helluva fire. Brenda comes in a couple minutes later. I see she's upset. She tells me to come out to look at the TV in the waiting area.

Well, you remember that day. All these attacks, hundreds, all at once, all over the country. And there's stuff in Philly too – the sirens I heard were those bastards hitting a junior high down the road, though I didn't know that until later. If I had, I'd have gotten the Smith & Wesson 686 .357 revolver out of my desk and gone over there.

Brenda and I both get on the phone and start calling our people, telling them to cancel their calls and go home. I was worried one of them might stumble into a gunfight. We closed up and I drove home with my magnum on my lap. Grady was the gate guard, and he looked scared as he let me in. When I got to the house, I called every one of my people to make sure they got home okay, and thank the Lord, all of them did.

Gail had gotten the kids home from school – apparently parents mobbed the place picking up their little ones the second it became known that the terrorists were attacking schools. I didn't understand it – hurting kids? Hurting innocent people was crossing a line.

Just in case, I got out some guns. The kids were too young for much above a .22, but I got one of the Remington 870s out and loaded it with alternate slugs and double-aught for Gail. One of our first dates was hunting, so she knew how to use it.

My gun took some thinking. I loved my bolt-action hunting rifles, but if something bad happened here in Crowne Pointe Estates – and I did not really think it would – I needed something with a higher rate of fire. I settled on a .308 SOCOM 16, basically a shorter, improved semiauto M14. I had an optic on it, but it was hard to miss even with iron sights. You basically had to try not to hit your target.

I put the weapons aside – the kids grew up around guns so they knew not to mess with them – and, like the rest of the country, we watched the tube. Gail was crying. I had to make the kids go upstairs because they were getting scared and asking if the terrorists would be coming for them too.

The next morning, it looked like it was pretty much over, except for some hostage situations. We never thought it might not even be half-done. The Army was called out and, of course, the company was closed. Everyone was staying home from work and school – I not sure if the stay-at-home order was on yet. I remember the Vice President coming on to speak to the country and wondering what the hell she was talking about.

"That woman is dumb even for a politician," Gail said.

Gail was in the kitchen at noon making us peanut butter and jelly sandwiches. That was the kids' favorite and they were still pretty upset.

I heard the shots coming from the front of the subdivision. A lot of shots, fast – automatic. I was never in the Army, but I watch YouTube gun videos. That was a machine gun. I looked at the TV – nothing about new attacks. Of course, they all started at twelve Eastern and it was noon on the dot.

In a way, attacking a place like Crowne Point Estates was…I don't want to say "smart," but it made sense if you are a terrorist. The Estates was off on its own, far from where the police would be expecting attacks. It would be packed with regular families, about 2000 people who probably did not have a lot of experience fighting or with guns. There was a wall running all around the subdivision, and it had one entrance and exit that was easy to block off to trap the victims. They did that. They killed Grady and they used their cars to block the gates shut.

It was like a private hunting preserve, and we were the deer.

I handed Gail the shotgun and told her to get in the cellar with the kids and Bess, our old beagle. There was a cellar door in the backyard that they could use to escape if the terrorists came and burned down the house – I remembered the terrorists did that in Israel. They set the houses on fire to make the people come out of their shelters, and then they killed them. I told her if anyone came in who was not me, unload that scattergun into his belly.

She did not ask me where I was going to be. She knew what I had to do. At the time, I did not know there were twenty terrorists.

I took up a bandolier of 20-round magazines loaded with Winchester Deer Season XP 150 grain Extreme Point .308 rounds. These were designed to hit hard and expand to take down the biggest bucks. I figured they would work just as good on a jihadi if it came to that.

There was a lot of shooting and screaming from all around the subdivision. Apparently, some of them drove to the back of the subdivision and started there. People were running and screaming and I saw smoke coming from houses. I went to the sound of the nearest gunfire.

It was a massacre. Dead people everywhere, some I knew, some I didn't. Old people, kids, moms. Dogs too. I tried not to think about it. I still try not to.

I just knew I had to try to stop it, though the odds were way against me. I was determined to do what I could no matter what. I was going to do what I did best.

Deer hunting takes patience. You don't chase deer down. You wait for them to come to you. You take careful aim. You are stealthy and quiet. I had never been in a shootout, but I never once considered being Rambo. I would stalk them.

I was hunting terrorists, and there was no bag limit.

I knew they would be coming down Ben Franklin Lane – all the streets were named after the Founders, and they stayed named after the Founders even after some silly lady tried to get the HOA to change them because they "celebrated racist cis holders of enslaved persons." I found a good position behind a porch with good sight lines down the street and set up.

They walked down the street without a care in the world, out in the open, taking their time. They were in black shirts with vests on and wearing green headbands around their heads. They carried their guns casually – I know they were Kalashnikovs, those Russian guns you always see on the news – and would shoot into houses or at people in the yards, or at dogs. They always shot the dogs.

I heard later they did that on purpose because they knew how we feel about our pets. I knew how it all made me feel.

I waited for this group of four to come along into the open, and I took aim at the one in back. It took me a minute to decide where to aim. You try to hit a buck in the heart, right behind the front leg, halfway down. It makes it quick for the animal, and you don't have to chase it through the woods until it drops of blood loss.

But people? I never shot a person before, of course. I did not really know exactly where to aim. They had those vests and maybe Kevlar chest plates. I was not sure if that would stop my .308 round, but it might. I could go for headshots, but that was much harder than center mass. I decided to go high on the chest and hope for the best.

I took aim through my optic. The guy was young and smiling – really smiling, like this was the greatest day of his life. But it was the worst. I exhaled and squeezed. The SOCOM 16 was loud and deep, deeper than the AK sound. The round hit him and took him off his feet, and when he went down he stayed down.

The other three froze – this did not compute. They also did not realize that their tail man was down – which is why I started with the guy at the rear.

The SOCOM is a semiauto, so it fires once per pull of the trigger. I drew a bead on the new tail man, carefully, not rushing. In shooting, fast is slow and slow is fast.

He was looking around and I squeezed. Boom. That round hit him in the face, and true to the ads, it penetrated and expanded. Seeing his head kind of disappear might have made me think twice earlier that morning, but not after what I saw. When I shoot deer, I respect them. That's why I ensure somebody eats the meat. It's respect. But these bastards? No way.

The others finally reacted and scattered for cover. You know, things change when someone is shooting at you. A big buck with a big rack is the king of the forest, but you start sending lead in his direction and he's got to react to you. Same with these guys. It was all fun and games when it was women and kids and collies, but now someone was shooting back and it was a whole different thing. I distracted them from killing folks because now they had to react to me.

And did they react. They must have both blown off a mag at me, but I was gone. I had another advantage. I knew the ground. They did not. I knew where the good spots were, where there were fences, and what was on the other side. This was my territory.

I stalked through the neighborhood for what seemed like hours, taking a shot when I could, then fading away as they tried to find me. I came across a lot of scared people and tried to direct them to where I knew the bastards were not at. I came across a lot of dead ones too, and worse than dead. I went into an open door looking to get up on the second floor to get a shot out of the back bedroom window and I saw a family there, all dead. They tied up the parents, slaughtered the kids in front of them, raped the wife, killed the husband last. They broadcast it – it's on the internet somewhere, which ought to be illegal.

I saw a lot of things like that. I was going to do what I could to stop it until they stopped me, which I figured was only a matter of time.

After all, I was only one guy, at least at first. Then, running past a swimming pool with a boy floating in it, I came across a guy in his sixties with an AR-15 and a real determined look. I knew him because he drove a Mercedes with a Purple Heart license plate whose holder said, "ARMY DESERT STORM VET." We didn't even discuss it – we just started to work together, hunting the bastards.

He was my security while I was the sniper. I kept shooting high center mass, and they kept dropping. We had some close calls. I took a shot from a kitchen window – the family was dead on the floor – when two of the terrorists came in the front door. My vet buddy shot them both, though his 5.56mm rounds did not kill one of them instantly. The headshot as the bastard lay twitching sure did.

The cops never showed up while the terrorists were alive. In their defense, they were being pulled every which way and were targeted themselves. The National Guard guys did show up. We acted as guides as this whole unit of infantry cleared Crowne Pointe Estates house by house. They actually took two prisoners alive, and they had to hustle them away before the civilians lynched them.

I had called Gail a couple times on her cell phone and, at one point, she and the kids had heard some of them upstairs, but the terrorists left and they were all right. My house was in the last section that the soldiers cleared, and when we got there I went first into the backyard, and there was this terrorist lying on the grass with a hole in his belly you could put your fist through. As the soldiers had swept that way, he tried to get down through the outside doors into the basement and had shot down inside when he heard something. He missed. Gail did not.

We were lucky. They killed or hurt hundreds of people in Crowne Pointe Estates; my vet buddy's wife got shot in the calf but recovered. They are good friends now. The only problem with the vet is that he doesn't like deer hunting – he says he's spent enough time in the woods with a gun. But he's not shy about sharing my venison. After all, I make sure someone eats what I hunt. Well, most of the time.

20.

Portland, Oregon

Sheena is not her real name. She has not yet availed herself of the booming tattoo removal industry, and the designs on her neck and face are still visible against her pale skin. So are the holes where she used to have studs piercing her lips, nose, and cheek. Her parole conditions require her to "maintain a normal appearance" and also prevent her from identifying as any gender but the one she was born into.

Sheena has a degree from Evergreen State in Decolonial Studies. That, and her presence on the Radical Persons Registry, have ensured that the job she has is about the only one available to her. She brings two mugs, with almond cream and yucca essence sweetener, from behind the counter of the Solid Grounds coffee house and sits by the window. Many of the buildings outside have been repaired, but the funkiness of the neighborhood is gone along with many of its most radical inhabitants. In fact, it was that drastic change in the neighborhood that convinced her parole officer to let her return here after her release from the federal prison camp.

Though she is not using her real name, she is reticent when she speaks, understanding that she could be prosecuted again if she admits to something that she was not already convicted of by the military commission. The statute of limitations on some *crimes is more than five years, and there is no statute of limitations for murder.*

I was an odd kid in high school, not a lot of friends, uncomfortable with myself. I was never going to be a cheerleader. I never saw a normal life as a possibility even if my parents did. So, Evergreen was transformative. And I was vulnerable. Looking back, it is like I was a different person. The choices I made were mine and I am responsible for them, but I was misled by people who pretended to care for me and I listened to them instead of the people who actually did.

I was in college during the George Floyd direct actions. Evergreen is a radical place, and when I got there I learned that pretty much everything I grew up thinking I knew was a lie. My family was part of the system, a willing part. We went to church, they had good jobs. We had a nice house. But it was all built on a lie. Literally. Our house was not our house. It was built on land literally stolen from the Muckleshoot, Snoqualmie, and Stillaguamish peoples. We were colonists, settlers, oppressors.

I learned about my privilege, how my projection as cis made me literally complicit in the genocide of trans and gender nonconforming beings. I felt the anger erupt in me, and it combined with the trauma I experienced from being unvalidated.

All that is what I really thought. These were not ideas that I adopted by choice. They were the only ideas we were allowed to have on campus, and they were everywhere there. It was not like I picked them. They took hold. After I left college, I never talked to my parents again.

I did not need my old family. I had a new family of beautiful, passionate people who rejected their assumed place in the patriarchy and in the system that literally murdered us. Some people called it "Antifa," though we never did except to annoy the fascists. We had smaller organizations that came together and faded away, then came back. People's Action Collective, Spartacist League, Indigenous Underground – one day we were part of one, the next day another. It was not one thing, but many things that made one thing. I found a home in that world with people who appreciated me for how I existed, not someone else's vision of my own being.

I stopped attending classes, though I was later given my degree. My real school was the streets. It was clear that direct action on behalf of the environment, oppressed peoples, and against capitalism was the way. I was in the street actions at the Portland federal courthouse. I destroyed construction equipment that was to be used to scar the land and take down trees in California. I went to Atlanta to fight against Cop City. I fought in the streets, and I found that hurting people made me feel good.

Our purpose was to dismantle the machinery of oppression. No to prisons. No to cops. But more and more I saw that the injustice done indigenous peoples through the paradigm of settler culture demanded a real response and not half-measures. Decolonialization was not just a slogan. It was action, and actions have consequences. Actions sometimes require blood. Some people refused to see that. But I saw clearly what was required. Fascists only understand force. And you have no right to question the response of the oppressed to their oppressors.

Don't you see that in our minds there was no other way? They were murdering the Earth. They were murdering people of color. They were enjoying the fruits of their land thefts while consigning indigenous folx to misery and death. What alternative did we have other than violence? We did not see one.

When the Palestinian people struck back on October 7th, we knew such joy. The Zionists and their lackies lied about it, of course. We were told they invented atrocities to turn the people against the struggle, and to make legitimate acts of armed struggle into crimes. Violence is the cry of the oppressed, and the Palestinian people lived under occupation in an open-air prison as the Israelis murdered their children.

The war crimes of the Zionist entity united us in ways we had not seen since the George Floyd rebellion. We took to the streets and confronted the Zionists and tore down their lying posters. Their claims that we were anti-Semitic might have worked in the past, but we rejected them now. We told ourselves that Palestine would be cleansed of settlers, from the river to the sea.

We told ourselves that this was not genocide. They could leave. Those that did not had chosen their fate. You could not blame the Palestinian people for armed struggle against settlers. No settler is ever a civilian. They are legitimate targets.

Even as we celebrated the attack, we also denied it, claiming the Jews – we were supposed to say the Zionists, but we would often say "the Jews" and laugh because that is what we meant – lied when they said the freedom fighters attacked children and women. We said it was propaganda to cover the real genocide, that of the people of Gaza.

We grew louder and more forceful, waiting for the pushback. We were not crazy. We did not want to be arrested or hurt. We would have found something else if there had been consequences, but like in the Floyd riots, there were no consequences. And this time, even more national leaders outright supported us. We tested the limits by shoving, then by punching, then with bats, then with firebombs and so on – and there were no limits. So we kept pushing.

The struggle did not fade this time. It grew. Our actions grew bolder as the Israelis' war continued. More and more Democrat politicians stood with us, and the FBI never bothered us. We understood that we had the tacit approval of some in power to continue, so we did.

This struggle was different. The tension with the Jews caused some members to leave us. We called them traitors, and the ones who remained had to denounce other Jews all the harder to allay our suspicions.

Our movement grew more organized and better funded. We had always had the money to do what we needed to do. Not to live, mind you. We slept in flop houses, wore dirty clothes, ate bad food. Our only luxuries were drugs, and those were less luxuries than necessities.

But when we had needed money to go somewhere or organize an action, it appeared. I am not sure where it came from. I was not a leader. We really were not supposed to have leaders, but we did. How they got enough money for a bus to cross the country or for the equipment we used during demonstrations, I don't know. Word was it was rich donors subsidizing the revolution. Of course, we laughed about that. They would be first against the wall when the revolution came.

After October 7th, there was even more money, and more...I guess the word is "organization." The structure of our groups became more rigid. It was more disciplined, and some people chafed at that. They were expelled or sometimes beaten up as an example to the rest.

Most of us went along with it because the feeling was that the revolution really was coming. We became more and more violent with no real pushback. Our enemies were weak and vulnerable, while we were aggressive and sure of our ideology. The settler dynamic became the central theme, even taking precedence over the trans focus we used to have. And we came to identify more and more with Hamas.

We saw some people who were not radicals working with our leaders. No one was really sure who they were. They were professionals. These were not street fighters. We never talked to them directly. They worked through our leaders – I think they helped select them. They pushed the most ruthless and the most charismatic into leader roles.

As we entered the summer, we were told that the time would soon come to take action, and that we needed to look inside ourselves and see who was truly down with the decolonialization agenda. Of course we all said we were. There was a cult-like feeling inside the groups that made up what you would call "Antifa." You were manipulated into thinking there is no possibility to be other than what the collective demanded. And it is hard to explain, but that made us feel good. We were doing something beyond ourselves.

I remember they got hold of an hour of the October 7th footage taken by Hamas fighters. We watched it together, with plenty of drugs, including the blowtorch and infant video footage. And we accepted it as necessary. We talked about how decolonialization was not a theory but a reality. The murder and rape and torture we saw was a necessary part of it. Hamas showed commitment. Would we be as truly committed when the time came?

Of course we would. It was exciting because we were beyond bourgeois morality.

On August 27th, the Attack began in Portland at 9:00 a.m. Of course, none of us were awake. We were strewn all over some squat house that the cops refused to evict us from for fear of our retaliation. We heard the boom of the bomb that hit the police station and the shooting of the terrorist teams. When someone finally found out by looking on his iPhone that they had essentially neutralized the police force, we cheered.

What I did not think about until later was how ready our leaders were for this. They did not seem surprised. Rather, they told us that now was the time for action. The revolution was here.

That afternoon the call went out. So did the weapons. Knives and guns. We did not ask where they came from. The guns were not the machine guns imported by the terrorists. These were American guns obtained and cached for just this occasion over a long period. We gathered *en masse* in the center of town and declared it a liberated zone. There were still killing teams loose, and what cops were left were fighting them. We had no opposition.

There were several thousand of us. We owned Portland. We burned what was left of the police station, and the courts. We freed the prisoners. That was the first night. There was no pushback. We heard the Oregon National Guard was called, but we did not see them then.

Regular people from the neighborhoods joined us in looting. There was so much beer! Most of us were drunk or high or both. And there was no authority, none.

The next morning, we were told that only the most dedicated of us should gather off to the side. We all wanted to be that, but we were not all allowed. The craziest and most violent were selected and they went away with the leaders. These are the ones who joined the attacks on the people in their homes in the suburbs.

I was selected to make calls. We would call the 911 lines in the suburbs and send the police running all over. Of course, while they were doing that, terrorists and their Antifa allies would be entering homes and killing people, then broadcasting it online – just like Hamas had done.

We were giddy with excitement. To us, it was fun. We totally alienated ourselves from the reality. I mean, most of us were distant from the second day's killings, but we knew it was happening. We were so deep inside that none of us left.

The third day we had new instructions – it was only in retrospect that I realized our actions were coordinated with the terrorists' plan. We were sent to destroy things not just in Portland but all over, using cars confiscated from people in the areas we liberated. Some of us started fires, others attacked the power transformers near the dams on the Columbia River. I helped burn down some supermarkets, not thinking about how the people we were supposedly liberating were supposed to eat.

We had ignored the stay-home order, so we laughed off the martial law order. Portland was our town. The homeless and the criminals were free to do as they pleased. They looted and stole and so did we. People who objected got hurt. When the power went out, we laughed that off too.

Later on the third day, the military showed up on the edge of town, and we scoffed. We knew how to handle riot cops, and now we had some guns too. Let them come, we told ourselves.

They did come. There was no hesitation, no negotiations. There was a mass of us and a line of them in vehicles with weapons. They told us, through a bullhorn, "Drop your weapons and raise your hands now."

I felt sick to my stomach. This was not normal. But my comrades were certain it was all another bluff. After all, the authorities always backed down. Our riots ended when *we* chose to go home. If you got arrested, they printed you, took a photo and let you go, and you ignored your court date and the charges got dismissed.

I looked at the soldiers that day and they looked like us. Angry and ready to fight. Other comrades pushed past me. Some had firebombs. Some had weapons. I was now to the rear of the mob, and I am grateful for that.

In our excitement of the last three days of our revolution, we had not internalized just what had happened. We felt joy and freedom in the chaos, and the pain of the people we called "the settlers" was not merely abstract but unworthy of consideration. We never considered it.

But those soldiers lived it. They had seen the uploaded videos not just of terrorists torturing and murdering citizens but of college students and Antifa participating in it – eagerly. Who knows how many had had friends or family maimed or raped or killed?

And yet our group still believed this was just a regular action, perhaps one where we had gone farther than ever before, but one where the regular rules still applied. We would be indulged, treated gently, patted on the head and allowed to go free only to repeat our actions again and again. It never occurred to us that the people we called "fascists" and "oppressors" might not treat us with kid gloves. Of course, most of us had grown up never being told "No."

I do not know who shot first. My comrades, stunned and terrified and on the run, insisted it was the Army. So what? Was there some cosmic referee who was going to come and make it right? For all their hatred of the system, I found it amusing how they still believed that they were owed, and how they expected to receive, fairness.

The roar of the gunfire was like nothing I had ever heard. It was a wall of noise that almost physically pushed us back. The first ranks of the mob just fell, shot to pieces. A girl next to me who had brought a finger back from her murder expedition to the suburbs, took a bullet in the stomach and sat down on the street Indian style – we were not supposed to call it that – and cried. She could not believe that she had been shot by the government.

A few of the mob tried to fire back. They died. Those without the flight instinct froze and they died too.

I chose flight. I ran, dropping the bat I had carried, and I did not stop for a dozen blocks. The shooting went on and on. I did not see, but I heard, that the soldiers killed the wounded. We would have in their position.

Our organization disintegrated in that first round of shots. There was no group left – it was every one of us on our own. We, of course, had no plan for where to go if the action went wrong. I went back to the flophouse, looking for our leaders and some guidance on what to do next. But our leaders were gone.

Where was I going to go?

I looked at my phone and the internet was wonky. Then I saw a pay phone. I had coins that I had stolen and made a call to my home. No answer. I later, from prison, reached my sister, who told me my parents had nothing to say to me and not to call again.

The Army swept through the streets. I saw them shoot people. I hid. When the police came, I ran to them to give up. They beat the hell out of me and took me to a military police prison camp.

The camp was cold and terrifying. The guards had no pity. The system had no pity. It was the system that we had claimed the judicial system from before was. They were using facial recognition from uploaded videos to catch the ones doing the killing. The accused would get hauled out and come back in an hour, sentenced to be shot. And then the next day, when their appeals were denied, they would be. We heard them, one shot, to the back of the head.

I realized I did not want to die.

My lawyer had dozens of cases. He told me my only hope was a confession and full debrief. I nodded. Yes. Anything they wanted.

I got four years. I told them everything. I named our leaders, all of whom were later caught and shot. I was not the only one, though. Lots of people informed on them.

Prison was hard. There were no excuses, no tolerance. My piercings were pulled. If you used some gender pronoun but the one you assigned at birth, you got beat. They reeducated us, and I resisted. But one day, during footage of a family like mine being tortured by laughing radicals, I started crying. That was when I began to heal.

But I don't know if I will ever fully heal. I am just lucky to be alive.

21.

Houston, Texas

Jace Gillette and Clement Willis seem a superficially unlikely pair. Jace is dressed with edgy flair, with a light blue blazer and expensive sneakers befitting his position as an art gallery manager. Clem, with a shaggy red beard, wears a gray work shirt bearing the logo of the tire store he owns. While Jace drives a Tesla, Clem has a Ford F-150 with a Texas flag sticker on the tailgate, along with one that reads, "Faith, Family, Flag and Fishin'."

Jace: Face it. We're a couple of stereotypes come to life! And I'm comfortable with that.

Clem: The only good thing about all this was us meeting Jace and his friends and he and them meeting the congregation and finding out that, you know, we're pretty different but we got a lot in common even if we don't agree on everything.

Jace: How did this all happen? Well, the thing about Houston is that there's no zoning. You can have an Arby's, a mattress store, and a strip club on the same block.

Clem: We all live in a small neighborhood southwest of downtown. Rosewood Avenue is the main way to enter the neighborhood. The Rosewood Avenue Church of Christ is right there on the edge of the quiet, more family-oriented part, and across the way it's a little funkier. Lots of people who are not so traditional live there.

Jace: He means gay! Anyway, the Cellar is a club just across the street from the Church, and as you might expect there was some tension. I'm not pointing fingers about who started it.

Clem: We could have been nicer, more Christian and neighborly.

Jace: And some of us went out of our way to get a rise out of the church people. We did not have to moon them.

Clem: We mostly ignored each other. We thought they were sinners and they thought we were a bunch of hicks, and I kind of am. Proud of it too. No one was throwing fists, but we didn't like each other.

Jace: I was at the gallery in Montrose when the Attack started on the 27th. We are on Central Time here in Texas, so it was about eleven. I was already thinking about this new Bangladeshi place I was going for lunch.

Clem: Bangladeshi? What do they eat?

Jace: I tried it later, and frankly, gimme a Whataburger. Anyway, I start hearing shooting outside. Now, I am from Texas, so I know the difference between a backfire, a firecracker, and a gunshot. This was gunshots, and lots of them. I thought it was some kook on a shooting spree, but it just went on and on. Now, I was the president of Gays With Guns because I was never going to be a victim. I had my CZ75 pistol and you know I had it out.

Clem: The attacks started kind of far from my shop, but we saw it reported because we have Fox on in the waiting area. My front desk guys yells, "Clem, there's some kind of terrorist thing going on." We all go in to watch and it's happening everywhere. Houston too. We actually saw a car full of terrorists roar by doing at least sixty, shooting and everything, with a whole pack of squad cars following. A round cracked my front window. I told everyone to go home. I got in my truck, put my Smith & Wesson Model 29 .44 Magnum on my passenger seat, and drove home.

Jace: I got to my house and just sat and watched cable news until midnight. I could not believe what was happening.

Clem: It was bad, like 9/11 but way worse. I went into the Marines after 9/11, ended up in Iraq. When they started talking about tens of thousands of dead, I thought I might get called back.

Jace: That first day, by the end of the day, we thought it was over. But it wasn't. I got up the next morning, but of course the stay-home order was in effect. No citizens on the streets without an emergency. So I started watching CNN on the big screen again. The Vice President came on. Now, I voted for her, but I was listening to her speech and I was thinking, "Oh, we are so...."

Well, for Clem's benefit, I won't use the language I used to myself that morning, but I was more worried *after* she talked than before.

Clem: Me and the family just sat at home, watching the coverage, praying for the victims, our first responders, our leaders, and especially our troops, because we figured they'd be going in somewhere soon to get some payback. I had three kids, all little then, and they were asking me if the terrorists were going to come to our neighborhood.

I told them that no, everything was fine now. Remember that at that time, we thought it really was all over. One and done. But then eleven o'clock came around and pretty soon Fox is reporting attacks on regular people in their homes all over the country. See, the first day they attacked out in public knowing from COVID that the government would lock us down in an emergency. That way, regular people were sitting ducks alone in their houses. I don't think they counted on the Second Amendment, though.

Jace: I saw what was happening and I was never under any illusion about this jihad crap. When it comes to intersectionality, the guy in the intersection gets run over. First the Jews, then us. I know what they did to gays in Iran and Gaza before Israel cleared it out. I figured that we in our neighborhood were a target they could not resist. Of course, I was right.

Clem: We were both right. I figured that we had a nice Christian community and these guys would love to come and cut some Christian throats. Like I said, I was in Iraq and I knew what these guys did given the chance. Plus, there were reports that there were attacks going on in Houston right then. The police chief came on TV and told citizens to arm themselves.

Jace: I was ahead of him. I figured that we definitely needed to protect ourselves, but the cops were stretched thin and the military was just coming out – this was still a day before martial law was declared. So I called around to my gun group and told them to meet up at The Cellar because it was right where Rosewood entered the neighborhood.

Clem: I was thinking the same thing – seal off our neighborhood. I activated the parish phone tree and told our guys to rally up at the Church. I gave my wife the Remington 870 and my Beretta and left. She's a better shot than me. And then I drove to the Church, ready to tell any cop who asked that hell yeah, it was an emergency.

Jace: We had about ten of us at The Cellar, all armed. AR-15s mostly. You need to understand. We are Texans, and we are not going to be victims. Then I look across the way and see Clem and about a dozen of his congregation there with all sorts of long guns.

Clem: I knew that more folks were coming, but right then we did not have enough parishioners to do the job. I was listening to the police scanner app on my iPhone and there were a bunch of calls. Some were fake – damn college brats trying to confuse the cops. But some were real. The terrorists were hitting neighborhoods like ours. We already saw some of the footage they uploaded from the first day from what they did at schools or malls – horrible stuff. Now they were doing it again, but this time to people trapped in their homes.

Jace: I thought that we had to work together, and Clem must have thought the same thing. We met in the middle of Rosewood Avenue – of course the streets were pretty much empty – and kind of looked at each other for a moment, suspicious.

Clem: I told Jace that we should work together and he asked me if we had a plan. I told him I used to be a Marine, and he said a few of his guys were Marines too. I kind of took charge since I was oldest, and we set up an L-shaped ambush on Rosewood. We blocked the street with cars, but set shooters on the north side with sectors of fire across the road.

Jace: We got some Motorola walkie-talkies and used them for communications. Then we had the guys not in the ambush doing a roving patrol through the neighborhood in trucks. We needed something to ID them as friendly, so they flew big American and

Texas flags. People were coming out of their houses, waving, thanking us, wanting to join up.

Clem: We just all worked together, and we kind of forgot our differences. Everyone was just a Texan and an American that day.

Jace: It was this whole cross-section of the community. I mean, everybody from the Church kind of looked the same, but we had every part of our community there. Twinks, otters, daddies, bears, borgnines...

Clem: I don't know what those are.

Jace: I think that on the spectrum, you're in between a daddy and a bear.

Clem: Okay. Is that good?

Jace: To each his own. Anyway, what were the chances the terrorists would come to our neighborhood?

Clem: We see this black Toyota Tundra barreling down Rosewood, and there are guys in the back and they start shooting at the roadblock with their AKs as they come. And I'm ducking down next to Jace behind a Mustang that is getting shot to ribbons, and talking into the Motorola saying, "Wait, wait."
The bad guys were totally focused on us at the roadblock and they were not paying any attention to their flank.

Jace: L-shaped ambush.

Clem: I gave the go for the guys on the flank to initiate and it was on. ARs, deer rifles, shotguns.

Jace: And then we popped up from behind the roadblock and joined in.

Clem: I almost felt bad for them.

Jace: Almost, but not quite. Not long after, a patrol of cops and soldiers comes by and looks at this shot-up Suburban and the five dead terrorists we laid out in the street and asks us what the hell happened.

Clem: I just said, "They messed with Texas."

Jace: The cops thought that was funny. So did I. Clem is a funny guy once you get to know him. But it was all true. We weren't anything but Texans and Americans that day, and these bastards fooled around and found out. See Clem, kept the language G-rated for you.

Clem: Appreciate it. You know, the cops didn't even investigate. They just called a meat wagon.

Jace: We kept up security for another week, until we were sure it was over. Even now, we have a community patrol that everybody in the community helps out with.

Clem: When it got real, we put aside our differences. We don't agree on everything, of course. I'm still trying to get Jace into a pew.

Jace: And I'm still trying to get Clem in The Cellar to dance.

Clem: I do like Jason Aldean. You saw what happened when they tried it in our small town.

Jace: Maybe we can compromise. Shania Twain?

Clem: She's a talented lady.

Jace: I'll tell you one thing. I know who my friends are. Once it was over, I tore that COEXIST bumper sticker off my Tesla and I put on one with a Texas flag.

22.

Trenton, New Jersey

The Kettner Home for Children of the Attack has 39 patients, children whose need for treatment and care is so great they cannot be adopted out. Some have been returned after initial attempts at adoption failed. Fifteen-year-old Millie was originally adopted by her uncle's family, but the house was near a road and the sound of passing cars would sometimes send her into a violent panic. After one outburst ended with her injuring one of her cousins, she came here. She will remain here, receiving treatment, until she is eighteen.

Her counselor sits with her as she talks, holding her hand. Within certain limits, the therapy calls for the children to discuss the events that brought them there. There is a scar on the girl's face from her forehead down to her cheek.

I was ten a few days before and we had a party a few days before it happened. I was in fifth grade at Seaton Elementary. Ms. Whirly was my teacher and she was nice. Mom would drop me off out front every morning and pick me up. I liked school.

We were in the classroom doing math problems. It was going to be lunch soon and I wanted to go outside because it was so nice. The principal came to the door and everyone was saying, "Uh oh, someone is in trouble!" But the principal looked scared, not angry. She took Ms. Whirly outside and they talked. Then Ms.

Whirly came back in and told us we were going home. We were happy to be getting out of school but I thought something had to be wrong.

Out front, all these cars were there with moms and dads. It was like it was pick-up time but it was not even lunch yet. All the parents were scared too. There was a police car with two policemen outside and they had guns.

The teachers made us wait by the buildings until our parents came, even the kids who could walk home. I asked Ms. Whirly what was happening and she said, "Something bad." Then I saw mom's car and Ms. Whirly said to go get in her car, to run. I said I would see her tomorrow and she said, "Oh honey, there's not going to be school for a while."

Mom was upset. I think she had been crying. She was listening to the radio where they had news instead of music like she usually did. The radio was talking about how there were people shooting people, including in some schools. Mom told me we would go home and that dad would come home from work soon. He was in New York.

She would not let me watch TV with her downstairs, but I saw some of it. There were reporters talking about people being shot and hostages and airplanes crashing. It was scary and I went upstairs and played video games on my iPad.

Dad came home and he and mom talked. He was very upset and he was talking to mom quietly and she was upset. I came down and saw he had blood on his shirt, but he told me it was not his. I started crying and he told me it would be all right but that was not true. He could not have known that.

I asked if I could take our poodle Doodle out for a walk but mom said I had to stay inside.

When I came downstairs for dinner, the TV was off and mom made us chicken. They did not talk about the terrorist thing that was going on. They tried to talk about other things, I think so I would not get upset. But I was already upset, since I knew they were. Mom told me there would be no school for the rest of the week and I should have been happy but I wasn't because I knew things had to be bad if there was no school.

I went to bed and dad came in to tuck me in and he told me everything was going to be fine and that I was safe here. Why would he say that if it wasn't true?

We got up in the morning early and I went downstairs to get some cereal and mom and dad were watching the second president – the Vice President – on the TV. I did not understand what she was saying and dad called her an "Idiot" and that scared me because it was a word we were not supposed to say because it was mean.

I had Lucky Charms and I gave Doodles some toast. Then I heard some cars. The cars were loud. I heard the cars out front. I did not know what it was. There were bangs, a lot of them, like guns. I heard people yelling.

Dad rushed to the window and looked out at the streets, then he came running back yelling, "You've got to hide!" to me and mom.

Now he was scared and that scared me and I cried and asked why and mom grabbed me and took me upstairs. She was crying, and looking around for a place to hide. There was her closet, She pushed me inside then came in and closed the doors.

There was shooting and screaming from outdoors. My neighbors were the McKenzies and I heard Mrs. McKenzie yelling, "No no no no," and then more guns shooting.

Downstairs someone started pounding on the front door and Doodles was barking and there was kicking and the door got kicked open and I heard Doodles bark and then someone yelled in a language I did not understand and there was shooting and I heard Doodles cry and then more shooting.

I heard fighting downstairs, and a gunshot and dad yelled out like he was hurt. Mom was crying and telling me I had to be quiet, I had to be quiet, and I tried not to cry but I could not help it.

They came up the stairs and I was crying and they heard me even though mom put her hands on my mouth and they opened the door. It was two men with black shirts and they had green headbands on their heads and big guns and they were yelling at us in a language I didn't know.

They had cameras on their belts, like the GoPros some kids use while riding bikes.

Mom was crying and asking them to let us go and not to hurt us and they grabbed her by the hair and punched her face and she bled out of her mouth. Another one grabbed me and I cried and mom yelled to them to stop and they hit her again.

They dragged us downstairs and Doodles was on the floor and covered in blood and I knew he was dead and dad was sitting against the wall and his hands were tied with a plastic thing. He had blood on his stomach and he was asking them to leave us alone and they laughed and hit him. They put a plastic thing on mom and one on me too.

They took mom and she was crying and telling them to leave us alone and not hurt us and they were laughing and one said, "You whore" in English and they hit her again and started ripping her clothes off. They started ripping off my pajamas and mom said they should take her and not me and dad is shouting and they hit both of them until they stop yelling and their faces are bleeding.

One had a knife and he said, "Shut up" and then they made mom get on the floor in front of dad and they hurt her, and then they hurt me.

The counselor holds Millie closer. Millie's affect is flat. The counselor asks her to move on to tell me what happened after.

Dad is crying and mom is not really moving and I was hurt. The one with the knife takes mom's head and cuts her across the throat with his knife and there's more blood and dad moans and they reach down to me but I move and he cuts my face here and there's blood and I can't see. I hear shooting and the two men start talking in their foreign language and they are looking outside and pointing their guns and then they both shoot outside.

My dad looks over at me and his face is purple and bloody and he is missing teeth and he says, "Run."

They can't hear him over their shooting and dad says, "Run!" again and red spits of blood come out of his mouth and I get up, I have no clothes on and my hands are tied with that plastic thing.

They are still shooting outside.

"I don't want to leave you," I tell dad, and he says, "Run!" again, louder. I get up and start running back to the kitchen because it has a door to the backyard, but I look behind me and one of the men saw I was gone and he kicks dad and shoots his head and there is blood everywhere.

I just ran, and there was more shooting behind me and I ran out the door and I just kept running through the backyards. I thought about going into the woods but I had no shoes.

There were police around front with guns and they were shooting at the terrorists. I saw some running around the neighborhood, shooting. The policemen shot one of them and he fell and they kept shooting him.

I ran and ran through the backyards between the houses and the woods past a bunch of houses and then an old man and his wife came outside as I came onto their property. He had a gun and she grabbed me and said, "Come in here, you poor thing!" I had seen her walking her German Shepherd in the neighborhood but I did not know her name.

She put a blanket around me because I was naked and then put a bandage on my face. She asked me my name and I could not say it. I just said that I wanted to go get my mom and that the terrorists had killed my dad and my dog.

I was there a long time. The man stood guard with his gun. There was a lot of shooting but after a while it died down and the man went outside and called the police inside. They looked at me and the woman whispered to them and what she said made them very angry. A fireman came and looked at me. I could not say my name, only that I wanted to go find my mom.

They took me to an ambulance and we drove by my house, There were police cars and firemen there and I saw the terrorist with the knife on our driveway with one of those plastic things that tied up his arms. I did not see mom. The man in the ambulance wrote down my address, but I still could not tell him my name.

They took me to the hospital and the nurses and doctors took care of me. My face hurt, and so did the rest of me. I kept asking for my mom, and my Uncle Rick eventually came to see me and he was crying and he said mom was dead too. I was talking again and I asked if there would be a funeral and he said yes, but he did not know when.

A lady detective came to talk to me. She had pictures of mom and dad that the men took and asked me who they were. The pictures made me cry, but I said that they were my mom and dad. The detective showed me a picture of the man with the knife. He looked like his face was beat up. The detective told me not to worry about that and she asked was he the man who hurt us. I said yes. She asked me if I was sure, if he had hurt mom and then hurt me the same way. I knew what he meant and I told her, "Yes." I told her he shot my dad.

The detective's eyes got red, like she was going to cry, and she hugged me, and thanked me for telling her what happened and said I was brave. I asked her if I was in trouble for crying because they heard me crying found us and she said no that I did nothing wrong and I that I was very brave.

I asked about the other man because there were two. She said he was dead, but the man with the knife was still alive and would have a trial. I said I wanted him to die. She said he will. Then I said I wanted to be the one to kill him, that I wanted to kill them all, and then she started crying and she hugged me.

I still want to kill them.

23.

Scottsdale, Arizona

Lucian Dunwoody is a deputy in the Arizona Citizen Posse (ACP). He wears a tactical vest and a badge, and a locked-and-cocked .45 M1911A1 pistol.

Founded in the wake of the Attack, the ACP represents a formal step between armed citizens – and everyone in Arizona is armed – and law enforcement. The Posse members undergo some basic training and have limited powers of arrest; many are veterans and want to continue to serve.

Others just want to be ready next time.

Those dumb sons of bitches had no idea what kind of woodchipper they were reaching into when they came out here.

Scottsdale is a nice town full of nice people. And, of course, there are ex-Californians who decided to get out of that hellhole and move here without getting rid of their dumb politics that turned the Golden State into a cesspool. I mean, some of the Californians came here and acted like Arizonans, and some of them are in the Posse.

We are nice people, until you push us. Arizonans do not go looking for trouble, but if you come looking for trouble you are going to get all the trouble you ever wanted in spades.

I was recently retired from the insurance business. I was a risk specialist and I did pretty well. We had a nice house here in

Scottsdale, not too far from Phoenix. It was and is an upscale suburb. We keep it nice, and have our own small police department. We do not tolerate nonsense. The biggest problem was how those damn Californians ran up the housing prices – I should be thanking them, maybe. It was changing a bit, with more frou-frou new places, though we always had Taliesin West, which was Frank Lloyd Wright's western home. But this is still the frontier in most of our minds. The Wild West, if you will, except after the Earps cleaned things up.

On that first day I was just living my normal life as a newly retired gentleman of leisure, kind of bored out of my gourd as it were. I was listening to Larry O'Connor's podcast because I like politics and that guy is funny, though I can't really agree with his love of show tunes and problems with Val Kilmer. Anyway, my daughter called me and I answered.

"Daddy?" she asked. "What do you think is happening? Is it terrorism?"

I had to ask her what she meant. It was August 27th and they were hitting us all over the country, including in Phoenix. I turned on the idiot box and saw they went after a couple police stations and that there were several attacks. The cops were stretched to the limit.

She lived in the city and I told her to hunker down with that .38 I gave her. She knew how to shoot it too.

I did not expect anything in Scottsdale, but best be prepared. I got out my Daniel Defense AR-15 and a bunch of 30-round mags and strapped on this .45 here. It was my EDC – everyday carry – gun. I rounded up a half-dozen extra mags.

I'm watching the tube – Fox, because I can't stand CNN – and the doorbell rings. It's Chuck from next door. He's got a rifle and a SIG in his holster. Good man.

"You seeing this?" he says. "I think it's those damn jihadis."

Chuck was a Marine. I was Air Force – I fixed jet engines at Ramstein to get my G.I. Bill back in the early eighties.

I told him that our cops were probably stretched to the limit. We knew a lot of them and liked them. He says, "What we need to do is to form a posse."

That seemed like a great idea. I don't know the last time anyone formed a posse in Arizona but if there was a time when law enforcement needed help, it was now.

Well, open carry is legal because it's America here in Arizona. Still, because things were unsettled, I called the department and got a sergeant who I knew from around town and told him some of us are going to form up and pull some security around our neighborhoods. He told me half the department was on mutual aid hunting shooters in Phoenix so we citizens should go for it.

So Chuck and I went down the street, looking for guys to join the posse and patrol the area. We got a good bunch of men. All of them were coming home from work early. We got a few ladies too. And everyone brought their own gun.

We skipped the Californians, at least the ones with signs in their front yards about loving science and hating hatred.

Some folks thought we were overdoing it, and I get how they might think so. But I worked with risk in my career. It's not just the chance of a bad thing happening you need to consider. It's how bad the thing is. It's basically one times the other. A big risk of something small requires the same level of protection as a small risk of a big thing.

Here, we had killers still on the loose. There was a small chance they would come here. If they did, the damage they could cause was huge. Hell, the news was saying around a hundred people were dead just in Phoenix.

So, we had a small but non-zero chance of a really bad outcome. That meant it was worth it to mount up and take precautions. If that means walking or driving around town for a day or two, okay, just in case. Of course, just in case was the case.

Now, we were not a gaggle. There were almost a hundred of us. We were organized into teams and shifts so we could go 24/7. We reviewed basic gun safety rules and use of force laws because the last thing we needed was somebody doing something dumb and hurting someone who did not need to be hurt. We tried to put people with law enforcement or military experience in charge of small groups and we set up a phone list so we could call each other. No one had radios but we all had an iPhone or an Android or a Jitterbug. Yeah, some of us were pretty high mileage.

We found the guys with SUVs and set up patrols, watching for strangers coming into town. There were a few – some of the people were trying to get away from the city because there were still several shooters loose and the whole place was getting locked down. That was before the stay-home order. But they were decent people.

The next morning the Phoenix police chief announced that they believed they had hunted down the killers, though several officers had been killed. We considered standing down but decided not to after the local department asked us to keep it up while they got their strength back up. We got a special exemption from the stay-home order, and we identified ourselves with U.S. and Arizona flags on our vehicles.

I remember watching that numbskull Veep give her address and thinking that we were in a lot of trouble. It was only that morning that the true extent of the Attack was becoming clear. We were all pretty stunned, and we decided to give it another twenty-four hours just to be safe.

Thank God we did.

The second day attacks were supposed to start on the hour, noon Eastern. That meant 9:00 a.m. Pacific time, though Arizona time can be tricky because we refuse to do that Daylight Savings Time nonsense. But they needed to get in position, so the first contact between the terrorists and the posse was about 8:40 a.m. when my patrol – me and two other folks – saw this older gray minivan coming into town and started following it.

It was driving badly, which was nothing unusual, but there were four Arab-looking guys in it. That seemed weird. Yeah, I know people whine about profiling, but its wasn't Samoans doing the killing. Then they started driving back into the residential areas. That was weird too.

Now, we had no authority to stop anyone. We were not cops, but who knew? Maybe these folks were lost and just needed a helping hand. So I accelerated up beside them, looked them over, and if these guys were not jihadis it was Halloween and they were on their way to pick up their "Best Costume" trophy.

Black shirts, headbands, tac vests, and AKs. Now, if they had two of those, I might still think they were locals, but four?

We're driving side-by-side northbound on North Pima Road and I locked eyes with the head honcho and I knew. And he knew I knew. He brings up that rifle and I, well, I hit the brakes.

They fly past and he leans out the window with his weapon. I swing right and bring up my .45. My guys are getting their own weapons up. He sprays and prays my way. I aim and squeeze off a couple, but they are moving and this is a pistol. Behind me, one of my guys starts popping 7.62mm rounds their way. The other guy is calling it in to the others. It was not even nine and we fired the first shots fired on the second day.

My people start converging. We are following but not too close. The shooter keeps shooting back at us and put one in my hood. Then we get a call that they are following the blue Chevy sedan with the terrorists in it. What? *I'm* following the terrorists in a gray Dodge Caravan. Wait, is there more than one team?

They actually sent four four-man teams into Scottsdale. Later, they figured that the terrorists probably thought that well-to-do folks were better targets because they were higher profile and less likely to fight back. Wrong answer, Achmed.

Pretty soon there were four of our cars following the gray minivan, and we are shooting back as the chase goes down. They tried to cut through a Whole Foods parking lot and hit a light post. They spill out of the vehicle and we roll up. I empty out my pistol from the driver's seat then pull up my AR. There is lead flying and these guys are barely aiming. I don't think that getting shot at by guys who know how to shoot and who are protecting their homes was on their bingo card. One by one, they fall as we circle them and close in. They keep shooting until we put them down. I looked at them on the parking lot asphalt and they all had knives. Thank the Lord we led them away from those families.

The others got surrounded too. The blue Chevrolet got stopped when someone put a round into the driver's brain stem. The others tried to shoot it out from the car and that was a bad move. Everyone knows you clear the vehicle to fight. That car looked like Swiss cheese when I rolled by.

We blocked off the town's main roads and another set got smoked trying to run the block. The last bunch did get loose. They split up and ran through a condominium development on East Chaparral Road with us following the front passenger. He winged Chuck in the arm. We put him down. Another kicked in the wrong door and got shot by the homeowners. We shot the third one down in front of the apartment where Bob Crane got murdered.

The last one got into a house and killed a dad, a mom, and a couple little girls before he ran out the back. We caught up with him and he got a round in the thigh. We took him and zip-tied his ass and threw him in the back of my SUV.

I'll tell you, I had to get pretty aggressive to keep the folks from taking care of business. We had trees and we had a rope and it was all I could do to keep the posse from putting those together to do justice after we found the family.

Now, I am not saying we were gentle to him when he started running his mouth. Let's just say his English was not the only thing that was broken. But we got him to the department and they put him in a cell. A week or so later, I actually testified at the military commission trial that we caught him with a recently fired AK-47 running out of a house with a dead family in it. I didn't need to. He started shouting that he was proud to have killed the infidels and vile crap like that. The verdict was easy and they shot him the next day.

The posse got a lot of credit for defending its town. I don't think we did anything special, or at least anything that should have been special. It became official a little later as a supplement to law enforcement. We do training and we have radios now. But I don't think that's all necessary. What's necessary is just for Americans to stick together and stick up for themselves. After all, that's why we have the Second Amendment.

24.

Evanston, Illinois

Sandra "Sandy" Chalmers speaks to the author as she sits at a picnic bench in the sun waiting her turn. She is in her mid-forties, thin and somewhat intense, though that is to be expected. Her left hand is missing most of her pinky.

Nothing bad ever happened in Evanston. We are a half-hour from Chicago, but we thought we were a world away. Northwestern University is here, and that contributed to our mindset. People called us "the People's Republic of Evanston." We had a climate action plan, and in 2021 we even agreed to pay reparations even though there was never a slave in our city.

I literally had a sign in the front yard that read, "Hate has no home here." It also explained that I believed in science and that no one was illegal. Ironic, huh? I remember putting up pictures of crying Palestinian kids on my Facebook during the Gaza war. That was who I was.

I lived in a sheltered world, safe and totally illusory. Violence and hate was out there, far away. I had never been in a physical confrontation in my life – none of the other moms that I hung out with, reading Ibram Kendi for our book club or whatever, had ever been in a fight either.

On August 27th, my ex-husband Dan Dunwoody – I was Sandy Chalmers-Dunwoody at the time – was in Atlanta on business. He worked for a marketing company and he was there doing a presentation on some sort of new hard drink that tasted like Dr. Pepper and vodka. I still remember that it was called Comrade Pepsky. I was not worried about not having him home – this was Evanston, not Chicago. We had our own police, who we bitched at for being racist but never defunded.

Of course, there was no gun in our house. I told Dan I would not allow it, and he did not object. That was probably true for most of our neighborhood, and I was proud of it. I remember driving my Audi back from Trader Joe's past what were some of the less affluent neighborhoods, the kind with trucks out front and lots of flags, and thinking we needed to take those assault weapons away from those knuckle-draggers. I sure voted my feelings – all Democrat, and the more strident the better about the climate and insurrection and, above all, guns.

I lived in a safe and secure bubble and did not appreciate it. The kids, Ulysses, 12, and Anastasia, 10, – no one called her "Annie" – were at the middle school. I was waiting for Pilar, our housekeeper, and listening to MSNBC in the background, just doing this and that, when the first report came on. A mass shooting, I forget where. I remember muttering something about the NRA and their damn thoughts and prayers. Then there was another, and another, and then the first plane crash. It was at O'Hare. I sat and watched for a minute, horrified. It was clearly coordinated. There were more reports, including an attack on a school somewhere. I got up and rushed out to the Q5 to go bring my kids home.

Everyone else seemed to have the same idea. The street in front of the school was packed, and there were three cop cars out front. The officers had rifles, which normally would have horrified me. The administration was trying to get parents to sign out their kids, but eventually they gave in and just released the kids *en masse*. I found mine after looking for a little while, and we drove home. We passed the poor part of town again and some of the locals were at the head of the street with long guns. I actually considered calling the police on them. That's who I was then.

I got Dan on the phone, finally, and told him that he needed to come home now. But the airspace closure order was in effect – nothing was flying but the Air Force. I told him he needed to get a car and drive home, but there was already talk of a national stay-at-home order. I got mad at him even though I knew that it was not his fault he was trapped in Atlanta.

You remember the first day, watching it all happen? It just got worse and worse. Nothing was coming out of the White House even though the attack on it was beaten back. I was a big supporter of the President and Vice President, but even I was angry. Where was the leadership? I was texting and calling other people I knew all over the country. There was nothing going on in Evanston, but I had a cousin who barely escaped being shot in a mall in Des Moines. I blamed the NRA for the availability of the guns and suspected it was all white supremacist insurrectionists. That was before we knew for certain who was behind it and how they smuggled in the killers and their weapons. But that was my mindset then.

The kids were terrified, but I told them we were safe. We just needed to stay put. I really believed that I just sat there with Rufus, my allergy-free colliedoodle, watching it all unfold on our family room big screen.

School the next day was canceled, of course – school was canceled everywhere – but the kids both went to bed early anyway. Anastasia was crying, and I told her that the Attack was over. I went to tuck in Ulysses and he had his Little League baseball bat out.

I woke up in the morning, and I felt a little better. It was a beautiful day. We did not bother to get dressed. Of course, the news was all about the Attack and I have to admit, there was a small part of me that was disappointed it was Islamic radicals and not homegrown white supremacists behind it. Isn't that awful?

The scale of the Attack was stunning to me – many thousands were dead, though we really had no idea yet how many – but at least it was over except for some hostage situations and tracking down the killers who had survived the first day. I made the kids steel-cut oats and tried to reassure them. I told them everything would be fine, that there were some bad people who believed in a twisted form of a peaceful religion who lashed out and that they would be held accountable by the authorities. That the President was nowhere to be seen nagged at me, but at the time, I never went against my home team.

I coped hard. I rationalized that violence had to be inspired by the Islamophobia cultivated by the Republicans and their mindless support of Israel and its war crimes. But even as I told myself all this while watching the coverage, the carnage and the way the killers broadcast their murders made me feel a little ashamed for excusing them.

Around 11:00 a.m. Central, we heard the explosion. The Evanston Police Department had about two dozen officers and it was located in a red brick building that was right there by the street. It was not designed as a fortress. It was designed to make it easy to come in and report a lost bike or that neighbor who keeps parking in front of your house. It was also easy to drive a car bomb up against it. The explosion took off the front of the structure, and then some of the terrorists went in with guns to finish the job. The police force for a city of 80,000 was effectively eliminated.

The kids were asking me what the noise was, and I told them it was nothing even though I did not know. Rufus the colliedoodle was getting upset. I was just getting myself calmed down again when I heard the shots. Not that I knew what gunshots were, but I knew firecrackers and these were different. These were in our neighborhood. They were close. And they did not stop.

I was breathing fast, terrified, when my phone buzzed with a text. It was my friend Allison from down the street. Her message said, "They are here" with a sad-face emoji. I slid the piddly little bolt shut on our blue front door.

I tried to dial 911. Busy – I got a busy signal. I found out later that some radical students at Northwestern had started calling 911 to clog the lines or report false attacks so that the few police left alive or who other departments could spare to support their neighbors would be drawn away and distracted from the real killing going on in our neighborhood.

Our neighborhood was full of leafy trees and beautiful houses. It was peaceful and quiet, but now all hell was breaking loose. There were shots, and then screaming. I told the kids to come with me, back to the kitchen. But the dog ran to the front window, so I went up to get him and looked outside.

The first thing I saw was people running, some still in robes and PJs too. Then I saw the terrorists. There were at least a half-dozen that I could see. Later we would learn there were 20 or 30 who went into Evanston on the second day. Some were walking calmly down the sidewalk or the middle of the street, then they would turn and go into a house. Others were shooting the running people. A man I knew from up the street fell dead on the sidewalk in front of my house, and a terrorist came along and shot him again several times as he lay there. He had a helmet on with a little camera on a holder so he could film it all.

It's hard to describe how utterly helpless I felt at that moment, but also humiliated at my impotence. I spent my whole life in affluent America and I had totally outsourced security for my life and the life of my family to others. And when I needed them to protect us, because I was unable to protect myself, they were not there for us.

I pulled the barking dog back to the kitchen with me, but maybe the terrorist saw me in the window, or maybe he was just being complete. He walked into the yard. I remember his face. It was so full of hate. I had never seen anything like it.

I ran back to the kids and he kicked the front door. When it didn't give, he shot through it. The kids screamed, and I probably did too. He kicked it again and it came open.

Rufus wanted to get at him and was pulling. I let go of the dog so I could push the kids out the back door – no shoes, just robes and pajamas. I heard the dog bark and then gunfire, then Rufus cried and there was more shooting.

We ran through the back lawn. There was no back fence and I could see the street ahead past the McGillicuddy's house. Then it happened.

We were all running, with Ulysses ahead and me pulling Anastasia along. There was shooting and I heard what I somehow knew to be bullets cracking around us.

It is like it is happening in slow motion. Ulysses staggers and falls and I see his face, I still see it. Bloody, a hole in the forehead where the bullet passed through. I knew without a doubt he was dead.

You see in movies where people lose control and scream and hug the dead, but some kind of strength in me told me he was gone and that I needed to save Anastasia. Maybe it was in my genes – my grandfather got some medal in Vietnam and I never really appreciated it. But I left my dead son on the ground and I pulled Anastatia along with me as we ran to the street. More bullets passed by us. I don't know how we are not dead. It was not until a couple minutes later that I felt a tingle in my hand and saw that he had shot off my left pinky.

It was chaos in the streets and we just kept running. Getting Anastasia to safety was all I could think of, all I could focus on, even as the fact that my son was dead and left behind was there waiting to come back to the forefront of my mind when the danger passed.

You know what happened in Evanston, just like what happened in dozens of other suburbs. They knocked out the local police departments first and tried to confuse any first responders so they would have time. They killed everyone they saw, babies to the elderly, and as horribly as they could. They raped when they had the chance. They sometimes had bodycams uploading the footage in real time to pre-arranged Facebook and Instagram accounts. There's footage out there of the terrorist shooting at us and laughing, and of him emptying his gun into my son's body after we had run away.

I ran and ran with Anastasia. My white robe was covered in the blood from my hand. After a while, the adrenaline faded and I started crying and screaming. But we kept running.

I stopped running when I turned a corner and came face-to-face with a dozen armed men and women. I thought we were dead, that all that running was for nothing. I saw one of them had a patch, a white skull that I found out later was The Punisher symbol, on his gear. The man had a beard and long red hair.

"Ma'am," he said. "Are you hurt?"

I managed to blurt out, "They killed my son!" before I collapsed. A woman medic helped me. The others moved out in some kind of formation and went toward the gunfire. They were an ad hoc unit of civilian militia from that neighborhood across the tracks that I had looked down on. They are the ones, with their assault rifles, who hunted down and killed the terrorists who invaded Evanston.

The next few days are a blur. I was in shock. We were sent to a refugee center where they cleaned up my hand. As much as I suffered, at least I had some family left.

Dan eventually got home and broke down when he heard about Ulyssess, but at some level he blamed me for what happened. I blamed myself too – I grew up being told I was empowered and when it counted I was helpless. Dan and I split up not long after. I saw this with a lot of victims. Not all our wounds are on our bodies.

Now, I am on my own with Anastasia, and I will damn well never be helpless again.

The rangemaster calls Sandy and Anastasia to take their turn on the firing line. Anastasia is already walking over. Sandy gets up from the picnic table and picks up her Wilson Recon Tactical 5.56mm rifle, a fancy version of the AR-15 platform, as well as her tactical vest. On the front, attached to a Velcro field, is a patch with the white skull of the Punisher.

THE THIRD DAY

AUGUST 29TH

25.

Malibu, California

A beachside restaurant by the Pacific Ocean seems an odd place to meet a United States Forest Service Ranger, but the Santa Monica Mountains National Recreation Area is just to the north up Malibu Canyon Road. The mountains are green again now, though many of the trees seem stunted, and few of the buildings that were up in the heights have been rebuilt even half a decade later.

Ranger Shannon Christensen, wearing her tan USFS ranger uniform among the shorts n' flip-flops crowd, has left her utility vest in the green and white Chevy SUV parked outside. Her Glock is holstered at her waist.

The author tries not to stare at the left side of her face. It is severely scarred.

I love nature, I guess. Always did. I liked helping people. I did not want to be a cop, but you know how it is. We rangers all carry firearms now. It was not like that before. Only some of us did before, but today everyone on the job does. It added time to our training, but the government wants more guns out there. I can't say I blame them. After the Attack, we understood that anything could happen anytime, anywhere.

You see those hills? They burn every few years. Fire season is in the fall, October and November. When it's getting cool everywhere else, in California it's getting hot and the fire danger is the worst. Remember in 2007, how San Diego nearly got burned off the map? That was around Halloween. But late August is still dangerous. It was that year, hot and dry after a wet winter.

August 27th was a pretty normal Tuesday. I came down from the hills into Malibu to get a snack. The only thing unusual was I saw a B-2 bomber flying overhead out toward the ocean, which was pretty cool. I saw it again a few hours later when it flew back over LA afterward to show us our military was on the job. I understand that plane was one of the ones that got us payback.

I patrolled alone, and I was law enforcement-qualified so I had my weapon – just my pistol, not an AR-15 like we all carry in the car now. Anyway, I was at a Jack-in-the-Box drive-thru at about quarter after nine because they will make burgers before lunch. I was really pissed. See, Governor Newsom had decreed that fast food workers had to be paid $20 an hour, and my Jumbo Jack with cheese, medium fries, medium Diet Coke, came to $24.38.

Well, since it was worth a king's ransom, I'm at the end of the driveway digging into the bag to make sure I'm not shorted and when I look up, I see a Sheriff's cruiser – the LA County Sheriff's Department patrols Malibu – flying by, lights and sirens. That was weird. Malibu is all, well, people like the ones in here with us now. Lots of people with money who dress like life is one big Jimmy Buffet concert.

Movie stars live out here, businesspeople too. Pepperdine is here, with college kids. Lots of nice cars. There are some upscale places, but it's generally chill. Even my beat in the rec area was relaxed. Some kids partying, that kind of stuff. Occasionally, we would come across some people growing dope – which is weird because it's pretty much legal in Cali – and they were usually mellow. Not a lot of crime, not like you would get down PCH

(*Note: Pacific Coast Highway*) in Santa Monica and Los Angeles proper.

Then I hear shots in the direction the deputies were going. I'm thinking, "What the hell? Maybe it's a robbery gone bad." I knew I did not need this. Still, it was the job. I pulled out onto PCH, hit my lights, and followed.

I call into dispatch to tell them my status and our dispatcher, a nice lady, was just losing it. She's talking nonsense about some kind of attack. I give her my status and focused on driving.

Up ahead, deeper in town with more buildings on the east side and oceanfront mansions on the seaside, the cruiser is sitting there in the middle of the road at a weird angle, lights flashing. I can't see the deputies. Now I see people running, cars hauling ass in my direction. I have no idea what is going on.

I stop, get out, and then my windshield just blows out. I hear automatic weapons fire. I'm not soldier, but I've seen movies. Someone is shooting at me with a machine gun.

I duck down and get out my Glock. I'd never been in a shootout and I could not see who was firing at me.

Then, I spot them – some assholes in black, shooting anyone they see with their rifles. There are bodies everywhere. They are at least 100 meters away and I rise up and take aim and blast away.

I miss, but the good thing – well, the sort of good thing – is they start shooting at me and only me. My Chevy is taking hell – it looks like Swiss cheese and I am trying to keep down. But they are not shooting civilians, which is something.

Anyway, I'm thinking this is it, that I'm gone, when I hear this BLAM. Not the pops like the terrorists' rifles but a big BLAM. One of them goes down, and it's messy. I had no idea who was shooting at the time, but he sure put that one away.

Now more Sheriff's cars are coming. The bad guys are retreating and I'm blazing away, missing, but they are running out of targets because the surviving civilians have run away.

Long story short, the deputies hunted them down. None taken alive. It was a four-man cell. Afterward, lots of civilians were mixing with the deputies and there were lots of guns – lots. Man, they might be liberal Californians but they had some firepower and, of course, citizens were forming up all over the country to secure their towns while the police were the mobile response force.

I saw one handsome older guy with the biggest gun I'd ever seen just walking down the street. I'm not a gun gal, but I later learned it was called a Barrett .50 cal. Anyway, you would recognize this guy. He's played action heroes since before I was born. I know he's had some trouble, but man, he was a lethal weapon that day and he saved my ass.

The next couple days were chaos, as you remember. They sealed off Malibu and no one was getting into town. For us rangers, we were doubled up and they issued a shotgun to each car. I got assigned a rookie who looked like Mr. Rogers with glasses and used to do our night sky talks for the campers. I thought I was no fighter, but then I met him and I felt like Arnold Schwarzenegger.

Not much happened with us on the 28th – we put up barriers, evicted the campers, and closed the park, then patrolled the empty roads. It was eighteen on, six off. I remember joking about how we at least did not have to worry about a fire – the "FIRE DANGER" sign with Smokey the Bear had him pointing to "EXTREME" right then, and it was at least 85 degrees.

The only people who got into the park were LEOs or Army, which was showing up and moving through. There was this tension in the air because we knew the terrorists were now focusing on residences, and when they hit Calabasas next door, well, we thought we might see some action.

It was the 29th when they flexed again. Everyone was expecting more mass shootings and more attacks on homes and assassinations, but they were smart, not that I want to compliment them. I mean they did the unexpected and hit us where we were not expecting it.

They came up 101 from LA, and got off at Los Virgenes to come south on Malibu Canyon Road. That should not have happened the next day because of martial law and the shelter in place order, but on the third day a lot of people still moved. There were not enough police to stop everyone.

What gets me is that the UCLA students who helped drove their own cars. It was like there were no plate readers on the 101 that would let the FBI trace them later. They were so fixated and radical that they just wanted a piece of the Attack. The organizers with them shot up a Forest Service SUV at the park entrance, killing two of our people, and then they all drove inside and split up, at least seven cars of college kids helping the terrorists.

They spread through the park. They all had downloaded Google maps and the spots were all planned. They took gas cans, splashed the gas on the brush, and lit it. They set dozens of fires. Even in normal times we could not have stopped it. The park went up in flames.

My partner and I heard the radio calls. We chased one car, a BMW 4-series – working near Malibu, you get familiar with them. The driver was a fat girl with a keffiyeh around her neck – I found out she was the first-generation daughter of a prominent oncologist in San Jose. She's got her boyfriend and another girl with her. She blows a corner and hits a tree.

We roll out, guns up, and they dump out. I swear, the daughter has her iPhone out and is filming us while the other girl is shouting, "From the river to the sea, Palestine will be free!"

The boyfriend is wearing a jacket, in 85 degrees heat mind you, and he gets out. I'm yelling for them to get face down in the dirt and they are screaming back at me and the boyfriend twitches his hand like he's going for his waistband and Mr. Rogers dumps a load of buckshot in his chest. He's all of a buck-thirty, so he flies backwards like he's been hit by a bus.

The girls shriek and Mr. Rogers points the barrel at the passenger and she pisses herself. We move up and tell the daughter to drop the iPhone but she's now yelling about police murder and WHAM – Mr. Rogers buttstrokes her to the jaw. That shut her up, at least for a little while.

We hook them up and load them up. We just leave their dead buddy twitching on his back. He's not going anywhere, and we have to move because the fire is coming.

We turned them over to the Army MPs. They were screaming about their rights and lawyers. The MPs took them away and they pretty soon stopped yelling. I never saw them in person again, but me and Mr. Rogers testified by Skype at their summary court-martial a week or so later. Judging from their expressions, it had dawned on them that they were in deep doo-doo. I asked Mr. Rogers, who is still on the job and who I don't call Mr. Rogers anymore, what happened to them. He did the pull the finger across the throat thing. Oh well.

As for us, no one ever came back at us about the shooting. No investigation. No one even recovered the boyfriend's body. The fire swept though. It destroyed everything. It almost burned down to the Pacific – the civilians playing cops to guard their town had to put down their guns and pick up hoses and shovels to play firefighters. But everything up in the hills was gone. They just let it burn. They had to. There was no one to fight the fire.

Of course, that was just one fire. The bastards set hundreds. Pretty much every major national forest and park got hit. Who would be looking for that? We were expecting more of the same killings in the cities and suburbs. They went where we did not expect. The fires went on for months. There was no way to fight that many. The biggest wildfire in American history was the 1825 Miramichi Fire in Maine, about three million acres and 160 dead. The Attack fires burned eight million acres and killed over five thousand, mostly because they spread to communities built in and around the forests – and because we failed to maintain the forests properly and let them turn into firebombs.

A lot of us with fire experience, like me, got called up to go help with the fires – the soldiers guarded the park. I went to Tehama County, up north. California is fire country, and it was going off. I was working with a bunch of prisoners – they got a promise of time off if they did a few days training and went on the line. We were fighting in a canyon, trying to clear brush, and they did not know what to look out for.

The fire swooped down on us and we all had to go into our fire shelters. They look like aluminum foil sleeping bags, and they are designed to radiate heat back and to trap air, because it's breathing the hot gases that kills you. Well, in that canyon we were in an oven. The fire swept over us and, well, look at my face and understand that I was one of the lucky ones. We lost a dozen of our prisoner-firefighters.

I found out later that it was brats from Chico State's Students For Justice for Palestine that set that fire. And I testified at that trial too.

Ranger Christensen draws her hand across her throat.

26.

Undisclosed Location

Wen "William" Feng is in hiding somewhere in the United States – maybe. Perhaps he is not in the United States at all. A condition of meeting the only publicly acknowledged Chinese sleeper cell agent to date was that his current location be kept secret. The Chinese Communist Party was most displeased when he went public after spending several years in the United States awaiting the command to strike. The Chinese government denied his claims that he was an agent, and also labeled him a traitor.

After extensive debriefing by U.S. counterintelligence agencies, Wen was allowed to make some limited media appearances. His English is flawless, if anything reflecting the Southern California beach vibe of San Diego, where he lived as a sleeper agent. In his brief prior interviews – this is his most extensive public statement to date – Wen gave two reasons for defecting. The first was that he met and secretly married an American woman. The other is that he experienced and survived the Attack.

I was not born poor, nor rich. My father was an office worker. He did not get rich like many others, but we were always comfortable. He was a communist in the sense that everyone was a communist. It was just assumed, even if you ran a business like a capitalist.

I was not a particularly good student except for languages. I studied English in school and did well. It is such a different language, and I think that the structure of a language becomes the structure of how you think. Learning English opened me to new possibilities.

I was patriotic, again because what else would I be? I also excelled at the military training during my elementary and secondary schooling. When I graduated what you would call high school, I had to make a decision about my future, since I had no interest in regular college. I could follow my father's footsteps, but I dreaded that. Perhaps I could go into business. No, that was not what I wanted. I was very physically fit, and I wanted a challenge. I applied for officer training in the People's Liberation Army Ground Forces (PLAGF).

I excelled, and I was commissioned a lieutenant. I continued to study English on my own and worked hard to perfect my accent. I would watch YouTube videos, those that were not censored, to try to mimic the sound of the voices. Occasionally, I would see foreigners and try my English with them, and I was proud when they complimented me on my American accent. But to me, it was more of a hobby than anything.

My superiors gave me good evaluations and they must have noticed my fluency in English because after three years, when I considered becoming a civilian again, I was approached by a colonel. He was different than the colonels I worked for, less stiff and formal. I remember his hair – it was a bit longer than the regulations technically allowed.

He spoke to me in English – American English – and asked if I was interested in "a new challenge." I was. I received orders to a base far away in Xinjaing, in the west of China. It was one I had never heard of. I was there with a dozen other first lieutenants and captains, all fit, all speaking English. In fact, we were told we could not speak Mandarin.

Our assessment course was three weeks of endless ruck marches, exercise, and sleep deprivation. No one told us what we were doing it for. No one shouted. They would politely say, "Please gather your equipment and weapon," then hand us a compass and a map with a marked location and say, "Go there." They did not tell us how long we had, or how to accomplish the task. We had to push ourselves to our limits in every training iteration. And when you finished, they did not tell you if you passed or failed. They simply allowed you to eat or sleep for a few hours, and then the next task began.

At the end of three weeks there were two of us left. They continued to give us tasks and we continued to do them until one day there were no more tasks. My comrade, Jiang Changming, and I were accepted for special forces training.

That was another year of harsh training, but this time we were told what we needed to accomplish. We learned foreign weapons and advanced hand-to-hand combat, as well as tradecraft and many other skills. We also had to learn an "enemy" language even as we trained on the tactical skills. It was easy for me and for Jaing because we both spoke English already.

Afterwards, I was assigned to the famous Guangzhou Military Region Special Forces Unit, called "South Blade." We were primarily a reconnaissance unit with some direct action capabilities. A major part of the unit's mission was moving cross-country to surveil and take out targets. We also did security for dignitaries. A good portion of our work was in foreign countries, often undercover. Because I spoke English, I would often be given a passport and backstory as a Chinese-American. It was interesting work, occasionally dangerous, especially in Africa. I got in my first firefight when some bandits tried to kidnap the diplomat I was protecting.

I did this for several years and grew restless again. I never thought about making it a career, so I was considering leaving the PLAGF. You could do well in private security with my background. Then that same colonel – now a general – came to me and offered me a new challenge. Would I embed in the United States, to be ready in case the homeland required my services?

Clearly, this had been the plan years before when I was recruited for the special forces. They had identified and cultivated me, and I must have passed their tests since they were now making this offer. I would be under deep cover in the United States, living as an American, ready to fight on enemy soil if war came. It was a challenge I could not pass up. Plus, by then my parents had passed away and I had no family left that would miss me – this was actually unusual, since they preferred sleepers with family back in China to keep them from going native.

I spent another year in training learning how to be an American. We studied everything – how to get a doctor appointment, use a McDonald's drive-thru, open a bank account. I learned to do all the things you learned growing up American. And I studied popular culture – it would not do to have someone mention "Captain Kirk" and to stand there with a blank stare.

I would be an illegal. That is, I would have no official cover. Instead, I would assume an identity carefully prepared for me by our agents in America. I flew in under a false name and vanished. I appeared in San Diego, where I was assigned as Thomas Evan Chang, a traveling salesman. I was handed my documents, including credit cards and the keys to both a Pacific Beach apartment and a Toyota Camry. My cover was that I recently moved to California from "back east." In a way, I guess that was true!

I actually worked the sales job, selling industrial piping and pumping equipment, which allowed me to move about the West Coast. San Diego had many military installations, but I assessed vulnerabilities and selected targets throughout the western United States. For example, I saw how unsecure the refineries were, and we certainly targeted those. The attacks by the terrorists on petroleum facilities proved us right.

I reported these targets back to China through a coded internet protocol. I also memorized certain preselected infrastructure targets, including power stations and so forth, that I might be called upon to strike in a crisis.

I was delighted to find that Jiang – or Doug, as he was known – was also in California and that if the time came we would work together. He also came as an illegal, but once the borders opened it was simpler to send large numbers of agents in through Mexico. With the Taiwan crisis heating up, the Party decided to prioritize the quantity of agents over the quality. One of my tasks was to maintain contact with these men, who were not as well-trained as Jiang and me. Unlike us deep cover sleepers, they stayed in the Chinese expatriate community while we lived as, and mingled with, Americans.

One thing I was shocked at was how vulnerable American infrastructure was to sabotage. I mentioned the refineries, but there were many other vulnerabilities. Like any normal American, I immediately bought several large-caliber hunting rifles which, if called upon, I could use to destroy critical infrastructure. For instance, a big transformer can be effectively destroyed with a few gunshots in just minutes, but it will take months or more to replace – and they usually came from China. This was only one of many vulnerabilities we identified. Sadly, during the Attack it became obvious that the terrorists had identified them too.

I met an American woman and we began to date. This was normal and even encouraged to solidify our identity. I did not tell her who I really was, of course. She thought I was an orphan because my family back east had passed away. I tried to ignore the fact that my situation meant we really could not be together forever and enjoy the present. But I still married her at city hall – I just did not tell my superiors.

Pacific Beach is a funky area of San Diego next to the ocean, with plenty of coffee houses and restaurants. I miss it! I made my own hours as a salesman, and on the morning of August 27th, I decided to take my bride for breakfast. I loved American steak and scrambled eggs with black coffee. We were at our favorite spot, The Noble Yolk, on Ingraham Street, just a couple blocks from my apartment, at 9:00 a.m.

What were the chances it would happen to us, that we would be in the center of one of the attacks? It was crowded along the street, with few police, and therefore very vulnerable. I had seen that myself, but I saw the neighborhood as vulnerable to *us*, not to these Islamic fanatics.

I had just received my food and I was pouring Heinz ketchup on my scrambled eggs – very American – when I heard the sound of an AK-47. I knew it by heart. Though the PLAGF was using newer rifles, the AK was still around.

It was close, as in next door. And I heard a shout – "Allahu Akbar!"

Then bullets ripped through the restaurant over our heads, missing us but killing our waiter and some other patrons.

I had been in combat situations before, but never without a weapon. Still, my training kicked in. I pulled my wife to the floor and told her, "Stay down!"

She looked at me as if I was a different person, and I was – certainly different from the gentle salesman she had just married.

I grabbed my steak knife off the table, ignored the screaming and rushing patrons around me, and moved toward the sound of the guns.

I saw the shooter outside, in a black shirt with a vest and a green headband with some Arabic-looking script written on it, probably with a Sharpie. He was pulling the empty magazine from his weapon. He was not smooth – he needed practice. I charged him as everyone else scrambled to get away. He looked up as I was on him.

I grabbed his hair and forced his head backwards. Then I cut his throat with the steak knife. The blood spurted out and some landed on me. He fell backwards in the street and I took his rifle and pulled off his web gear – he had a Kevlar plate in the front. I slipped it on, and reloaded the rifle.

I looked up and my wife was in the window of the restaurant, mouth open, staring.

"Get back down!" I yelled. And then I put the weapon to my shoulder and began to move. I did not realize I was being filmed by a dozen iPhone cameras.

The terrorists were not professionals. I was. There were five shooters in Pacific Beach, killing anyone they saw with barely any resistance except for some outgunned police and me.

I began hunting them down, but only after I put two rounds in the head of the man whose throat I cut. On 9/11, they attacked where people could not fight back, but this time Americans, and I, could return fire. I do not think they truly understood that many of them would go from hunters to hunted very quickly.

The first one I encountered was coming out of a diner. I shot him in the face and then again in the head as he lay there. Further up the street, a grenade went off inside another restaurant. I shot the thrower as he prepared to toss another. It blew up next to him and I did not need an insurance headshot since he had no head left to speak of.

I killed the next one as he tried to carjack a Honda SUV from a screaming mother. One moment she had a barrel in her face and the next I had put the terrorist down. I walked up to the driver's window and told her, "Drive home!" She said, "Thank you!" and then I shot the terrorist again just to be sure.

The last one had turned a corner up ahead and was running, though he was still firing at anyone he saw. I followed, passing a shot-up police cruiser and two dead officers, then turned the corner and took aim. The AK-47 is not particularly accurate, particularly with the stock folded, but I was a good shot. I had it on semi and fired three times center mass. On the third shot, he staggered and fell. I walked over to him as he crawled to his weapon and shot him twice in the back of the head.

I turned and walked back to the restaurant where my wife was waiting. In the distance, I could hear shooting from other incidents. There were bodies everywhere, as well as wounded civilians. I still had the rifle, but no one thought I was a terrorist. A few people thanked me.

I went back inside the restaurant and found my wife. I tossed the weapon and the vest to the floor and picked her up and started walking home. I did not know what was happening in the rest of San Diego, much less the rest of the country. I just wanted to get out of there before the police showed up, but for some reason no police came. I found out later one of the killer teams had bombed the department.

At home, I had to explain the truth to my wife, who wondered how her husband had transformed into a special forces operator before her eyes. The TV was on and one of the first local images was me, taken by a civilian, slitting the first terrorist's throat, securing his weapon, and systematically killing the others.

My wife wanted me to turn myself in. I refused, until the third day. That was when the terrorists focused on infrastructure. At that point, I knew I could not sit aside as my adopted home was attacked.

I went to the FBI, and somehow managed to get past the guards at the front door and talk to a couple counterintelligence agents. They seemed prepared to ignore me completely – they probably thought I was insane – until one recognized me from the video taken in Pacific Beach. Then they listened.

The infrastructure attacks were underway already, but I began telling them the targets and vulnerabilities we had identified so they could secure them. I do not know if that helped stop any attacks, but it earned me credibility. When things calmed down, I made my defection official and submitted to extensive debriefing. The only thing I made them do was promise not to arrest and prosecute Jiang but to send him home, which they did. After all, he was just a soldier defending his country in his own way.

Now I live quietly with my wife, consulting occasionally. I consider myself an American, and I will become a citizen soon. There is something that worries me, though. The infrastructure attacks by the terrorists caused a great deal of damage, but they were quite superficial compared to what we were prepared to do to the United States if given the order.

We were prepared to do much, much worse. And there are still thousands of Chinese sleeper agents in the United States waiting for that order.

27.

Belmont, California

Jared Sokolov is the founder and chief technical officer of Helm's Deep, one of many cyber defense companies that have sprung up since the Attack. Capitalism is about finding a need and filling it. The myriad cyber vulnerabilities America's enemies found and exploited during the Attack were far too extensive for government agencies to address alone. Jared worked at one of those agencies then – he is coy about which one but it seems likely that it was an agency working on national security located at Fort Meade, Maryland.

The Cyber National Defense Act really created this industry. Before the Attack, companies and government agencies talked a good game on cyber, but the threat was so hypothetical that most companies just hired a few nerds to try to put up some basic defenses and that was it. Banks, financial companies, and that sort of thing took it very seriously. They had money and people would try to steal it. But some trucking company that shipped food all over half the country? Their margins were already tight and they weren't going to spend cash on cyber defense until someone made them.

The cyber-attacks on the third day were part of the infrastructure assault. With cyber, it's not walking into a mall and gunning down everyone you see, or going house to house massacring families. The cyber-attack was really designed to both rub our faces in our own vulnerability and to fuel the social upheaval they hoped to provoke. There are many tactics for doing that. You can blow up infrastructure with a truck bomb, or try to kill the people who run it, or you can try to disrupt it from a keyboard on the other side of the world.

Some people wondered why there were no cyber-attacks on August 27 or 28. Why did they wait until the 29th to initiate it? It was simple. They *wanted* the internet up. They wanted to allow the radical assets in America like Antifa and the college left the ability to mobilize and coordinate, sure, but that was only the supporting rationale for their plan. They mainly wanted what they were doing on the first and second days to be seen.

The killers used all of social media as well as the dark web to upload their atrocities. Plus, the American media was covering it non-stop and they wanted that too. Did you know that not a single TV station, radio station, or antenna farm was targeted during the Attack? They were all vulnerable targets, but the terrorists never touched them. They wanted the American people, and people around the world, to see exactly what they were doing. And they waited until the third day because they figured, correctly, that the American reaction to a massive cyber assault would be to do what it did after 9/11 with the civilian aviation system – essentially, pull the plug.

The attacks were, primarily, an information operation. Sure, there was a kinetic component where certain people and property were targeted in order to affect America's strength – think about the attack on Whiteman Air Force Base's B-2 bombers. But the real purpose of the Attack was to compel America to abandon not just Israel and the Middle East, but any kind of world leadership. And then, once Europe was picked off by jihadis, they would come again for America, assisted by the homegrown supporters invigorated by the Attack and America's humiliation.

The preparations for the cyber warfare component began long before the Attack, decades in fact. The Iranians, of course, were active in the cyber battlespace, frequently probing and testing American and other countries' defenses. What they did was take a very close look at American infrastructure and identify mundane and routine types of enterprises that were, nevertheless, critical. To cite my prior examples, banks were hard targets for cyber. They avoided hard targets. They would look for the trucking company that delivered dairy to a region. They would test the defenses of its operating system, record any weaknesses, and place it on the target list. They would find critical supporting components of the power grid that were not part of the power companies themselves – they were hardened – but that *supported* the power company. For instance, in California the environmental mandates required the power company to use fifty percent electric vehicles. They targeted the third-party company that maintained the fleet's software. With a stroke of a key, suddenly half of the company's repair capacity was knocked out. The vehicles were bricks with their software scrambled.

It was asymmetry. They avoided our strength and placed their strength in cyber against our profound weaknesses. And it was not just them. Obviously, the Iranians were deeply involved in the actual attack but they needed to spread the tasks around. It was too much for them to do alone and besides, they could not have all of the cyber assaults originate in one place. They ended up hiring a whole army of hackers, to use the common parlance, including other governments, without disclosing exactly what the collective purpose was. A lot of Macedonian, Estonian, Chinese, Korean, and even American hackers ended up unknowingly helping the Iranian assault. All they knew is they were getting paid in Bitcoin to perform some discrete tasks. A few figured out that they were being used and pulled out, but most did what they were paid to do. And we all saw the consequences of the cyber component of the Attack.

There was a lot written in the unclassified portion of the Attack Commission Report about the cyber component, and a lot of criticism of our failure to detect what was happening. I will not speak to anything classified – at Helm's Deep, we do classified work for certain government agencies – but what I can say is that we saw pieces of the puzzle but not the whole.

Our AI looked at patterns within the internet, trying to detect anomalies that we would then investigate further. Obviously, the trick for them was to not appear to be doing anything unusual. You avoid detection by looking normal. Much of their probing and initial work to set up the cyber assault was disguised as typical phishing, hacking, and scamming. We saw tons of that every day, so much that we generally ignored it at our level. A probe of that trucking company would seem to be nothing more than an attempt to get in and place ransomware that was foiled by basic malware defenses. But it was not foiled because these were very sophisticated tools. Instead of ransomware, they would plant malware that activated on command.

We track Bitcoin – that's public knowledge – and we know it is a currency of choice to the sketchy and the actively criminal elements out there. We saw some anomalies, transfers that looked unusual. We did not tie it to the other things we were seeing in the cyber world, much less the things other agencies were seeing in the real world, like the transport of military-age males into the USA. That's why cyber is a key part of NORTHCOM's Intelligence Synthesis Cell, so we can look at how the digital world and the real world are relating.

We did not anticipate anything happening that day. It was normal – perfectly normal, which was the plan. I remember the first day as just a normal day, hot and muggy. I brought my lunch so I did not have to leave to eat because I hate humidity – one of the reasons I built Helm's Deep on the San Francisco Peninsula instead of moving to Austin or Miami like everyone else.

They did not hit the post directly. Fort Meade is an Army base and because the National Security Agency and the United States Cyber Command are on the post, and because there were a lot of crazies who thought we were blasting mind control lasers in their direction, there was a ton of security. Serious security, not a couple of contract guards with handguns but tough dudes who were ready to fight. So we all felt pretty safe.

But the security was not there in the towns next door like Odenton. The main drag has a lot of restaurants, and people who did not brown bag it or want to eat in the cafeteria would go off-post for lunch. None of them were armed because at the time you could not bring your weapon on base even with a concealed carry permit. That meant a significant number of unarmed workers at two of our key cyber defense agencies were sitting ducks when several terrorist kill teams hit at noon. I lost several friends and co-workers. My team was down a quarter of its people.

We were scrambling to deal with the Attack on our end. It became clear almost immediately that this was not a single attack or even several attacks like 9/11. This was *thousands* of attacks. Who conducts thousands of attacks without coordination? We began looking for communications, both signal and cyber, trying to find out who was running this, to detect their command-and-control lines so we could interdict them digitally or feed the targeting to the military to do it kinetically. But what we did not realize immediately is that they did not need command and control. All they needed was clear instructions and people to go carry them out hoping to be killed in the process and win their virgin jackpot.

Of course, we trained to interdict communications, observation capabilities, and logistics lines. That's how we fought. You render the enemy confused, blind, and unable to resupply, and then destroy him in detail. But what if the enemy does not need any of those things you usually target? We want to be inside the enemy's OODA loop – OODA is "Observe, Orient,

Decide, Act." That's the warfare decision-making process, and you want to be inside the enemy's loop observing, orienting, deciding, and acting faster. But what if there is no OODA loop to get inside? What if all the decisions have already been made and all there is to do is act by executing the plan? They chose the time, place, and manner of the individual fights and we were left to react. They got inside our OODA loop.

The Army locked us down on the post. I was working twenty hours a day, sleeping on the floor. We were physically exhausted, emotionally exhausted by the deaths of our co-workers, and our morale was crap. We were watching the enemy in real-time uploading their propaganda and essentially setting the terms of the information fight. We actually had visibility on terrorists uploading across the country as they killed. We knew where they were, but there was no process to feed that location info to ground elements – cops, soldiers, whatever – to go out and kill these people. The second day, when they attacked residences, was particularly hard on us because we were able to graphically depict the individual atrocity locations as red dots on a screen and the country looked like it was covered with blood.

The third day, we thought it was over. We were looking inside the United States mostly, starting to really see the American radicals beginning to mobilize in force, and we were not looking outward as much as we typically would. Then, at noon, it hit. The whole board lit up. Thousands and thousands of attacks, many preprogrammed, others in real time. Signals were going out to pre-planted malware. And it was coming from everywhere, including China. China denies that it knew what was happening or that government actors participated in it. I tend to think it did not, but there is no doubt it took advantage of the chaos to tick a few things off its cyber bucket list while we were busy with our electronic tsunami.

We fought back to the extent we could, but the sheer volume of the assault overwhelmed us and Cyber Command. The companies that were already hardened did fine. The enemy mostly avoided spending time and effort on hard targets they would likely never breach and the hardened ones they did assault usually beat off the attacks. It was targets like those trucking companies that did not, the smaller but crucial components of the system that make America work that no one thinks about until they are knocked offline. Well, the enemy thought about it.

The power went off in much of the country thanks to the cyber and the physical attacks. The logistical system essentially collapsed as the companies that haul goods and services found that their software was corrupted. Repair parts companies were hard hit – suddenly there was no way to fix cars because no one could get a replacement alternator or whatever. Some train systems were taken offline, traffic lights in smaller towns were disrupted, all sorts of things.

Nothing worked. Things kept going down. There was a leadership vacuum. Until the new president was sworn-in, we had no guidance. Back at Meade, we made our recommendations and then nothing happened until finally the order came through – shut down the American internet and cut it off from the rest of the world.

People online had always speculated whether there was an internet kill switch, and the answer was "sort of." We had the capacity, never used, to essentially air-gap America's internet from the rest of the world. The new president told us to do it, and we did. That largely stopped the cyber part of the Attack, but also all business and other transactions. And that helped send the stock markets around the world even deeper into the red. Ours, of course, had been shut down on the first day.

We all know the chaos that followed as food ran out in some cities and rationing went into effect. People had to go to paper and clipboard logistics and it was hard. The lack of gas and diesel and the rationing made it worse. But martial law made it much easier to address. People got the message pretty quick that they needed to behave. It was ugly but necessary.

I did not see it personally because it was three weeks before I got a chance to go home and change and water my dying plants. We worked nonstop to undo the damage and put up defenses against a repeat. The internet went back up after three days and we counterattacked. Of course, one of the nuke targets was an Iranian Republican Guard Corps bunker that included a huge cyber cell. Our H-bomb trumped their malware. In the end, digital is important, but physical is real.

Repairing the physical and digital damage took forever. Remember how, for the longest time, the supermarkets were bare? Rationing went on in some places for months. Of course, gas rationing went on for a year because the refineries were down. We learned just how much of our lives is enabled by digital. With it gone, we were a mess. It was only the harsh discipline of martial law and the American spirit we had thought might have been gone forever, but wasn't, that kept us from falling apart. We got through the infrastructure attacks, but like Wellington said about winning the battle of Waterloo, it was a close-run thing.

Even before the Attack Commission Report, it was abundantly clear that Uncle Sam could not be everyone's digital babysitter. The Cyber National Defense Act mandated that a broad range of companies that are part of our infrastructure must take certain steps to harden themselves, including hiring cyber defense consulting services. I left my agency a year later and founded Helm's Deep.

I wish I could tell you everything is hunky-dory now. The Iranians were good, but the Chinese and Russians are exponentially better. And we have yet to see what the hell they can do to us.

28.

Galveston, Texas

Ted Cooper hands over a hardhat and an orange vest. This safety gear is required to walk through the Chalmers East refinery, one of the larger refineries in the South Texas area. Getting inside the facility was like going through security to see the president – it required advance notice so that the security office could complete a background check with federal law enforcement, then a physical search at the gate. The author's car was parked far from the actual facility – Cooper picked him up with a golf cart.

Two guards follow the author and Cooper as he shows off the facility. They carry rifles. The perimeter is secured by an electrified fence, with signs on it that read, "This Facility Is Protected Under The Infrastructure National Security Act. Deadly Force Is Authorized." The author spots anti-drone defense systems on the top of the gun towers. Petroleum fumes waft through the pipes and girders, most of them brand new.

I used to joke that that smell, that gasoline smell, smelled like victory. Of course, that changed. But before the Attack, it did. This is where American prosperity began, here in the petroleum refineries. There are about 130 in America, most old, with about one new refinery coming on-line every year. This is where we take the black gold, the Texas tea, and make it into pretty much everything that fuels the country. All that climate change crap, that's all gone now – at least in America – because we had our own taste of what life without fossil fuels was like and we did not enjoy it. American dominance started right here, and now we know it.

Here's the thing about oil refineries. They are pretty much bombs. You are always hearing about fires and explosions at refineries, a lot fewer than there used to be, but these are still dangerous places. Fuel works by releasing chemical energy. It explodes, for lack of a better word. Internal combustion engines? Well, the oil products – like gasoline or kerosene of JP8 or whatever – combust. And there are millions of gallons here, though we measure it in barrels – barrels are 42 gallons.

So, each of these facilities is a bomb. It's a bomb we spend a lot of time keeping from exploding. We are good at it, but they are dangerous, and that's why no one wants them around. There are not going to be any new ones built around people. In the past, we built them off on the fringes of cities, but over time people moved in closer. It's so hard to build new ones that much of our increased capacity comes from building up the facilities we have.

Of course, they were a special target during the infrastructure attacks on August 29th. They were soft targets where the results were spectacular and the attacks did real damage to the country. It's one thing to make a big show that has no real impact, or to do something that no one really notices, but attacking a refinery checked both boxes.

You saw the footage of the fires and explosions. And then you felt the impact when the gas stopped flowing. No wonder they hit the refineries. It was their biggest bang for their buck, other than the people they murdered.

Look at the size of this place. It's huge, and Chalmers East is not even in the top half of refineries in terms of acreage. It has a lot of fence line to be secured, but it was not like it is now back then. We had guards, our own little police force. And while we knew there could be sabotage, we were really looking for thieves trying to steal metal or kids who thought it would be cool to explore. Our guards had handguns. They had some shotguns in lockers back at the guard building, but they were not expecting organized attacks.

Well, that's not entirely true. We got briefed on Chinese special ops sleepers that might come in. But that was only if Taiwan was heating up. And no one had any solutions. All we got was a warning to watch out because some Chi-Com snake eaters might show up if things get tense in the Eastern Pacific. No new training or equipment. And who wanted to spend money fortifying a place no one in his right mind wanted to break into? Oil companies make a lot in terms of gross, but the margins are thin. Every buck you spend on overhead costs the shareholders. So no one did anything, and we paid for it.

The first day, there were attacks in Houston out in public. That's where the police and soldiers focused the next day, when the terrorists switched to attacking residential suburbs. So, on the third day, the cops and soldiers were mostly in residential areas. That's when the terrorists changed again and focused on infrastructure.

They hit twenty-five refineries around the country, including Chalmers East. They hit only ones open for business – remember, about five to ten percent of the refineries are down for repair or maintenance or expansion at any given time. And they chose the places with the most impact, specifically the ones making gasoline. That should not have been a surprise. The Iranians did the targeting and they know refining.

They took about 300 of their guys and put them in special training, not the mass shooter schools most of them went to but one inside Iran itself that trained them for just this mission. They actually trained inside the refineries back there so they knew what they were looking for. And their sleepers here, some in the industry, gave them photos and maps of our facilities. They really planned it for maximum effect. They even got a team into

Hawaii to not only hit the one refinery in Honolulu, but to also hit the Navy fuel bunkers at Red Hill that fed Pearl Harbor. That was at least a little better defended because it held the fuel reserves for the Pacific Fleet and those boys took the Chinese threat seriously. They actually fought off the attackers – imagine 250 million gallons going up? Move over, December 7th. But everywhere else? Holy crap, what a cluster.

These guys were the terrorist elites, like the airport missile guys or the ones assigned to assassinate specific targets. These guys were inserted into the country last and watched closely. If they somehow got caught and spilled, these guys could actually do damage to the plan, unlike the shooters who did not know anything about the big picture.

They had teams of about a dozen terrorists for each refinery they targeted. The guards were on duty and the places were operating, but there was no extra security. Like I said, the cops and Army were out in the suburbs trying to stop another massacre. No one really expected to be hit. The bad guys counted on that.

They shot their way through the front gates and knew right where to go in their vehicles. They would leave a couple guys with machine guns at the gates to lock them and hold them, basically to keep everyone in and any first responders out.

They shot anyone they passed on the way, but the shooting was secondary. They knew where to go. They headed for tanks and pipes that processed the most volatile compounds. Crude oil? No. That burns if you ignite it, but they wanted explosions. They wanted fireworks that would be on the news to send the message that they could do what they wanted and America could not stop them, but they also wanted to take out the machinery and the systems to physically destroy them. They knew how long it would take to repair. And during that time, American gasoline capacity would be slashed.

It was 11:00 a.m. when they hit here. I was not out in the main processing facility at the time. If it had been, they would have shot me too, or I would have burned. There was no finesse – they would shoot bullets or rocket-propelled grenades at the structures. And the structures would go up – sometimes in pretty spectacular fashion. They knew what to shoot and did. Now, normal people would never do that. Why? They could easily die too. And a lot of these guys did. You only need finesse if you are planning to come out of it alive. If not, you can get right up to the tank and blast it and if you get caught in the fireball, fine, 72 virgins, coming right up.

Pretty soon everything was burning. The whole main facility was going up. Like I said, a petroleum refinery is a giant bomb. Hell, both what we make and the byproducts are all explosive. You see those fires coming up out of the towers sometimes? That's methane burning off. We have to burn it under control or else it would burn uncontrolled.

We had our own fire department, but even if they could get close without getting shot, this was beyond their abilities. There was no one else coming until the gates were retaken, which took a couple hours. By that time, the central facility was toast. I mean gone. Most of us who were not shot got out through side gates. I went out through the gates that the tanker trains use, running along the tracks to get away from the bullets and the fires.

Just putting out one fire is hard. But ten in this area around Houston? They burned for days. There was nothing left. It was unsalvageable. The same at most of the other refineries. They cut America's gas and diesel refining capacity by a third in a morning.

America runs on gas and diesel. Electric cars and trucks are nice, but they are a rounding error in the scheme of things. How do you move goods to people without fuel?

It was a nightmare, and it was not like we could just fix everything. First, you need to design the new facilities. A lot of the design documents actually burned in the fires. Plus we were only building one smallish facility a year. The design capacity was totally inadequate. How many petroleum engineering architects are there? I'll tell you – not very damn many.

Second, a lot of the equipment we were fixing or replacing was old. It was not made anymore. You essentially had to build stuff from scratch. But the problem was that America did not build stuff from scratch anymore.

Third, there were the regulations. The refineries are already contaminated ground. That's just how it is. But these were now super contaminated. You had millions of gallons of products spilled. The Environmental Protection Agency and other bureaucracies immediately swung in and told us that before we could rebuild we had to remediate. And to remediate, we needed environmental impact reports and the whole nine yards. And then environmental groups threatened to sue. It was insane – the country had just been attacked, tens of thousands killed, our fuel capacity was crippled, and these jokers were acting like it was business as usual.

Oh, and fourth, someone had to pay for all this. Every one of these places was a couple billion bucks. Sure, we were insured, but who underwrites against something like the Attack? You can have all the insurance coverage you want – assuming it does not exclude terrorist action, which we discovered some policies did – but that means nothing if your insurance company and its re-insurers go bankrupt.

Like I said, what a nightmare.

The fuel shortages hit and rationing went into effect. That focused the federal government's mind pretty fast. The new president took all the heat for pushing through the federal backing for the rebuilding costs. Hell, he was leaving office in January and retiring, so let him be the guy bailing out big oil. The smart thing we did was creating common plans. In the past, all the refineries were bespoke, custom jobs, all different. We came up with one refinery plan that we could adapt to each site. That made stuff a lot simpler.

We had to go to Europe, Japan, and South Korea, to get some of the parts and piping fabricated. We did not want to use China. We also tried to buy American as much as we could as a way to jumpstart rebuilding manufacturing capability at the same time we rebuilt the refineries.

And then the President essentially told the bureaucracy to lay off and the climate nuts to shut the hell up. Part of the Infrastructure National Security Act was a cancellation of any and all legal and bureaucratic challenges to the rebuilding. No more holding it up because the Texas Hairless Swamp Mole might be offended. Get it built! And we did, astonishingly fast. One thing that helped was the tax incentives for getting up to speed quickly. Again, tax breaks for Big Oil? Only a guy who promised that this was his last political job could have pushed that through.

The Act also turned refineries into national security sites. Now we take security seriously. We even have anti-drone capability because we assessed that that could be a threat. We have the same security here as at nuclear power plants, and the terrorists left them alone because they were hard targets. So are we, now.

It was a miracle that we got up and running as fast as we did. Other refineries increased capacity to try to help, but we only really got back to normal after the first repaired and rebuilt facilities came online. We worked 24/7 to get back up. As a result, gas and diesel rationing for regular drivers only lasted a year. My only regret is that now the traffic is getting as bad as it was before the Attack.

29.

Chicago, Illinois

Professor Drew Dillingham was once that rarest of unicorns, an unrepentant conservative and advocate of the free market within elite academia. The administration and his fellow faculty at the University of Chicago tried to force him out after his research and publications repeatedly attacked and undermined leftist shibboleths. But he refused to budge, defiantly resisting by leveraging his tenure even as he argued that tenure was economically wasteful and ultimately counterproductive.

Called a "hypocrite" by his outraged opponents, he would shrug. "I played by their rules, thereby demonstrating the flaws of their paradigm. But also, screw them." His non-professorial language was not surprising. He grew up with a family that ran a chain of grocery stores in Minnesota, and by the time he was a senior in high school, the precocious teen had learned most of the aspects of operating that kind of challenging business. He started sweeping out backrooms at thirteen and was working beside his father during high school, seeing exactly how business worked.

"I went to college because I got a scholarship and assessed that taking four years to complete college would be better economically for me in the long run than sticking around the stores," he explains, adding, "Also, I liked beer and Notre Dame was kind of a party school."

I got famous for the Dillingham Postulate. It's actually a formula, but in layman's terms, and the way people usually put it, is that a business's proximity to government is inversely related to its efficiency in a theoretical free market, thereby requiring ever closer proximity to the government. What it really means is that the closer you are connected to the government, the worse your business will be as a pure business and the more you will have to glom on to the government to keep making money.

We saw that with the crony capitalist corporations over the last few decades – they got worse and worse as companies, to the point they could not function except in proximity to the government. Which the government liked because it could co-opt the corporations' power for its own purposes. Take, for example, how the government outsourced limitations on free speech it could not directly impose because of the First Amendment to social media companies.

No one in academia or government wanted to hear that. I became one of the most hated economists in America. I expected that. The University had many radicals. I tried to ignore the woke nonsense around me except when it was focused on me. I wish I could say I was shocked by the active participation of so many faculty and students. Look at it as an economist. It made economic sense for the kind of maladjusted, fringy characters who gravitated to radical leftism to do so. It was the best a lot of them could do socially – jocks and cheerleaders had better options. What was the cost to being radical in peacetime? None. But the upside – in social cachet, meaning, comradery – was huge. So, they were rational actors on that score, if on no other.

I was taken aback by the Attack. I did not see it coming, but then I did not know what to look for. National security issues are not my bailiwick. In light of the information the enemy had, however, it was rational to launch it. In retrospect, if America had reacted as they expected us to instead of how we did, they would have had an incredible return on investment. But they had bad information and it turned out to be a disastrous miscalculation.

The key problem of economics is information. When you have better information, you make better economic decisions. The problem for the American leftists is that they had bad information, and that manifested most clearly among the ones who took an active role in the Attack. They were being told that some sort of revolution was in the offing that was going to tear down the United States as we knew it. They were themselves going to form the cadre that would take power. They would not be held accountable for their actions. That was all bad information.

When the attacks happened on the first day, the campus was terrified. A distraught young woman came into my lecture and started shouting about mass shooters. I thought, for a second, that we had one at the University. It took me a moment to get from her that it was happening all over the country, but not on our campus even though there were obviously attacks in the city and places like nearby Evanston. I dismissed class and went back to my campus apartment.

It made sense for the terrorists not to attack the University – they wanted the help of the student radicals. They got it. That evening, as normal students had prayer vigils for the dead, the radicals tested the waters with demonstrations demanding no more Islamophobia, as if that was the issue, and blaming Israel. Nothing happened from the administration, and they soon got violent, damaging property and then beating up students at the vigils.

The administration still did not push back and some of them went even further with direct actions the next day. Their cost-benefit analysis was flawed – they lacked information on the costs of their acts.

I was the subject of one of these direct actions. A gang of radicals came to my office, because I had gone in even though the campus was closed, and told me I was to be held accountable for my "settler imperialism." I got stabbed in the gut and might have died if a couple cops had not run them off and gotten me to the crowded emergency room to be sewed up. That day and the next, the radicals swept through campus, killing or hurting Jewish and conservative students. They briefly took control of the campus. I was lucky to be in the hospital.

The police had to violently restore order. They were not in any mood for nonsense and when the radicals resisted the authorities hit back hard. These sheltered students who were used to being politely asked to behave when they acted out previously were now facing working-class police and military with zero patience for affluent brats after the horrors they had seen. And there was no kabuki arrest and release nonsense. These radicals were being detained under martial law rules. Because they had never had anyone in authority resist their whims, they incorrectly believed this would remain true after the Attack. Big mistake. They did not factor the chance of getting shot into their calculations. The killers, who often filmed and uploaded their crimes, should have.

Five days after the Attack began, I was recovering at home and watching the chaos after the violence was suppressed. The infrastructure strikes had been very effective. Big pieces of the Jenga tower that was the American economy were missing, and it was teetering and in danger of collapse. Something had to be done, and I assumed what would be done would be the dumbest possible thing because the government was involved.

You need to understand that the government's purpose is not to solve problems. It is to accumulate power and money for those operating its levers, and that means *perpetuating* problems. I assumed that whatever government-led response was coming would take us further down the road to socialism or just impoverished anarchy. Pessimism is a necessary attribute of any competent economist.

I confess that I was *slightly* heartened by the new president, who I had spoken to when some conservative members of Congress had invited me to a GOP Caucus retreat. Someone asked me what was the most important thing for Congress to do to make America prosperous, and I said, "Nothing." They laughed, but I was serious.

I guess the new president remembered me because some Air Force gentlemen showed up at my apartment and told me the President wanted to see me. I threw some clothes in a bag and they whooshed me to O'Hare, where the wreckage of a shot-down airliner was still smoking on the ground, and flew me to D.C. in an Air Force jet. This was while the ground-stop was still in effect, so it was serious.

The new president wanted me to be his secret advisor for the coming rebuild. It had to be secret, because I was polarizing and he was trying to keep things bipartisan. I looked around the Oval Office and saw bullet pockmarks in the window. "Sure," I said. I figured that, worst case, I would not be stabbed again. Of course, that was before I started dealing with the bureaucracy.

America was effectively frozen. Stay-home orders, martial law, the ground-stop. We did something like it in COVID with the lockdowns, and it was a disaster. A big problem was that the government enjoyed its COVID power and had no incentive to give it up. It instead tried to use borrowed money to defray the costs.

My initial advice boiled down to "Normality now." If things were perceived as going back to normal, things would go back to normal. The intel people said the actual fighting was done, except for a few random get-aways. I said to POTUS that the best thing to do would be to let people out of their houses and end martial law going forward, though he should keep the military commissions. They were fast and efficient and dragging out trials for months or years would be counter to our message of normality.

The bureaucrats *hated* that idea. They defaulted to accumulating more power. All these restrictions needed to stay for reasons and because – yada yada yada. The President, to his credit, saw it my way. The stay-home order was lifted, martial law canceled, and the aviation ground-stop stopped. People were free again.

But we had the fuel and food crises. Our supply chain infrastructure was a mess. It is a finely tuned machine and the terrorists had taken a sledgehammer to it. The bureaucrats, of course, were eager to step up and take charge of rebuilding what they had never built or operated before and did not understand. They could only make things worse. We had to let the market forces do it. We had to incentivize the supply chain to fix itself.

I told two stories to the President. The first was about the original colonists. They tried to build a socialist commune where everything was owned in common and centrally planned. They nearly starved. But, in desperation, they let people tend their own plots and sell what they grew. They prospered because people work most effectively when free to pursue their own self-interest.

Next, I told him about the Interstate 10 bridge that fell down in Los Angeles in the 1994 Earthquake. Experts estimated that it would take months to fix. The governor, a Republican, told a contractor it would get paid extra for every day the contractor completed work under the estimate. That bridge went up in record time.

We told the oil companies and the trucking companies and the food companies to get it done how they thought best. We pulled the bureaucrats off them, waived environmental rules, and spent some money where we needed. Mostly, we told them they would not get taxed on what they delivered during the emergency, creating a massive incentive to deliver the needed goods.

And we let them price gouge. Oh, the bitching about that! But price gouging is simply economic efficiency. Yeah, the first week a gallon of gas in Chicago was $15 bucks. Outrageous! But then everybody and his brother was sending gas to Chicago to get $15 a gallon, and suddenly there was no shortage. Because the supply increased, the price of gas...wait for it...declined. Supply and demand is a thing.

We were stuck rationing food and gas for a while. That was just political reality. We ended the food rationing quickly as the logistics folks figured out how to get food where it needed to be – for a price. Rationing lasted much longer for gas, though after a few months people just started ignoring the rationing because the supply was back up. Companies squeezed all the refining capacity they could out of the undamaged plants and found creative ways to repair and replace the damaged ones.

Of course, the assault on the power grid caused massive power outages across the country. Wrecked transformers had to be replaced, which was not easy because they take time to make and America did not make them anymore. Here, our size helped. We have *lots* of transformers, far too many to be all taken out. We were able to identify and cannibalize transformers to take and use to replace critical ones that were destroyed. Of course, the folks whose power went out when we took their transformers got pissed. We incentivized building new transformer plants here by essentially making them tax-free. America now makes transformers again.

Our plan was to let the people doing the things we needed done to pursue the almighty dollar, and it worked. The bureaucrats, if they had been given the control they wanted, would have screwed it up – we would still be rationing everything and living in the dark. A lot of people got mad at our reliance on the market instead of on Washington hacks.

I got outed as the guy behind the plan and I did some CNBC show to explain it. The host was outraged that food and trucking and gas and power companies were all making record profits. I pointed out it was because they were making record sales. Wasn't the goal to get the goods and services to the people? I thought she was going to stab me and finish what the radicals started.

There were a lot of challenges. The industrial base that made America an economic powerhouse during World War II and thereafter was largely gone. It had been outsourced to countries with lower wage costs and less concern about the environment. We needed to rebuild our industrial base. Yet, as an economist, outsourcing seemed to me to be the right answer – it was economically efficient.

But in Washington, I had to work with other people with other interests besides pure efficiency. That really expanded my view because there are priorities besides purely generating dollars. Making sure we were not vulnerable to another attack was a national security issue. I guess you could put a dollar value on that, but your valuation would be arbitrary. It is its own thing.

I became a bit less doctrinaire. I understood why we might not want to lean on China for our rebuild. I recognized that in some cases, tariffs supported vital interests. I got why we would need to guarantee some loans to the critical companies that were on the verge of failure. But my first inclination was always minimal governmental involvement, let the folks in the market make money and they will make the problem go away. And they largely did.

30.

Nampa, Idaho

Travis McKinley does not look like a vintner, though he owns a winery that specializes in Italian varietals in the Snake River Valley.

"This place was created by a disaster," he observed. "About 14,500 years ago, there was a giant lake in the basin where the Great Salt Lake is now called Lake Bonneville. It was huge and over time it eroded away the natural dams that held back the water. A 400-foot wave came down the path where the Snake River is now at seventy miles per hour. Re-carved the whole landscape. Disasters make us who we are. Natural and unnatural."

He offers the author a glass of his current vintage of cannonau, a Sardinian take on grenache. The vineyards are peaceful and quiet. His AR-15 rifle seems out of place in the calm.

"You gotta be prepared," he says, savoring a sip. "We weren't. Well, I was. But America wasn't."

It's weird how many people got into prepping because of zombies. Remember the zombie craze? It started with Max Brooks's *World War Z* book in the 2000s, and then there was that dumb *Walking Dead* show. I guess it started to make people think about what happens if all this falls down. I mean civilization.

Well, I knew. I saw it. It was 1992 and I was a TV writer in Hollywood. I wrote sit-coms. Made a good living, had a nice house. That's where I got my wine habit. And the residuals from *Wacky Neighbors* – it still kills on Hulu – actually defray the costs of my vineyard. A vineyard is a patch of dirt that you throw money into and get cirrhosis out of. That's a winemaker joke.

Anyway, I'm at the Culver City studio finishing up a script meeting one afternoon and somebody comes in and says we gotta see what's on TV. The Rodney King cops had been acquitted in Simi Valley, and there's this mob beating up a truck driver at Florence and Normandie, just a few miles south. Suddenly, one of them throws this brick into his head and starts cheering. No cops. What the hell?

We go back to our meeting – we were trying to sassy-up the female lead's gay friend – and it never occurs to us that it might spread and involve us. Well, it did. I leave the lot and there's smoke. There are people on the street and you can feel the mood. It's angry and scary. I had never been in anything like that before. I grew up in the *Brady Bunch* suburbs. I wasn't in the Army. The last fight I was in was when I got in a shoving match in third grade with Tommy Jansen over whether or not The Six Million Dollar Man could beat Rocky. Of course, I didn't have a gun. I had never shot one.

I saw plenty of chaos on the way home. Looting, fires. People running around. I was driving all over the place to get away from crowds. I still got surrounded by a mob and had to gun my engine to get away. Cops? Are you kidding? I saw squad cars rushing this way and that, but there was no authority on the street. The only people who looked like they were safe were the Koreans on the roofs with their rifles. Those boys were prepared.

I was not. I finally got home, locked myself in my house, and got out a golf club to brain anyone coming in. No one came that time, but I was done being a victim. Once things got under control, I replaced my nine-iron with a nine-millimeter. I have been a prepper ever since.

I learned about guns, of course. I learned to shoot, then to make my own ammo, then to gunsmith. I learned survival medicine – I am basically an EMT. I learned about food in an austere environment, and how to get safe water. There is this whole plethora of skills our pioneer ancestors knew, but we forgot. We outsourced them to other people, which is fine – when everything works. When it doesn't, then you have a problem.

We had some close calls in society – 9/11, the Wall Street meltdown, the BLM riots – but things never went quite to hell the same way as in the LA Riots. Not until the Attack.

Some people say us preppers wanted an Attack, or at least some kind of disaster. I get what they are saying. If you train for years to be a firefighter, you eventually want a chance to put out a fire, right? But how we felt is kind of immaterial. The people behind the Attack did not ask our permission. In fact, a lot of us were pretty damn opposed to the administration. I went from a pretty liberal guy to one who Genghis Khan would tell to dial it back a little – one of many reasons I drifted away from Hollywood and toward high-test grape juice.

We saw the problems because we were looking for them. You had an administration basically allowing crime and chaos on the streets if you happened to align with the administration politically. They hated us – as if our guns were the problem. The border was wide open. We watched the supply chain nearly collapse during COVID. The prepper community saw that our establishment just did not have the basic competence to keep it together. I went and doubled my food and ammo stocks at my bug-out location in the mountains north of the city. And nobody but me and my family knew about it.

I was between writing gigs when it happened. On August 27th, I was having these orange scrambled eggs I liked with bacon at Farm Shop in Brentwood when nine o'clock struck. I heard shooting, lots of it. Turns out a kill team was coming through town.

Time to get out of there. I had a black Ford Bronco, which looked fine in town but could take rough roads. And I had my Glock 19 in it. I had no concealed carry permit. LA made it a pain in the ass even after *Bruen*. My thought was better judged by twelve than carried by six.

I always had an exit route in mind anywhere I went. At the time, that sounded crazy to most folks. Even in a theater – Okay, there's the exit door down there and if things go off we move left then down and out. It was a habit I learned from the special ops guys and the cops I knew from the community. It became a habit. So, when I needed to drive away, I had a tentative plan and followed it. I avoided trouble that day. Like Kenny Rogers said, you gotta know when to walk away and know when to run.

Maybe I could have intervened and gone toward the gunshots, but there's a layer to preppers those outside do not really get. We're in it for ourselves, like the ant that worked all summer putting up food while the grasshopper played and then winter comes and the grasshopper is out of luck. I prep for me and my family. You can prep for you and your family, and I hope you do. But if you aren't prepared, that's a problem, and it's your problem.

I got home and talked with my wife, who was all in with the community and probably more hardcore than me, if that's possible. We discussed bugging out to the redoubt, but figured the situation would be under control that day. Still, there was a damn arsenal laid out on the kitchen table – and not golf clubs this time.

The second day starts with Vice President Numbskull's speech and we look at each other and thirty years of prepping was validated. There was nobody in control. And there was a stay-home order, though there were so many exceptions it was pretty much meaningless. If anyone asked, my fifty-year-old wife was in labor. We decided to call the kids – they were all grown up – and give them the codeword – "Rutabaga." That meant meet us at the redoubt. We did that just as nine a.m. rolled around.

We had bug-out boxes that fit in the truck with the stuff we needed to have for the trip. We loaded those, and we loaded our guns.

We got on the road at about 9:30 a.m. and we turn on the news station and they are reporting a new wave of attacks. What was weird is that they were not happening in public places. They were happening in residential areas – just after our genius government told everyone to stay home. And they were happening in LA. All over LA, in fact.

I felt like I was back in time thirty years. I thought about heading to Koreatown for some backup.

We're going through the streets and there are people out running around, not rioters but panicked regular folks. Then we saw the first body. Some guy was dead on the sidewalk and his dog was right there. He still had the leash in his hand.

Now I'm keeping my head on a swivel because bad guys are around. "Was that a gunshot?" my wife asks. I hear a bunch more. Yeah, those were gunshots.

More dead people, I am going fast, as fast as I can without running down panicking Los Angelenos. I'm looking at them, unarmed, terrified, and I remember that was me in the Riots. They thought civilization would protect them. Well, civilization teeters on the edge of a cliff and it only takes a little to push it off into chaos.

This was the chaos.

I go fast through a light – no one is paying attention to traffic lights, which is probably the best indicator of social chaos – and this Toyota truck is in front of us. I hit the brakes but we still collide. My truck had a front push bar, and it was fine. The Toyota was wasted. It was full of guys in black shirts with headbands and rifles.

We were driving with the windows down. Not only does it give you better situational awareness in an urban environment but if you shoot a gun in a closed-up car, you're deaf. It will blow out your eardrums. It's bad enough with the windows open.

We shot first. We just opened up with handguns. Bullets fired through a windshield outward deflect up, so you need to shoot low. We had learned that in training. We shot low. A couple of them got hit and the rest scrambled. Maybe the guys we shot died – we don't know. We got the hell out of there.

The stay-home order was in effect but no one bothered us. Like the cops were not busy enough, especially with those college jerks calling in false reports to 911. We're driving in violation of the law and with bullet holes in our windshield and the authorities thought nothing of it. Kind of tells you how much law and order there was.

We got to the redoubt. Within a few hours, my kids got there. One of their wives had lost a brother in Philadelphia and of course she could not go back there – no air travel. We hunkered down, assigned security duties and turned on the surveillance system. That night, as the attacks died down, I remember thinking something else was coming the next day.

There was. We noticed when the power flickered. The generators kicked right in when the power grid went down. We also had satellite internet – thanks Elon! – but pretty soon that went down. They shut it off. And if the internet was down, that meant the supply chain was down.

This was it, what we had been waiting for. Except we had months of food and lots of ammo.

Our big worry was people coming out of the city looking for food. A city only has a few days' supply because it's more efficient to continually restock than keep a lot on hand. But no one was going to be stocking for a while.

The old redoubt – we sold it when we moved up here to Idaho and now we have another – was back at the end of a long road. There is a gate where it connects with the public road, but except for a big "KEEP OUT" sign there is no real indication from the road about what is back there. The problem for us was GPS. The global positioning system is a bunch of geosynchronous satellites that each send electronic signals and your phone or car or whatever can read them and determine your exact position on Earth to a few meters. Our problem was that some of the devices would show maps of the ground, real maps, not just roads, even without the internet. That meant people could see the house inside our redoubt.

We had to rotate security, two folks at a time, down at the gate, with ARs because people from the city would start trying to get through. Now, our local cops were overwhelmed. We were on our own. And we are looking out for our own.

Here's the thing about prepping. I lay in my food, and that will hold me for a while, and I have plans to grow more over time, but I have an alternative food source. It's people who are not prepared. I got the guns and the training. That means I got anything I want. Sound hard? It is. Welcome to Darwintown, population only the strongest, because it is survival of the fittest.

I remember one family in a minivan came by and the dad gets out and tells us his kids are hungry. I tell him politely to move on. He starts swearing at me, screaming about his kids. Hey, if he cared so much about his kids, why didn't he have food laid up? Why didn't he have a gun? I can't care more about his family than he does, or more than I do about mine.

I told him he needed to leave. Pretty clearly. He was smart enough to go. It's a big national forest and there are lots of places to dig holes.

I guess that sounds hard, but maybe if we were all a little harder it might not have gone down the way things did. If more people had been harder on illegal aliens and enforcing the law. If more people had been harder on those jihadi freaks. If more people had done what I did and gone out and bought guns and ammunition and trained up for the worst-case scenario.

But we have to understand that the Attack was not the worst-case scenario. It was bad, but we recovered. But what if Iran had nuked us back? What if China decides to in the future? How about it sends us another COVID, only worse? How about if there are zombies?

Disasters made our world, literally here in the Snake Valley. There will be another. I have new redoubt. It has more fuel, more food, more guns and ammo. Got a helluva a wine cellar too. I'm ready. My family and I are prepared. And while I like you, and while you seem like a good guy, I'm still not telling you where my redoubt is. But if you figure it out, and if all hell breaks loose again, don't come knocking.

31.

Nashville, Tennessee

Ted Sorenson lives in a quiet residential area of the city. It is affluent, but not rich. There are decent restaurants, both chain and non-chain. The schools are good, not terrible as in the inner city. The neighborhood could be anywhere in America.

Have you seen *Office Space*? That old movie with that guy and Jennifer Aniston and she has flair on her waitress uniform? Pretty funny movie.

My job is not exactly like the one the guy in that had. I am in middle management in a big corporation that does boring stuff. I won't mention the name but you know it. We don't have a TPS report, but we have other things that are pretty much the same. I am not an exciting guy. I'm not some special forces vet. I don't jump out of airplanes. I did not marry a model. I'm just a guy, a regular American guy. I had two kids, a dog, and a Dodge Caravan minivan. I like beers and grilling and video games. I hate politics, but I love football – go Titans! I am normal and boring.

I like being normal and boring. And I never thought my world would be anything else. I didn't ask for it to be. There are people who are supposed to keep things boring, you know? That's their job. They are supposed to keep us safe and they didn't and guys like me paid for it.

The first day, there were a lot of attacks at business parks. Our security was a gal making minimum wage in a blue blazer who sat at the entrance and said, "Good morning." She couldn't stop a pack of Cub Scouts, much less a bunch of terrorists with machine guns.

They did not attack my office complex, but they could have. They hurt a lot of people at other places around the country, some other big companies. I guess attacking ours would not make the same splash as attacking a kids' movie company or a tech company or a car company.

The first day we all stopped working to follow the news on our phones. I went home early – we closed the office – and I guess everyone else got out early too because the roads were packed. I sat in my car listening to the news station and I felt sick. I was scared too. There were all these people stuck in traffic. The terrorists were still in the city and we were sitting ducks. I never thought of myself like that. I knew about wars in faraway places but that was, well, far away. It was never *here*. But now it was.

I figured the government would take care of it. That's what I paid taxes for, right? I thought the president was too old, but the other guy he was running against was too loud. My wife and her friends hated him. I was probably not even going to vote. Like I said, I hate politics. Like I said, I'm a normal guy.

I knew about the Palestinian stuff and the stuff about Israel. I thought the Israelis were pretty hard on the Palestinians. I saw all these pictures of dead kids and you just wanted to make it all stop. I knew they had attacked Israel first, but I was still upset by it. I tried not to pay attention to it.

I never expected that to happen here, though. I thought the trouble was only over there. I mean, we elect politicians to make sure these things don't happen but they let it. We expect them to take care of us and they left us on our own.

I got home and Majorie was really upset. She had already gotten the kids home from school. They were attacking schools and hurting kids. They were uploading it on the internet. I did not do the Twitter or X or whatever it was, or the Tik Tok, though the kids did. They came to me really upset about what they were seeing. The videos showed terrorists shooting people, cutting them, burning them. There were rapes. I was wondering how the government was letting this get on the internet. I made my kids stop looking at their screens. They got mad at me, so I let them after they promised no to look at bad stuff.

We watched the network news. It was one of those Special Reports, but all day and into the night. The terrorists were attacking everywhere. It was scary. We did not know what to do. Our neighborhood was always pretty safe, maybe some kids break into a car or something, but nothing bad. I thought our police would handle it. That's their job, right? It's not my job to do that. I did not have any guns – Marjorie would never let me. She thought no one should have guns and I agreed because regular people can't be expected to be safe with them.

Marjorie said the terrorists must have gotten the guns through the gun show loophole and said that this was more blood on the NRA's hands. She was saying it was probably insurrectionists, and she was surprised when we found out it was crazy Muslims. But after a while, she was talking about how she hoped they all got killed. That was not like her. I guess what they did really got her mad. I just wanted it to be over.

Our neighbors came by. They were pretty upset too. Bill hunts, and Marjorie said maybe we should all go to his place because he would protect us since he had guns. Everyone laughed, but I felt kind of disrespected by that. I locked our front door and shut the curtains that night, but I thought it was mostly over except for some terrorists who were still loose.

Marjorie had the kids come down to watch the President. She said it would be historic. But it was not the President. It was the Vice President. She was doing the speech because the president was sick or something. We watched with the kids and, well, you know what happened. It was like watching someone do a presentation at a meeting and you know they are in way over their heads. I mean, even the kids were asking if she was okay. But at least she said it was over and I wanted to believe that.

Work was shut down and so were the schools. There was a stay-home order. The kids went upstairs to go play video games. I watched the news. Things were a lot calmer, but there were a lot of dead people. I was in grade school when 9/11 happened and it felt kind of like that. It's weird when something happens to the country that everyone experiences, like when JFK got shot or the first space shuttle blew up. Those were before I was born.

Then there are reports about new attacks, but these were against people's houses and apartments. There was footage coming over the air, and the neighborhoods where there were attacks looked like ours. Some were even in Nashville, but not so close.

Marjorie was freaking out, asking what we should do. I don't know. I'm not a cop or a green beret. She said I should go borrow a gun from Bill, but that was crazy. I told her that I didn't know how guns worked, and that I was not even sure I could shoot someone. She got mad and we just watched TV without talking.

Some of the men in our subdivision blocked off the streets with their cars. Others were walking around with their own guns. I put on my shoes and went out with them and we waited on the street in case something happened. Nothing did. The second day passed and the terrorists never came to our neighborhood. They did kill a lot of people in one about ten miles away. I think we got lucky.

That night we watched the television news again. It looked like it was over, finally. I locked the door and closed the curtains again and went to bed.

The third morning we got up and the Attack finally looked over. They were catching the last killers and ending the last hostage situations. The number of dead people was so high. We could not believe it. We did not know anyone personally ourselves who was involved, but my sister had a friend whose brother-in-law was murdered. That really brings it home.

Right at eleven, because we were Central Time, the power flickers and goes out. I said something about how this was a bad time for a blackout and Marjorie told me it was the terrorists. She guessed right.

The AC was out without power and it was August, so that was miserable. We tried to keep the fridge closed to keep the cold in. At night, we had to use birthday candles. I did not have any lanterns or things like that, and the one flashlight we had had dead batteries.

The power came on and off for days as the power company tried to fix the damage. When it came on, we found the internet was out. Later, it started coming back intermittently.

By then, there was martial law. Army trucks with soldiers were patrolling. The neighborhood watch was still up for a few days before we really believed the killing part was done.

But we were not back to normal. Not even close. What happened in Iran was scary – I was worried the whole world would get caught up in World War III. I think it was kind of an overreaction. Maybe we should have asked the U.N. to get involved.

The stay-home order got lifted after a few days and the new president said we were going back to normal. The internet was coming back and I got an email saying to come back to work. I did not get paid for the time off, and that was a problem. Money was tight. I wanted to go to work, but I needed gas.

Except there was no gas. I drove around all day, wasting gas looking for gas. Where there was some, there was a mile-long line and then the tanks would be empty before you got to a pump. How would I get to work?

And how would we get food? Putting aside that I was not getting paid, there was very little food to get. People panicked when there were reports the supply chain was going down – remember having to hunt for toilet paper and then stocking up when you found it during COVID? They rushed the stores and cleaned out the shelves. All there was left were store-brand lima beans and packages of liver in the meat case.

We started eating stuff in the freezer before it thawed and went bad. Freezer-burned ground beef is no good no matter how well-done you make it.

We did not have any supplies laid in, like food. I mean, we had the old forgotten stuff at the back of the pantry. We used it up. Before rationing started and you could get something, we were to the point where she was making kidney bean pasta. The kids were complaining and I probably was too. It wasn't her fault, but she did the shopping and food stuff. It was probably unfair and I felt bad about it. After all, it was not her fault. The government should have been looking out for us.

We stood in line half a day to get our ration cards for food and fuel, and then the rest of the day she stood in line at the Kroger while I sat in the car all afternoon and waited at the Union 76. I got tired of listening to the news and looked around the dial until this guy with an accent came on. His name was Doctor Something, and he basically said we needed to destroy the terrorists. He kept talking about how we needed to hunt down the terrorists and I just felt like we ought to move on.

I finally started going into work, and schools started up again. The grade school now had a parents' patrol with dads and some moms with those AR-15s that Marjorie and I used to think ought to be banned acting as guards. Of course, I couldn't do it myself since I did not have any guns.

Marjorie spent all her time getting us food. That meant standing in lines for hours. She and the other moms would text around whenever they found a place with something in stock and everyone would show up and buy as much as their ration cards allowed. If someone stumbled on something in stock, they always bought the max and then traded with other moms who had extras of something else. They might trade soap for some oranges. All she talked about was her food wrangling.

And it was expensive! I could not believe the government let people charge so much for stuff. It should have banned price gouging. Milk at $20 a carton? But after a while you would see prices drop. It still really ticked me off.

This went on for a while. Life was not normal. Restaurants closed and you couldn't just order something for delivery to your door. There was so much standing in lines. I mean, don't get me wrong – the killing was bad. Horrible. But for most people, life was much harder for months afterwards. It was like COVID in a way, except you did not get to sit home watching *Downton Abbey* and ordering DoorDash Thai food.

Things got back to normal slowly, but in some ways they haven't at all. Marjorie and I grew apart. I think she resented me not being able to get enough the food and stuff, but how could I? And I think she resented me for not having a gun, which was bull because she didn't believe in guns either.

I live in a nice apartment near her and the kids. I see them a lot, mostly on weekends. After we divorced, she married a guy who had been a soldier. That's good though, you know, because if there's trouble he can be there to protect the kids.

32.

Linn, Missouri

The Paw Pals Rescue Farm lies among the rolling, wooded hills of central Missouri just a few miles southeast of Jefferson City. It is spare but clean, with several work buildings, dozens of kennels, and plenty of grassland for its furry residents to use. And, in fact, the fields are full of dogs of all breeds running, playing, and barking at the stranger who just drove up the winding dirt drive.

Most of the kennels are empty now, with many of their original occupants adopted out or passing on from causes natural or unnatural. Jackson Breed, the 46-year-old proprietor, currently has 62 "orphans," as he refers to them, down from the high of 253 during the first year after the Attack.

Jackson is lean and tan, wearing work clothes and a Las Vegas Raiders ballcap. He has a .45 pistol in a holster on his hip. A golden retriever follows him – Rex has the run of the farm. He also has three legs, though that does not seem to slow him down.

With all the thousands of people they murdered, it's easy to forget the dogs. And the cats – there are some facilities for them as well. It's not disrespectful to the dead to think of the dogs too, especially when you hear some of their stories. I think we owe it to their owners.

On the second day, when the terrorists targeted Americans in their homes, many of those victims had dogs. About 40% of American households had a dog. So, when the bastards switched from big public attacks to going house to house in the suburbs just killing people, for every couple of murdered families there was a dog or two.

And with everything going on, with terrorists still on the loose and dead and injured and homeless humans to care for, that's a lot of dogs orphaned. The pounds and shelters, even when they were opened back up, could not handle the numbers. Tens of thousands of dogs wandering the streets, and the authorities could not spare any effort on them. So people took them in. Your neighbors got machine-gunned, but you somehow got passed by, and pretty soon their little dachshund is out on the street crying. You take it in, feed it, but that's not a permanent solution.

And a lot of the dogs were injured. You need to understand that the terrorists hated our dogs as much as our people. They bought into the dogs as dirty and evil teachings they learned back home. I'm no expert on Islam, and some people have told me it's not that clear-cut. Whatever. I'm not a mullah. I just know what the terrorists did.

Part of their plan was to target dogs, pet dogs. That was one of the things they trained the killers to do. They understood how much Americans loved animals. That's why they went after them specifically. It was a message. I'm not sure if they were happy about the message we sent back, though.

They would often shoot the animals – you've seen the videos of that big lab coming up, wagging his tail, and the bastards blasting him and laughing. Or they would hurt them. Wound them with guns, cut them. There were families that would be upstairs, dad with his pistol, and downstairs they would be breaking the dog's legs and letting it cry to get the father to throw out his weapon and give up. And sometimes it worked. Many times it did.

Americans could just not come to grips with that kind of evil. The children, the rapes – it was almost abstract it was so horrible, but somehow when the terrorists hurt animals, it humanized the evil. And it drove Americans into a frenzy. I heard about a citizen militia team in one Texas town that caught up with one terrorist who still had the axe he used on a litter of puppies. They used it on him. And the war crimes prosecutors would always, always, make sure to show the military commission any GoPro footage of the accused hurting an animal.

I later adopted a terrier to one of the Judge Advocate General prosecutors. He'd seen what these animals did to animals – I guess I'm insulting animals, right? – and he specifically wanted an orphan doggie. Now, technically, the war crime is not murdering or torturing an animal. The crime is actually called "Destruction of property in violation of the law of war." So, your beagle is "property," but that's enough for a slug in the back of their head from an American military war crime commission. He told me he never got anything but a death sentence when there was evidence of hurting an animal.

The JAG captain was a mess. He had to look at the evidence, day after day, and he sent a lot of terrorists on the short walk to bullet city. He said he wanted a dog because he had to be reminded that there is something good in this world. I know what he means.

I had a used car dealership in Las Vegas pretty close to the Strip. It was not a small, cheesy place but a nice one. High-end models. I was expanding. I was doing fine. I bought a lot of BMWs and Porsches and such very cheap from gamblers trying to get back into the casinos to recoup their losses. You'd be surprised at the rockers and movie stars who would roll in eager to take 50 cents on the dollar for their ride as long as it was in cash right then and there. That's why I was at the dealership at 9 a.m. Pacific on a Tuesday – to take advantage of the guys who had a rough night.

I was sifting through DMV paperwork when I heard the bomb go off at the Mirage, and then the others too. I had no idea what was happening. I just knew it was bad. There was shooting. Cops were rolling Code 3, lights and sirens, but in all directions. That first day, we didn't understand that they were everywhere, all over the country, hitting public targets. We just watched the TV in the office – that's when I realized they had truck-bombed the casinos – and I finally closed up and told everyone to go home.

Of course, that's just what they wanted us to do, what they planned for. We didn't know. We didn't understand what the Attack was then.

So I go home, a nice house in Summerlin, and I get my .45 out. Jesse was my second wife, and our kid was Tom. He was three. I had him when I was 38. I want to tell you they were my everything, but there was the dealership too. I stayed home overnight, watching the coverage, but the cash I kept on hand in the dealership safe just gnawed at me. It was a lot of money, but I would not have missed it. I just kept thinking not so much that the terrorists might take it, but that one of my employees – I employed a few gamblers – might get the idea to use the Attack as cover to get flush with my cash.

So, the morning of the second day, I tell Jesse I'm going in to clean out the safe. She doesn't want me to go. I tell her it's Summerlin, nothing is going to happen here, and anyway the news is reporting that the attacks stopped overnight and the government is busy just clearing up all the terrorists still on the run.

I took my .45. There was the shelter-in-place order, but I figured if a cop pulled me over, I probably knew him, and if I didn't I could either talk my way out of a problem or buy my way out. I pass all sorts of things – wreaked cars, dead bodies. The casinos are surrounded by the Army and they are starting recovery operations. You see it on the tube and it's one thing. You see it in real life and it's another. I thought I was going to puke, and I thought about going home, but I didn't.

I get to the dealership and it's fine – not a scratch on a single car. I feel better. I go in with a duffel, pop the safe and shovel in a couple hundred grand in stacks. Then I'm getting into the car, and I start hearing sirens again. I head west on Charleston Boulevard toward home and there's a cruiser behind me, lights and siren.

Shit, I think, and pull over. He rips past me. I start up again and then there are more, hauling ass west. I start feeling sick again. I start driving faster.

I come up to a bunch of Las Vegas Sheriff's deputies on Charleston, all with big guns and tactical gear, their cruisers parked with lights flashing. It's right outside a gated community but the gate is open. There's a cop on the ground and he's clearly hurt because they are working on him. And there's a guy in black lying on the ground, obviously hurt, arms waving. He looks like one of them from the television.

A deputy walks over, yells something down at him, and just starts pumping bullets into the guy. And the other deputies don't seem to care.

I drive past. There are people running around, civilians, panicked.

I call home. It picks up and goes dead.

I'm tearing through the streets now, swerving around people, trying to get home.

I get a ping on the phone. A message from Jesse.

I'm relieved. I look at it. It's a video.

Why would she send me a video?

I'm still driving even as I am playing it. It's shaky – someone's filming her. There's blood on her face. Little Tom is in her arms crying. She cries out, "Jackson!" and then there's a noise and they fall out of frame. The video cuts off.

I'm frantic now. I'm five or ten minutes away.

I get home and there are people on my street, walking around like in a daze. Some are bloody. It looks like a zombie movie.

No cops, no terrorists.

I pull into my driveway and run into the house.

I found what so many people found. Maybe it was better, since it was quick. They used a lot of bullets.

I walk outside, one of the zombies now. I'm totally helpless. What can I do? I don't even notice that the rest of the neighborhood, those that are alive, are in my same boat.

I sit on the curb. I'm numb. I hear shooting in the distance – the Sheriffs intercepted the killers and none got away. But I was trying to process it all. Tears are rolling down my face. I don't know if I even realized it.

I felt something lick my face.

It's Rex here.

He was the Goldmans's dog. I don't know how he survived. The family didn't, and the terrorists were especially bad because they saw the mezuzah on the door. The terrorists did not know what that was. The little Antifa bastards with them told them, "Hey, these people are Jewish." I don't want to talk about what the bastards did.

Rex was their dog. I was never a dog guy, but Rex was a big, floppy puppy, and I'd pet him. I turn to look at him and he's licking my face, trying to help *me*. Then I realize his front paw is smashed. Bone is poking out of it. But he's licking *me*, helping me.

We were all each other had left, and I was not going to lose him. I got him in the car and took him to the vet hospital I used to pass on the way to work. It was open. There were a couple guys with big guns out front. The doctor, who had his own gun, later told me he would be damned if he wasn't going to do his part, and, after what he had seen, woe to any terrorists that came along.

Rex's foot had to come off. The doc said it looked like someone had hit it with a sledgehammer. But you see, today, he's good to go with three legs. At least someone knew him. There have been a lot of orphan doggies who were not only injured but whose names we never found out. This one guy from Michigan adopted a tripod terrier and named him "Bob Crane."

There was nothing I could do after that for Rex right then – I paid the vet cash from my duffel – and got ready to leave. I had told the story to the vet, and he told me I should come back in three days to pick him up. It never occurred to me that I would keep him, but Rex needed me and I think I knew I needed him.

I went home and after the Army mortuary affairs team gently and respectfully took Jesse and Tom – those poor kids probably enlisted for college money and ended up with that job – I realized I was alone. I guess I could have sat and cried, but instead I got off my ass and cried. I started going through the neighborhood picking up strays. I got a dozen dogs, took them to my house, and blew off the stay-at-home order again to go get them some food.

Things started returning to normal, but I was never going back to the dealership. The economy tanked bad, and I sold it for about 50 cents on the dollar – serves me right. But it was enough money to do what I knew I needed to do. I picked up Rex and loaded up my dogs and headed to an old breeder farm out in Missouri I found on the internet. That became Paw Pals.

I took in every dog I got offered and used everything I knew about marketing to find them real homes. We had a lot of senior dogs who were confused and scared. Many were physically hurt. All of them missed their families. They would howl sometimes. It made you cry. I just wanted to find them someone to love them again.

And they deserved it. They never hurt anyone. They just loved us, and those bastards used that to hurt them and us.

But there were some great stories out there of dogs protecting their families. There was Rambo, the corgi who attacked the ankle of a terrorist coming up to a house where a mom had three kids. The bastards shot the doggie, but Rambo gave the mom time to grab a Glock and blow the bastard away in her front yard.

Eddie was an Australian shepherd who actually herded a couple toddlers away from some bastards who had broken into their house.

And there was Gibson, a Belgian Malinois named after the dog hero of some novel series, who literally ripped the throats out of two terrorists who threatened his family – *after* they shot him. He lived, they didn't.

Good doggies.

But mine are orphans. They can't tell their stories or what they have been through. Sometimes you could see it in their injuries. That duffel of money and more went fast. I have enough to keep this running as long as we have dogs who need us. A lot of the ones still here are older or badly injured, so that may not be that long.

Hey, you seem a little down. Maybe you'd like a friend to take home?

AFTERMATH

33.

Louisiana

For a guest to get inside the compound requires passing through three gates, with ID checks and a biometric scan. To get even that far, you have already passed a Secret Service background check. The protection detail is supported by a company of Army light infantry soldiers who rotate in for a month at a time to patrol the perimeter and the surrounding swamps. They are in full battle gear, and the author's escort assures him that their weapons are loaded and that the use of deadly force against intruders is not merely authorized but directed.

The main house and the several outbuildings are not particularly impressive. The United States government owns them all. When their occupant needed a place to live, the fact that he was famously unwealthy created a conundrum for the federal government. He could not afford to buy the kind of palatial and easily defended estate that other past officeholders could. Because of the security nightmare of him and his family living in the kind of mid-scale suburban house that he could actually buy, the Congress bought this place and will allow the family to remain there permanently.

If the isolation bothers him, he does not show it. If the death threats and attempts around the world to prosecute him for his alleged crimes bother him, he does not show that either. In person, he is the same pleasant and humble man whose direct and honest personality allowed him to assume his remarkable tenure while his country convulsed in horror at the greatest terrorist attack it, or perhaps any country, had ever suffered.

My presidency was the second shortest, probably. The consensus is that the shortest was that of William Henry Harrison, who served 31 days before going to the Lord, and the second shortest was James Garfield, who had served six months, fifteen days, when he finally died after being shot 79 days earlier by Charles J. Guiteau. Now, there are those who say that a couple of vice presidents were acting president for a few hours here and there while the real president was under anesthesia. But I think I am probably the second shortest, at 144 days.

I am certainly the unlikeliest.

I was really a backbencher when my party had a minor coup that threw out the previous speaker. Candidates were designated, but failed to meet the threshold in vote after vote. Someone suggested me, and for some reason I felt I should at least throw my hat in the ring. Was it divine inspiration? I don't know. I have an ego like everyone else. I do know I got a lot of grief because I am a Christian first. Much of the media treated me like some kind of nut because I believe in God. Somehow, I won.

Suddenly, I was in the spotlight, and I thought the best way to serve was to step out of it. I felt there were plenty of people who could go make the case on *Hannity* or with Hugh Hewitt or wherever. I felt my job was to serve quietly, to get things done. Oh, I am a conservative, but I tried to treat the other side with respect, to treat them how I wanted to be treated – you know, the Golden Rule. I never lied to them – my word was solid. I just felt that was the way to be, and I think that trust I built helped make what happened possible.

Most of Congress was out campaigning that week, even the two-thirds of the Senate not up that year. The terrorists who attacked the Capitol only managed to wound one local member who was there to meet some school kids from her district for a tour. My family and I were not in Washington on the 27th either, thank the Lord. They sent hit teams to the homes of the Big Four, the Speaker of the House, the House minority leader, and the Senate majority and minority leaders. It was a miracle that not one of us was home. Sadly, they proceeded to slaughter many of our neighbors before they were stopped.

I was camping with my family out at Pine Grove Furnace State Park in Western Pennsylvania on a one-afternoon break from my election appearances in that swing state. We had some security, but they stayed back and let the family be. Sometime after noon, our Capital Police detail suddenly came into the campsite carrying their rifles and I knew something was up. But I had no idea at all that it was as bad as it was. I was privy to a lot of intelligence as a result of my position, but the intelligence community was totally blindsided. We were stunned by the Attack, though in retrospect we should not have been.

They packed us up and we headed back to DC, not sure exactly where we would go that was safe. I had a secure phone and I was trying to call the White House and I could not get through. I knew they had been under actual attack earlier, and I worried that maybe the terrorists had taken the place. The scale of it all was staggering. But it turns out that the President's handlers were simply stonewalling, hoping his injuries were not as serious as they turned out to be.

I got back to Washington later that afternoon and I called the House back into session, not realizing that between the airspace ground stop and the federal stay-home order, well over half of the Congress was not going to be able to come back quickly. My home having been attacked, I had the Capitol Police secure my family and I met with the few congressional folks who were already back in the District. Even the guys from the other side of the aisle had not spoken to the President, and the Vice President was apparently missing in action too.

This was terrible, The American people needed to see their president was in control. So did foreign governments, friendly and unfriendly. But there was nothing. Total stonewall. I did not find out he had broken his hip and was in emergency surgery in the White House clinic until nearly 6:00 p.m., when the Secretary of Defense called me.

I asked him who did this to us. He obfuscated. I asked if America's armed forces were on alert. He did not give me a straight answer. I asked him what his orders from the commander-in-chief were, and he told me, "I don't know."

I remember that evening hearing the first White House statement read on television – I still had not talked to anyone at the White House – and I was horrified. It was not the President from the Oval Office but the press secretary, whose voice cracked as she read the short press release: "We have suffered a terrible tragedy and now, together, America grieves. But be assured that there will be accountability and that the crisis is over."

Of course, the Attack had only just begun.

At about eight o'clock on the 27th, the Big Four from Congress, with a few other trustworthy members who had trickled back into the District, the SecDef, the Secretaries of State, Homeland Security, and others, all met at Fort Belvoir because that was the most defensible location. Of course, the Pentagon had been attacked that day with massive casualties. It was a whole building full of soldiers, and almost no one had a gun. Tragic.

At the meeting, the White House staffers told us for the first time about the President's condition, focusing on his broken hip. They played up that he was recovering well from surgery, but one of my members, a former Special Ops doctor, pulled me in and told me that there was no way a man his age in his already deteriorated condition could serve. The mental strain was too much.

I said what everyone else was thinking, and brought up the 25th Amendment. Everyone demurred, saying we were not ready for that step, but I think the real reason was they were even more scared of having the fully functional veep in charge than the unconscious old man.

We agreed to hold off on taking any action on removing the President under the 25th Amendment, but we all agreed that someone would have to go to the Vice President and get her to go on camera with a statement to the nation.

Well, you know how that went. It was a disaster. The speech was set for 10:00 a.m. Eastern the next morning. It took hours to get her to come out of her safe room – literally – and do it, and when she did, she read this speech her own people wrote and, well, the whole country was terrified that she was apparently in charge. And not two hours after she promised us the crisis was over, they hit us again.

After that, she completely became non-responsive. No one – not us, not the military, not Homeland Security – could get a decision out of the White House as we came under attack again.

And worst of all, not only did Iran take credit for the Attack, but our intel assets and Israel's were telling us that the mullahs had seen our non-response and decided to crash out and test a nuke. Once they did, they would be untouchable. We had not weeks but days.

The group of us at Belvoir began issuing orders based on consensus. It was not our right to do it, but someone had to. By the afternoon of the 28th, it was clear that the country was nearing an existential crisis. We had had two days of massacres, tens of thousands murdered in horrible ways and had it been uploaded all over the internet. Our transportation infrastructure was frozen, and our enemies overseas were circling. China and Russia were on high alert; we only brought our military alert to DEFCON 2, enemy attack imminent, *after* they did.

We needed to act. And that's when we made the deal. The 25th Amendment required all sorts of complex actions that were impractical under the circumstances. And we would have had to do it twice.

As Speaker of the House, I was next in the line of succession under the Presidential Succession Act of 1947, and I volunteered to take the job because there was no one else. I freely admit that I made a deal. We had a presidential election in six weeks, and the Democrat candidate was in a hospital bed unable to continue, so they wanted a law to let them switch him out on the ballot. Okay, I would get my people to back it and I would sign it. Also, I would pardon him and his low-life son – but also the Republican candidate. I agreed not to appoint any Supreme Court member to replace the two the terrorists murdered. That would be for the next president.

I would serve until the winner of the election was sworn in on January 20th, and then retire from public life. They did not want someone with the gravitas of an ex-president to contend with down the road, and I agreed to that too. The understanding was that I would be a pure caretaker, but that I would take the actions necessary to respond to this disaster. Just as importantly, I would take the blame.

Our ad hoc group agreed – now the issue was getting the President and Vice President to resign.

I have heard all the rumors and stories about how the President thought he was actually signing a proclamation for "National Ice Cream Cone Day." Let me just say that I am informed that after the First Lady was called away upstairs to the family quarters, he was presented with the papers in his sickbed and, to his great credit, he put country first and signed the letter of resignation. I attribute his later claims that he was somehow tricked or misled to his age, injuries, and infirmities.

The Vice President actually signed her resignation first, so there was no question of succession. Her staff tried to bar access to her by the Democrats who were coming to her to explain what was going to happen; the Secret Service removed the flunkies, and the Democrats had a face-to-face discussion with her. You have to admit, they have party discipline. I do not know what they told her that convinced her to resign, but she signed those papers. I pardoned her too.

Justice Clarence Thomas had been on the road in his RV on vacation and he headed back when the disaster happened. A huge team of federal marshals brought him to Belvoir, where he swore me in as president on August 29th just as the third day of the Attack began.

I am a committed Christian, and I prayed about this new responsibility. I believe Jesus bears the weight of our sins. As I embarked on the task, I realized that I was going to have to take on the weight of what our country had to do in response to the Attack. I had already given up my career, which was especially hard since, unlike almost everyone else in government, I had no money to speak of. But I was also going to give up more.

I was the one who had to make the hard, nearly impossible calls necessary in the wake of the Attack. I declared martial law. I directed summary court-martials to punish the killers and terrorists. I sealed the borders, deported millions in just months, and crushed the cartels with our troops. I sent out the Reaper Teams. And I ordered Operation Beirut, the tactical nuclear strikes on Iran's nuclear program and terrorist infrastructure.

It is me that our enemies have at the top of their kill list, which means that me and my family have to live here like this forever. I am the one who leftist prosecutors in Third World countries purport to indict for crimes against humanity – though my successors have been good about that. When some Brazilian judge/prosecutor indicted me, the United States cut off diplomatic relations, ordered every Brazilian out of the country in 48 hours, banned all Brazilian imports, and locked them out of the international monetary system. The next day, the judge and the indictment went away.

And I am the one the leftists hate here at home. There still are not many, but in the last couple years they have poked their heads up, testing the waters to see if they can get away with attacking the United States for its response to the atrocities. As memories fade, it will become fashionable to despise me among the so-called intellectuals and academics. In 1945, everyone knew someone who was bobbing around on a ship off Japan waiting to go ashore and probably die. Nobody complained about Hiroshima or Nagasaki until some time had passed and memories had faded. That's my fate too. People will forget what we endured and remember only what we did in response.

I am here forever. Of course, I gave up politics. That's okay, but I cannot participate in life much because I am a target — I don't want to speak somewhere or attend some event and be the reason terrorists attack it. A Little League game? Nope. A movie or a McDonald's drive-thru? Never again.

But it was important that someone did the job, and that someone made the hard calls and accepted the consequences of them. In a way, I gave up my life when I took on the presidency. I'm not saying that to paint myself as a hero. I think of myself as a patriot, but more importantly, as a Christian. I think of John 15:13 often: "Greater love hath no man than this, that a man lay down his life for his friends."

34.

Lawrence, Kansas

He looks fit and able for a 64-year-old man, with short gray hair and a full agenda of speaking and other engagements all over the country. He is extremely busy, and rigorously maintains the very tight schedule he has observed since retiring from the United States Army as one of its most celebrated warfighters since General "Stormin' Norman" Schwarzkopf.

General John "Black Jack" Cutworth is still accompanied by a full personal security detachment of military police everywhere he goes. And he still carries his own M17 pistol, a tan SIG Sauer P320 variant issued to him as a general officer. He became famous for carrying it, and he was allowed to buy it when he retired.

But it was more than just image enhancement for a notably aggressive cavalry officer who commanded Operation Border Justice, the invasion of northern Mexico designed to eliminate the drug cartels. "We're still putting them down," he says. "And there's a possibility they might try to take me down. I don't intend to go down without a fight."

I was just about to rotate out of command of III Armored Corps at what was then called Fort Cavazos, but was just recently changed back to Fort Hood when all the woke name changes were undone. I was in line for my fourth star and going into command at SOUTHCOM. Southern Command oversees all U.S. military forces in Central and South America, and in the Caribbean too. But not Mexico – that was in NORTHCOM, and that became an issue.

For us, the Attack started when they hit the main gate, which is in Killeen. There were twelve of them and they shot up the gate guards and some folks in their vehicles, but my guys got a couple of them there. The survivors drove inside with their vehicles and were heading to the PX and the dependent day care center and such, and were basically shooting everyone they saw.

Now, years ago some major went off and killed a dozen or so of our folks. He was a jihadi, and he knew all our weapons were locked away. Of course, Army regs said no concealed carry on base, so ironically a military base is a giant, vulnerable gun-free zone.

I did not have the authority to overrule that, but I did have the authority to require that every company charge of quarters and runner be armed, and have bullets and the ability to open their arms rooms in an emergency. And I ordered them to have emergency ammo on hand in each arms room – the Army mindset was to lock it all up at a central location because it was easier to count.

So, basically, we had a couple hundred armed soldiers in addition to MPs and civilian security, plus the ability to get to our rifles. And our guys did, fast, once we blasted out the mass shooter alert. The terrorists killed fifty-two folks before we got them, but they never got into a school or a hospital or a store.

My guys and gals closed with them and took them down. That's the aggressive mentality I had in III Corps. Our people did not waver. We did our jobs, though many of us had personally lost so much in the Attack. We knew we had a mission and we focused on that. Focus on the mission got us through our grief.

With martial law in effect, I was deploying whole divisions out to U.S. cities. NORTHCOM was my higher command, and it was overwhelmed because it was not really a tactical command. I had a lot of authority. The post was about empty, but everyone still here was in tactical uniform with a loaded weapon. My troops performed magnificently. They killed 93 terrorists and captured 18. As a court-martial convening authority, my folks ran the commissions and I approved death sentences for all 18, plus a bunch of others that other folks caught. That includes some American radicals who joined in. I tried to be fair. Obviously, I had my own biases, but I put them aside because it was my duty to. I looked at the evidence, like the footage they uploaded. But when I did, the decision was easy.

After a few days, I got called to Washington and flew out – as a corps commander, I had a plane. I did not know I was going to see the new president.

Apparently, I did a good job during the Attack and he wanted to meet me. I went to the Pentagon and got briefed first on the intel we had gathered so far. A lot is still classified, but I can say some of it was info we got from pretty forceful interrogations of captured terrorists. We got a lot from law enforcement too, including from the DEA. It was clear that the cartels in Mexico had facilitated the insertion of the vast majority of the terrorists and their weapons. It was also clear that the border needed to be closed, but that was impossible with the cartels intact.

The President said he was giving Mexico an ultimatum that he expected would be ignored. We were going in. As SOUTHCOM commander, I would be in charge of all forces going into Mexico. To make that happen, they switched Mexico from NORTHCOM to SOUTHCOM's AOR – area of responsibility – because NORTHCOM had enough to do in CONUS, which is Army-speak for the continental United States.

Before I left, he asked me how I was doing personally. Was I able to do the job? I told him I was, and he shook my hand and told me the country was behind me and my troops. He never once failed to have my back, no matter how hard the media and the politicians cried.

I went back to the Pentagon to see what we had already. There are CONOP – contingency operation – plans for everywhere. There is one for Antarctica! There are whole rooms of majors and colonels updating them. To my surprise, the ones we had for northern Mexico were actually pretty good.

My objective was to destroy the cartels, to root them out, kill or capture their key members, and reestablish law and order along the border. We anticipated some resistance from the Mexican military but that would not stop us. The cartels themselves were primarily light infantry mounted in civilian vehicles. They could operate in platoon strength at best. We anticipated they would revert, along with Mexican patriots angry that we had invaded, to an insurgency model. Our goal was therefore to knock them out rapidly and reestablish control before a guerilla movement could develop, then turn the whole thing back over to the Mexicans and go home once we took out the trash.

I had fifteen divisions, including mobilized Guard units. We would seize the big border cities first – Tijuana, Nogales, Ciudad Juárez, Nuevo Laredo, and Matamoros – with smaller incursions in between. We would start with airstrikes on key cartel facilities and individuals. And our special operations teams would capture or kill high-value targets. Mostly kill.

We started moving forces even as we planned. The Mexican government was in a panic. We told it to pull back its units, to stay out of our way. They could not do that – too humiliating. So they went on the target list.

You hear a lot about asymmetrical warfare, but usually in the context of a weaker force attacking a stronger one. The Attack was asymmetrical warfare. But so was our assault on Mexico. Our strength was firepower. Their weakness was that neither the official army nor the *sicarios* were organized or trained to conduct modern, high-intensity combat. I told the President that I intended to unleash hell, to break them hard and fast as the best way to end it quickly and avoid something like the Iraq insurgency, which I fought as a company-grade officer. He told me to win. Just win.

The cartels threatened to bring their retaliation to American soil, but if anything, that made us more determined. We issued a warning to Mexican civilians to leave the border areas. About a million did, and we actually held off three extra days to let them clear out.

When D-Day arrived, they did not know what hit them. We had developed a detailed target list of people and places. Over half were within 15 miles of the border. I could service those targets with 155mm artillery. My aircraft could do five to ten sorties a day because the airfields were only minutes from the targets. That made it easy for me. And then there were rockets, AH-64 Apache gunships, cruise missiles, planes, and drones that could hit deeper into the country. Hell, I had ships off Tijuana and Matamoros providing naval gunfire.

We had the fires plan down to the gnat's ass. The target list was a list of things to destroy, hundreds of them, developed by our intelligence/targeting cell, and there was a time schedule attached. You just go down it, service every target with a bomb or shells, and then hit the next one.

The first night, we blew the living snot out of Mexican military and cartel targets, over 2000 of them. I did not hold back. If there was a big drug processing facility, it was not just one shell. It was a battalion fire mission, dozens of shells. Remember shock and awe? Well, that is a thing. Believe me, my guys had no hesitation. A lot of us had suffered, though we put that aside for the moment to do our jobs.

When it started, I was in San Diego with I Corps, which was a joint Army-Marine formation that included the 1st Marine Division from Camp Pendleton, the 7th Infantry Division from Fort Lewis, and the mobilized 40th Infantry Division of the California Army National Guard. There are artillery pieces firing, rocket launchers, air strikes, and destroyers out in the Pacific lighting up targets. It looked like a Bosch painting.

We were watching the explosions erupt all in and around Tijuana, and the reporters were standing there, mouths open, just stunned. They had no idea what American forces could do. That was where that viral clip came from, where that scrawny guy with the goatee for the *Los Angeles Times* asked me, "General, why are you using all this firepower on Mexico?" and I answered, "Because I can."

Our operators were already inside the country – many of our targets had come from our recon missions. The cartels had actually caught two SEALs and unwisely murdered them and uploaded it to try to scare us. Big mistake. They made it personal. A lot of cartel guys woke up dead that night, and for many nights to come.

The invasion met only sporadic resistance. They would try to use light weapons against tanks, firing off bursts of 7.62mm rounds and getting a volley of 120mm cannon shells in return. We hunted them relentlessly through the houses and buildings. There were civilian casualties – there always are. We warned people to leave, but the cartel fighters tried to hide behind the ones who didn't. We were not like the Israelis. We did not recognize human shields. It was hard, but if you give in you incentivize them to keep doing it, and there is no moral or legal obligation under the law of war to allow illegal combatants like the *sicarios* to set the parameters of the fight. Note that we treated Mexican military as prisoners of war for purposes of the Geneva Convention; we did not try them like we did the cartel thugs, and they were eventually repatriated home.

We expected an insurgency and there was one. Mexicans are a proud and patriotic people who felt they were being invaded unjustly. I was not there to convince them but to defeat them, yet those guys I respected. If we captured a guerilla who was only fighting, not committing any atrocities, and not connected to the cartels, I directed he be treated as a POW instead of an illegal combatant. I am not going to shoot a prisoner for fighting for his country.

We are able to keep the insurgency to a low-level and focus on the task of rebuilding. We reactivated the Mexican government and ordered the government workers to report for work. We tried to clean out the corrupt ones, but I was in Iraq and Afghanistan – we Americans are never going to make a Third World country into a democratic copy of some town in New Hampshire. Our mission was not to "fix" Mexico. It was to make sure Mexico could no longer be a base from which our enemies killed Americans.

We did that. And then we got the hell out. But we still have our capture or kill list of cartel bums, and we will never stop hunting them down. These gentlemen with me are in case they attempt to return the favor.

We assessed that the cartels were 96% defeated. But that 4% will metastasize. Our analysts think that in a decade there will be a substantial cartel presence along the border again, though the wall and the U.S. Border Force are making their job exponentially harder.

That is the nature of borders. Someone is always going to try to cross it without asking. We just want to make sure they don't ever again smuggle in a bunch of terrorists and weapons to kill our families. Never again.

The author considers asking the general about his wife Rebecca, who was shot to death by a terrorist kill team at a mall in Dallas during the first hour of the Attack, but the old soldier is already departing for his next event. It occurs to the author that if the general immerses himself in his work, perhaps he is able to avoid thinking about what he lost. At least for a while.

35.

Whiteman Air Force Base, Missouri

Security is tight at the home of the base's squadron of new B-21 Raider bombers, probably the last manned bomber aircraft the United States Air Force will ever operate. You enter the base through a large gate under the watchful eyes of at least a dozen combat-equipped security police and their guns. Near the entrance you can see why. There is the memorial to the 123 dead the base suffered on the third day, when a 42-terrorist kill team attacked the base in order to destroy as many of America's 20 B-2 Spirit bombers, then stationed only at Whiteman AFB, as possible.

They managed to destroy four on the ground, the rest having been deployed. The USAF subsequently distributed the 97 B-21s, which were rushed into service 18 months after the Attack, at multiple bases, including Ellsworth Air Force Base in South Dakota and Dyess Air Force Base in Texas. That a reinforced platoon of guerillas could take out 20% of America's air leg of the nuclear triad using AK-47s and rocket-propelled grenades was intolerable and could never be allowed to be repeated.

Colonel David Gray commands the bomb wing that flies the nuclear-capable bombers. He came up in bombers, flying the B-1, then the B-2, and now the Raider. A USAF Academy graduate, his original callsign was "Butch."

I was not at Whiteman when the Attack happened. I was on TDY, temporary duty. We had done an overflight on Sunday at a Rams football game in Los Angeles and instead of doing it as a round-trip mission and heading home, we landed at Edwards north of LA to do some training off the West Coast over the next few days. Our support crew had flown in with us. The Spirit, like the Raider, is a stealth bomber, and it takes a lot of TLC. At the time, it was certainly the most complex atmospheric aircraft to ever fly, but as expensive and high maintenance as it was, the Spirit could get in and out of places nothing else could.

My plane was the *Spirit of Ohio*, which was built in 1992. It was still a damn potent bomber. My co-pilot Major Jerry Gordon and I were actually out over the Pacific the morning of August 27th doing training with the Navy when it all began. I can tell you the exercise was China-focused. About 0946 hours – I remember looking at the digital clock – we get this call telling us that U.S. airspace is closed.

"Closed?" Jerry says. "What the hell does that mean?"

But I knew it was ugly. I was a smack at the Zoo – a freshman at the Air Force Academy, for you civilians – when 9/11 happened. They shut down the whole United States to aviation that day, and now it was happening again. We were not monitoring the civilian channels. If we had been, we would have already known what was going on, especially at Los Angeles International, which was not that far from us.

I answered and asked for information and orders. Traffic control told us there was a "national emergency," a "terrorist event," and directed that we loiter off the coast no closer to land than 50 miles. We had plenty of fuel, so that was no issue, but why loiter and not come back to Edwards?

Turns out the terrorists had been using MANPADS – Man-Portable Air Defense Systems, essentially one-man ground-to-air missiles – to shoot down airliners at different airports, including LAX. They could not hit us at the altitudes we flew, nor could they even get a lock on us because of our stealth and countermeasures, but no one knew what was happening and a B-2 is a helluva an asset, so better to keep it far away.

We flew circles for three hours before getting word to come back to Edwards. But we got tasked to fly back over the LA basin on the way, at 20,000 feet. That was above the max ceiling for the Russian-made SA-29 Gizmos they were using, so even if they could have locked on us, we were still good to go. Us flying overhead in an empty sky was a message to the people that we were in charge. Of course, that wasn't true at all.

I remember looking down at Los Angeles International and seeing two burning wrecks on the runways, and two more at the gates. Apparently, they had used the SA-29s to bring down two aircraft as they were landing and rocket-propelled grenades on the loaded jumbo jets as they were waiting to take off. They were full of passengers and jet fuel. Even from eight miles up it was horrible.

Anyway, we got to Edwards but we did not go home. The 509th Bomb Wing was surging. Six were going to Guam. We were ordered to Diego Garcia with seven other Spirits and me as the commander of the element. We started prepping for that. The rest of the airframes were all in maintenance at Whitman or the depot. I knew it was serious because we were surging everything.

We were still at Edwards on the third day, getting ready to deploy. The funny thing is that we never felt personally threatened. We were on an Air Force base, right? Most of us had family back at Whiteman and we were just happy because we thought they were safe. It never occurred to us that they were not.

On the third day, when everyone thought things were dying down, the terrorists fought through the Whiteman front gate and hit the housing area first. The base was on Force Protection Condition Charlie, terrorist attack likely, but there were only so many SPs. The security police responded in force to the housing area where the terrorists were killing anyone they saw. The other half of the terrorists fought through and headed to the airfield. They got to the remaining aircraft and started pumping RPGs into them. Eventually, the SPs killed or captured the attackers, but they did a lot of damage to people and to planes.

Of course, we heard about that at Edwards and all of us wanted to fly right home. We all lost friends, but several of us had family injured or killed. Jerry's 15-year-old daughter got shot in the back. He requested emergency leave. Denied. I know he was pissed at me, and I also know he knew I was right. You cannot just replace B-2 crew. So we flew to Diego Garcia, in the middle of the Indian Ocean with his daughter in critical condition. She still cannot walk.

At Diego Garcia, we waited and spent time reviewing attack plans on Iran. We focused on conventional strikes, but it was SOP – standard operating procedure – to review the nuclear target package too. It never occurred to us we might have to execute Operation Beirut. It was only later that we learned the name for the coordinated nuclear attack plan on Iran was chosen because of the 1983 Beirut Marine barracks bombing that the mullahs were was behind.

There was the drama in Washington and we got a new president. He got the intelligence that showed Iran was behind it all, and that Iran knew we knew and was doing its last dash to finish a nuke. I can say, because it is now public information, that they were planning to detonate a test on September 13th. On the 5th, we get told we are going in, eight of us, to wipe out their nuclear program, their missile program, and the Iranian Revolutionary Guard Corps high command, and that we are dropping hot rocks.

Talk about a sphincter tightener.

It had to be bombers doing it. The nuke and missile factories, and the IRGC command center, were all in bunkers deep underground. We carried B63-11 deep-penetrating gravity bombs that would dig in and detonate, crushing underground facilities with the shock wave. The submarine and land-based missiles could not dig, and besides, if we launched those the Russians and Chi-Coms might think we are attacking them.

I do not know how the air crews would react if we had not just had over a hundred thousand fellow Americans murdered, but there was nothing but focus and professionalism in the 509th as we got ready. We traced our lineage to the 509th Composite Bomb Group, the special B-29 unit that dropped the A-bombs on Hiroshima and Nagasaki. We would get it done, no hesitation.

Diego Garcia is this pleasant tropical island out in the middle of the Indian Ocean. All the natives got shipped away years ago. It belongs to the Brits, but we use it too. Apparently, the new president called the prime minister and told him what was going to happen. The British did not object. They helpfully cut off the internet comms from the island so there could be no leaks.

We were supposed to go on the 10th, but weather was bad – high winds that would carry fallout further than necessary. We got the go order on September 11th, an irony not lost on any of us.

We got in our aircraft after making our final checks. I looked at the B63-11 hanging in the bomb bay and it was surreal. We were actually going to do this. It was not only retribution but a strategic necessity. If we did not do it, the Iranians would have the bomb. Colonel Paul Tibbets did not hesitate in 1945, and neither did I when my time came.

As we pulled out, the entire ground crew lined up to see us off. Sergeant Coolridge was allowed to give us the final salute, which he did tearfully. I returned it. His whole family was shot dead in their base apartment.

It was several hours north over the Indian Ocean at 40,000 feet. The sun was just going down – we did not want to hit them too late. This was no attack on an empty aspirin factory. We wanted the targets as full of enemy as possible, though it would still be in the evening because we needed to transit the country in the dark. We flew in radio silence, and Jerry and I were silent too, lost in our thoughts. Mine were entirely about the mission. I was intent on doing it right.

We would cross the coast just after sunset, each aircraft synchronized so we would hit our targets nearly simultaneously at 8:25 p.m. local time. The plan was that a coordinated cyberstrike and electronic warfare operation – which I cannot discuss in detail even today – would happen as the first aircraft approached the border. That was ours, since our target was the deepest inside – our target was on the north side of the country, so we had to fly over the length of it at about 630 knots and 40,000 feet.

The power was out across the country when we entered Iranian airspace. We could see a few lights, cars, and generator-supported lights, but it was mostly black. The air defense system was up intermittently. We read them scanning the skies, but we were invisible to radar. We could not send signals, but we could receive them. The SATCOM system informed us that the Iranian air defense grid was essentially blinded by whatever computer and electronic magic was going on. Rumor has it our Israeli friends were active on the ground adding fuel to the enemy's confusion.

It was the Mossad that identified the target originally, though American intel confirmed it. The IRGC was not dumb. It understood that someday someone would come for an accounting of its legacy of murder and terror. The killing of Qasem Soleimani by the Trump administration had been a warning, and they had dug a deep command and control bunker in the mountains near the town of Gorshan about 250 miles east of Tehran.

The Mossad secretly pilfered the plans from the construction company – which, of course, was owned by the brother of some general. It was several hundred feet deep in a mountain, with luxury accommodations for the entire IGRC senior command to live and work in for an extended period. They were pretty comfortable with it, according to the detailed target package our intel folks had prepared on it. They correctly believed that no conventional bomb could reach them as they hid. And they went into hiding the day before the Attack. The rumor is that they planned to come out the day after Iran declared itself a nuclear power, and therefore effectively immune from attack.

As we approached, we went into strike mode. Jerry and I ran through our checklists as we drew closer. We checked the bomb – which itself is a very complex machine – and it was a "GO." I entered the target solution in the attack computer and sat back. There was no dramatic pushing of a button or the like. The bay doors swung open and the bomb dropped out, then the doors shut again and we peeled off immediately on a new heading.

The opening of the doors and the appearance of the bomb in the sky broke the stealth mode for a moment. Suddenly, the Iranian air defense system was active again, looking for the source of the blip it had detected for just a few seconds. But the blip was headed due north and we were now heading northwest toward the nearby Caspian Sea.

We detected a launch of a ground-to-air missile, but it was heading away from us. The attack computer was counting down to the strike. We did not say anything. We were too busy flying away.

The attack computer's countdown rolled down to zero and ... nothing. You see movies like *Fail-Safe* or *Dr. Strangelove*, and you expect this massive flash and shaking, but there was nothing that we could see. The warhead detonated deep underground, so the dirt absorbed the flash. The B63-11 is a "dial-a-nuke." You can set it for various detonation strengths. Publicly, the range is something like 10 kilotons – thousand tons of TNT – to 300KT. Hiroshima, for comparison, was about 15KT. The strength setting at Gorshan is still classified, but I can tell you it was probably on the low end in order to dampen the fallout from the ground burst.

But even on the low end, it was enough to do the job. The scientists tell me that the shock wave was so powerful that it crushed the bunker so hard and fast that the air in the tunnels exploded and flash-fried everyone inside, like that homemade submersible that imploded near the *Titanic*. It was so quick that it is likely that they never knew what hit them, unless you believe a rumor I heard that about thirty seconds before impact our cyber folks put a message on all their monitors that read, in Farsi, "We just dropped an H-bomb on you" and had a little thirty-second countdown clock. Like I said, I don't know if that is true. I just hope it is.

The aircraft all hit their targets within the same sixty-second window. Obviously, it worked in more ways than one. The mullahs never got a nuke, and the people of Iran rebelled – this time with us supplying weapons and enforcing a no-fly zone. All the targets were at remote sites, and all targeted the regime. We were not attacking the people, and after they overthrew the mullahs, Iran and America began building a new relationship.

We flew out over the Caspian Sea, over a bunch of countries that had no idea we were there, and refueled over the Mediterranean and went home to Whiteman. It was a helluva a flight, but we did not want any other country to have to explain why it allowed the planes that just conducted the first nuclear attack in nearly 80 years to land on their territory.

It was a huge deal. A lot of people, even at home, were outraged. Like after the October 7th Hamas attacks, the original atrocity got forgotten by some people who focused on the retribution. But America was not in the mood to be lectured about restraint.

I remember the new president being asked by some *New York Times* reporter how he felt having ordered the use of nuclear weapons, and he responded, "I feel like justice has been done, and that the rest of the world now understands what happens if they kill Americans."

That's how I feel, too. My conscience is clear. This was no city. This was a purely military target full of the bastards who murdered my friends and countrymen. Whether it was a conventional bomb or a bullet or a club or a B63-11 kind of makes no difference to me. Just as long as they're dead. That's how I feel.

The only thing I regret is that after the strike, the guys in the unit changed my callsign to "Oppenheimer."

36.

Fort Lauderdale, Florida

Terry Bonfilio looks like a beach bum, and he sort of is one. He is blonde, 40-ish, with a deep tan, wearing a green and red Hawaiian shirt, cargo shorts, and flip-flops. He is not bulky, but he is clearly muscular. There are no tattoos on his arms, in contrast to many of his contemporaries, and his hair is short but not quite regulation. He teaches scuba and water sports at a high-end beach club that faces the Atlantic.

Bonfilio sips a Heineken, having acquired a taste for it in Europe. As he talks, he greets passing club members by name. He is popular with his clients, but also the media, as he is the only Reaper Team member to go on the record to date.

Of course, the United States government still denies the existence of the Reapers and will not comment on him or his activities. But people inside the U.S. government will, strictly off the record, confirm that *Chief Petty Officer Bonfilio was part of the American program to hunt down and kill foreigners (and, allegedly, some expatriate Americans) on foreign soil who were significantly involved in the Attack.* There is some speculation that the U.S. actually wants him talking, to send a message about what happens to those who help murder Americans.

For his part, Bonfilio apparently believes that he has earned some enemies. His tan cargo shorts betray the outline of a SIG Sauer P320 Compact .45 pistol.

I grew up surfing in Torrance, California. I was at the tail end of the era when kids still went outside and actually did things instead of staying inside watching screens. I was very physical, but not very good in school. I was good at languages, though. I picked up Spanish and, for laughs, took German at South Torrance High. Ended up fluent.

When I graduated was about the time when you started to actually need a good GPA and SAT to get into college. I did not even bother applying. I decided to go into the Navy, because I thought the Navy SEALs seemed cool based on the movies and all the publicity about the war – 9/11 happened when I was in middle school.

I applied for BUDS, the Basic Underwater Demolition School, and got in. I ate it up – the cold, the tired, all good. I was cool. I just did what they told me, graduated, then went through more training and got on a team. It was hard, but I got through.

I did Iraq, I did Afghanistan. Gnarly shit. Ugly stuff. I'm from sunny SoCal, so a lot of what I saw was really alien to me. I did not get it, the hate and the corruption and how people treated each other. But I did my job, moved up the ladder. Then the wars wound down and we stopped deploying all the time.

I liked deploying. I wasn't married. No kids. The guys who had families went through hell, but for me it was – I don't want it to sound wrong – fun. There's a feeling you get in the middle of a mission that's like nothing else. That's what I did it for, really, I mean besides my country and buddies and that stuff. My only regret was that I was not on the team that took out Bin Laden. I later joined those guys, though.

When the Attack happened, I'm at Coronado on the BUDs faculty, and we're just wearing out this new class. By then, most of the guys joining are total trident chasers. They want to be

SEALs not because of the mission, but because SEALs are badass. Not saying that's not a factor, but you have to get the guys in for the wrong reason out. So we had them up all night, and then ran them three miles in sand, then did some boat carries. It's about oh-nine thirty and we've got them in the surf freezing, doing flutter kicks, and the schoolhouse master chief petty officer rolls up. I'm an E-8 and in charge, so I go to see him and find out what's up.

We called him Shrimpy because he was a short aquatic creature. Well, only I called him that, because we were pals and I dragged his ass out of the line of fire when some ISIS asshole popped him in the thigh in Syria. Shrimpy was tight – he's got arterial bleeding and he still shoots that asswipe. But I see him and he looks like I ran over his beagle.

"Terry, it's on here, in America," he says. "Worst case."

"What?" I have no idea what he's saying.

"Massive attack, everywhere. Freaking here, and everywhere else. Shooters in the Gaslamp, at the colleges. Drop the students, load-out, rack-up, and be ready to move. We're fighting today."

Not two hours later I'm at UC San Diego in a freaking firefight with terrorists in the Tioga Hall dorm at Muir College. Animals. They killed everyone. They didn't care. I cleared a room with a Palestinian flag on the door and the kid inside had a dozen bullet holes in him.

I remember having to keep the San Diego cops from executing the two we captured alive. Had to explain that the tangos would be better alive and talking. One of them spoke good English. He said something about my mom and how he would never talk. I went back into Iraq mode, wheeled around, and shot out his kneecap. Now that bitch would not shut up. And good thing I did. After he talked, we raided his higher's apartment in Mira Mesa and tagged him out before he could organize the second day's attacks. Saved a lot of families in the suburbs by putting him down.

Of course, with martial law and everything, school was out. We were the QRF, the quick reaction force, for the military in San Deigo during martial law. Then the cartel war started and that was a whole different thing than we were used to. A JAG lawyer came in to explain the new rules of engagement and said, "They killed over a hundred thousand American civilians. You kill them all." And we did.

Not long after, I volunteered – well, actually I was volun-told – to join a Reaper Team. The wanted me mostly because I had no tatts. Tatts made you distinctive. They needed generic people, people who did not stand out. That sucked for a lot of guys who wanted the mission. Most of the guys had ink, sleeves and stuff, but I did not like it. I thought that it looked painful, and I had enough pain already, plus it was going to look like hell when I was fifty.

Without tatts, I clean up nice. The Bonfilio side is northern Italian, almost Swiss. My mom was a Lindstrom, Swedish. I got assigned to a European team, and speaking *Deutsche* helped.

Our mission was simple. Anyone with a hand in the Attack needed to die. Some guys could not handle that. They went away fast. I could. I figured that this was that game and if you chose to play, don't hate the game. Did I mention I watched all five seasons of *The Wire* on deployment?

A Reaper Team was about ten folks, though it varied. A commander, two logistics, two intel and ops, one comms, one computer, and three muscle. Everyone could do surveillance, or even security, but we tried to leave the trigger pulling to the muscle. The muscle was usually ex- or active SEALs, Delta, Marine Recon, Rangers, but occasionally others. Not all the teams were even military. We had civilians who got a sheep dip of cover stories and sixty-day wonder training. Some rose to the occasion, others sucked.

We were northern Europe, mostly white with blue eyes – we looked like a Mitt Romney family reunion. But we also had a couple folks of Arab extraction because the assholes would hide out in local immigrant communities. Of course, some of them did not bother hiding. The leftist Norwegian government made a big deal of providing sanctuary to wrongly accused victims of American persecution. The bastards lived out in the open. So, we got to know Oslo well.

Our first job was a Palestinian spokesman who had gone on BBC the first night of the Attack to praise the brave warriors of Allah. Intel said he was helping with coordinating the propaganda piece, which was key to the Attack. Obviously, reoccupied Gaza was not going to have him back, and no Arab country was dumb enough to let his ass in, so he went to the Norwegians and their feminist prime minister personally approved him based on his fear of American persecution.

Well, she was right about that.

This guy was a Class-A douche. He raped at least one local girl within a week, which the government covered up by telling the poor girl that if she told anyone she would be helping create Islamophobia and that she should suck it up.

We thought for sure they would have eyes on him, but no, no one was watching him. So *we* watched him and got his daily battle rhythm down. For a devout Muslim, he sure loved vodka. He had this nice apartment and every night would walk about three hundred meters to this little bar in the Grünerløkka, which is kind of Oslo's Silverlake, in LA terms. Very artsy.

We made our plan. I carried a suppressed Wilson Combat CQB – Wilson had given the government a bunch of them. Pity we had to dump them after each hit. It was important to use .45 because only Americans really used that caliber. It was telling the world that "America killed this piece of crap" without actually saying it.

One of our guys had him leaving his place and followed. We knew the route. There was a place on his route that that was dark, and that we made darker by popping out the streetlight with a silenced .22.

He's trucking along, smiling, like he's King Turd of Shit Mountain. I step out of the alley in front of him, weapon in hand,

and he stops and starts begging in Arabic. I knew enough Arabic to know begging. I also know what happened to those kids in Tioga Hall.

I put two in his chest and one in his forehead. Then we executed our out and we were gone from Norway in two hours.

We did targets all over northern Europe. If you had anything to do with the Attack, no matter how remote, your ass was forfeit. I think one guy on the team had a problem with it. He went away. I didn't. I saw what they did to those college kids. You ever see a girl raped to death? I have. It was ISIS-level shit, and they filmed it. They were *proud* of it. So did I hesitate? No. I shot them all, and I am *proud* of it.

There was killing going on all over the place. Everyone knew it was Americans, but after our popping couple hot rocks on the Iranians, no one was in the mood to cross Uncle Sam. We were not playing.

Once, some *polizei* in Heidelberg swarmed us as we were tracking a money guy for the Iranians. Our commander, a former Special Forces colonel, took the lead cop aside and said, in perfect German, which I understood, "If we're still in custody in five minutes, the next team is going to your house."

I don't know if he meant it or not, but neither did the kraut cop. What was clear was that we were not playing. They let us go. And three days later, I shot that terrorist banker and dumped his carcass into the Neckar River.

There was not a lot of controversy about the Reaper Teams killing foreigners, at least in America. But there was a little about us doing Americans. I think it was less about citizenship than the fact that most of the expatriate targets were rich kids radicalized in college who managed to get overseas one step ahead of a military commission death sentence. They would go on local media talking about how America was a fascist state and whining that they could not go home. Nothing about the victims, just them.

There was a pretty girl from Yale who had headed an Antifa outfit that ended up killing a bunch of folks in Washington, DC. She got out and off to Denmark. We tracked her there.

The girl was the subject of a slobbering profile in *Rolling Stone* – "Hunted By Her Own Country" – where she was the victim. There was not a word about the victims of the group she organized in the 2000-word toe-suck of an article.

She was speaking at a club, and we decided to make the hit public. We got a very tight out organized first. Me and my buddy went into the club as she took the stage, speaking English, talking about how America deserved the righteous retribution of the Attack. We just walked down the center aisle and stopped in front of and below her. She looked down at us and said, "What do you want?"

We drew and unloaded. The place went nuts, but not in our direction. She's lying on the stage, gasping with a couple sucking chest wounds. I was frankly surprised she was still alive.

I looked her in the eye and said, "America sends her regards" and shot her in the face. We watched all of *Game of Thrones* too.

Later, I decided to go public even though our combat record is sealed for fifty years, or so I was told. I think America needs to know what we did. Several Reaper Teams got hit themselves. We paid a price. But the important thing is that those bastards did too.

Our motto was, "America remembers." And we did.

37.

New York, New York

The second-floor walk-up's walls are covered with framed posters, placards, and photos, as well as some eclectic pieces of art and a diploma. The owner of this Soho flat is famous – or infamous, depending on your perspective – but she clearly did not choose the path of fortune to go with her fame. The posters all announce protests and marches from the seventies up until the present, while the placards demand justice for various peoples and demand that the U.S. get out of wherever. The photos are of living and dead – mostly dead – icons of the left. There she is with Castro, and Arafat, and Obama. In another one, she raises fists with Rashida Tlaib and Ilhan Omar in happier times, before they were expelled from Congress.

The art is mostly works sent to her by her clients, painted or sculpted in prison art studios.

Her diploma from Harvard Law hangs on the wall too – she was a legacy, her father having graduated from there as well. He made himself similarly famous/infamous defending communists, terrorists, and the like from the McCarthy days through the eighties.

Inessa Jacinda Merchant is in her seventies now, but she still crackles with the restless energy of a true believer in a failed ideology. After the Attack, progressive politics went from the vanguard to fighting a rear-guard action. She still advocates for *her passion, but about personal matters she is guarded. For example, she denies knowing her father's mind when he named her "Inessa," shrugging when asked if it was in honor of Lenin's revolutionary lover Inessa Fyodorovna Armand, and she quickly changes the subject to her clients.*

The overreaction to the events of that August was perhaps the greatest injustice ever perpetrated by the United States of America, and that is saying something. In the future, this nation will be deeply ashamed not only of its inexcusable atrocities overseas, but by its total abandonment of any pretense of justice here.

I understand the anger that regular people felt. They suffered greatly for the crimes of our ruling class. But if they had understood the anger that oppressed people around the world felt, none of it would have happened. It was inevitable. I am not attempting to justify it, just to explain it.

I represented the people the government hated. I used the law to try to protect them, to the extent I could in a system that was utterly unjust and built upon a system of ingrained racism, sexism, Islamophobia, homophobia, and capitalism. I represented what you might call "criminals," but who I call "victims." People stripped of dignity and a future, condemned to oppression – society labeled them as evil, but I would ask jurors what choice these prisoners really had. Did they steal? What was the alternative? Did they lash out? Can they truly be blamed? The organized violence not just of the police but of the capitalist system the cops protect dwarfs whatever actions some frustrated and justifiably angry young man might take in a moment of crisis.

I represented political prisoners and so-called terrorists too, even before the events of August. If you were a Muslim, if you were trying to resist the climate murder of the planet, if you fought racism in the streets, you received that label. But America was born of terrorists. What do you think the so-called Founding

Fathers were? No different, except they had slaves. And if you want to talk about terrorists, let's talk about the children murdered by American bombs and drones.

For doing this, I was hated. The Department of Justice tried to disqualify me, and they accused me of passing messages from my clients in custody to the outside. They tried to gag me. I fought all that. And sometimes I won, even with the deck so massively stacked against me.

When the Attack happened, I was here in my flat working. I had cut back some, but I still had a few clients and a trial coming up in September. It was a man unjustly persecuted because he dared to stand up for the right to follow his heart as the leader of the New England Man-Boy Love Association.

I heard shooting and bombs. People outside my window were in a panic. I flipped on the television. The coverage was supposed to make me want vengeance, but I wanted to know why these people felt it necessary to take these kinds of direct actions. And from the beginning, I feared that their message would be lost beneath the superficial violence of the actions, and that this would simply be an excuse for more Islamophobia.

And events proved me correct. When martial law was declared on the third day, I knew one thing for sure. Those in power finally had the excuse they had always needed to take off their mask of civilization. They wanted this, they did everything possible to make it inevitable, and once their handiwork was manifest, they struck. I was no fan of the President or Vice President – they were not as bad as the fascist troglodytes of the Republican right, but they flirted with fascism, nonetheless. When the President became unable to perform his duties, I was mildly hopeful that the Vice President might stand up and reject punitive violence and vengeance, but then she was gone too, and that monster was installed.

His name will go down in history with Hitler and Pinochet.

A few days after, I was listening to NPR, although my favorite announcer had regrettably been accidentally killed during the events. Obviously, censorship was in effect, and even NPR succumbed to the overwhelming pressure to repeat propaganda emphasizing casualties and alleged acts of brutality instead of illuminating the root causes of the militants' actions. In any case, the NPR report mentioned that there were prisoners, hundreds of them. That had never occurred to me – and I knew what I had to do. I planned to contact the federal public defender and offer my services to those facing charges in federal court.

But then the regime announced that the prisoners would not be tried in courts, real courts, but by military commissions under the Military Commissions Act of 2006 and the subsequent amendments to the law. That was the same law they used to attempt to prosecute those poor, tortured souls in Guantanamo Bay. And they were going to do it in a summary fashion. Moreover, they were going to use the same process on American citizens caught up in the actions.

You have to understand what this means. The Military Commissions Act of 2006 does not mean a fair trial, especially with the changes that Congress voted on and the new president signed into law less than a week later. It allowed the United States military to try captured persons in front of a military judge with a five-soldier military commission as the jury. And the specific charges were set out in the Act, but came from both the Law of War and the Uniform Code of Military Justice, the UCMJ – I had no familiarity with that before then.

The argument in favor of these drumhead tribunals was that these defendants were unlawful combatants, not uniformed members of a state military engaging in combat. You have to treat lawful combatants as prisoners of war and cannot punish them for acts within the Law of War, but the theory goes that you *can* prosecute unlawful combatants as criminals.

Previously, America had generally done this using the regular courts, which were soon up and running even after the loss of so many judges and justices during the events. Until then, the US only used the commissions for a few so-called Al-Qaida terrorists, and there was a great deal of frustration that defense attorneys in Gitmo – many of whom were my friends or were lawyers from big law corporate firms – had tied the government up in knots and kept it from lynching the detainees for over two decades.

But the government was determined not to let this happen again. It decided to turn due process into an assembly-line kangaroo court.

I got a call from a desperate criminal attorney friend who was positively frantic. The government had contacted her and asked her to represent some of the accused. But the trials – if you could call them that – would be in three days. Worse, the government was seeking the death penalty.

And there were thousands of people in custody who needed lawyers. She said she needed me. I immediately told my friend we should gum up the works by refusing to participate because even with the new changes to the Act they had a right to a lawyer. But she had thought of that, and when she made the threat the government told her that if civilians would not do it, junior judge advocates would be assigned to do it – lawyers with no real experience and a huge bias against their own clients.

I agreed to help and went down to the Meadowlands, where there was a giant military base in the parking lot. The trials were not in a courthouse but in five large tents, each holding one commission. There were so many prisoners, American and migrant, that they were kept in tents surrounded by barbed wire, floodlights, and machine guns. Even if there had been room in the jails, the other prisoners would kill the militants given the chance.

My first client was Ahmad Al-Suzeri, from Jordan but of Palestinian extraction. He was wounded in the leg and getting utterly inadequate medical care. His story of living adjacent to occupation and apartheid was deeply moving. He was accused of several counts under Title 10, United States Code Section 950v(b), including murder, rape, attacking civilians, taking hostages, using protected persons – civilians – as shields, torture, mutilating, and maiming, and others.

He was a sweet young man of 24, articulate, strong in his faith, dedicated to the freedom of his people. I wanted to tell that story to the commission, though I cannot say that would have swayed the officers on the commission even if the judge had not ruled that vital background evidence inadmissible. And I had the challenge of explaining the footage in the GoPro Ahmad was supposedly caught with that allegedly showed the acts he was charged with. I pointed out that you could not tell for certain that the people in the video were actually dead, or that the women depicted had failed to give their consent. I had no chance to supply any of the context the raw forage required.

I argued there should not even be a trial, that he was a lawful combatant. See, he wore a black shirt and had a green headband. That was a uniform. He was a soldier. They rejected that argument. The trial by military commission went forward.

It was a sham trial. The commission admitted evidence of a written statement of some policeman declaring that he had arrested Ahmad bleeding on the ground after a firefight and that the footage was from the camera he was wearing. This was rank hearsay, but it was admissible under the Amended Act's rules in effect during a national emergency. And, of course, this was declared to be a national emergency.

The trial, such as it was, lasted 90 minutes. The commission deliberated for ten, and returned to pronounce Ahmad guilty of all charges and to recommend death. I asked for time to prepare a report prior to sentencing. That was denied. The judge not only sentenced him to death right then, but directed that his sentence be carried out in 24 hours.

I was staggered by the injustice of this kangaroo court, but I resolved to appeal. A Guantanamo case, *Boumediene v. Bush* (2008) 553 U.S. 723, held that detainees had a right to challenge their imprisonment in federal court. But there was frightening precedent too. In *Ex parte Quirin* (1942) 317 U.S. 1, the U.S, had prosecuted and executed German saboteurs for violating the law of war and upheld trial by military commission for unlawful combatants. Ominously, it also said – let me read it, from page 38: "[C]itizens who associate themselves with the military arm of an enemy government, and with its aid, guidance, and direction enter this country bent on hostile acts are enemy belligerents within the meaning of the Hague Convention and the law of war." That was how the government used the Act to try American citizens accused of participating in the events.

The problem was that the Amended Act stripped the Article III courts of the power of review. In other words, the civilian courts had no jurisdiction. That jurisdictional provision itself got challenged by lawyers a couple days before, and the Amended Act provided the Supreme Court with original jurisdiction to rule on the issue of the Amended Act's constitutionality. The surviving members of the Supreme Court took it up and upheld the Amended Act in a short *per curium* opinion 24 hours after it was filed. The commissions were unleashed.

The only review of a conviction available to a condemned defendant was an informal one by the convening officer, some general who would review all the findings each evening and either approve or disapprove them. But who wants to be the general who spares the Muslim – or college student – whose GoPro showed him or her mowing down a classroom of schoolkids?

I tried to keep Ahmad's spirits up. He prayed a lot. The next morning, I was told that his appeal to the convening authority was denied. He began to cry when I told him. Sometime that afternoon, a team of MPs dragged him out of the prisoners' compound, took him behind a screen in the parking lot, and shot him in the back of the head.

No last words, no last meal. If a prisoner was lucky, he would mail off a last letter to his family – after the intelligence agents read it through. It was brutal. They took a page from the

Russians during Stalin's purges of the counterrevolutionaries and just shot them, then buried the bodies.

I defended 101 accused, both foreign militants and American citizen militants. I was well aware of the existence of privilege, and I tried not to treat the Americans as more important than young men from the Middle East who came here to fight for their people's freedom. But with the Americans – almost all young people, college students or so-called "Antifa" and the like – you had their frantic parents calling you. It was hard telling them the reality of the situation, that their son or daughter or gender non-binary child had uploaded video of themselves dancing around fresh corpses while chanting "From the river to the sea, Palestine will be free!" and was certain to be executed.

I got two accused off. One was an 18-year-old Muslim from Afghanistan who I showed was clearly – can I say this word? – retarded. I did not get an outright acquittal. They just did not sentence him to die. Another was a girl from Wellesley who was captured in Brookline, Massachusetts, with several other members of the Student Movement for Decolonialization Action. The prosecutor said she and her comrades were going from McMansion to McMansion killing families, and emphasizing the killing of toddlers and pets. Part of the reason she got off is that she was caught on another girl's bodycam crying and saying, "I don't want to do this anymore," before her friends stabbed one of the families to death. But I think the real reason was that she was a senator's niece. The commission condemned her, but the general decided she would get her sentence commuted. She and the retarded boy are both doing life in federal prison. The girl's surviving friends were all shot.

I tried to do the best I could for my clients. I tried to explain the militants' motivations. I tried to bring up the root causes of the violence and explain how it was the cry of the unheard. I questioned the evidence. I flat-out begged for mercy. But there was never going to be justice. The commissions were a machine that fed America's bloodthirsty appetite for vengeance. There was no way that the American people, humiliated and angry by militants who struck a blow against a century of American oppression, would let it go unavenged. And they flat-out judicially murdered nearly 3,500 people. They even murdered the 9/11 prisoners still at Guantanamo Bay.

If you ask me, that was the real terrorism, not the legitimate resistance of oppressed people. I was disgusted by so many supposed progressives who refused to confront the truth. What do they think resistance to settler colonialism means? Do they think they can get an omelet without breaking a few eggs?

Wait, where are you going? I have more to say...

38.

Atlanta, Georgia

This is a poor area of the city. Several crying aliens sit on the curb in zip-ties, waiting to be loaded into the idling Federal Alien Removal Agency (FARA) van for "expedited processing." The parents came from Egypt ten years ago, overstaying a visa. Now, they will be taken to a FARA facility and be presented to an administrative judge who will evaluate any possible claims they have for remaining in the United States. If their claim is denied – as 98.3% of them are – they will be expelled from the U.S. within 48 hours. Their minor children were born here and are U.S. citizens. They will go with their parents unless a legal guardian with executed papers claims custody before they are sent away.

Lieutenant Victor Conrad is overseeing the sweep, which was the result of an anonymous tip. Tipsters who reveal the presence of illegal aliens are awarded $250 per alien identified to FARA officers – more if the alien is specifically wanted for a crime or is on the Priority Removal List of aliens that the government particularly wants expelled. Citizens of most of the Middle East nations, but others with high terrorist propensity – like Somalia, Niger, and Afghanistan – are on that list.

There were at least twenty, and maybe twenty-five, million illegal aliens in the United States at the time of the Attack. Nobody cared, except us and regular citizens. Like a lot of FARA officers, I worked for Immigration and Customs Enforcement, which was part of U.S. Department of Homeland Security. We were not allowed to do our jobs. Hell, we were not allowed to call illegal aliens "illegal aliens," though that is the term in the statutes. Millions came in illegally over the southern border. Millions more made false asylum requests. And millions overstayed or abused their visas. Worse, the Government gave these people cash while citizens like you and me got the bill.

As for us, our orders were clear – do not do your job. It was pretty frustrating.

I did interior enforcement, which meant I was inside the country, not on the border. We would grab serious criminals – I mean murderers and rapists – and deport them. Lesser criminals got a pass. I don't know how many drunk drivers we would try to expel with five or six DUIs and we would be told to turn them loose. I remember several that went on to kill Americans. No one cared. Americans were expendable. And illegals were untouchable.

We had this giant list of people who had been processed through the broken asylum system and ordered out, but they just would not go. We would not be allowed to go get them, assuming we knew where they even were. It was a joke.

The ones that really burned me were the college visa holders. They got to come into this country to go to school, get an education, and better themselves. A lot did, but a lot decided to stay here and crap on this country. You know that it always was an expellable offense for a visa holder to support a terrorist organization? Well, after the Gaza War started, these aliens would be supporting Hamas – a terrorist group – openly. They would tear down the posters of kidnapped Jewish babies, destroy property, attack Jews. And no school would suspend or expel the little creeps because that might hurt their visa status. Ha! Even when they were expelled, which was pretty damn rare, we were told by headquarters in no uncertain terms that these guys were untouchable. I watched guys on TV who I knew were visa holders rioting and I could not do a thing about it.

Am I surprised they smuggled in over 10,000 terrorists? I mean, you look at that number and it sounds crazy. But the administration, after it undid the previous administration's policies, let in eight million illegals at least, including the fake asylum claims. With just one in eight hundred being bad, you have an Army division. That's just 35 or so a day for the year after October 7th, not counting the sleepers already here. I'm surprised there weren't more.

They just waited for orders. Their asylum hearings were not until 2029. No one was looking for them. ICE was closed down after the Attack, of course, and all of us were transferred to FARA or the United States Border Force. But it was not our fault. We were *ordered* not to do our job. It was no accident that we failed. Failure was the plan. The administration wanted aliens in to be new voters down the road, and the corporations wanted new, cheap workers. What the rest of us wanted did not matter, and a lot of people died because of it.

I was on the job when it started. I was in downtown Atlanta, running down an MS-13 guy. By some miracle we were going to be able to expel him back to El Salvador even though we did not have a conviction here. Now, El Sal used to be terrible, the highest per capita murder rate in the world. It was wall-to-wall gangs, and when they came here they behaved the same way. Lots of murders, including of civilians, people outside of the game. The members were just brutal animals. But their new president, Nayib Bukele, turned it around. He sent in the army. The ones who fooled around with the soldiers found out. They got dead. The rest got locked up at a special new prison. It was not one of those South American party prisons where you can walk your girlfriend in and out and buy whatever. It was Pelican freakin' Bay – no games, no slack, just hard, hard time for a long time.

As you might expect, our little cholo was probably not going to be too excited about his upcoming one-way trip south because he was going straight to jail. We were ready. There were ten of us in four vehicles, long weapons and gear, and we were in a Hardee's parking lot making our final plans before rolling out to his crib. Intel told us the guy got up at the crack of noon, so we were hoping to take him fast and clean while he was getting ready for another day of being a useless piece of trash.

Our guy lived on the east side of Mechanicsville in a crappy apartment in the shadow of Interstate 85. Mechanicsville is a trash pit, really bad. The crime rate is through the roof, so our guy felt right at home.

We were supposed to rally at noon and my partner and I got in there early, so we futzed around, grabbed a Famous Star, and waited. The other tac team members showed up and we did one last sanity check of the plan. We were not rushing. We had this.

Of course, the police scanner was on. Atlanta PD knew we were pulling the raid, but we needed situational awareness – what if someone said, "All units, armed home invaders at 123 Fake Street?" We had to be able to say, "Whoa, it's just us ICE boys, so chill out" before we got in some serious blue-on-blue trouble.

We have the AAA street map and some photos of the apartment out on the hood of one of the white Ford Explorers, and we are going over them. It is all as routine as routine gets. And then we hear the call – shots fired at the Zoo. One guy pipes up, "Is it hunting season?" and we laugh. I mean, Atlanta metro – somebody is always busting caps at someone.

Then there is another call and we hear the magic words – "Mass shooting, mass casualties."

No more jokes – we all know that on a weekday that place is packed with kids on field trips. I look at the map. The Zoo is half a mile straight east on Summerhill.

We are in our vehicles in a flash, code three, and I am calling Atlanta PD dispatch that there is an ICE tac team inbound, ETA two mikes.

The Zoo is big, almost a mile long and wide. I ask Atlanta dispatch, "Where is the shooter?"

She says, and I'll never forget her voice, "*Shooters*. There are shooters, multiple."

"Two?" I say, forgetting radio procedure.

"More," she says.

"Where?"

"All over. Everywhere."

We're weaving in and out of traffic, my partner Earl driving. He takes the side mirror off some guy in a Porsche who did not get out of the way fast enough. That was Earl – nothing was going to stop him from getting to those kids.

Now we're hearing calls from APD units on the scene. Shots fired, officer down. No, *officers* down. Automatic weapons.

I have no idea that what is happening is happening everywhere. I pull up my M4 and check the chamber. I'm ready to rock. We drive into the Zoo parking lot. Hundreds of people are running out. Some are bloody.

The mass shooter protocol has changed. In the past, you would secure the perimeter, get the negotiators in, try to talk it out. But mass shooters don't want to talk. They want to kill until they kill themselves or get killed. The new protocol is simple.

You find them and engage them until you or they are dead.

That's what we did.

I knew the layout from taking my own kids there. We rolled right up to the main entrance. People are running out, panicked. A lot of kids. I see bodies all over the little plaza. You gotta ignore them until the killer is down. Or killers.

We heard fire and a round hit my window. We spilled out and determined the fire was coming from up near the elephant pen. Earl and I start moving with a couple of our guys. The other guys got engaged from the kid's playground and assaulted that way.

There's a terrorist in black, with his headband. He's spraying at us and there are civvies all around us. Earl and I start firing. The other two of my guys come up and help. We smoked the terrorist. I told the other guys to confirm the kill and then to move north.

There is a lot of shooting from the kid's playground, so we head there. We are running toward the gunfire, dodging dead and wounded people. Then we come on a familiar body on the ground, one of ours, headshot, so we knew he was gone. We had to press forward, to put it out of our minds. But his wife and my wife were friends.

We get to the kid's playground and five of my guys are shooting it out with three of the terrorists across the playground. I can't describe the playground to you. Murdered kids, teachers, some wounded, screaming. Not just a few. It seemed like hundreds. They caught them inside and emptied mag after mag into them.

I motion to Earl to follow me to flank them. There's a lot of shooting. They are not so tough when they have to face trained pros. My guys cap one and he falls. The other terrorists split up.

We follow one. He sprays at us and we take cover behind a low cement wall. Earl and I are engaging the guy, trying not to hit any of the civilians. The terrorist is shooting everywhere. Civilians are falling. I think Earl realized he could not see us to shoot at us, so he stands up to engage. The guys sees him, stops shooting kids, and starts shooting at Earl. Earl falls back – I see the arterial spurt from his neck – but I have my shot and take the terrorist with two center-mass hits outside of his Kevlar.

Earl looks at me and mouths something – I knew what it was, and I did it. I walked up to the terrorist, who was cockroaching on the ground, and put two shots in his brainpan. Lights out.

I walked back to Earl but he was gone. He drew fire from the kids. He was a damn hero.

We fought for two hours that day, killed a couple more ourselves. There were nearly six hundred dead and wounded at the Atlanta Zoo, mostly kids, and eight law enforcement, including ICE Officer Earl Walters.

After the Attacks ended and martial law happened, we got a new president, and we got new orders. No slack.

The new president went on TV and ordered all illegals out. All pending asylum applications were denied – they were free to refile them somewhere other than in America.

No more games. Leave now, on your own terms, or leave on ours. But you will leave. Every one of you.

It was like that movie, *The Untouchables*. Everyone knew where the liquor was, they just did not want to cross Capone. Well, we knew where the illegals were. So we went there. Mass sweeps. With martial law, everyone had to display ID, and if you did not have one, get on the freakin' bus.

And he cut off their money – no illegal would get a dime. he cut off the money to the NGOs too. Man, they howled. Oh well. He did keep the law that hospitals had to treat everyone, even illegals. He just ordered us to place agents in the ERs. Take two aspirins and get in the van, pal.

Some people were scandalized. The media tried to tug our heartstrings with a bunch of sob stories. Poor Joe Illegal had been here for years and was only trying to make it and climate change made him leave his village blah blah blah. That fell flat. Most of us Americans were burying dead family and friends and we did not want to hear it.

Some Hawaiian judge put out an injunction on mass deportations. The president said he was doing it anyway as commander-in-chief in time of war. The Ninth Circuit upheld the judge in a day, and then the Supreme Court knocked that nonsense off the next. Not a shock since two of their own got murdered the first day. As for us, we kept deporting them.

Many left on their own. They could tie up their affairs, that sort of thing, then get on a free flight to wherever. But many tried to hide, thinking it would all die down and we would go back to business as usual. Nope. There were too many dead from not securing our borders.

Then Congress passed the laws that enabled the new tough hearing rules and set up FARA expressly to toss illegal aliens out. We got the power to offer rewards for tips – we're not supposed to call them bounties – and a lot of people made a pretty good living narcing them out.

And we made it unprofitable for businesses to hire illegals. The new laws let any American citizen sue a company for damages and attorney's fees if they hire illegals. It was like those handicap lawsuits where shysters sue Quickie Marts for having the bathroom towel dispenser mounted too high. As soon as companies found out they would have to pay big bucks to skeevy lawyers if they hired illegals, they stopped hiring them. No welfare and no worky, no reason to stay. The 50% tax on remittances to the folks back home helps fund it all.

I have read that the movement home of illegals in the last five years, nearly seventeen million that we know of, is one of the largest migrations in human history. Good. Now, it's kind of hard to find illegals. The ones still here are hiding pretty well and have good documents, but we will get them.

People sometimes ask me if I feel bad about what I do, but then I remember Earl and those murdered kids, and you know what? I feel pretty damn good.

39.

New York, New York

Max Zimmerman is interrupted twelve times during his interview by phone calls, and those are only the ones he did not send off to voicemail. As one of the senior Democrats in the United States Senate, everyone wants a few minutes of his attention. But he felt it was important to devote an hour of it to telling his, and his party's, story.

We thought we had the Republicans on the ropes. I have been doing this for a long time, and sometimes you are up and sometimes you are down, but this was different. This was something unlike anything since the Whigs were cracking up a century and a half ago. You had the old-school Republicans who understood the importance of institutions and who were reasonable. We could work with them. And you had the new GOP, the crazies. The MAGA stuff was just too much. They did not care about institutions and they refused to play ball. They developed this distrust of American power. They eventually refused to help Ukraine. We painted them as antisemites, and you say what you need to say to get elected, but when Israel needed them they were there, except for a fringe.

It was a party in chaos.

The GOP was paralyzed by two irreconcilable factions when reconciling factions is how you get power in the United States.

Our Constitution does not expressly require two parties, but having two parties is the inevitable effect of its design. Third parties never win anything – they just influence which of the two parties win and lose. It is all about getting 50% and one vote. This means America had two broad parties that were coalitions packed with competing factions.

But the GOP's factions just could not work together to retain power. The two factions were falling apart, kicking out one Speaker for another for no reason and, on top of everything, the extremists' polarizing leader was about to go to prison.

We just laughed. I remember thinking that we had a generation of being in charge ahead of us before they got their act together. I understand this business is cyclical and that one cycle you are up and the next down, but they were such a mess that many of us were sure we were on the verge of a couple decades of power. I was a little worried about our own left fringe, but I thought the adults would stay in control. The only problem was our president at the time should have gone off to Sunny Acres. And his veep – she was never the sharpest knife in the drawer. They dropped the ball a lot, but they beat the guy the Republicans insisted on putting forward. We knew they were not good, but they were good enough.

Then October 7th happened. I was seeing these images of murders and torture and I was horrified as a human being but also as a Jew. After all, the terrorists were not targeting Baptists. Of course the IDF had to respond, hard. And I expected we Democrats would unite with the Republicans and support our ally against these fanatics.

What I did not expect was that we would be unable to unite with fellow Democrats. I knew about the woke stuff, the intersectionality, and the progressives. We had fought it out in primaries. Parties do that. But I did not imagine that they would embrace this kind of evil. We had congresswomen chanting, "From the river to the sea, Palestine would be free." I mean, they knew that, at best, it meant clearing every Jew out of Israel and, at worst, it meant October 7th across the whole country.

There are a lot of liberal Jews in the Democratic Party, both as candidates and donors, and most – not all, because some choose progressivism over survival – who were outraged. We prided ourselves about being the party that protected minorities, and the progressives were not shy about wanting to withdraw that protection from Jews. They usually called it anti-Zionism, but we knew the score. They didn't rip down pictures of kidnapped Jews, attack Jewish students, and damage Jewish businesses because of Zionism. They did it because they hated Jews. We had seen this movie before.

The President could have shut that down in a heartbeat. Put the FBI on the hate criminals, deport the student visa holders, tell the universities, "Nice endowments you got there – pity if they were to become taxable." But the election polls were tight – the guy going to jail was beating him in some battlegrounds, and there were an awful lot of Muslims in swing states like Michigan as well as progressives all over. He did not want to alienate either group when he needed every vote in November.

He had been playing footsie with Iran before the Attack – an Obama holdover policy a lot of us were mad about already – and when Hamas invaded Israel he would not call out the mullahs by name. His Departments of Justice and Education ignored the attacks on Jews here at home, but he put a lot of heat on Netanyahu to "pause" the retribution. Pause it? They had 200 hostages, including Americans!

The press played along too. They never counted the days they were held hostage or even named the hostages. It just never spoke of them – they were like Voldemort, They Who Shall Not Be Named.

It suddenly became clear that we had a huge fracture in our own party. And it was worse than the Republican schism because, in their case, one faction disliked the other and in our case, one faction wanted the other to be slaughtered.

It got worse and worse and the protests and unrest grew on the streets and campuses. Moreover, the border crisis was a real issue, but he refused to really change the asylum procedures even after another "compromise." It was practically a holy writ on the left of the Democratic Party that there should be no barrier to immigration. We moderates saw that was starting to hurt us with other voters, but the President and the progressives would not budge. He needed that base rock solid, and the progressive side was ascendant.

I can tell you that we never saw what was coming. The intelligence community never warned us, and we all know about the Attack Commission Report's conclusions. In retrospect, yes, we should have been more vigilant. But our focus was inward, with an election and the prosecutions of the ex-president and the left-wing, pro-Palestine unrest on the streets. No one saw it coming, not us or the Republicans. It was just our bad luck that we held the presidency. As a mainstream Democrat from long ago once said, "The buck stops here."

They hit my house the first morning. Thankfully, I was out and my family was back in New York. Any of us they found there would be dead now, and their murders probably posted on YouTube. As it were, they went through my Georgetown neighborhood killing people for several hours and uploading it all. There was no one to stop them. The police were overwhelmed. They are not trained for this. I personally knew so many people murdered, not just the big names but the regular people. There was a nice older lady who walked her poodle every afternoon and always said hello and they killed her and her dog.

I was deep in the negotiations after it became clear that the President was incapacitated and that the Vice President was incapable of handling the task. We needed leadership immediately – we could not wait for the 25th Amendment process – but even at the end of that process, assuming it was successful, we still would have gotten the Speaker since he is third in line. I helped negotiate the concessions – no SCOTUS nominations, pardons for everyone, the agreement to a law to let us sub in a new nominee for the November election. We also got him to agree to retire from politics after the January inauguration. Making that deal got us some criticism, but again, if we had the 25th Amendment process we would have had the same guy and no guardrails or concessions.

What was clear was that the veep could not be president, not in that crisis. The woman was never going to be confused with a brain surgeon, but she was utterly emotionally unstable because of the attempt on her life and she was totally confused. This was the most serious attack on our country in its history. We needed a leader. You remember her speech the second day – the woman was not just in over her head, she was down on the ocean floor with the *Titanic.*

I was one of the people sent to tell her she was quitting for the good of the country. It was a lot easier than I expected. I told her, "You are resigning. The only question is whether you are doing it the easy way or the hard way." I told her that if she signed right now, she got a doubled pension, a pardon, and protection. I also told her if she didn't sign right away, she got none of the above plus a ticket to the penitentiary for dereliction of duty. I was talking out of my ass, but like I said – she's as dumb as a box of rocks. She just started nodding and asked for the letter of resignation and a pen. I kept the pen – it's a piece of history.

Then we got to work. I never thought I would see America under martial law, but I never thought I would have seen tens of thousands of Americans killed in our country by foreigners. A bare majority of Democrats went along with it, and we passed the enabling legislation to make sure this kind of thing never happened again.

The current problem for our party is that not everyone changed after August 27th. You know that famous clip of the baby and the blowtorch in that yard in Marin Country with the

"Hate has no home here" sign? Of all the clips the terrorists uploaded, that one really made people choose a side. Most chose our own side, but there was this progressive fringe, shrunken but still there, that would not budge. They went nuts over the deportations, for example. But we managed to moderate it a little bit at least here. Hell, we all saw what the French and Germans did with their immigrants after seeing what happened here – remember the news pictures of soldiers loading migrants onto trains in Stuttgart and Paris? Scary.

Our party had a real problem. So, we had to choose between the Republicans who wanted to kill the people who wanted to kill us, and the people who wanted to give a free pass to the people who wanted to kill us. And we had to face the voters about six weeks later.

One thing everyone agreed on was that the election had to go forward. We had to show that those bastards were not going to defeat democracy. In fact, if we had tried to postpone it to give our guy a better shot, the GOP would have thrown the "protecting Our Democracy" stuff we had been talking about for almost four years right back in our faces.

Our new candidate for November made what I think was a huge mistake in trying to moderate his response to the Attack. Americans, including most of our party, were in no mood for moderation. The terrorists really read us wrong. We were not going to give in. We were going to hit back. But our candidate, a handsome but not-too-bright guy who had never had to run outside a state where everyone votes like Manhattan, tried to appeal a little to the hard left. He lost.

It did not help us that the elections were carried out completely differently than they had been four years before. The Republicans were fixated on fake election fraud claims and they wanted one-day elections with photo IDs and paper ballots. Well, that's what they got. Everyone was carrying ID everywhere anyway under martial law, and they claimed that demanding ID was necessary "for security." We could not count on electronic voting machines with the power system unstable, and the cyber-attacks had made people distrustful of any voting machines – if people could hack the grid, they could hack your ballot. So, all the Republicans and a bunch of our people – under pressure from their constituents – voted for the reforms that made Elections Day a one-day event again. It also allowed people to carry guns into a polling place – no one wanted to be caught with a bunch of people in a "gun-free zone" again.

The election reforms probably helped, but we lost because the voters held us responsible to some extent, rightly or wrongly. We could not get past the fact that we Democrats had the presidency when it happened. We had left the borders open and the terrorists and the guns got in on our watch. Our intelligence agencies and military did not see it coming. A lot of these were longstanding problems. The border crisis began decades before. Our agencies have been problematic for decades as well. It was not fair, and I am convinced that it probably would have happened anyway even if there was a Republican in the White House, but it didn't. In politics, you play the hand you are dealt, and sometimes that hand sucks.

The Republican Party's fissures healed over immediately, or rather, they were painted over. The party generally tossed out their isolationism fixation in favor of a consensus behind getting retribution for the Attack. And the party demographics changed. I cannot tell you how many Jewish voters I have had tell me they are going register Republican, and when I argue with them, they tell me they are choosing life over liberalism.

I think the GOP probably generally has the edge for the next few cycles, to be honest. I think there is some chance, as the memories fade and time passes, that some of the more economic populist elements might come back to us. We had been dancing with the corporate interests for a while, but they have gone back to the GOP and some of the people in that party might not be comfortable about that.

The problem for us is the same one the Republicans had on abortion when we were in safe and secure enough times for that to be a dominant issue. All of the Democrats were for more liberal abortion laws and some of the GOP was too, meaning we had the majority. Well, today, all of the GOP is fire and brimstone on any foreigner who even hints at looking at us cross-eyed, and some of the Democrats are too, meaning we are in the minority. That's bad when the big issue for voters is self-preservation.

40.

Herndon, Virginia

The Bureau of Attack Historical Analysis is in a heavily guarded high-rise office building in suburban Virginia. There was some controversy at first over which department it would fall under – Defense, Health and Human Services, or Homeland Security. None wanted it. HHS ended up with it. The Department generally leaves it be to operate on its own.

The Bureau consists of about 200 government employees plus some contractors, most of whom sit in front of computer terminals on two floors gathering, collating, and processing information about the Attack and entering it into the Bureau's enormous database.

The AHA's entire purpose is to gather statistical, historical, and other relevant information related to the Attack, and then to put it into a form that can be used both by the government and accessed by the citizens. Part of its legislative mandate was adopted as the Bureau's motto – "To remember and understand."

Dr. Marcus Chapman, formerly a professor of history at Notre Dame, is the head of the bureau. "History is a story," he says, "and that's what we are doing here – preserving and telling the stories of the Attack one individual at a time."

Balding with glasses, his calm demeanor and academic's objectivity seem to contrast with a job in which, with surprising frequency, workers will spontaneously burst into tears and run out of the building.

He guides your author to a seat in a cubicle that faces a monitor and opens up the Bureau's website dashboard. It displays the cold statistics that quantify the horror of the Attack.

Before you can truly tell the story of one individual, you must have an idea of the bigger picture. That means knowing the numbers. The most important number today – as of right now – is 172,385. That is 172,385 dead innocents. Not just Americans – that number is 162,172. You can see it right there on the Bureau dashboard. The other dead are non-US citizens. What we call the "innocents" are anyone who was not a terrorist or an active conspirator who joined in the slaughter. "Innocents" also includes soldiers, police, and so forth, killed in America during the attacks. It also includes 473 missing who we presume are dead.

The terrorists and terrorist-adjacent dead number today is 13,133. That includes the executed, but not those enemies killed in the foreign actions that followed. That number is hard to know and hard to define. Do the low-yield nuclear strikes on the underground Iranian missile and nuclear facilities count, or the conventional strikes on the mullahs' military? What about the Mexican incursions during the counter-cartel police action? We have chosen, perhaps arbitrarily, not to count the American military dead in those post-Attack actions against the total.

The numbers change daily. There were about 235,000 wounded in the Attack, we think. We cannot know. Some never sought treatment, while sometimes the doctors working the mass casualty events simply kept no records. They were too busy trying to stop the bleeding and save life and limbs. Oh, we have that statistic too – 6,336 people lost limbs or were blinded.

As I said, the number changes. People still die of their wounds every day, usually between one and three. The law requires that when someone dies of a cause linked to the Attack we be alerted and that we determine if the deceased is or is not to be counted. That can be important to the family because there are government benefits. But here, our focus is on accuracy. We want to make sure that all our dead are remembered.

The people in these cubicles are tasked with making sure that each victim is identified and that his or her webpage is properly updated. That's where we preserve and tell the innocents' stories. Eventually, we will begin accepting and collating stories of survivors – they already send them to us without us even asking.

Just memorializing the dead has been a huge undertaking. We had to first identify the dead to generate the list, and we are still in the process of gathering information on each of the names. We go through open-source information on the web, and usually talk to the surviving relatives. Most are happy to speak about their relatives, but some tell us to go to hell and hang up. We get photos and histories and enter them. If the whole family was murdered – which is common – we try to get photos from happier times off of social media accounts.

We also try to identify the manner of their death and we include it. Some families want us to include post-mortem pictures. We honor the families' decisions. We feel we owe them the truth. That is truly the traumatic part for our workers. Obviously, we all know how the terrorists made a point of maximizing the shock effect with savagery.

Our workers are exposed to the mayhem every day. We try to be honest and complete in our records – as I said, we feel we owe the dead that. But when you must see the photos and hear the stories, then process them, of babies being cut apart in front of their bound mothers, and the like, it has an effect. And most all of these workers have people they knew on the list. Many have close family members, even wives or husbands or kids. We cannot tell who knows who. The cases are assigned randomly, with only cases with the same last names redirected. Maybe your raped and murdered sister comes across your screen under her married name. That has happened.

We have three therapists on staff to counsel our people and we still have people run out and never come back. We had a suicide two months ago. And yes, she went on the list as part of the total.

The total is staggering. And that plus the deportations, self and forced, that followed meant that America's population experienced a significant drop that year for the first time in our history. It overwhelms us emotionally now, but at the time the sheer logistical challenge of it was immense. There were tens of thousands of crime scenes. There was no way to process them. No way to do postmortems. No CSI. Our mortuary system was not set up for this. Even if people were willing to gather in groups for funerals, there was no way to process that many bodies. And the power outages limited refrigeration capacity.

We try to list the final resting place of the victims in the database, but for many of them we have nothing. If the whole family was killed, who would there be to call to ask?

The intent of mass murder on that scale was to shock America into a complete retreat from the world. It shocked us, but we eventually lashed out instead. You look at the number of dead, which is just less than half the losses from World War II, and it is mind-boggling. Of course, America had a population of 140,000,000 in 1945, and at the time of the Attack, we were at about 335,000,000. As a percentage, the Attack was much smaller in terms of deaths per capita, but World War II happened over three-and-one-half years. Ninety percent of the Attack casualties happened during the first three days, and they were overwhelmingly civilians.

The sheer scale of the murder is stunning, considering there were only 10,000-11,000 terrorists plus many thousands of American and alien participants. Putting them aside, this means essentially 17 dead per terrorist, a hellish ratio, but it proved possible. Put aside the aircraft attacks – 16 airliners shot down in the sky and four packed jets destroyed on the ground for a total of 5,872 dead. They initially chose targets to maximize casualties. Schools, conventions, campsites, campuses, business parks – places where there were many people but little or no security because we never imagined we would be attacked here by a dedicated force willing to kill, savagely, until killed. They used automatic weapons, bombs, and ground-to-air missiles. And then, when our responders converged on the targets, the terrorists faded back and went on decentralized killing sprees. It was all designed to kill as many people as possible as fast as possible, and as horrifically as possible. And it worked.

Many of the victim pages read similarly. Machine gunned in his classroom. On a plane that was shot down. Blown apart in a bombing. Killed in the street. Shot fighting back with his concealed pistol. Normal people, just going about their lives. They walked out the door – or were sometimes killed within their homes – and they were murdered.

Every religion and ethnic group was represented. The terrorists attacked a reservation and killed three American Indians, and the Indians have the distinction of killing more terrorists than their losses. Same with the Sikhs – three Sikhs were murdered but they killed nearly a dozen terrorists at one temple. There were 403 innocents we identified as Muslim. We identified 22 Muslim soldiers, police officers, and armed citizens killed fighting the terrorists.

For total first responders, there were 4,376 cops killed, 421 firefighters, 403 EMS. There were also 1,234 soldiers killed, some National Guard and then active-duty troops after martial law was declared.

The scale of it was the point. They wanted a number so high, so horrific, that we would be paralyzed as a nation. That was their intention. And we were, for a time.

One of our statisticians did a calculation on degrees of separation of regular Americans and those killed. The first degree was personally knowing a fatality. The second degree was knowing someone who knew someone who was a fatality. He calculated that 84% of Americans knew someone – personally – who was murdered. Not the celebrities or politicians the terrorists targeted, but someone they were related to, worked with, went to school with, a neighbor. And 98% were within the second degree of separation. Pretty much everyone was impacted directly.

I was. My brother and his family were driving home from a vacation and stopped at a roadside rest westbound on I-80 in Nebraska. They were in their camper finishing breakfast when a cell pulled in and began shooting at 11:00 a.m. Mountain Time. They were killed along with 32 other people – families, truckers, just normal folks. I wrote their websites myself. I felt it was the least I could do.

We have no idea which cell it was that did the killing. We assume the terrorists were killed in Omaha or thereabout. I hope they were. We have pages for each of the dead terrorists. Most have very little information. They came into the US without identification, gave fake names, and disappeared. Most who were processed a large number were "gotaways" who were never processed at all – gave biometric data, but a fat lot of good that was to us. Like there was some Gaza or Aleppo database to compare their eyeball scans and fingerprints to.

Some who were taken alive gave their real names when it became clear what was going to happen to them, hoping to get word to their families. We know that people from the Middle East log in and check our terrorist pages. Those pages look different from those of victims. They are against a black background, and the terrorists are called "Terrorist." We call things by their true names at the Bureau.

There was a minor controversy in the media over including the Antifa and other radicals who joined in the killing. It was never controversial for us. The ones we could reliably show who joined in the Attack will be remembered for what they are, terrorist traitors. They are actually among the easiest to write up

– they are among the most active on social media and many did not hesitate to tweet out their crimes. Imagine being the college student who joined in the "decolonialization" spree only to find yourself in front of a military tribunal and condemned to be shot because you posted yourself scalping an elderly "settler" on Tik Tok.

There are no pictures of the terrorists from happier days taken off their Facebook or whatever. If we have a picture of their corpse, that goes up, unlike for victims unless the family directs it. If it's ugly and graphic, it still goes up. We are not concerned with the tender feelings of their loved ones. The most complete pages are of those who were executed. We usually have an accurate name, some good information on the terrorist's specific crimes, and a pretty good photo, unless the bullet exited his skull through the face, in which case it goes up anyway. It will hopefully encourage the others.

You know, I really hate this job. I enjoyed being a professor. I love history, love reading it, and love teaching it. But I'm no soldier. This is what I could contribute. If a family takes some solace in what we do to remember their loved one, that makes it worthwhile.

And there's another thing. We cannot change the past. We can only learn from it, so maybe we can prevent it from ever happening again. America did not learn from our own history. At the turn of the century, we received a harsh warning on 9/11. But people forget that we had a warning a few years before that when these same people bombed the World Trade Center. We did not learn from either of those. Maybe I can do my part to help us learn from the Attack so that we never have another.

One of the workers rushes by, hands over her face, in tears. Dr. Chapman stands and excuses himself, then follows after her.

Your author is alone in the cubicle. He reaches for the mouse and moves the cursor into the "SEARCH" box. He pulls the keyboard close and types in a name.

The screen flickers, and there is a smiling face of a man in his sixties in a 49er's cap, on a fishing boat, smiling broadly in the sun. There are more photos, of the man playing high school basketball, getting married, proudly posing with a '71 Dodge.

There is a bio, but your author knows it already. He scrolls to the bottom of the screen. A final paragraph explains that the man and his wife were shot to death holding each other in their arms in a Safeway supermarket on August 27th. There is a hyperlink under the woman's name to her own page, but your author has seen enough. He does not hit the link to his mother's memorial page.

Maybe someday he will, but not today.

ABOUT THE AUTHOR

Kurt Schlichter is a senior columnist for *Townhall*. He is also a Los Angeles trial lawyer admitted in California, Texas, and Washington, DC, and a retired Army Infantry colonel.

A Twitter activist (@KurtSchlichter) with over 490,000 followers, Kurt was personally recruited by his friend Andrew Breitbart to write for his Breitbart sites. His writings on political and cultural issues have also been published in *The Federalist*, the *New York Post*, the *Washington Examiner*, the *Los Angeles Times*, the *Boston Globe*, the *Washington Times*, *Army Times*, the *San Francisco Examiner*, and elsewhere.

Kurt serves as a news source, an on-screen commentator, and a guest host on TV and on nationally syndicated radio programs regarding political, military, and legal issues, at outlets including Fox News, Fox Business News, CNN, Newsmax, One America Network, and on shows hosted by Hugh Hewitt, Larry O'Connor, Cam Edwards, Chris Stigall, Seb Gorka, Dennis Prager, Tony Katz, Dana Loesch, Mark Levin, Dan Bongino, and Derek Hunter, among others.

Kurt was a stand-up comic for several years, which led him to write three e-books that each reached number one on the Amazon Kindle "Political Humor" bestsellers list: *I Am a Conservative: Uncensored, Undiluted, and Absolutely Un-PC, I Am a Liberal: A Conservative's Guide to Dealing with Nature's*

Most Irritating Mistake, and *Fetch My Latte: Sharing Feelings with Stupid People*.

In 2014, his book *Conservative Insurgency: The Struggle to Take America Back 2013-2041* was published by Post Hill Press.

His 2016 novel *People's Republic* and its 2017 prequel *Indian Country* reached No. 1 and No. 2 on the Amazon Kindle "Political Thriller" bestsellers list. *Wildfire*, the third book in the series, hit No. 1 on the Amazon "Thrillers – Espionage" bestsellers list and No. 122 in all Amazon Kindle books. *Collapse*, the fourth book, hit 121, while *Crisis* hit 29. His previous novel, *The Split*, hit at least 43. Both *Inferno* and *Overlord* hit No. 1 on the "Political Thrillers" and "Military Thrillers lists respectively.

His nonfiction book *Militant Normals: How Regular Americans Are Rebelling Against the Elite to Reclaim Our Democracy* was published by Center Street Books in October 2018. It made the USA Today Bestsellers List.

His Regnery book *The 21 Biggest Lies About Donald Trump (and You)* was released in 2020 and hit Number 1 on an Amazon list.

His Regnery book *We'll Be Back: The Fall and Rise of America* was released in July 2022 and hit Number 1 on an Amazon list.

Kurt is a successful trial lawyer and name partner in a Los Angeles law firm representing Fortune 500 companies and individuals in matters ranging from routine business cases to confidential Hollywood disputes and political controversies. A member of the Million Dollar Advocates Forum, which recognizes attorneys who have won trial verdicts in excess of $1 million, his litigation strategy and legal analysis articles have been published in legal publications such as the *Los Angeles Daily Journal* and *California Lawyer*.

He is frequently engaged by noted conservatives in need of legal representation, and he was counsel for political commentator and author Ben Shapiro in the widely publicized "Clock Boy" defamation lawsuit, which resulted in the case being dismissed and the victory being upheld on appeal.

Kurt is a 1994 graduate of Loyola Law School, where he was a law review editor. He majored in communications and political science as an undergraduate at the University of California, San Diego, co-editing the conservative student paper *California Review* while also writing a regular column in the student humor paper *The Koala*.

Kurt served as a US Army infantry officer on active duty and in the California Army National Guard, retiring at the rank of full colonel. He wears the silver "jump wings" of a paratrooper and commanded the 1st Squadron, 18th Cavalry Regiment (Reconnaissance-Surveillance-Target Acquisition). A veteran of both the Persian Gulf War and Operation Enduring Freedom (Kosovo), he is a graduate of the Army's Combined Arms and Services Staff School, the Command and General Staff College, and the United States Army War College, where he received a master's degree in strategic studies.

He lives with his wife Irina and their monstrous dogs Bitey and Barkey in the Los Angeles area, and he enjoys sarcasm and red meat.

His favorite caliber is .45.

The Kelly Turnbull Novels

People's Republic (2016)

Indian Country (2017)

Wildfire (2018)

Collapse (2019)

Crisis (2020)

The Split (2021)

Inferno (2022)

Overlord (2023)

Also By Kurt Schlichter

Conservative Insurgency: The Struggle to Take America Back 2013-2041 (Post Hill Press, 2014)

Militant Normals: How Regular Americans Are Rebelling Against the Elite to Reclaim Our Democracy (Center Street Books, 2018)

The 21 Biggest Lies About Donald Trump (and You) (Regnery, 2020)

We'll Be Back: The Fall and Rise of America (Regnery, 2022)

Made in the USA
Coppell, TX
29 January 2024

28345699R00187